W9-BEP-232

The Silver Compass

OTHER NAL ACCENT TITLES
BY HOLLY KENNEDY

The Penny Tree

The Silver Compass

Holly Kennedy

Doubleday Large Print
Home Library Edition

This Large Print Edition, prepared especially for Doubleday Large Print Home Library, contains the complete, unabridged text of the original Publisher's Edition.

NAL Accent
Published by New American Library, a division of Penguin Group (USA) Inc., 375 Hudson Street, New York, New York 10014, USA
Penguin Group (Canada), 90 Eglinton Avenue East, Suite 700, Toronto, Ontario M4P 2Y3, Canada (a division of Pearson Penguin Canada Inc.)
Penguin Books Ltd., 80 Strand, London WC2R 0RL, England
Penguin Ireland, 25 St. Stephen's Green, Dublin 2, Ireland (a division of Penguin Books Ltd.)
Penguin Group (Australia), 250 Camberwell Road, Camberwell, Victoria 3124, Australia (a division of Pearson Australia Group Pty. Ltd.)
Penguin Books India Pvt. Ltd., 11 Community Centre, Panchsheel Park, New Delhi - 110 017, India
Penguin Group (NZ), 67 Apollo Drive, Rosedale, North Shore 0632,
New Zealand (a division of Pearson New Zealand Ltd.)
Penguin Books (South Africa) (Pty.) Ltd., 24 Sturdee Avenue, Rosebank, Johannesburg 2196, South Africa

Penguin Books Ltd., Registered Offices:
80 Strand, London WC2R 0RL, England

First published by NAL Accent, an imprint of New American Library,
a division of Penguin Group (USA) Inc.

ISBN 978-0-7394-9542-1

Printed in the United States of America

PUBLISHER'S NOTE
This is a work of fiction. Names, characters, places, and incidents either are the product of the author's imagination or are used fictitiously, and any resemblance to actual persons, living or dead, business establishments, events, or locales is entirely coincidental.

The publisher does not have any control over and does not assume any responsibility for author or third-party Web sites or their content.

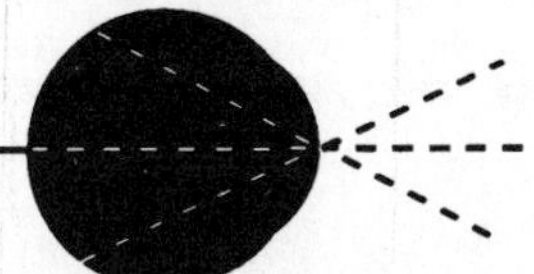

This Large Print Book carries the Seal of Approval of N.A.V.H.

For my father, with love.

Acknowledgments

I would like to express my deep appreciation to my editor, Ellen Edwards. I could not have finished this book if you hadn't so patiently coaxed the story out of me, and for that I cannot thank you enough. In addition, I am grateful to all the people at New American Library, who work so hard to keep everything moving in the right direction, including Becky Vinter.

Thanks to my agent, Liza Dawson, for being so wise and steadfast. You are, as always, my voice of reason. Also Chandler Crawford, my foreign rights agent. An author couldn't ask for better representation.

Fellow authors, great writers, good friends: Jacquelyn Mitchard, an industry icon who is unfailingly supportive of my work; Susan Wiggs, one of my first teachers and a class act I'm honored to call my friend; Karen Joy Fowler, whom I have admired for years and who graciously offered input on sections of this novel; Patricia Wood, who listened during my whiniest rants and never once hung up; and my first-ever creative writing instructor, Linda Holeman, with whom I regularly share great chats about the business of writing.

A respectful bow to the Maui Writers Retreat and Conference, as well as everyone in Athabasca, Alberta, especially Bob Tannas, Mrs. Olson (my high school English teacher), and Cynthia at the Alice B. Donahue Library and Archives. I also owe a special thank-you to Evan Read Armstrong for her input on how the mind of a teenage girl works.

For their support and encouragement, I'd like to mention my mom, Ann Holt, Al Finlayson, Jim Kennedy, Sally Weingartner, Jana from Montana (aka Jana Felt), Eric and Marilyn Holt, Ron and Marilyn Edwards, Randy and Karen Holt, Ian and

Sydney Holt, Karen Veloso, Roberta Talmage, Julie Block, Andrea Kennedy, and Russ Kennedy.

Last of all, I am blessed to have the love and support of my husband, Rick, who talks me off the ledge at regular intervals, and my children, Thomas and Marcus, who are truly the reason for it all.

I find the great thing in this world
is not so much where we stand,
as in what direction we are moving.

—Johann Wolfgang von Goethe

PROLOGUE

Before sneaking out of the house that morning, Ellis Williams pulled a baggy sweater over her T-shirt and gathered her hair back in an elastic band. She was making her way down the alley when the band broke and snapped against the tender skin of her neck. Blinking once, long and hard, she ignored the sharp sting and hugged her elbows, keeping her eyes on her feet crunching robotic-like over dead leaves littering the ground.

It took her half an hour to reach the bridge—not the small one that goes over the creek on the east side of town, the big one that takes people north over the river, the one they string Christmas lights from every year. She leaned over the railing and stared down at the river, noticing for the first time that it was the color of dirty dishwater. It was mid-October. The water would be cold. Once she jumped there would be no turning back. Undeterred, she made her way to the halfway point she'd marked with a felt pen the day before. She had chosen Sunday morning, long before church services began and when half the town would still be asleep. She had walked the length of the bridge three times, calculating how far down it was to the water, how deep it would be, and if there were any hidden boulders beneath the surface. She wanted to drown, not end up crippled for life.

Wedging herself into a narrow space between two of the bridge's steel posts, she pulled out the silver compass that went everywhere with her, rubbing her thumb in circles against the inscription on the back. It was a gift her dad had given her four years ago, on her thirteenth birthday, so treasured that she couldn't leave it behind.

All of her senses were on high alert, amplified a thousand times beyond normal, but even so, not a single car or truck passed in either direction. There were no sudden unexplained gusts of wind, no smoke rising up through the trees in the distance from some wayward forest fire, no migrating Canada geese choosing precisely that moment to fly over. *Not a single sign that tells me I shouldn't do this,* she thought, pulling her sweater over her head. Dropping the sweater on the ground at her feet, she stuffed the silver compass back into the front pocket of her jeans, grabbed one of the bridge's steel posts, and heaved herself up onto the guardrail. Then she stared down at the river and positioned her feet just so.

Late the night before, she'd flipped through her diary, lingering on certain pages. On some, she'd simply written "Happy" across the entire page. Just happy. Nothing else. But then they'd started to fill up again, each one crammed from top to bottom with her anguish, concluding with the words she'd written over and over weeks ago: *I can't do this anymore.* After her mom went to bed, she'd ripped out the pages one by one and burned them in the fireplace, and when there was nothing left but ashes, she wrote out a note and propped it against the toaster. Then she'd curled up on the couch, waiting for the watery light of morning to come.

Now, as she tilted her head back, teetering on the bridge's narrow railing, the reality of her situation hit her. Tears welled in her eyes and she willed them back. If anything was going to stop her, it would have to happen now.

Seconds passed in silence, but nothing happened.

There was no thunder, no lightning, and certainly no voices—clipped, impatient, gentle, or otherwise—trying to talk her down. A few drops of rain landed on her face, though, enough to make her hesitate. Hanging on to the post, she swung herself out and around it in one fluid motion, landing safely on the other side. No slipping or sliding, no frantic scramble to balance her body against the steel railing, just one perfect airborne arc before she landed; two seconds of weightlessness and grace that made her feel strong and sure and in control, two seconds that gave her a surge of confidence.

She pushed her hair off her face, only vaguely aware of the greasy residue that came away on her hands. Then she counted to ten—her voice rising in volume and pitch—and held her breath, waiting for a sense of peacefulness to come over her. But her heart was still pounding and now her hands were shaking, too. She wondered if this had happened to others. In their last few seconds, did they freeze, too scared to jump, but too sad to turn back? Or was it worse? Were their loneliness and despair so raw and real and painful that they couldn't push past them long enough to bother getting scared?

She studied her shoes. In gym class the week before, when it was her turn to cross the rope bridge over the ravine behind the high school, someone had whispered, "Watch this. She's gonna choke." And, in fact, she had. At the last second, she had choked big-time, pushing to the back of the line, feeling sick. *But this is different,* she thought. Her heart constricted and an involuntary sob rose in her throat. For as long as she could remember, she'd been terrified of water. Even wearing a lifejacket, surrounded by adults who could swim, she used to be scared that the boat they were in would flip over. And now here she was.

She closed her eyes and whispered, "Now."

She turned and jumped, letting go of the steel post and throwing her arms over her head. When she hit the water, she hit hard, slamming into it with an unforgiving force that caught her off guard. Within seconds, it engulfed her. At first panic set in and her arms and legs flailed against its weight. Pushing back toward the surface, she sucked in a mouthful of air, then went under again. The current was strong, so when she came up a second time, she was quickly pulled down yet again, her legs sluggish and ineffective in the cold water, hampered even more by the weight of her clothes. Soon she sagged from exhaustion and her shoulders began to curl in on themselves, her arms offering only weak, spasmodic movements.

The rest happened fast.

Something caught a handful of her hair, jerked hard, and then let go. Her head snapped back and she reflexively opened her mouth to scream. Water shot up her nose where air had just been, burning her nostrils. She started to choke, her shoulders bucking convulsively under the water, and then a whole new level of panic set in when something grabbed her arm in a viselike grip. Suddenly she was being pulled from the water and she heard a string of curses, followed by the heavy pant of someone breathing hard. Drenched and sputtering, she landed on her backside in the bottom of a small boat, automatically lifting an arm in the air, pulling back from whoever was standing over her.

"Unbelievable! Ten more seconds and you would've landed on top of me."

Slowly, she lowered her arm and felt her face go slack. Standing in front of her, legs spread for balance, was Louie Johnson, brow furrowed with concern and hands open in a friend's welcome. "What the hell you doing, Ellis? Trying to get yourself killed?"

She squinted up at him, transfixed and disbelieving, struggling to comprehend that she was sitting in a puddle of water at her next-door neighbor's feet instead of bobbing down the river to meet her maker. Her mouth opened, but nothing came out. There might have been a few excuses she could have invented, but she didn't have the energy. Her shoulders dropped and she turned away.

Yes, she thought. *That's exactly what I'm trying to do.*

Nothing about him looked happy. "Jumping from a bridge is no joke, young lady!"

This was unarguable logic, and yet Ellis said nothing. *Stupid, stupid man,* she thought, shivering as she folded her arms across the front of her blouse.

Water trickled down her forehead and she wiped it away with the back of one wrist. It had taken her weeks of planning and she'd done so with great care. What she hadn't planned on was Louie. That of all mornings he would choose this one to take his boat out on the river, or that he'd drift along, not bothering to use the motor because he hated polluting the water. Worse yet, that she hadn't noticed him when she'd climbed up onto the guardrail.

She sneaked a look at him, silently cursing her bad luck. It had always been this way, her anticipating one of those incredible jaw-dropping moments you see in movies, and life dishing up something rotten instead. This wasn't the kind of divine intervention she'd had in mind earlier. A lone dove cooing down at her from the bridge's steel girders might have worked, or maybe a butterfly landing inexplicably on the tip of her nose. Even a swarm of bees attacking her out of the blue may have made her rethink things, but not getting hauled out of the river *after* she'd already jumped.

As Louie stared at her, realization dawned in his eyes. He pulled off his black skullcap, which made him look like an aging cat burglar, reached into the canvas bag at his feet, and pulled out a towel that looked startlingly white against his dark skin. "When something's bothering me," he said, setting the towel on the seat next to her, "I often go for a swim. I recommend it, by the way—swimming—just not here. The water's too cold and—"

"Please leave me alone." Her voice came out as a whisper.

Water slapped against the boat in a soothing rhythm as they drifted down the river. Louie stared at her as if trying to decide what he was supposed to do with this wet teenager shivering on the bottom of his boat. Then he squatted in front of her, resting one hand on the seat between them for balance.

"Are things really that bad?" he asked, rubbing the stubble on his face.

Ellis looked up at him, and he looked back with such genuine concern that she had to glance away. She could tell he was essentially a kind man, and she should probably say something, but she just couldn't. *Yes,* she thought, biting down on her trembling bottom lip. *They are.* To her horror, the girl who never cried started crying, huge gulping sobs that made her nose run and her shoulders heave. She hid her face in her hands, wishing she could undo what she had just done, that she hadn't picked that exact moment to jump, that Louie would go away. More important, that he wouldn't tell anyone.

Louie straightened. "I'm sure everything'll look better tomorrow."

Ellis didn't look at him, but she could tell by his voice that he wished he were anywhere but here. Maybe sitting on his sagging porch reading the newspaper, or sifting through photos of the sunflowers he planted in his yard each summer. She wiped her nose on her sleeve. She was cold and wet and miserable, and she didn't know what to do next.

Seconds later, her eyes widened in alarm. Somewhere in the distance, she could hear the distinctive clank and groan of a truck's gears grinding as it lumbered down the gravel road that followed the river. Her hands tightened into fists and her stomach constricted with dread.

Oh, no. Please don't let anyone see us!

The truck was hidden from view by the trees, but she heard the heavy rumble get louder, and then it slowed to a crawl and stopped not far down the river from where they were drifting. Ellis's back tensed as she waited and watched. Garbled radio messages crackled through the crisp morning air, and a man's urgent voice called out, "Is everyone all right? I just saw a girl jump from the bridge."

"Looks like we got company," Louie said, standing up.

Every muscle in Ellis's body went slack. "This is my worst nightmare," she whispered, hearing the wobble in her voice as clearly as Louie must have. "Before the end of the day, it'll be all over town."

Louie frowned at the shoreline and Ellis slid down farther in the boat, trying to make herself small and unnoticeable. Taking deep breaths, she imagined next week's front-page story in the *Barrow Gazette*: LOCAL GIRL BOTCHES SUICIDE.

Quickly, and without warning, the boat tilted, throwing her off balance.

She slid sideways, slamming into the opposite side, then, as she scrambled to grab hold, the boat seesawed and dropped down again. A mountain of water hit her and she crabbed backward, sputtering. She sat up and saw Louie in the water ten feet away. *Oh, no! Did he slip? Did he have a heart attack or something?* She reached over the side of the boat, stretching a hand toward him. "Here! Grab on to me!"

He went under, then came back up, arms flapping just out of reach.

Trying again, Ellis stretched one arm out as far as she could. Somehow she managed to grab on to him. Bracing her feet against the inside of the boat, she got a good grip and leaned back, but he was too heavy, and she quickly realized that she'd never be able to pull him back into the boat. Panting, she looked over her shoulder, hoping now that whoever was coming would hurry up so they could help her.

What happened next happened too fast for her to process until later.

When she turned back to Louie, he had both hands wrapped around her wrists. “Are you okay?” she asked, adjusting her feet again. Louie didn’t answer. Instead, he cracked a smile, one glorious flash of mischief and white teeth before giving her arm a sharp tug. Ellis gasped, eyes widening with confusion. He tugged again, harder this time, and in a heartbeat she was in the water next to him. She landed facedown, but somehow managed to straighten herself out. Anger surged through her as she came up for air, struggling to keep her head above water.

“What are you *doing*?” she sputtered.

Louie didn’t answer. Instead, he seemed strangely calm as he grabbed her by the arm and pulled her over to where the boat was now drifting.

At that moment, a heavyset man with a good-sized paunch and a head of leonine white hair burst through the trees on shore, stumbling to catch his balance. “Try to catch this!” he yelled, throwing a towrope out into the water. It fell short, so he yanked it back in and tried a second time. Louie finally grabbed it and passed the end to Ellis, who was holding on to the boat.

"Hang on," the man called out, bracing one foot against a rock as he pulled them in.

When they were close enough to shore for their feet to touch bottom, Ellis followed Louie up the rocky riverbank, half walking, half crawling, and dropped to her knees. Their rescuer was breathless from exertion. "That scared the crap outta me," he said, stabbing a meaty finger in Louie's face. "You okay?"

Louie leaned forward with his head bent and one hand on his knee.

The heavyset man jerked a thumb in Ellis's direction, sounding more exhilarated than concerned, talking as though she wasn't kneeling right there beside them five feet away. "I was unlocking the gate up at the dump when I looked down the hill and saw her jump from the bridge. I can't see the river from up there so I didn't know you were in the water, too. You sure you're okay, Louie?"

“I’m fine, Roy,” Louie coughed out, waving a hand.

Great, Ellis thought, flushing. *They know each other.*

She dropped her head forward, trying to hide behind a tangled mass of wet hair. She wanted to disappear, to dissolve into the silt and muck she was kneeling in the way Sasquatches blended into the bark of a tree, becoming the tree, so no one could find them. When she glanced up, she saw Roy frowning as he studied her. Clearly he was trying to piece everything together, but he seemed so rattled that nothing was making sense.

“Louie, is she sick or something?” he half whispered, brushing mud off his pants. “Why would she jump off the bridge like that?”

Despair overcame Ellis. *My life’s ruined,* she thought, wiping her nose with the back of her hand. She pushed back onto her haunches and clutched her arms around her middle. She was about to explain that it was all her fault, but before she could say anything, Louie straightened and stepped in front of her.

"She didn't jump to *jump*, Roy," he said. "She jumped to save me." Louie pointed to his boat, looking genuinely embarrassed as he rubbed the back of his neck. "Someone must've greased the bottom of that thing. I stood up to grab an oar and—boom!—I was in the water. Smucked my head pretty good, too."

Ellis froze, staring at him in disbelief. There was a difference between a good lie and a bad lie, and she immediately recognized this one for what it was—this was a beautiful lie, a lie unlike any other she'd heard before.

Louie walked around behind her and put a hand on her shoulder, pressing down hard as he carried on. "I must've got disoriented after that. When I came up for air, she grabbed me and pulled me over to the boat." He sounded amused, as though the very idea of some teenage girl saving his sorry ass was one for the record books.

Roy stared at Ellis, rubbing his chin. He seemed suspicious, not fully convinced that Louie was being up front with him. Flushing with guilt, Ellis dropped her eyes. All she had to do was say, "No, that's not right. That's not what happened," but in the lie Louie had just offered up she saw the same solution he had seen—a way to save her from the town-wide humiliation that would surely follow if she told the truth.

Louie introduced them, maybe in an effort to distract Roy from his own confusion. "Ellis Williams, meet Roy Ballard. Roy, this here's Ellis." He walked over to Roy and clapped a hand on his shoulder. "Look, I feel stupid about this," he said, lowering his voice. "So let's keep it between us, okay? No need going off telling half the town."

Roy looked over at Ellis, then back to Louie.

"Sure," he said and shrugged. "I won't say nothing."

Moments later, after Louie said he'd come back and pick up his boat that afternoon, they started climbing the embankment to Roy's truck. The ground was thick with scrubby trees and wild rosebushes, so the three formed a line with Roy leading the way, Louie and Ellis following. As they parted branches and carefully worked their way up the hill, Roy complained about his back, how it hurt like hell from saving them the way he had. Louie thanked him more than once, but Ellis stayed quiet, shivering as she kept her head down.

When they got to the top, Roy flopped forward against the hood of his old truck, muttering that Louie sure owed him a few beers for this one.

"Done," Louie said agreeably, slapping the truck's fender. Then he looked back at Ellis, put a finger to his lips, and winked.

After Louie helped her up into the truck, Ellis kept her eyes riveted on her fingernails, comparing them, trying to decide which were longer, doing everything she could not to cry. Overwhelmed with emotions she couldn't put into words, she took in the earthy smells that drifted in through Louie's open window. Clearly she wasn't meant to die today. She was alive, and the world around her was churning with sights and sounds and smells that would forever mark this day. Unable to hold them back, she let a few tears slide down her cheeks, and as they did a quiet resolve came over her, a crisp sense of purpose that rose up from somewhere deep inside. It was as though destiny had pointed her in a new direction, saying, "Okay, then, here's that movie moment you've been waiting for. What you do with it is your choice."

Later, when she thought about this day, recalling it often in the months and years to come, she would remember two things with remarkable clarity: an unexpected relief that made her light-headed, followed by the profound realization that she owed Louie Johnson for saving her life. Ellis glanced sideways at him and he caught her looking. For a moment she pretended to be absorbed in the scenery outside his window, but then she shifted and stared straight at him, trying to make her face say, *Thank you*. And as she did, she experienced an unexpected rush of gratitude. *Because you didn't just save my life. You saved two lives—something I won't be able to hide much longer.*

One

FIFTEEN YEARS LATER

It was snowing as Ellis drove around the final bend of highway leading into Barrow, Montana, typical weather for this part of the country in November. She just wasn't used to it after living in Dallas for fourteen years. She crested the long, winding hill and turned on the wipers. The windshield suddenly became a theater-sized screen, the oval bowl of winking lights in the valley below holding a definite Norman Rockwell appeal. An hour south of the Canadian border and slightly northwest of the Big Belt Mountains, the town of Barrow was no more than a blip on the map, known mostly for a man who'd had the hiccups for five weeks straight and got himself invited onto the Late Show with David Letterman. "No-man's-land," her dad used to say. "God's country," her mom often countered. As a child, Ellis probably would have sided with her dad, but now that she was older, she could see her mom's point of view. Either way, the closer she got, the more her heart raced. She had successfully stayed away for years, but now circumstances had forced her to come back.

Ellis pulled over and stared at the rusty metal road sign illuminated by her headlights: WELCOME TO BARROW: POPULATION 2138. It'd been there for as long as she could remember. One corner was bent, probably from when it'd been hit by a passing snow plow, and there were gunshot holes on the far side from when someone had used it for target practice.

Wonderful, she thought. *I'm back where I started, in almost the same situation I was in when I grew up here, helpless and miserable.* She turned and looked at her daughter, Hadley, asleep next to her, looking deceptively serene with her hair tousled and mouth open. *The only difference is now I have you to worry about, too.*

She pulled back onto the highway and slowly accelerated. *What would Mark say?* Would he give her a hug and say, "I know you can do this," or would he think she hadn't tried hard enough to stay in Dallas? Her mind stayed empty for a while, and then her head slowly began to pound, the way it often did now when she thought about her husband, torn between missing him and wishing he were here so she could give him a piece of her mind.

Five months ago, he'd begun complaining that he wasn't feeling well. She'd pushed him to see a doctor, but he'd dismissed her worries, chalking it up to a bad strain of the flu. Not even two weeks later, while on a business trip in Houston, with his partner, Lance, Mark had collapsed and died from what was initially diagnosed as a heart attack.

When Lance phoned to tell her that day, Ellis had illogically found herself wanting to change the subject, to ask what the weather was like in Houston. It had seemed, at the time, a reasonable question, so surreal was their conversation.

"He grabbed my arm and said he wasn't feeling good," Lance had explained, his voice quavering. "He said he wanted to lie down. . . ."

Ellis closed her eyes, feeling dizzy as she listened to the wind thrum around their house, signaling an oncoming storm.

"I called an ambulance, but it was too late. . . ."

She clamped a hand over her mouth and her shoulders began to shake in a strange, uncontrollable way. Inexplicably, she suddenly realized how often Mark had let her pretend she was in charge, even though they both knew she wasn't.

"Ellis, are you there?! Are you okay?" Lance's voice said over the phone.

"Yes," she managed, choking back a sob. "Yes, I'm okay."

But, of course, she wasn't. Not really. Mark was her husband, and Hadley's dad, and the bustling force of nature that had kept their family humming along so harmoniously for years. How could he be gone? *How strange,* she thought. *I can't remember important memories right now. No milestones or major events, just his arms wrapped around me, the smell of him after he's been puttering around the yard outside, the sound of him and Hadley laughing.*

Even when she flew to Houston to have his body released, it hadn't seemed real. Not Lance leading her into the hospital, holding her by the elbow as they had walked into that bare, windowless room. Not the sight of the gurney with a sheet-covered body on it, just like you'd see on television. Not the coroner, kindly asking if she was ready before pulling the sheet back. And certainly not Mark's face, mouth slightly open as though he were asleep, the small scar on his left shoulder from a childhood bike accident exactly where it had always been. At first, she had stood there, squinting at him in disbelief, and then she'd doubled over and quickly backed away, bumping into the table behind her. She felt her insides convulse and she squeezed her eyes shut, clutching her stomach. Vomit exploded from her mouth, splattering Lance's pants and the coroner's shoes and the salmon-colored floor tiles.

Only then had she let herself cry, sobbing into splayed hands as Lance helped her into an empty chair.

Only then had she finally realized it was real.

She didn't learn about the financial problems Mark had been keeping from her until after his funeral. It'd been humiliating to admit to Lance that, no, she hadn't known anything about them. Three years earlier, Mark had left his secure management job with Tesco Oil and invested everything they had in a consulting firm with Lance. At first business was good, but apparently they had been struggling for a while. Mark hadn't told her they had recently lost their biggest contract, that if they didn't find one to replace it soon they'd personally lose everything, which is what happened after he died.

Mark's life insurance covered some of the debt, but there wasn't enough. The financial problems were too big and pressing, and Ellis had no choice but to sell their home and both of their cars, a process that was mostly a blur now, thanks to the medication her doctor had put her on.

She bought an old bare-bones Toyota Corolla, put her last eighteen hundred dollars in the bank, and took a hard look at the future. What to do about the rest of her life and what clothes to wear that morning were equally daunting questions. Even now, there were days when all she wanted to do was curl into a ball. But then she'd think of Hadley and tell herself to keep moving, pushing aside the illogical sensation that Mark was going to come through the door any day and tell her this was all a big mistake, that she and Hadley were still the center of his world, that together they'd bring it all back on track.

After digging through his desk at home, she'd pulled out a yellow notepad and had made a list that she carried with her everywhere. She needed a job and they needed somewhere to live. New owners would be taking possession of their house in a month, the house she and Mark had bought years ago, believing they would grow old there. She wrote "boxes" on the list, pretending to be concerned with how many she should get. When her mind said, *You need sleep*, she wrote, "Buy espresso," and when Hadley's private school phoned and suggested a monthly payment plan option for her daughter's outstanding tuition, she scribbled "Need a school nurse?" at the top of her list.

Ellis was an LPN, a licensed practical nurse, a profession commonly known to be in demand, but the health-care situation in Texas wasn't any better than it was in other states, and with all of the cutbacks, she'd only been able to find work on an as-needed or contract basis for the last few years. Studying the want ads one weekend, she wrote "Consider retail job" on her yellow notepad, and then quickly scratched it out, knowing it wouldn't pay enough to support them.

In the midst of those urgent financial problems, Hadley began behaving as she never had before. After dinner, she would immediately retreat to her room. Hours later, Ellis would knock on her door and get a muffled "I want to be alone, okay?"

"Hadley, I'm worried about you."

"Don't be," she'd reply. "I'm fine."

I'm not, Ellis thought, wishing her daughter would open up and talk to her, desperate to know the pieces of Hadley that Mark once had so she could lay claim to them before they were lost forever in this new, quieter version of a daughter she barely recognized.

Ellis was too preoccupied with the problems Mark's death had created to notice that Hadley was cutting classes. Nor did it occur to her that Hadley was lying when she said she was sleeping over at Rhea's or Leslie's, two friends she'd had since grade school. Yes, she was quiet and withdrawn, but wasn't that normal given what she'd been through? Then one day Hadley walked through the door after school and Ellis slowly lowered herself into a chair, slack-jawed. Gone was the long blond hair she and Mark had loved; in its place was a punk layered style, dyed Goth black.

"I decided to get it cut," Hadley said, with a hint of defiance. "Like it?"

"Yes," Ellis said after hesitating long enough that Hadley probably knew she didn't.

Over the next few months, they argued about everything, from Hadley's lack of effort at school to what she was and wasn't allowed to wear each morning when she left the house. Black leotards with strategic holes ripped in them and skimpy miniskirts weren't negotiable, although Ellis agreed to the combat boots. By then, they had moved into a two-bedroom apartment and Ellis had finally found a buyer for Mark's treasured BMW Z3 roadster—the last thing she owned of any value. Ellis had already signed the bill of sale, and the buyer, a man in his late twenties, was writing out a certified check, when Hadley came storming up the sidewalk after school.

"What are you doing with Dad's car?!" she demanded, dropping her knapsack.

Ellis held up her hands in a let's-calm-down gesture.

"Dad promised it to me," Hadley reminded her. "He said when I was old enough, he'd teach me how to drive using that car."

"I don't have a choice, Hadley," Ellis said. "We can't keep it." Then to the buyer, in a lower voice, Ellis said, "I'm sorry. Her father passed away recently and she's having a hard time—"

"*I'm* having a hard time?" Hadley said, stepping closer. "Oh, that's rich, Mom! What about you? Have you told this guy how you've got Dad's clothes boxed up in your bedroom, or that you still keep his shaving things in the medicine cabinet?"

Ellis felt her face grow hot with embarrassment. "Hadley, that's enough."

The BMW Z3 buyer took a few steps away, looking uncomfortable. "Maybe I should come back another time," he suggested.

Ellis shook her head no. This had to be done. She accepted his check and handed him the keys, hands trembling.

"Thanks," he said, walking backward to the car. "I'll take good care of it."

Two weeks later, Ellis came home one afternoon and found Rhea and Leslie waiting on the front steps. Pale and somber, Rhea stood and handed Ellis an envelope. "Mrs. Semple? I found this in my locker today." Ellis opened it and unfolded a letter inside, decorated with dozens of black cartoonish crosses. In small, neat letters, Hadley had written: *Tell my mom I won't be coming home for a while, okay?*

A breeze came up, blowing a strand of hair across Ellis's face. She immediately felt something harden inside, fueled by a distant memory she'd spent years trying to forget. *Oh, yes, you will,* she thought, giving herself no time for contemplation. She drilled Rhea and Leslie, pushing for answers they couldn't give her. "Did she discuss this with you? Did she mention where she was going? Did she say why?"

"Hadley barely talks to us anymore," Rhea said.

Leslie lifted a shoulder, let it drop. "She's been acting . . . different since her dad died."

Ellis phoned everyone she knew, everyone Hadley knew, anyone either of them had ever known, with no luck. She called the police, but because of Hadley's note, they said they had to treat her as a runaway, giving it a lower priority than they would have if she had been abducted. Ellis was told to phone back if she hadn't heard from her in a week.

She checked and rechecked Hadley's room, underneath her bed, through her closet and all her drawers. Finally, using her hip, she'd shoved Hadley's oak dresser out of the way and lifted a loose floorboard Mark had shown her when they'd moved in years ago. Taking a flashlight, she got down on her knees, reached inside, and pulled out two empty bottles of rum and a ziplock bag with the remnants of pot in the bottom.

She stared at them in stunned silence. *There,* she thought, hands shaking as she lined them up on Hadley's dresser. *Evidence.*

And yet finding these things only added to her worries. How had this been going on and she hadn't noticed? What else was Hadley hiding from her?

On the second night that Hadley didn't come home, Leslie phoned. "Mrs. Semple? A guy in my class said he saw Hadley catching a ride with Adam Peterson after school on Wednesday."

Ellis searched her memory, trying to place Adam Peterson. Leslie explained that he'd dropped out of school the year before; that his parents traveled a lot.

Within an hour, Ellis had his parents' address.

Jumping into her car, she drove across town to an upscale neighborhood. It didn't take long to find the house, a veritable mansion built among a handful of others on a hillside. She parked on the circular driveway out front. It was Friday night, and as she walked to the front door, she could hear music through an open window, followed by swells of laughter from somewhere out back, and then the sound of breaking glass.

Dread blossomed in her stomach when she rang the doorbell and no one answered. Taking a breath, she turned the knob and found it unlocked. Pushing the door open, she stepped into a large tiled foyer. As though sensing her presence, a handful of people turned their heads—one choreographed movement—to look at her with frank curiosity. They were standing in a massive room with floor-to-ceiling windows that overlooked a swimming pool outside. The pool was filled with people, all of them a lot older than Hadley, and near it was a crowded dance area, a stompfest of pounding feet and flying elbows as music pulsed at an earsplitting volume.

"Is Adam Peterson here?" she asked, raising her voice.

A young girl with excessive facial piercing nodded toward a skinny guy on the far side of the room. His back to Ellis, he was mixing drinks at an ornate glass and marble bar. When he turned around, she saw that he was wearing a black T-shirt—"The Doors" on it—that looked too big on him, like it belonged to someone else. *Probably his father's,* she caught herself thinking.

She gave him a cold stare. "I'm looking for my daughter, Hadley Semple."

He frowned and shook his head, annoyed by the intrusion, but by the time Ellis had made it across the room, he'd assumed a polite expression. "Last I saw," he said, jerking a thumb over his shoulder, "she was in the pool."

Ellis walked past him, opened a set of sliding glass doors, and stepped outside, scanning the crowd. There were people everywhere, some seated at tables around the pool, others on the dance floor, more clustered around a swim-up bar. Most of the guys were overdressed, and the girls were flashing more skin than seemed appropriate for any age. And then she saw Hadley sitting on the grass, elbows resting on her knees as she stared at her hands, a picture of misery. She was wearing a red bikini that made her look years older than fourteen, and her hair was wet and dripping from its spiky ends.

Ellis's throat closed and she had to tilt her head back so her tears wouldn't fall.

Thank God she's okay.

Pulling herself together, she weaved her way through the crowd to the far side of the pool, a few kids rearing away in exaggerated alarm when they saw the look on her face. All at once her determination equaled Hadley's. They were going home. Now.

She walked up to Hadley and waited. Her favorite skinny jeans were lying on the chair behind her, as was the British racing green duffel bag she always used for swim club. After a moment, Hadley lifted her gaze and slowly focused on her mom. Her eyes widened briefly and then her face collapsed with disappointment, a slight flush spreading up her neck.

Ellis let ten seconds pass. "Come on," she said, grabbing her jeans. "We're going home. We need to get our lives back to normal."

"Define normal," Hadley mumbled.

"All right, Hadley," Ellis said, meaning, *That's enough*.

Outwardly, she remained calm, but inside Ellis realized she was holding her breath, hoping Hadley wouldn't create a scene.

An older girl dropped her cigarette on the cement a few feet away and ground it under the heel of her shoe. "You really going?" she asked Hadley.

"Looks like it," Hadley said, shrugging.

She made a halfhearted effort to get up, and that was when Ellis realized she'd been drinking. Her balance was off, her speech slightly slurred. Swearing under her breath, Hadley struggled into her jeans and swatted her mom's hand away when Ellis tried to pull her sweatshirt out of her duffel bag. Keeping her head down, she put on her flip-flops, and although she didn't exactly walk in a straight line, she independently maneuvered her way down a stone path to a gate that led to the Petersons' front yard, refusing any help. Behind them, as Ellis followed her out of the yard, someone called out, "See ya, Hadley," and she raised an arm in the air like an afterthought, singularly focused on opening the gate.

They were in the car, Hadley strapping on her seatbelt, when Ellis noticed two long scratches on her left arm, blood beading from them. "What happened?" she asked, trying to keep her voice level and calm.

Hadley stared at them for a long moment, seemingly transfixed. "You mean to my arm?" she said in a half whisper. "Or to us?"

"Both," Ellis heard herself say.

Hadley wiped her nose with the back of her wrist. "I had a few drinks," she said, shrugging. "And then I tripped and fell against a stucco wall."

Ellis shifted sideways to study her. "And us?"

Looking perilously close to tears, Hadley locked eyes with her. "Dad died," she said simply, as though that explained everything.

Ellis turned away to stare out her window. Whenever she and Hadley were arguing—over homework, help with the dishes, Hadley's refusal to clean her room—Mark used to step in and calm them both down. He would start singing "Angie" by the Rolling Stones. At first, his voice would be timorous and off-key; then he'd throw all of his personality into it, and soon neither of them were paying attention to how badly he was singing it because he was enjoying it so much, drowning out the loudest parts of their argument. By the time he finished, despite themselves, she and Hadley would be shaking with laughter.

Closing her eyes, Ellis tried to imagine him singing that song now. She almost thought she could hear his voice.

Two weeks later, she told Hadley she couldn't find a full-time job she could count on to pay the bills; so they'd have to live with Grandma for a while. They were moving to Barrow. Hadley begged her to reconsider. She would get a part-time job to help out, she would stop skipping class, she wouldn't hang around with the crowd she'd been hanging around with. But Ellis refused to change her mind, working hard to keep her thoughts turned inward and her face blank so Hadley wouldn't sense her own simmering anger over the fact that they had no choice.

"How long are we gonna live in Barrow?" Hadley had asked.

"I don't know," Ellis replied.

"Six months?" she pressed. "A year?!"

Ellis turned away. "As long as it takes to get back on our feet."

Ellis, too, longed to stay in Dallas, worried that a past she had buried long ago would rise up and destroy her if she moved back to Barrow. Rationally, she knew moving back was the only option left, and yet, even after she'd phoned her mom and made all the arrangements, she'd released a shaky breath and set the receiver gently back in its cradle, praying she hadn't made a mistake.

Since then, Hadley had barely spoken to her.

No doubt about it, Ellis thought, turning off the radio, *we're off to a good start*.

During a crisis many people might welcome going home, to a haven filled with soothing voices, supportive family, and fond memories; the first place you would want to run to. But it wasn't that way for Ellis. When she recalled memories from her childhood in Barrow, she often found herself teetering between love and hate. So much had gone wrong there, and yet, after she'd had Hadley, so much had gone right.

Ellis had left fourteen years ago, rarely coming back, preferring to fly her mom to Dallas a few times each year instead. There'd always been a good excuse—Mark couldn't take time off work; Hadley didn't want to miss a swim meet; it would be so much easier if her mom came to Dallas. Other than Mark, no one knew about the ghosts Ellis had left behind in Barrow. Not even her mom. For years, Ellis had worked hard to forget them herself, creating family traditions of their own that were as rich as any she could have imagined as a child. Mark and Hadley had always been her top priority, but now that he was gone and she was on her way back to Montana, the terrible reality of her situation seemed sharper than before.

She slowed as she reached the bottom of the hill leading into town, trying to focus her thoughts. It was late and she was exhausted, about to begin a whole new phase of her life, but in no hurry to do so. Up ahead, Main Street ended two hundred yards before running into the Dearborn River. To her left was Save-On-Foods, a bakery with a crooked DAY OLD BREAD sign taped to the window, the always "Under Renovation" Chinese restaurant, the drugstore, and the town lumberyard. On her right was Mercer's Clothing, the bank, the post office, the regional health clinic, the liquor store, and the infamous Rockhead Hotel, which had been built in 1959, burned to the ground, and was rebuilt in 1973.

When she hit the end of Main Street, she turned left, drove four more blocks, made another left and drove up a steep tree-lined street. Halfway to the top, on a long flat stretch, she parked in front of an old two-story house. Twenty years ago, before her mom had been financially able to buy it and fix it up, it had been a dilapidated rental home, almost completely stripped of its original paint and with bald patches on the roof where shingles had fallen off. Today, it was sap green with white trim and it had a front porch. The roof had long ago been reshingled. One side was covered in lush vines that blossomed every summer with cherry-colored flowers, and the other had an ivy-covered trellis with a stone walkway leading into the backyard.

Ellis turned off the ignition and rested her forehead against the steering wheel, listening to the soft tick of the engine. She and Hadley had left Dallas four days before. Mostly, they'd traveled without speaking, the sadness between them mixing with Hadley's simmering hostility, and the long drive and Hadley's silence had made Ellis feel terribly alone. They had stayed in a motel in Santa Fe with a glossy cardboard sign taped to the TV advertising in-room adult movies, at a Super 8 in Boulder with a toilet that wouldn't flush, at a bed-and-breakfast in Wyoming that only had bunk beds. Other than stopping for gas today, they'd driven twelve hours straight.

It was almost one in the morning. Ellis's eyes were burning, there was a crick in her neck, and her back ached from sitting in the same position for so long. She suddenly felt years older than thirty-two, but when Hadley sat up and yawned, she quickly composed herself.

"Hey, you," she said, trying to sound upbeat as she rolled the window down and stuck her hand outside to catch a few snowflakes. "We're finally here."

Hadley stared out at all the snow, a stony gaze taking hold of her face. "God, this is hard," she said in a half whisper, lifting an arm to bury her face in her sweatshirt. It was her dad's, and for weeks now she'd worn it over whatever she had on, refusing to wash it, trying to hold on to the lingering scent of him.

Ellis rubbed her eyes, thinking, *Harder than you can imagine*.

When she looked up, her mom was silhouetted in the doorway, a hall light on behind her, one arm raised in welcome. Ellis felt Hadley's gaze on her as she unbuckled her seatbelt and rolled her shoulders.

"We'd better go in," she said, motioning to the house. "Grandma's waiting."

Hadley got out of the car, and her grandmother ran down the steps and met her on the sidewalk, wrapping her in a warm embrace. At sixty-three, Paulina Williams was a tall, thin woman who moved with an old-fashioned grace. She had exquisite silver hair and the sort of natural elegance that made people stare appreciatively. Growing up, Ellis had often marveled at how polished and cultured she seemed. *But fragile, too,* she thought, remembering how her habit of working through her rosary beads after mass every Sunday had blossomed into a nightly ritual after Ellis's dad left.

Eventually, her mom had suffered a deep depression. There were many nights when Ellis would slap together a peanut butter sandwich and sit cross-legged outside her mom's bedroom door, listening to her cry as she asked God to give her strength. Sadly, though, more often than not her mom's prayers didn't seem to help half as much as the pills did, and to a large extent Ellis was left with the responsibility of taking care of herself.

Until Ellis met Mark and got pregnant, she spent a lot of time on her own. If she didn't want to do her homework, her mom didn't make her. If she came home late, beyond what normal parents considered reasonable, her mom was usually asleep. And when she slipped out at night, slinking among the trees along the river as invisible as a Sasquatch, no one ever knew she was gone. She did well at school, but was preoccupied with waiting for her dad to return, something she didn't fully recognize until one day, voice thick with emotion, her mom announced that he had "stopped in for a visit" while Ellis was in school. "He's living in Canada," she said. "He wants a divorce."

That got Ellis's attention. Outraged, she tried to stare her mom down, the burning need to defend him overshadowing all logic. She wanted to point out that he would never stop in for a visit without seeing her, but instead she retreated to her room and shut the door. A month later, she got drunk for the first time at a party, and three weeks after that she put the small of her hand against Mark Semple's chest and kissed him back, meaning business as they stretched out on a circle of tamped-down grass next to the river.

Ellis's thoughts returned to the present as Paulina put her hands on either side of Hadley's face. "What in the world did you do to your hair?" Not waiting for an answer, she gave her only grandchild a kiss and said, "Lord, though, but you are beautiful," shaking her head in wonder.

She turned to Ellis, eyes misty with unspoken worry. "I'm so glad you're both here," she said, moving closer to hug her, too. Ellis squeezed her back, and when her mom's embrace grew tighter and went on longer than usual, she felt her composure start to slip.

"So where do you want us?" Ellis asked.

"Right," Paulina said, tenting her fingers against her lips. "We'll talk more in the morning." Taking Hadley by the elbow, she guided her up the steps and into the house. "Let's get you to bed. You must be exhausted."

Ellis grabbed two suitcases out of the backseat and carried them inside.

She stopped in the kitchen to take in her surroundings before following them upstairs. For years, this place had been home—she and her mom drinking tea with honey whenever it rained; making fish patties with their meat grinder every fall to "stock up" for winter; rolling quarters and dimes to pay the power bill. Today, on the porch, was the same life-size cardboard cutout of a Sasquatch her mom had bought her the year she'd turned thirteen.

Upstairs, Paulina opened the corner bedroom door and waved Hadley inside. Ellis leaned against the frame. The room had been freshly painted cobalt blue and was equipped with every convenience her mom could manage on her meager income: a small television set and used books filled a floor-to-ceiling bookcase. There was also a wrought-iron bed and a refurbished skylight Paulina had "bought at an auction and hired someone to install the week before." It wasn't a big room—it had a slanted ceiling and two small windows—but with the gleaming hardwood floor and funky IKEA throw rug, it looked cozy and welcoming.

"Do you like it?" Paulina asked.

Hadley slowly circled the room before sinking onto the bed. "I do," she whispered with a kind of polite wonder. "Thanks, Grandma."

Feeling an unexpected flash of irritation, Ellis set Hadley's suitcase down. "Look, you guys, I'm going to bed," she said. "I'll see you in the morning." She retreated to her old bedroom, set her suitcase on the mattress and flipped it open.

Moments later, there was a soft knock at the door.

"Come in."

"Ellis?"

Paulina stuck her head inside, her face serious and intent, as though she was about to say something she'd given a lot of thought. "I just . . . I want you to know I'm here if you need someone to talk to."

At first, Ellis wasn't sure if she'd heard her right. Chewing on her lip, she looked away, at the lace curtains covering the window, at the oatmeal-colored chenille bedspread, at the age-worn hardwood floor. If only her mom had been there for her after her dad left, instead of retreating into her own little world, leaving Ellis to deal with problems on her own. There weren't a lot of memories from those years Ellis liked to recall. She and her mom weren't close the way some mothers and daughters were, but she was happy with the relationship they'd managed to cobble together and saw no need to change it now.

"In some ways I know what you're going through," Paulina said quietly. "Losing Mark when you didn't see it coming, I mean . . ."

Ellis sniffed hard and looked up at the ceiling. "Mom?"

"Uh-huh?"

"It's not the same."

"I know," Paulina said. "All I'm saying is—"

Ellis held a hand out. "Stop, okay?" She

tried to keep her voice steady. "Dad walked out on us. Mark didn't. There are no parallels here. Mark died from an aortic dissection. The main blood vessel leading out of his heart tore—" She stopped, took a breath, and then started again. "Damn it, Mom, his aorta exploded like a ticking time bomb. He was sick and he didn't know it and there is no way he would have left me and Hadley if he'd had the choice. Dad was healthy as a horse, he just wasn't as happy as he thought he had the right to be. How can you possibly know what I'm going through?"

It went so quiet that Ellis could hear Hadley flush the toilet downstairs. Paulina turned and walked to the door. "Loss is loss. That's all I'm trying to say."

"Fair enough," Ellis said. "But I don't want to talk about it."

Minutes later, Ellis flicked off the light and hugged her pillow. As she drifted off to sleep, eyes heavy with exhaustion, she imagined Mark whispering to her that everything would be okay; that coming home to Barrow was the right thing to do; that it was time she faced the past instead of running away from it. *And maybe he's right,* she thought. *Maybe here, where it all began, I can get a new perspective on the past that helps me shape a solid future for myself and Hadley.*

Two

Ellis pulled in to her mom's driveway, parked, and took out her yellow notepad. She'd been in Barrow almost two weeks now and she suddenly realized she couldn't remember the last conversation she'd had with Mark. This sort of thing had been happening a lot. A simmering feeling of panic would set in during the day and she would stop whatever she was doing, grab her yellow notepad, and scribble down some notes. Things like: "How old was he when he first tried parachuting?" "What was the name of that British actor he liked so much?" "Did he break his right or left wrist playing hockey as a kid?" For reasons that didn't make sense to her, it was important that she accurately remember these things—imperative, in fact.

Outwardly, she had been putting on a game face, acting as though she was adjusting, but inside that wasn't exactly the case. Before moving to Barrow, she had been protected from hard reality by her own state of disbelief. Now, faced with the disheartening task of finding a job where there didn't seem to be any, she had more time to consider everything she had lost. Mark had died five months ago, yet she was still finding it hard to get any perspective on it. She had snipped at her mom over breakfast this morning when Paulina asked if she was all right, not wanting to lose her train of thought as she struggled to recall if she'd waved good-bye to him on that last morning.

She believed she had, that her wave was a genuine and honest memory she could treasure, but she also realized she may have invented it, dreamed it up later, because she couldn't handle not having said good-bye to him.

For months after the funeral, she'd had

the same recurring dream in which she would step outside with her morning coffee and find him crawling around their backyard looking for Hadley behind one tree and then the next, wearing only a green hospital gown and a plastic identification bracelet. She knew she should tell him he wouldn't find Hadley here, that something horrible had happened, that he was now dead, but when she looked into his eyes, the words wouldn't come. He looked so hopeful and happy that she couldn't bring herself to hurt his feelings, so instead she got down on her hands and knees and joined him, laughing like they used to when life was one big open-ended playground they had yet to explore.

She rubbed her fingers against her temples and thought hard. They had talked the day before he died, right? Yes. They were sitting outside on those horrible deck chairs, the ones that wobbled on the hard-baked earth around the fire pit in their backyard. Mark had reached over and held her hand very tightly; she remembered that. He'd said there were a few things he wanted to talk about, important things. One was that he thought they should stay home for Christmas instead of going somewhere exotic. Ellis was surprised. In all the years she had known him, Mark was the one who'd always pressed for a winter vacation, just the three of them. Before she could say anything, though, Hadley had burst through the back door and joined them, leaving Ellis to wonder what was going on. Only later, when Lance broke the news about their financial problems, had Mark's suggestion made sense.

One July, when Mark was fifteen and away for a weekend with a friend's family, a tornado had plowed through Topeka, Kansas, destroying three hundred homes, causing millions in property damage and killing twenty-seven people, including his parents and his two younger sisters. Because of this, he'd grown up faster than usual, raised by an aunt and uncle in Calgary, Alberta.

Family meant everything to Mark. For Christmas he had always insisted that they celebrate by doing something unforgettable. One year, they flew to Banff and went skiing with his cousins. The next, he took them to New Zealand, and Hadley saw her first kangaroo. Over the years, they traveled to Antigua, took a Blue Lagoon Cruise through the Yasawa Islands in Fiji, and explored the jungles of Belize.

Ellis slowly set her notepad down beside her on the front seat. Sometimes missing him was so intense, it bent her over as if she had been punched, and with each quiet return to old memories, a dull ache would follow, a sickening pain she had trouble hiding, especially now when she looked around Barrow and felt even older memories bumping around inside her, demanding attention.

"Did you like growing up here?" Hadley had asked the day before, pulling her feet out of her boots and propping them against the dashboard.

They were on their way to Motor Vehicles so Ellis could get new license plates. Hadley had looked at her in a pitying way, as though it hadn't occurred to her that they would be staying very long; that living in Barrow with her Grandma was only temporary. Inside, Ellis had flinched. *No, I didn't.*

But she had turned to her daughter and said, "Sure. It's not Dallas, but then again,

I'd never been to Dallas so I had nothing to compare it to, right?" It was a carefully phrased, casually delivered lie that had left her feeling both responsible and exhausted. What was done couldn't be undone, none of it, but the future stretched ahead of her like a foggy mist and she knew she had to guide Hadley through it alone now that Mark was gone. No way would she let herself succumb to weakness as her mom had when faced with a similar situation.

Making a snap decision, Ellis decided to pick Hadley up from school. Maybe that would take her mind off Mark and finding a job. When she arrived in Barrow her determination to find work had been fresh and strong, but as the first week slid into the second, her confidence had slipped and she'd found herself putting her coat on over her pajamas instead of getting dressed to drive Hadley to school each morning. After all, with no interviews lined up, there wasn't any reason to put on clothes, was there?

The regional health clinic told her they had no plans to hire anyone until their new fiscal year began in April. The hospital also had no openings, although they would keep her résumé on file. Positions as the receptionist with the town lumberyard and night clerk with the Best Western hotel had both been filled by other candidates. Then, this morning, frustrated and at her wit's end, Ellis had gone downtown to apply as a part-time cashier at Save-On-Foods. She needed a job, and right now any job would do.

On her way, she'd stopped to pick up the mail and shoved it inside her purse. She arrived at Save-On-Foods early, as the assistant manager, a young man with a bad case of acne, was unlocking the front doors. He told her to take a seat outside the manager's office next to the produce section. The store manager wouldn't be there for another twenty minutes.

"No problem," Ellis assured him. "I'll wait."

He began flicking on row after row of fluorescent lights, followed by a Christmas soundtrack that rang out across the store. Ellis pressed her back against the chair. *Oh, my God! Christmas is three weeks away and I haven't bought anything for Hadley. What kind of mother am I?*

She reached inside her purse for her yellow notepad and pulled out the mail instead. Mixed in with her mom's phone and water bills were two envelopes addressed to Ellis and a larger one to Mark, forwarded from Dallas. Setting her purse on the floor, Ellis ripped them open.

One contained the damage deposit for the apartment she had rented in Dallas after selling the house. *Good,* she thought. *Money for Christmas gifts.* There was also a sympathy card from Mark's cousin in Calgary, and Mark's *Travel + Leisure* magazine, which he'd subscribed to for as long as she could remember. Flipping slowly through it, she stumbled across a four-page spread of the Yasawa Islands in Fiji, including photos of a tiny resort where they'd stayed for a few nights years ago.

Her throat pinched shut and her hands began to tremble. Hadley had been eight. Mark had shown her a bunch of baby sea turtles hatching in the sand, and they had spent one entire day snorkeling. Ellis couldn't recall a more perfect vacation.

"I want to be cremated when I die," Mark had whispered against her ear one night after Hadley was asleep. They were sitting on the beach, watching the moon reflected against the water. It had caught her off guard, this talk of dying.

"What are you saying?" she'd said. "That you'd want your ashes spread here?"

"No," he said, giving her a nudge. "I'd want you and Hadley to pick a spot. Somewhere you both agree on."

A bum fluorescent bulb was buzzing and flickering above Ellis's head at Save-On-Foods, hidden behind rows of red and silver garland someone had taped in loops across the ceiling. Staring up at it, she felt nauseous and dizzy. She had managed to avoid thinking about the urn filled with Mark's ashes, wrapped in a towel inside a box at the back of her closet. She had taken it out after they'd first arrived and gently placed it on her dresser, pretending her hands weren't shaking. But the next morning, she had packed it back inside the box, unable to look at it.

Remembering, she felt sweat break out on her brow and her throat closed up. Her heart started to pound and she couldn't breathe. This had been happening a lot, too. "They're anxiety attacks," her doctor in Dallas had explained. "Perfectly normal given the sudden loss of your husband."

Cramming today's mail back into her purse, Ellis leaned forward and put her head between her knees, taking a series of long, slow breaths to calm herself.

The assistant manager's Nike-clad feet suddenly appeared to her left. "Ma'am? Are you okay?"

Keeping her head down, she gave him a thumbs-up, hoping he wouldn't tell anyone about her strange behavior. If he did, she'd never get the job. She scrunched her eyes shut for a moment, thinking. Wait. Had she introduced herself when he'd unlocked the front door earlier? Whew! Thank heavens, no. She'd said she wanted to speak to the manager about the part-time cashier's job she'd seen in the paper. Embarrassed, but relieved to be able to keep this unfortunate moment of humiliation between her and this no-name kid, she lifted her head and flashed him a cheery expression.

"Sorry," she said. "Got a little dizzy there."

"Hypoglycemic?" he said.

"Exactly," she replied, rising from her

chair and pointing to the exit doors. "I think I'll stop by tomorrow instead, when I'm feeling better."

Now, as Ellis parallel parked across the street from the high school and sat back to wait for the bell, she tried to wipe everything from her mind except Hadley. That morning, her daughter had had dark circles under her eyes when she came downstairs for breakfast, and when Ellis asked how things were going at school, she'd given a noncommittal shrug.

More than anything, Ellis was concerned that Hadley would hate going to school in Barrow as much as she herself had years ago. Back then, Ellis had been a chunky girl with angry clusters of acne on her face and back, the sort that made people stare and point, the kind that made her a target, especially after her dad left town and she went from wealthy and privileged to a coupon cutter on welfare.

For years she had endured verbal barbs and cruel jokes, telling herself they didn't matter even as they ate away at her self-esteem. The year she turned thirteen she found "Ellis Williams eats dog fud" scratched across her school locker. Her mom had seen it when she'd attended parent teacher interviews weeks later; she had slowly run her fingers over the words, then told Ellis to ignore it, that graffiti only counted if it was spelled correctly. Another time she'd stepped out of the shower after gym class and her clothes were missing, a note pinned to a hand towel left in their place that read, "We have cameras waiting for you outside." Being bullied wasn't only humiliating, it was socially alienating, and the sting of rejection had followed Ellis like an oppressive shadow, even after the acne had cleared and her body became curvy.

Hadley, on the other hand, had always been a natural leader: confident, charismatic, and at her best when given something or someone to organize. During gym class when Ellis was growing up, if someone had ever passed her the basketball, she'd panic and toss it to someone else—anyone else—even if they were on the other team, whereas Hadley was a girl who'd zip down the court, easily dominating the play as she called to other players, "You can do it!" or "Great pass!"

Still, Ellis worried about Hadley. She'd

just lost her dad, had had to leave the only school she'd ever attended, and was now living thousands of miles away in a small town she'd visited only a handful of times.

One after another, Ellis watched yellow school buses pull in to their assigned spots on the one-way access road built parallel to the street in front of the high school, doing so with a precision that came from practice. They would crest the hill one at a time and take a sharp left at the end of the street before parking.

The final bell sounded and the front doors burst open. A gaggle of kids pushed through, running to catch their rides. One guy jumped onto the back of another, laughing as he flattened his buddy into a snow bank. Then Ellis saw Hadley and for a few seconds her heart seized up. Hadley was holding her books against her chest the way Ellis used to carry hers, only Hadley didn't look vulnerable or lonely or lost. She looked like an untouchable ice queen, heart and soul safely curled up and tucked away where no one could reach them, eyes roving across the crowd, but not really *there* if anyone took the time to look at her.

Ellis unsnapped her seatbelt and fumbled for the door. Distracted, she pushed it open, forgetting how busy that street could be when school let out, how vehicles crested the top of the hill and whipped past.

Her car suddenly lurched forward, lifting up slightly as a piercing metal-on-metal screech filled the air, assaulting her ears. There was a loud, drawn-out snapping sound, and then the car dropped back down again, unceremoniously slamming Ellis against the seat.

A rush of cold air lashed past her.

"Holy shit!" someone yelled.

Time slowed down, and then it seemed to slow even more. Ellis felt as if she was in a vacuum where all of the sound had been sucked away. She brushed her hair off her face, raising her eyes in time to see the back end of a burgundy SUV fishtailing in the middle of the street. When she lowered her gaze, she noticed that her car door was no longer there, a gaping maw of a hole left in its place. She stared at it, dumbfounded, trying to connect these two important observations, fighting a flash of impatience at her sudden thickheadedness.

From far away she could hear voices yelling and what sounded like a crowd coming closer. That was when she saw her car door spinning in circles in the street, twenty feet away.

Another car crested the top of the hill and slammed on its brakes, skidding sideways before coming to a stop inches from the burgundy SUV. In the fog of her peripheral vision Ellis saw a man run out onto the road, waving his arms in the air, warning other drivers that something was amiss ahead. Through it all, she was acutely aware of voices coming at her from all directions, alarmed and concerned.

"Maybe someone should call an ambulance!"

"Oh, my God! Did you see what happened?"

"Lady, you all right?"

"Is she okay?"

Ellis looked at her hands. The heel of one was braced against the dash and the other was pressed flat against the steering wheel, the words "air bag" visible directly above it. Her mind distantly processed that the air bag hadn't deployed, and she caught herself wondering whether that was right or not, a tiny frown forming between her brows. When a car door gets ripped off, shouldn't the air bag inflate? Didn't they test cars for these things? Even old ones like hers?

Suddenly a man was squatting next to where her door had been, asking if she was hurt. He had chestnut hair and a mustache in need of a trim. He was wearing a brown sport coat with suede elbow patches. He looked a bit older than she was, with gasoline green eyes and—she couldn't help but notice—outrageously long eyelashes.

"Are you okay?" he asked, touching her arm.

Ellis put her fingers to her mouth, heart pounding. She looked past him at the crowd that had gathered around her car door.

"I'm sorry," he said, rubbing his face with both hands. "I didn't see you." He tilted his chin to the top of the hill. "I came up over the rise and—"

"It was your fault?" she said, a tremor in her voice.

"—*wham*, your door went flying!"

Ellis narrowed her eyes. The transition for her was immediate. All at once she went from feeling expansively sorry for herself to a slow boil. It was all suddenly too much. She lifted both hands to her face.

My daughter and I hardly know each other. I no longer have a husband. Or a job. Or any money. And now I don't have a fucking car door, either!

Pushing past the stranger, almost knocking him down in the process, she got out of her car and walked over to the burgundy SUV.

"This yours?" she said, swiveling to face him.

The chestnut-haired stranger got to his feet, shooting her a nervous look. "Uh . . . yes."

Ellis ran the palm of her hand down its length. "Nice," she said, raising an eyebrow. "Oh, and look, it has a driver's door. A nice shiny driver's door!"

He lifted both palms in the air. "Look, I said I was sorry."

Ellis turned sideways and gave the door a succession of quick kicks with the heel of her boot. "You jerk!" *Thunk.* "You ripped"—*thud*—"my door off!" *Crunch.* She was hot and flushed and her foot immediately began to throb, but she liked the feeling—although she couldn't quite understand what she liked about it, other than that it made her feel more alive than she'd felt in months.

Her hands started to tremble. She was staring at them when the stranger grabbed her arm from behind. "Okay," he said. "I don't blame you for being upset, but that's enough—"

Ellis's reaction was immediate and instinctive.

She lifted both arms high over her head and snapped them back down again, hitting him in the soft center of his stomach with one elbow. Turning to face him, she drew back her leg and kneed him in the crotch.

His eyes went wide and stayed that way as he dropped onto the snow-packed ground.

"Fight!" someone yelled. "Fight!"

Ellis yanked her jacket down and took a few steps back.

"Wh-what'd you do that for?" he choked out, rolling onto his side and pulling his knees up to his chest. "It's just a car door! I can get it fixed."

Ellis's eyes narrowed, and before she could stop herself she was in his face, unloading every thought that raced through her mind, going off on a rant that bordered on the hysterical. "Oh, sure, you'll get it fixed. You and your shiny SUV and your little worry-free life! Write the woman a check and the problem goes away, huh? Well, you know what, mister? Money can't fix everything. It can't stop crime and you can't use it to buy self-esteem and it won't bring back the people you love when they're gone."

He tilted his head and let his eyes crawl from the tips of her boots all the way up to her face. "You're crazy. You know that, lady?"

Her vision blurry with tears, Ellis turned away and walked over to her car door, sinking down cross-legged next to it. She watched him rise gingerly to his feet, one arm folded over his stomach, unable to straighten to his full height.

A murmur went through the crowd. "Did

you see what she did to him?" someone said.

"Mom? Are you okay?"

Glancing up, Ellis saw Hadley, her faced etched with disbelief as she pushed past two women who were now fussing over the man Ellis had just accosted, assuring him that this woman must be crazy, cooing that it was obviously an accident and she had no right to hit him like that.

"It's Hadley Semple's mom," someone said.

"Did you see that? It was like out of a movie!"

Ellis got to her feet, embarrassment hitting her like a tidal wave.

The crowd edged closer. One kid gave her car door a fresh spin with the toe of his boot. "That was unreal," he said. "Her door came right off."

Pushing through the crowd, a young girl came clumping over next to Hadley in thick platform shoes. "You gotta admit, it was sort of funny," she said. She was holding a toothpick and an open jar of maraschino cherries. She speared one and held it out in front of her, admiring it. After popping it into her mouth, she stabbed another and casually offered it to Hadley, who hesitated, then pulled it off with her fingers and ate it.

The girl was tiny, no more than five feet tall, but she moved as though she were completely at home in her own skin, unabashed at wearing a too-big down-filled jacket the color of a copper penny.

Shaking her head, the girl leaned down to examine Ellis's car door, still spinning in lazy circles, and then she threw her head back and snorted, which sent Hadley into hysterics. Before long, a few more kids had joined in, holding their stomachs as they pointed to the gaping hole where Ellis's car door had been.

"Okay, okay," the man with chestnut hair said. "That's enough. Let's give it a rest, all right, guys?" Still bent, he made his way to where Ellis was now standing, careful to keep his distance.

"It's okay," Ellis said. "Leave them." He looked at her as though she must be in shock. "Honestly," she assured him. "It's fine. Let them laugh."

He shook his head. "I don't get it. They can laugh hysterically, but when I try to offer you a sincere apology for what was clearly an accident, you beat the crap out of me?"

Ellis looked away from him. "I'm sorry. It's just, when you grabbed my arm from behind like that . . ." Her voice trailed off and she shrugged, desperately wanting to move on from this awkward conversation.

She lifted her chin to where her car door was lying. "If I pop the trunk, could you help me throw that in?"

The girl in platform shoes handed Hadley the jar of cherries so she could give a few stragglers an over-the-top reenactment of the stranger crumpling into a heap after Ellis had kneed him. Lolling her head to one side, she dropped to the ground as though she'd been shot. Then she writhed in pretend agony, clutching her midsection and groaning. Hadley was laughing so hard she had to wipe tears from her eyes.

"No problem," the stranger said. "And I meant what I said. I will get your door fixed. Just give me your name and number—"

"Did you hear that?" Hadley said to the girl in platform shoes. "We need a witness! He said he's gonna fix my mom's car door. Which is a good thing cause my dad died and we just moved here and Mom doesn't have a job yet so money's a little tight right now."

She was obviously playing for sympathy, basking in the attention the way she would have before everything in her life flipped upside down. Ellis drew her upper lip between her teeth, unwilling to say anything that would potentially throw Hadley back into the dark cloud of depression she had just crawled out of.

"You're looking for a job?" the man asked.

"I am," Ellis admitted.

"What kind of work do you do?"

She flushed under his scrutiny. "I'm an LPN."

His face lit up. "A nurse? No kidding?"

Hadley and her new friend rolled their eyes in unison. "She didn't say she was an astronaut," the girl in platform shoes pointed out. "She said she was a nurse, which isn't actually all that exciting, unless you're one of those guys who think nurses wear skimpy little lace outfits like they do in B movies."

Hadley clamped a hand over her mouth, muffling another laugh.

Ignoring them, the man took a few steps

back and studied Ellis as though considering something. "I'm probably going to regret this," he said, reaching into his pocket. He pulled out a wallet and handed Ellis a business card. "But why don't you stop by my office tomorrow afternoon for an interview?"

Ellis read the card: Pleasant View Manor—Ben Muldoon, Manager. She looked up at him in sudden understanding. "You're kidding, right?"

"No, and I'm also not suggesting it because of your car door. I've been thinking about hiring another aide for months."

"You run the nursing home?"

He nodded. "It's not technically an advanced dementia unit, although we do have a few heading in that direction. It's an assisted living complex for the elderly. I've been short-staffed for at least a year and everyone's been giving me a hard time about their shifts."

Ellis slipped the card into her pocket, mortified about what she'd done to him earlier. "Okay," she said. "I'll drop by tomorrow."

The girl in the platform shoes slowly

looked Ben up and down. "You manage the nursing home? The big one up on the hill?"

Ben nodded.

"Then you're the guy who had the hiccups for five weeks straight years ago, right? The one who went on the *Late Show with David Letterman*?"

"The one and only," he said, reddening slightly.

Looking impressed, the girl stepped back and struck a Vanna White pose for Hadley's benefit, one arm extended toward Ben as though he were the contestant and she'd just uncovered a million-dollar phrase.

"What'd he do?" Hadley asked, leaning in closer.

"He hiccupped for thirty-eight days straight," the girl said. "My mom told me after the first week, everyone in town was talking about it. Someone said he should drink pickle juice. Dr. Roberts suggested he try acupuncture and another woman had him use Lamaze breathing techniques every night. At the annual Fourth of July parade, one guy snuck up behind him and tried the Heimlich maneuver, but none of it worked. Then, when he was into his fourth week, the *Late Show* phoned, and everyone in Barrow went crazy, praying he wouldn't stop, that he'd hang in there and hiccup all the way to New York so he could put us on the map. Which is what happened. He met David Letterman, hiccupped through the Top Ten list for the night, and told everyone how great it was living here. Three days later, his hiccups stopped on their own and the town council voted to waive taxes on any home he ever owned within town limits."

"Okay," Ben said dryly, grabbing one side of the car door while Ellis took the other. "Let's get this into your trunk."

"Wait," Hadley said. "You had the hiccups for five weeks without stopping? Not even for a couple of minutes?"

"I did," he said. "And if I get them again because of what happened here today, I'm holding your mom accountable."

Ellis studied him intently, mortified at how she had reacted earlier. So this was Barrow's famous hiccup guy? She'd often wondered who he was and what had happened to him. She vaguely recalled seeing his face on the news one night around the time her dad had left: a gangly young guy with a deer-in-the-headlights look who seemed too old to be in high school but not old enough to have outgrown a few pimples on his forehead.

They loaded the door into her trunk, the lid held down with a bungee cord, and the crowd dissipated. "Thank you," Ellis said, dropping her gaze.

Ben laughed. "For what? Ripping your car door off?"

"No. For putting it in my trunk, and for being so . . . understanding."

"All right," he said, edging away. "I'll see you tomorrow."

Ellis surveyed the hole in her car, wondering if it was legal to drive a vehicle without a door. She could probably get away with it in Barrow, at least for a few days; this was a small town, after all. But she sure wouldn't want to take the car out on the highway.

"Want a ride home?" Hadley asked the girl in the platform shoes.

The girl glanced over both shoulders,

noticing that the buses were all gone. "I missed my bus, so that'd be great."

From the corner of her eye, Ellis watched them: Hadley talking more than she had since they'd left Dallas, and her friend hefting her knapsack onto her back, making her winter coat sag off her shoulders.

"Mom, this is Anissa," Hadley said, getting in the front seat. "Anissa, my mom."

"Nice name," Ellis said.

"It used to be Bitsy," Anissa admitted as she climbed into the back. "But I'm totally not into foo-foo names, and after complaining over and over how it was ruining my life, my parents finally let me change it last year."

Ellis swiveled to survey her, and Anissa heaved a long, theatrical sigh. "I know. Can you, like, imagine how hopped up on drugs my mom must've been the day I was born to come up with Bitsy? I mean, strap on a pair of pigtails and buy me a set of pompoms, right?"

Hadley burst out laughing. "You're hilarious!"

"By the way," Anissa added, "my mom and dad share joint custody. This week I'm staying with my dad. He lives ten miles east of town. Is that okay?"

The corners of Ellis's mouth twitched. For the first time in months, Hadley seemed able to negotiate the world with a smile on her face, at least for a few minutes, and for that reason alone, Ellis would have happily driven Anissa to the moon and back.

Three

Ellis pulled in to visitors' parking at Pleasant View Manor the next afternoon, positioning her vehicle so that the hole was facing a line of trees. It had taken her and Hadley almost an hour to cover it the night before using a roll of duct tape and a four-by-six strip of polyurethane construction plastic.

"I'm not riding in this until it's fixed," Hadley had said when they were done.

"Oh, it's not that bad," Ellis said.

"Excuse me?" Hadley said, rapping her knuckles against the hood. "Step back and take a good look, Mom. It sucks hard-core, okay? We're going to look like total losers driving around in this car."

To get in or out, Ellis now had to climb over the stick shift and use the passenger door, feeling juvenile and embarrassed as people rubbernecked. Worse yet, all day long—while loading groceries into the trunk, parking at the post office, filling up with gas—each time a vehicle had passed on her left, she'd caught herself jumping like a startled rabbit. *Great,* she thought. *Years from now, I'll probably still be leaping out of my skin every time a car drives by. Line me up for another round of therapy.*

Right now, she was more concerned with her impending job interview. Setting her purse on the trunk, she fished inside and pulled out a tiny box with a tortoise frame surrounding a hinged lid. Nestled inside on red satin lining was her old silver compass. It had been years since she'd carried it everywhere with her. Lifting it out, she rubbed the pad of her thumb in small circles across the back, trying to draw strength from the words inscribed there.

Okay, she thought. *Let's do this.*

Pleasant View Manor overlooked the river valley on one of the highest hills on the west side of town. Ellis's mom said it had a good reputation, that there was a list of people from counties all around them who were waiting to get in. A walkway wound across the grass to the front entrance, where a generous overhang was supported by two pillars. To one side was a cedar bench, and sitting in the middle was an old woman sipping from a cup of tea.

"Morning," Ellis said.

The woman lifted her gaze. "Morning, dear."

She looked frail and her white hair, as fine as mist, had been carefully combed to cover a few bald spots, but for a split second Ellis could see how lovely she would have been as a young woman. It was in the way she held herself, shoulders back, chin tilted slightly. Her small feet were encased in winter boots, she was wearing an eiderdown jacket that came all the way down to her knees, and a blanket was spread across her lap. Next to the bench was a hard brown suitcase covered with stickers from faraway places.

"Are you taking a trip?" Ellis asked.

The woman brightened. "Yes. My husband and I are going on a five-day polar bear sightseeing excursion."

"Polar bear sightseeing?"

The woman nodded. "In Churchill, Manitoba."

Ellis stared at her.

"That's in Canada," the woman added.

"I know," Ellis said.

"We travel a lot, though, so it can be very tiring. Last month we flew to Germany for a week to see what's left of the Berlin Wall."

"The Berlin Wall?"

"That's right. Roy took dozens of photographs. He even managed to buy me a small chunk of the wall. They're hard to find, but you can still get them at a few reputable agencies over there." She lowered her voice confidentially. "I keep it tucked away in my room. If you like, I can show it to you."

Before Ellis could reply, the front door swung open and a woman wearing an olive green uniform stuck her head outside. She was built like a compact warship—short, thick, no waist to speak of, and with sculpted arms and broad shoulders—but when she smiled, her face lit up in such a way that Ellis immediately sensed a generosity of spirit.

"How are we doing, Nina?"

"Fine, thank you," the old woman said, holding out her empty teacup.

The other woman took it and gave Ellis a welcoming smile. "Good morning. Are you here to visit someone?"

"No," Ellis said. "I have an interview with Ben Muldoon." The woman looked confused. "Apparently, he's hiring another aide?" Ellis added nervously.

Her expression quickly brightened and she pulled the door open. "Well, come on in then. My name's Murphy, by the way."

"Nice to meet you, Murphy. I'm Ellis Semple."

Holding the door, Murphy looked back over her shoulder. "I'll check on you in half an hour, Nina."

"Oh, I'll be gone by then," Nina replied.

Murphy glanced at her watch. "Probably, but I'll check anyhow in case he's running a little late." Not bothering to wait for an answer, she let the door close and refocused on Ellis, who was taking off her boots. "You can hang your coat there," she said, nodding to a row of empty wall hooks.

Seconds later, Murphy was hustling her past a chest-high reception desk that closely resembled a nurses' station. They took a right turn down a wide hallway. Along the way they passed a young man with tattoos curling up the length of both arms, also wearing an olive green uniform, who was helping an elderly woman with a severe dowager's hump maneuver down the hall with a walker.

"This here's Oliver," Murphy said, giving him a nod. "He double shifts every Monday. Couldn't ask for a better aide."

They passed a large dayroom on the left with interior floor-to-ceiling windows that made it easy to observe everything that was going on inside. Ellis saw two men playing cards, a woman sifting through a box of photos balanced on her knees, and three others watching a TV that hung suspended from the ceiling by a metal bracket.

Outside the dayroom were two women in wheelchairs, one yammering softly to herself, hands twitching in her lap, while the other stared with a vacant look on her face. They looked spidery and frail. As Ellis studied them, she felt an instinctive and unstoppable tenderness well up inside her.

Murphy gestured to a door on her right with the words "Staff Lounge" stenciled in black. "You can wait in here. Ben'll be free in a few minutes."

Ellis was about to thank her when a door at the end of the hallway opened and an old man shuffled out using a walker. He was short with fake shoe-polish black hair and clumpy gray eyebrows. "I'm serious, Ben," he said, slamming his walker against the floor. "I can't stand that mattress. I'll give you two weeks, but if you don't get me something decent to sleep on, you will have my resignation."

"You don't work here, Joseph," Ben gently replied. "But I'll look into it anyhow."

"Is everything okay?" Murphy asked.

Joseph turned and squinted at her. "Is everything okay?" he said, incredulous. "No, Murphy, everything's not *okay*. You ever sat on my mattress? I wouldn't donate it to a homeless shelter. A cardboard box would work better." He threw her a disgusted look and then caught Ellis's eye as he was turning away. He stopped to scrutinize her, then waggled a hand in the air that was missing half of one finger. “Mattress delivery gone wrong in ’eighty-seven,” he confided in a hushed voice. “They’re talking to a man who knows all about mattresses. No point in trying to pull the wool over my eyes.” He smoothed his hair, gave her a brisk nod, and shuffled into the dayroom.

Crepe-soled shoes *squeak-squeak-squeaked* around the corner from the lobby and another aide, a woman in her late twenties, appeared carrying an armful of bedding. She had blue-black hair weaved into one long braid that fell down her back, and as she went by, she gave Ellis and Murphy a polite nod.

Murphy set her hands on her hips. “That was Charlene. Other than Marcel, who works the night shift, that’s all we have for staff. There’s Ben, of course, and Denise, who works in the kitchen and answers phones. We have a service that does the housekeeping.” She stopped and studied Ellis closely. “Aides do a bit of everything around here. We bathe ’em, feed ’em their meals if they need help, hand out meds, cut toenails. Some have

Alzheimer's. Others have had strokes, head injuries, hip fractures. Right now we have two with multiple sclerosis, one with emphysema . . ."

Her voice trailed away as an old man in a wheelchair rolled out of the dayroom and came to a stop. He had a hooked nose, and was coughing fiercely, thumping his chest hard with each phlegmy expulsion. Murphy stepped behind him and wrapped both arms around his midsection.

"Breathe, Rolly," she said, lifting him halfway out of the chair and then gently lowering him again. "Breathe!"

Swatting at her, he wriggled free. "What do you think I'm trying to do, Murphy?" he said, looking embarrassed when he saw Ellis. "No one listens to me, but I'm telling you I'd breathe a lot easier if Louie stopped smoking those damned cigars. I'm allergic, remember?"

Murphy lifted an eyebrow. "You smoked for thirty years, Rolly," she reminded him.

He raised a hand as though swearing on the Bible. "I never smoked cigars. That's a whole other can of worms. Besides, we're supposed to be smoke-free here, but he's still sneaking them in his room and no one wants to deal with it."

Ellis's gaze, of its own volition, snaked down the hall, looking for Louie.

Rolly rolled himself toward the lobby. "When you talk to Ben," he called back to Murphy over his shoulder, "tell him I'm also not happy about our new room assignments. I don't give two hoots if it's my turn to spend six months living next to that old coot. I ain't happy about it."

Just then, Ben Muldoon came barreling out of his office at the end of the hallway, head bent over an open file folder. Murphy put out an arm to block his path. "Ben, this lady's here about a job."

He lifted his gaze, eyes widening in recognition. "You came," he said.

"You asked me to," Ellis reminded him.

"I did," he said. Distracted, he closed the folder and tucked it under his arm. "Uh . . . Murphy, can you do me a favor?" he said, running his thumb and forefinger down both sides of his mustache.

Murphy narrowed her eyes. "What sort of favor?"

Ben turned and gestured for Ellis to follow

him into his office. "Phone King's Auto Body and tell them I need to get a car door for . . ." He stirred the air with one hand, looking at Ellis expectantly.

". . . a 2000 Toyota Corolla."

"Right," he said. "For a 2000 Corolla."

Murphy frowned. "You don't drive a Corolla."

"True," he conceded. "But this lady here does, and if I told you that getting a car door for her 2000 Toyota Corolla was essential before I agreed to hire another aide to help out around here, would you take care of it for me anyhow?"

"Consider it done," Murphy said, spinning on her heel.

Next thing Ellis knew, she was sitting in one of two mismatched armchairs across from Ben Muldoon's desk. His jaw was covered with stubble and he was wearing a mauve button-down shirt with the sleeves rolled up his forearms.

"Here's my résumé and a reference letter," she said, handing him both.

He leaned back in his chair and read, his expression changing from interested to unmistakably impressed by the time he was done. "You spent three years working at Mary Shiels Hospital in Dallas?"

"Part-time," Ellis confirmed. "Two or three days a week."

He pulled on his mustache thoughtfully. "Why'd you leave?"

Ellis shifted in her chair. "It was a decision my husband and I made together. I wanted to spend more time with our daughter."

"I need someone full-time," he said, setting her resumé down. "Every aide works one Saturday and one Sunday each month, and when that happens, they get a day off midweek in lieu of."

"I'm fine with that," Ellis said.

"The pay's industry standard," he pointed out.

"Sounds good to me."

Ellis watched him, wondering if she should tell him she wasn't the best nurse on the planet, that she'd once passed out while helping to set a broken nose, that she was quite sure she could never do an emergency tracheotomy, but that working with a group of sedate elderly patients seemed right up her alley.

He leaned across the desk and extended his hand. "Can you start Monday?"

She fought an urge to leap out of her chair and hug him. "Sounds fine," she said.

On her way out, Murphy, Oliver, and Charlene were huddled at the front desk in the lobby. Murphy was casually moving papers around in an attempt to look busy, but Oliver and Charlene watched Ellis with undisguised anticipation as she approached.

"Could anyone tell me where I might find a few of those nifty green uniforms you're wearing?" Ellis asked.

Murphy's head snapped up. "He hired you?"

Ellis bit back a smile. "I start Monday."

Charlene lifted both arms in the air as though claiming victory. "Yes!"

Stepping back, Oliver gave Ellis a deep and respectful bow, as if to say, *Welcome*.

Murphy clapped a hand to her breast and looked skyward, unable to hide her relief. "Stop by tomorrow and I'll have two uniforms waiting for you," she said, radiating good cheer.

Their collective reaction startled Ellis and she felt a spot of color climb onto her cheeks. "Oh, before I forget." Murphy jumped up and handed her a slip of paper. "Dave at King's Auto Body said he'd be able to fix you up with a car door by the end of this week. You can give him a call anytime."

Ellis thanked her and said good-bye, happy and relieved. Two huge problems solved in one afternoon! She had a swift impulse to run full tilt across the parking lot and pump her arms in the air while taking a victory lap.

Outside, Nina still sat on the bench, her head tilted to one side and mouth drooping open as she dozed in the sun. Leaning closer, Ellis squinted to read a cardboard sign lying next to her. In bold letters someone had written, Seek the Unique—Churchill's Polar Bears Rule!

Ellis headed to her car, thinking about something she'd overheard Louie Johnson tell her mom years ago: that his life hadn't been defined by the days and weeks and months he'd lived, but by a mere handful of events that had happened along the way—a beating he had survived as a teenager from two white men at the Greyhound bus station in Kansas City; the morning his daughter was born; the night his wife had died. Ellis knew what he meant. Her life could also be boiled down to a handful of moments—the summer her dad left, the morning Louie pulled her out of the river, the moment she gave birth to Hadley, the day Mark died. She hadn't seen any of them coming, and yet each one had helped define who she was today.

And now this job, she thought, sensing on some level that this day, too, might mark a turning point.

Four

It was only six in the morning, but Ellis had already been awake for an hour. Her mind was racing and she couldn't sleep. She reached into the top drawer of her nightstand and pulled out her yellow notepad, crossed off "Find a job," and reassessed her list. She found doing so helped center her and made her realize she had more control over her life than she sometimes gave herself credit for.

Attend grief counseling (?)
Go through Mark's things
Save money
Get our own place

Flipping to the back of the notepad, she pulled out a pamphlet she'd tucked away before she and Hadley arrived in town. Her nursing girlfriend, Rita, had suggested Ellis try grief counseling. At first, she was skeptical, but when Rita hugged her the day they left, she'd pressed a pamphlet into Ellis's hand with the name of a bereavement group that met every Wednesday in Great Falls, only twenty minutes from Barrow.

"Give it a shot," she'd whispered. "What can it hurt?"

Reading the pamphlet now, Ellis saw that this particular group had been founded ten years ago. It met in a conference room at the local health clinic and was run by a licensed mental health clinician.

Many times when you are in the middle of your grief, you may feel that the world has moved on. Our bereavement group will provide you with a safe place to talk about your loss with others who are experiencing similar feelings.

Tucking the pamphlet away, she decided to give the group a try, determined not to let the feelings she had been struggling with remain a permanent fixture in her life; she was worried that if she didn't move on, history might repeat itself and one of her worst fears would be realized—she'd sink into depression like her own mom had years ago, leaving Hadley to fend for herself.

The first time Ellis attended the grief group, she arrived early. No one else was there yet except the leader, a woman wearing a crisp jacket and matching slacks, her hair pulled back in a clip at the base of her neck. In the center of a conference table a glass bowl was filled with peppermints. A coffee urn on a corner table was surrounded with foam cups, sugar cubes, and a handful of individual creamers. When Ellis slipped through the door, the group leader was writing on a blackboard at the front of the room.

1. Can you recall the last conversation you had with your loved one?
2. Name one trait you admired about him/her.
3. One you didn't.

Ellis felt her stomach clench. She dipped her hand into her pocket and grabbed her silver compass. This was going to be harder than she thought. She'd written some notes on her yellow pad in case she went blank when asked to introduce herself, but looking at them now, she had the sinking feeling that more was going to be required of her than she'd realized.

My husband died suddenly six months ago.
He was thirty-six years old.
I would prefer to listen and observe rather than spill my guts to a roomful of complete strangers.

The group leader put the chalk down and dusted off her hands. "Oh. Hello there," she said, turning around. "I'm Roma Clark. And you are . . . ?"

"Ellis Semple," she said. "I'm . . . uh, I'm here because—"

"You're here to work through a loss," Roma finished for her. "Everyone in the group is," she added.

Actually, Ellis wanted to say, *I'm here because I'm always tired. I'm here because every morning when I open my closet I pretend not to notice the towering shrine of boxes stacked inside containing Mark's things, and even though I can't afford it and I have never told anyone, I keep paying his monthly cell phone bill so I can dial his number and hear his voice on a prerecorded message. I've filled up voice mail more than once talking to him, and then had to delete all my messages to make room for more, which makes me tired all over again.*

Ellis slipped off her jacket. "I guess you could say that."

"The group starts in five minutes," Roma said. "I have to go across the street to buy donuts, but I'll be right back." She handed her a glossy brochure about grieving and Ellis slid into an empty chair and read it, entranced by the clinical description of what she was going through.

> Loss happens in a moment, but its aftermath lasts a lifetime. Grief is the internal part of loss, or how we feel, and it doesn't have a clear beginning or end. Rather, grief will ebb and flow throughout our life after a loss. We each grieve as long as we need to. We don't ever get over the loss of

someone, but we learn to live with loss. There are five stages of grief: denial, anger, bargaining, depression, and acceptance. All are part of the framework that helps teach us how to live without the one we have lost—tools to help frame and identify what we may be feeling, although we don't all experience them in the order described.

Denial is typically the first stage of grieving. For a person who has lost a loved one, denial usually means you simply can't fathom that he will never walk through that door again. In this stage, the world becomes meaningless and overwhelming. We try to find a way to simply get through each day. Denial helps us to pace our feelings of grief. There is a grace in denial. It is nature's way of letting in only as much as we can handle.

Well, I can sure relate to the denial, Ellis thought, thinking back to those first weeks after Mark died. How she would get up every morning and make his coffee. Or how, when the mail came, she'd toss it into the basket on his desk, because he had always been the one who paid the bills. But what about the anger? Was she there yet? Did kneeing a complete stranger in the groin suggest she was angry? Before Ellis could consider any further, Roma was back and the room began to fill with people.

Including Ellis and Roma, there were fourteen in the group. They all introduced themselves. There was a man in his thirties who'd lost his wife in a river rafting accident the year before. They'd spent six months planning the trip and now he couldn't stand driving past the river that claimed her life.

There was a woman in her twenties whose mother had died in a head-on collision eight months ago. She hadn't been able to drive since then and was worried about the long-term effects of taking medication to calm her fears. A middle-aged lady sitting next to her had lost her husband from liver failure sixteen months ago. Their sons were grown and now she missed taking care of her husband and pushing him around in his wheelchair. An old woman wearing red leggings tried three times to explain how her husband had died, but each time she had to stop and compose herself. “Please,” she finally said, “go on without me.”

Some in the group were clearly more seasoned than others, and by the time they got to Ellis, she was a bundle of nerves. She stared at a scratch on the table and decided to begin at the beginning, her voice high and wobbly. “I’m Ellis Semple and my husband died six months ago of an aortic dissection. He was thirty-six years old, and we have a daughter who is fourteen. . . .” She stopped.

“Please continue,” Roma urged gently.

Ellis shook her head. “That’s all for now.”

“Could you tell us one trait of your husband’s that you admired?” Roma asked.

Ellis blinked at her. “Like how he made great waffles?”

“If that’s what you’d like to share with us.”

“Okay. Then that, the waffle thing.”

An hour later, as she stood to leave, Ellis worried that she wasn’t any better at grieving in a group than she was on her own. Sitting in her car in the parking lot, she turned on the interior light and read yet another glossy handout Roma had given to her.

Do children grieve? Yes, if children are old enough to love, they are old enough to grieve. In our society children are often the forgotten grievers. For instance, when a parent dies, we expect the surviving parent to help the child with their grief, and yet that parent not only has their own grief to deal with, they are learning for the first time how to be a single parent. Like their child, they need support in their grieving, so we recommend parents and children attend grief counseling together, keeping in mind that children don't grieve the same way we do. They don't talk openly about how they are feeling. A death in their life usually causes them to feel isolated and alone. Some act out in ways that aren't typical because they are running away from their grief and fear. Bereavement groups can be extremely helpful for children, because they are able to listen to others who have also experienced and survived a loss.

Ellis turned off the interior light and sat thinking for a few minutes. Maybe she should bring Hadley with her. In Dallas, she'd taken her to her doctor a few times and he'd recommended a therapist who could help Hadley work through her feelings, but Hadley had adamantly refused to go.

"Why don't you go instead?" she'd said. "You need it more than I do."

After Mark died, there had been so much to do that Ellis hadn't known which way to turn, and because of it, she had put off grieving. There was the funeral, his life insurance, selling the house. There were papers to sign that shook in her hands, decisions to be made that she didn't want to make, boxes to pack when all she wanted to do was sleep. Thank heavens Lance and her friend Rita had been there to help her, but now that all those issues had been dealt with, why did she persistently feel as if she were running from a freight train? And if that was how she felt, then how must Hadley be feeling?

Late the night before, Ellis had slipped into Hadley's room to check on her, and as she'd stood there watching her sleep, she had faced a hard realization: Mark had been the glue that had held them together; without him, they were adrift from each other. That was why Hadley's behavior had changed so drastically after his death. She hadn't lost only her dad, she'd lost her moorings, something Ellis understood, given her own dad's desertion years ago.

Hadley had been fourteen and smack in the middle of puberty, but until Mark died she hadn't been interested in parties or drinking or dating. She was too busy. Every weekend, off she and her dad would go, mountain biking or bungee jumping or doing something else equally exciting. Ellis would go along to watch, but she didn't always participate. She enjoyed mountain biking, but you couldn't pay her to bungee jump. Instead, she would use their camcorder or camera to capture each experience, moved beyond words each time she saw Mark kiss Hadley on the forehead or give her an affectionate squeeze, thankful that Hadley had him in her life.

How did I let this happen? Ellis wondered. *How could I allow my relationship with my daughter to get pushed onto a back burner?*

When the answer came, she realized she wasn't an unfit parent. She had simply loved Hadley so much that she'd wanted to give her the very thing she herself had missed out on while growing up—a strong and loving relationship with her dad—even if that meant inadvertently sacrificing the quality of their own relationship.

Five

On her way downstairs, Ellis stopped to look at the pictures hanging from the walls that lined the staircase. Up one side were at least a dozen of herself—wearing pigtails at five, with a tooth missing at eight, dressed up for church at twelve—and up the other side were snapshots of Hadley, also hung chronologically, starting with one of Ellis when she was pregnant, a photograph her mom had taken a month before Hadley was born. She was on the couch asleep, one arm thrown back over her head and the other resting on the hill of her belly. On her bottom were a pair of flannel boxer shorts and on top an extra-large Edmonton Oilers hockey jersey Mark had given her. Ellis shook her head. Pictures could be so deceiving. She may have looked relaxed and rested, but in reality, she'd been a nervous wreck.

Not unlike how I feel today, she thought.

Anxious about starting work at Pleasant View Manor, she hurried down to the kitchen for breakfast, and as she did a thought suddenly came to her, as if someone had just poked her with the sharp end of a long stick. A sense of apprehension seeped through her.

"Mom?" she said.

"Uh-huh?" Paulina said, snapping open the newspaper.

"What ever happened to Louie Johnson?"

"What do you mean, what happened to him?"

Ellis slid into the empty chair next to Hadley. "I mean, where'd he go? He had to be almost sixty-five when I was in high school and he lived next door, so that'd make him close to eighty now, right?"

"He turned eighty months ago," Paulina said, distracted. "He lives at Pleasant View, has for eight years. I try to get up there to visit him a few times each month. I'm sure you'll see him when you go to work today. He hasn't changed much."

Hadley was spreading jam on her toast. "Who's Louie Johnson?"

"An old fellow who used to live next door to us," Paulina said.

"Do you remember him, Mom?" Hadley asked.

"Yes," Ellis said, keeping her voice impassive. "I do."

Ellis still felt uncomfortable thinking about the day Louie had saved her life. She could almost hear him artfully lying to cover for her. *She didn't jump to* jump, *Roy. She jumped to save me.*

And now I'm going to be working where he lives. Great. What am I supposed to say when I see him again? Hi there, Louie. By the way, have I ever thanked you for yanking me out of the river years ago? No? Well, let me thank you now. You won't believe how humiliated and embarrassed I feel looking back at that morning. She glanced at Hadley, taking in the tilt of her head, the freckles on her nose, the way her mouth fell open when she was not quite awake. *But grateful, too, Louie—grateful in spades*.

"Are you working today, Grandma?" Hadley asked, taking a bite of toast.

Paulina's part-time job at Bianca's Café had evolved over the years and now she was half owner, although she still worked there a few days each week. "Not today, honey," Paulina said. "I'm helping to deliver for Meals on Wheels this morning and I have a yoga class at the community center this afternoon."

Ellis got up to pour coffee. In all her previous life, she had never seen her mom exercise. Not one sit-up, knee bend, or ab crunch, but last week she'd come home from having her car door replaced and found Paulina doing step aerobics in the living room. The furniture had been pushed up against the walls and she was following along with a woman on television, a knee-raising, toe-touching, hip-swiveling routine that had left Ellis gaping. Up the step Paulina went, arms reaching high into the air, then back down with a quick side lunge to the right. On and on she went, barely breaking a sweat, until she'd finally noticed Ellis, stopped, and offered to make lunch for them.

Ellis had also noticed other changes. Paulina hadn't gone to church once since she and Hadley had arrived, and she no longer carried her rosary beads everywhere she went. She'd cultivated a whole new set of friends. One was an attractive older woman named Bonita who owned two Chihuahuas, Flora and Fauna. Often, Bonita and her husband would pick Paulina up and take her out for dinner. Ellis found herself struggling to reconcile this new Paulina with the mother she had known growing up.

The windshield wipers on Ellis's car were frozen. She brushed away enough snow so that she could see to drive and jumped into the blazing warmth of the interior. Anxious to make a good impression and determined to arrive at her new job early, she didn't bother clearing off the rest of the snow, so when she pulled into the street, it spilled down the back window. Once she pulled in to Pleasant View Manor, she checked her face in the rearview mirror and pulled out her silver compass. Over the last few weeks, she had rubbed her thumb in countless circles against its back, thinking about Mark and Hadley and how much she doubted her own abilities.

Years ago, when she'd decided to get her nursing degree, it had seemed like a good choice. After all, she was used to taking care of others. Still, Ellis hadn't foreseen how stressful and rigid nursing could be.

"Who here feels that ninety-nine percent accuracy is a good thing?" her supervisor had asked a group of them during their first week on the job, and to a person all of them had agreed it was.

"Really?" the woman said, raising her eyebrows. "Well, guess what. In the world of nursing, it's not acceptable. How are you going to feel when one out of one hundred of your patients dies because you made a mistake on the dosage of their medication? How long do you think you'll remain employed?"

Flawlessness at anything seemed an impossible goal to Ellis, and living with that kind of pressure day after day was exhausting. Beyond that, patients came and went so quickly, Ellis felt as though she were spinning in circles. She began to lose weight, her clothes became too big for her, her skin broke out in a rash. Eventually, she chose to work part-time, and yet she still felt as though she were playing a role for which she was ill equipped. With time, she became detached and desensitized, experiencing numerous lows and very few euphoric highs from her chosen profession.

I hope I don't feel that way here, she thought, slipping the compass back into its box.

When Ellis walked through the front doors of Pleasant View Manor at eight, Louie Johnson was the first person she saw. He was standing next to Rolly, the man who'd been complaining about Louie's cigar smoking the week before. Louie was wearing a ball cap, his corkscrew gray hair fanning out from underneath it. His nose was broad, his nostrils round, his eyes the color of inky coal. He had on a pair of burnt orange running shoes with brown dress slacks and a golf shirt open at the top, a mat of curly chest hair sticking out. He was cradling a newspaper and a FedEx box, and he was glaring at Rolly.

"No, I will not show you what's inside," he said in a way that implied Rolly was being a child. "It's none of your business whether I ordered cigars or scotch or dirty magazines." The sound of his voice struck a familiar chord inside Ellis. His lecture was short and clipped, and he didn't bother to make sure it found its mark. Instead, he tucked the FedEx box under one arm and started to walk away. "Go change your Depends, Rolly. I've got better things to do than fuss over you."

Eyes widening, Rolly tried to block Louie's way, doing some rusty karate moves with his arms and elbows. "I'm not kidding, Louie. Smoke one more cigar in your room," he warned. "Just one and I swear . . ."

Louie flipped him the bird, then closed his eyes and began singing "Feliz Navidad," moving his hips from side to side, snapping his fingers.

Ellis chewed on her bottom lip. Clearly he hadn't changed. He could be oddly charming and charismatic one minute and frustratingly small-minded the next, and if there was one thing Louie wasn't, it was a pushover. He had saved her life years ago, and because of that, to a certain degree she saw him in a different light, but on the hero barometer, Louie would fall short by most people's standards.

Rolly's attention swung away from Louie when he caught sight of Ellis. "This one's losing it upstairs, don't you think?" he said, tapping the side of his head with an index finger. "And he's got loads more of those funny impulses, too."

Ellis raised her eyebrows. "I can imagine."

Louie stopped singing. He looked at Ellis, edging closer to study her face, squinting against the sunlight shining through the windows behind her. There was a beat of silence before he said, "Do I know you?"

"Yes," she answered.

"I thought so."

Ellis looked him directly in the eye, searching for something more, an acknowledgment that he knew exactly who she was, but there was nothing. It had been years since they'd seen each other, and beyond the fact that she was now thirty-two, her hair no longer touched her backside and she'd gotten contact lenses.

"Are you here to visit me?" he asked.

"No," she said.

She opened her mouth to explain who she was, but he was already turning away, seemingly uninterested. After taking a few tentative steps, he stopped, looked back, and pointed a gnarled finger at her. "You're Paulina's daughter."

"Right," she said.

"Ellis Williams."

She felt her throat tighten. "Ellis Semple now," she said. "But close enough."

Seeing him reminded her of that time in her life she had spent years trying to forget. Days and weeks of anguish at seventeen when she'd fallen into despair and tried to hide the horrible secret of her pregnancy, then the shame and humiliation after Louie pulled her out of the river and she fully realized what she'd almost done to herself and her baby.

Another heartbeat of uncomfortable silence followed, broken by Rolly's voice. "Murphy, he's got another delivery of cigars!"

Murphy *squeak-squeak-squeaked* toward them with a clipboard, a hand raised in welcome. When Ellis glanced back at Louie, he had already turned away. She watched until he disappeared around a corner, then reached into her bag and pulled out her yellow notepad, scratching out "Offer to work extra shifts" and replacing it with "Make it through the day."

An hour later, during Ellis's first staff meeting, Ben handed her the names of those she'd been assigned to. "We have twenty-five residents," he explained to her. "Which means you, Charlene, and Oliver each have six, and Murphy will take seven. All three of you report directly to Murphy, although my door is always open as well."

Oliver grinned in approval as he read over his list. Charlene frowned once or twice, but then shrugged with what seemed like bored indifference.

Ben turned his attention back to Ellis. "If you have questions about your charges, feel free to ask any of us. Murphy's been here ten years, Oliver six, and Charlene going on three, so please use our combined experience to your advantage."

"Thanks," Ellis said.

Outside the staff lounge, someone let loose a string of curses, prompting Murphy and Ben to share a knowing look. Oliver pushed forward on his chair, eyes crinkling with undisguised delight. "I've gotta tell you, Murphy, having Rolly reassigned to you just made my year." Murphy rose to deal with the situation, wagging a finger at him.

Ben glanced at his watch. "I'm going to a funeral this morning, Ellis, so I'll introduce you to the residents when I get back this afternoon. Until then, tag along with Murphy and she'll show you some of the basics."

Ellis waited until he left before reading her list.

1. Nina Ballard—83 years old: Room 3
2. Joseph Millson—81 years old: Room 11
3. Vera-Lee Dale—77 years old: Room 9
4. Louie Johnson—80 years old: Room 6
5. Ed Notton—74 years old: Room 14
6. Fran Wilson—73 years old: Room 13

Twenty-five residents and she'd been assigned to Louie Johnson? What were the chances? Her stomach twisted into a nervous knot. *Maybe if I offer to take on this Rolly character, Murphy would take Louie for me.*

"Who'd you get?" Oliver said, sliding over next to her on the couch. Charlene quickly joined him, perching beside Ellis on the arm of the couch.

"Nina's no work at all," she offered, leaning over to scan the names. "And Vera-Lee's a hoot. Doesn't ever ask for much. She used to be a show girl dancer of some sort. Fran sticks to herself, but she does get preachy when it comes to religion. I think you'll like Ed Notton. He's a bit of a blowhard, but he means well. That guy knows more famous people than I'll ever hope to meet."

"Joseph's a nice man," Oliver pointed out. "His memory's getting worse all the time, though."

"What about Louie?" Ellis asked, steeling herself.

Oliver and Charlene exchanged an uneasy look, and then Charlene set her mug on the coffee table. “Louie’s not easy to categorize. He came here years ago after he fell and broke his hip. He had some heart trouble last year, and he does have all of his mental capacities, but he’s . . .” Her voice trailed away and she gestured to Oliver to give her a hand.

“High maintenance?” he said, offering Ellis an almost apologetic smile.

After lunch, Ellis knocked on Ben’s office door and asked if she could have a few minutes. He was busy with paperwork, head down, shirtsleeves rolled back to the elbows. He was wearing a steel gray tie, and a suit jacket hung on the chair behind him, a white carnation tucked into one of the buttonholes.

He motioned her in. “Ellis. How can I help?”

“I don’t want you to think I’m complaining,” she said, “especially because this is my first day on the job, but I was wondering if I could trade Louie Johnson for someone else.”

“Trade him?” Ben said, straightening.

“Yes. Could I switch him with Rolly?”

Ben shook his head. “Sorry, Ellis,” he

said, smiling. "All new hires get assigned to Louie."

She studied him for a few moments, then asked, "Did you assign him to me because of what happened last week?"

"You mean because you kneed me in the balls?" he deadpanned.

"Yes," she said, flushing. "Because of that." In her mind, she imagined him grinning as he marked Louie's name down next to hers, knowing what a handful he would be.

Ben sat back in his chair. "Not at all," he said. "I pride myself on being the consummate professional at work. Although I did set up an appointment with my doctor to have the bruising checked out," he added.

Ellis tried not to wince.

Letting her gaze flicker to the window, she waited until she felt properly composed. "I'm asking because I know Louie well. He used to live next door to me and my mom. He worked nights as the janitor at the high school for as long as I can remember, and then he spent most of his days from May to September either fishing down at the river or sitting in an old La-Z-Boy in front of Bianca's Café."

"I know," Ben said, his smile widening.

Ellis carried on, pacing across the length of Ben's office. "He had a neon pink golf umbrella soldered onto the back of his chair and a small drop-leaf table bolted onto one side. He used to till up his entire backyard and grow hundreds of massive sunflowers because he hated having to mow his lawn. He smoked two cigars a week and drank an ounce of scotch every Friday afternoon."

Ben tented his fingers, listening.

Her voice sped up. "The guy was a newspaper freak. He had annual subscriptions to at least six big-city newspapers, wouldn't hesitate to start a petition if something got him worked up, and he'd write these long, rambling letters to the editor of the *Barrow Gazette* when he felt his voice wasn't being heard. His wife died giving birth to stillborn twin boys and Louie had to raise his daughter Arla on his own, but she ran away after her high school graduation and I don't know if they've ever talked since. . . ."

Ben lifted a hand. "What's any of this got to do with you being assigned to him?"

Ellis gripped the back of a chair, determined to change Ben's mind. "I know him too well to remain impartial when it comes to serving his needs as a patient."

"I don't agree," Ben said. "Dealing with him can take patience, a rare quality given how cantankerous and difficult Louie can be, but knowing him the way you do is actually a bonus, not a hindrance. You should've seen him giving Charlene a run for her money last year. I swear, that girl didn't know which end was up."

Ben suddenly looked delighted as he stood and walked Ellis to the door. "Honestly, I think this might work even better than I'd hoped. Let's give it a try, all right? We'll consider making a change in six months if you still feel this way. Oh, Murphy did tell you Louie's on a short leash right now, didn't she?"

Ellis briefly closed her eyes. "No, she didn't."

Ben lowered his voice. "He started a bonfire in the parking lot last week to mark his eighth anniversary living in this hellhole, as he calls it. He dragged six broken chairs and an old card table out of the storage shed without anyone catching him.

Marcel was working the night shift when he saw the flames through the dayroom window. Said Louie sprinkled gasoline on the pile, then tossed a match on top and sat down to watch."

Wonderful, Ellis thought, smoothing her hair behind her ears. *He's a pyromaniac too.*

Six

By midafternoon, Ellis had been formally introduced to everyone except Louie. Touching her elbow, Ben nodded to the front doors. "He's probably outside. Let's go find him." He led the way, stopping in the lobby so they could put on their jackets. It had turned out to be an unusually warm day, and the snow was on the verge of melting under the afternoon sun.

They followed a winding sidewalk around the back of the building, and there was Louie in the same La-Z-Boy chair he used to sit in years ago, golf umbrella open and drop-leaf table up. There was a tarp folded on the ground next to it. Louie was wearing a plaid winter coat and a wool cap, his pants tucked into his boots.

Ellis couldn't believe he still had his old chair.

"Louie," Ben boomed, "this is Ellis Semple, our new aide."

"I heard all about it at lunch," Louie said, folding his newspaper.

"She's also been assigned to you," Ben said, sliding his hands into his pockets. "And she tells me you know each other, so I'm hoping that'll make it easier."

"Can't hurt," Louie agreed, a wisp of breath curling up from his mouth.

Ellis didn't know what to say so she just smiled at Louie and waited for him to smile back. He didn't, though. Instead, he squinted into her face, shrewdly assessing her. "Did you give her a copy of my list?" he asked Ben.

"List?" Ellis said.

Ben lifted a hand. "Louie, do we need to do this?"

"I believe I am *paying* to live here, Ben," he said. "So if this little lady's been assigned to me, then she should get a heads-up on a few things, don't you think?" Reaching down, he yanked the handle on the side of his chair. It folded in on itself and he pushed to his feet and held out a piece of paper to Ellis.

"Here you go."

"Thanks," Ellis said, taking it.

Ben's gaze wandered to a thermos on Louie's drop-leaf table. He opened his mouth, then seemed to think better of it. "You can read it over later," he said to Ellis, indicating with a tilt of his head that they should go back inside.

Ellis gave Louie a polite nod. "I'm looking forward to working with you."

"Can't say I blame you," Louie said, sliding back into his chair. "A lot of the others act like they've got one foot in the grave."

Ben tugged on her arm. "He's been pushing the envelope more this year than any other," he said when they were out of earshot. "Last summer, he disappeared for a few days. . . ."

"Disappeared?" Ellis said, alarmed.

"Like that," Ben said, snapping his fingers. "He surfaced four days later. Phoned me from some bird sanctuary in British Columbia."

Ellis smiled at a distant memory. "He always did like birds."

"Right," Ben said, swiping a cobweb from the windowsill. "He took a Greyhound bus. Brought pictures for everyone of hundreds and hundreds of bald eagles. I have to admit, I hadn't seen him that happy for a long time, but it was a stupid thing to do."

He held the front door open and motioned Ellis inside, checking his watch. "We'll talk more later, okay? If you've got questions and I'm not around, ask Murphy. She knows all of Louie's tricks." Inside, he hung up his jacket and left her in the lobby as he walked down the hallway to his office.

Ellis watched him go. Unfolding the paper Louie had given her, she blinked in surprise when she saw her name, inserted in handwriting on a typewritten form letter:

Dear Ellis Semple: Ben Muldoon and I have a few understandings you should be aware of now that you have been assigned to me:

1. I smoke cigars, and I don't want to be lectured about it. You're my aide, not my doctor.

2. There's no need to raise your voice when you speak to me. I might be old, but I'm not deaf or stupid, and I don't want you clucking at me like I am.
3. I don't need help shaving or bathing or using the commode and I won't be showing you my naked posterior any time soon.
4. I only use nonperfumed hand soap.
5. I prefer my clothes line-dried (even in the winter) and would like my sheets changed every Friday.
6. A Norwegian friend of mine, Hans Holt, brings me a bottle of scotch every three months. Do not give him a hard time when he visits. He's got enough problems; he doesn't need you bothering him, too.
7. If I decide to skip a meal, that's my choice. It's utter horse manure that a person needs three meals a day to be healthy, a monstrous flimflam of an excuse the obese in our country are far too hung up on.
8. My birthday is May twentieth, and it would be nice if you remembered.

9. I enjoy a little jig now and then to keep my joints from getting rusty, and when I do, Ben says you should supervise. I've come a long way since my hip fracture, but I'm not the man I once was.
10. I am color-blind, so my clothes don't always match, but I'd appreciate it if you didn't point this out and embarrass me.

He line dries his clothes? He's color-blind?

Ellis recalled times when she'd seen Louie wearing the oddest combinations: pumpkin-colored pants and a green golf shirt, or a coral suit jacket with a yellow dress shirt. "What do you think?" he'd say, turning this way and that so Ellis and her mom could get a better look. "I got 'em on sale."

She thought she knew Louie well, but these were things she hadn't known.

Growing up in Barrow, she'd often seen Louie around town, although she didn't meet him face-to-face until she was twelve and they became neighbors. Many people thought he was a delightful nonconformist, Ellis's mom being one of them, but to others he was simply an eccentric old fool. For days after she and her mom moved in, Ellis had watched him each night from her bedroom window. He would sit outside in his yard listening to Christmas music, eyes closed, one hand moving in the air like an orchestra conductor's.

Back then, her mom couldn't afford to send her to summer camps, which meant Ellis spent most of her time alone, exploring the riverbank or collecting empty pop bottles to earn extra money. Bored and listless, she would watch Louie go down to the river each morning, and now and then she'd follow him, placing her own feet carefully into the footsteps he left behind so she herself left no tracks, no sign that she had been there. Sometimes he'd carry a lawn chair and fish from shore, but other mornings he just sat reading the paper.

One morning, when Ellis was lying on her back under a lean-to she'd built near where Louie sat, the sun rose over the trees with a warm brilliance, slicing through the branches and landing against her skin. Hearing something, she rolled onto her stomach and craned her neck to look through a hole in the branches. A bald eagle was perched on a rotten tree trunk not far from Louie. It was the first bald eagle she'd ever seen and she was spellbound.

Louie turned his head, never taking his eyes off the bird. "Make sure you don't move," he said from the corner of his mouth.

Ellis glanced behind her to see if someone else was there. There wasn't. It was just her and Louie.

"I think he has a nest nearby. He comes here often."

Her face burned with embarrassment when she realized he knew she was there.

"Wait a few minutes," he said in a voice so quiet she had to strain to hear it, "and he'll stretch his wings and lift off, which is something every girl should see before she grows up."

Quiet as a mouse, Ellis had pushed up onto her knees, straining to get a closer look. Louie slowly folded his paper in half. "Did you know their nests can stretch eight feet across and weigh up to a ton?"

She shook her head, forgetting he couldn't see her.

Moments later, the eagle spread its

wings and lifted off, the drawn out *whffff, whffff, whffff* of air moving beneath them making Ellis's mouth fall open in awe.

Louie tilted his head back and watched it fly away, then stood and folded his lawn chair, whistling "White Christmas." On his way past the lean-to, as Ellis considered what a good whistler he was, he stopped and stood still for a moment, staring straight ahead. "When I was your age I used to match people up with the animals I thought they were most like," he said. "My dad used to run seven days a week, rain or shine, so to me he was a cheetah. My mother was a squirrel because she was always storing up for the winter. I don't think I ever saw her not cooking or baking or canning something. And my grandma? Now that lady was an owl. She was always awake at night, drinking tea or knitting, complaining about her joints seizing up. And I used to think of myself as a bald eagle, mostly because I felt as rare as they are, being black like I am and living in Montana like I do."

He paused, lost in thought. "Someone once told me there's an eagle reserve in Canada, north of Vancouver in the Tantalus

Mountain Range. It's in a place called Brackendale near Squamish and it's called the bald eagle capital of the world. I've heard tell most winters about two thousand bald eagles make their way there, and you know what? Someday before I die, I'm going to take a trip up there and see them."

Ellis peeked at him through the jumble of branches. *Did he want her to say something?*

"By the way, know what you remind me of?" Louie asked.

"What?" she said, before she could stop herself.

"A Sasquatch."

"But they're huge and hairy," she protested.

"I didn't say you *look* like a Sasquatch. I said you *remind* me of one." He was laughing, hand on his stomach and head thrown back. "Only difference is they're a heck of a lot better at the art of camouflage than you are. I've heard they like sneaking around and being invisible, too, though I can't say I've ever actually seen one myself."

That night, long after Ellis should've been asleep, she had grabbed some paper and made a list, jotting down the names of animals she felt best matched everyone in her life. Her old friends were easy. They were zebras, because they would never change their stripes, pretending they didn't know her anymore after she and her mom had had to go on welfare. Her mom was a gazelle, timid and easily scared, but breathtakingly beautiful. And after careful consideration, she decided her dad was a grizzly bear, because bears need their space (the same way her dad did), and the males take off and let the females raise the cubs (just like her dad had) and there were lots of them in Canada, which was where her mom said he'd found work at a fish hatchery. *And me?* Ellis thought with a growing sense of pride. *I am a Sasquatch, the queen of invisibility.*

One morning not long after she and her mom had moved into their rental house, Ellis pulled open the front door to go to school and there was Louie, standing on the front steps. She thought he was a dead ringer for the actor Morgan Freeman, only Louie had a high bald forehead and a hundred-watt smile.

"Morning," he said.

She glanced down at the navy beret he was fingering. “Morning.”

Following her gaze, he grinned. “I belong to the Kinsmen Club.” He quickly looked over both of his shoulders to make sure no one was listening and added with a smile, “I’m their token black guy.”

Ellis’s eyes widened; she was unsure of what to say.

“I’m here to extend an invitation to your mom,” he explained. “I’m making plans to decorate a float for the town parade and I wanted to know if she’d like to help. Last year, we bought a double-decker bus from an auto wrecker. Decorated it with ten thousand miniature lights. Won first prize, too. They put our group picture on the front page of the *Gazette*. The year before, we built a four-seater go-kart with a sail to propel it down Main Street, but we only got second prize with that one.”

Ellis stared at him, wishing he would go away.

Louie cleared his throat and pointed past her into the kitchen, moving his finger in circles. “Is your mom home?”

“Yes, I am.”

Ellis swung around to see her mom

walking across the kitchen, dressed for what seemed like the first time in months. Paulina waved Louie inside. "Louie, come in. Please."

Ellis moved to one side and let him pass.

"This is my daughter, Ellis. Ellis, this is our next-door neighbor, Louie Johnson. He tells me his daughter Arla is in twelfth grade at the high school. Apparently, she is the star of the school's drama club."

That's not the only thing she's known for, Ellis thought.

Everyone in town knew who Arla was, even a few men who weren't supposed to, from what Ellis had heard. Because she was the only black girl in the entire school, Arla was unique before you even bothered to consider her unusual beauty. She wasn't young and wholesome and pretty like a cheerleader. She was tall and thin and graceful like an exotic jungle cat, the kind of girl who looked older than her age, the sort who wasn't intimidated by anyone. Ellis had overheard her English teacher say to the principal, "That girl's so busy trying to be someone she's not that she's missing out on who she is."

"I think Arla's beautiful," Ellis had once confided to her mom.

"Self-absorbed is a better word," Paulina had countered quietly, one of the few times Ellis ever heard her run anyone down.

Back then, Ellis had needed someone to model herself after, and for the short time that Arla Johnson lived next door, she had been that person. At school, Ellis often studied her, trying to memorize the way she walked and talked and laughed, recognizing how huge the gap was between beautiful and not when she looked in the mirror and saw her own face staring back. During assemblies, Ellis would watch everyone else watch Arla: guys with their mouths hanging open, and girls who looked her up and down with disdain, unwilling to admit to themselves, or anyone else, how exotic she was.

Ellis had accidentally run into Arla a few nights after they'd moved in.

It was late and she couldn't sleep, so she'd slipped outside and sat on the back steps, watching her breaths change to cloudlike puffs in the cool night air. Their house backed onto a creek that ran through the west side of town, so there were no houses behind them, and late at night it was dead quiet other than the soft insect whine of electricity traveling through the power cables that stretched across their yard. It'd been months since Ellis's dad had left, and although she still missed him, lately she had been focused not on why he'd left, but on how his leaving had affected her and her mom. They had never had to worry about money before, or having enough of anything, but now they found themselves stretching and straining as they tried to get used to being welfare poor.

Ellis pulled on a chunk of her hair to stare at it. You couldn't call it auburn, more a rich copper; wavy, badly behaved, and so long it fell to the top of her hips. She wanted to get it cut, but couldn't bring herself to ask her mom for any money. Tossing it back over one shoulder, she frowned. She thought she heard a noise coming from the side of their house. After zipping up her jacket, she snuck down the steps and around the corner, coming to an abrupt stop.

The streetlight out front was situated so that the wide strip of grass between the houses was lit with a rich buttery yellow glow. Leaning against Louie's house with his arms crossed was the manager of Barrow's video store. Ellis recognized him right away. He was tall and burly and muscular, and at that moment his eyes were glued to Arla Johnson, who had tossed her cropped jacket onto the ground and was dancing toward him, doing a playful bump and grind.

Ellis stared at her, mouth agape.

Arla was wearing high heels and a barely-there dress, and as she gyrated toward the video store manager, who was a lot older, and *married* if Ellis remembered right, she slowly and seductively pulled the dress up her hips inch by inch. When she got closer to him, she hooked her thumbs into the waistband of her panties and took her time inching them down over her legs before kicking them off with the toe of one shoe. Unaware anyone was watching, the manager took Arla by the arm and pulled her up against his chest, skimming the length of her back with his hands and then grabbing her bare ass and giving it a squeeze like he owned it.

From his expression, Ellis could tell he thought he'd just won some kind of lottery.

Arla threw her head back, throat arched and exposed, corkscrew hair flying wild and crazy around her face as though she was enjoying what he was doing. Suddenly the video store manager stepped back, took hold of the front of her dress with both hands and tore it open, making all her buttons pop off and go flying like bullets from a toy gun.

Then Ellis saw him touch her *there* and her face prickled with heat.

She started to back away, but as she did, the heel of her foot bumped into the downspout from the drainpipe and she lost her balance. "Whups!" she cried out, reaching out for a handful of vines to steady herself.

Arla abruptly straightened. "What the—?"

Ellis froze, swallowing as Arla fixed her with a murderous stare. "My mom and I just moved in next door," Ellis said, jerking a thumb over her shoulder.

The video store manager ran a hand down his face and said, "Jesus Christ."

"We're your new neighbors," she added.

"Is that so?" Arla said, adjusting her dress and smoothing it down with her hands. "Well, excuse me while I find a container for my joy."

"I'm sorry," Ellis said. "It's just that I heard a noise and—"

Arla took two hip-thrusting steps forward, shaking a finger at her. "I don't care what you heard," she said, her voice dropping three octaves. "Just get out of here, and don't you even think about tellin' anyone what you saw tonight, understand?"

Ellis had been too stunned to reply.

Instead, she lifted two fingers in the air, scout's honor, and backed away, suddenly feeling like a six-year-old, not someone who would soon be thirteen.

After sneaking inside and up to her room, Ellis shut the door and stared at herself in the mirror, thinking about everything she had just seen. How even when Arla was doing something she shouldn't she still looked beautiful. Turning her head this way and that, Ellis made a snap decision. She reached under her bed, pulled out a cardboard box, and rummaged around in it. Finding a pair of scissors, she lifted half of her hair over her right shoulder and began cutting before she could change her mind.

Snip, snip, snip.

Her hair fell to the floor in chunks, and when she was done, she pulled the rest over her left shoulder and did it, too. When she was finished, she stepped back and frowned. Crap! One side was longer than the other.

Squinting into the mirror, she went at it again. *Snip, snip*.

Dropping the scissors on her bed, she grabbed a small hand mirror, turned around, and looked at herself from behind to make sure it was even.

It wasn't, so she decided to take another shot at fixing it. *Snip, snip.*

And so it went, on and on as she whittled away at her hair for half an hour, trying to make it straight. When she was finally finished, her hair was at least eighteen inches shorter than it had been. Now it skimmed the top of her shoulders, and upon closer inspection Ellis believed she looked much older and Arla-like.

Hands on hips, she practiced preening in front of the mirror. *I'm seventeen and every guy in school wants to date me,* she thought, thrusting her hips forward with Arla-like attitude as she strutted around her room. *I own a pet raccoon and I have a walk-in closet crammed with fancy clothes. Oh, and my dad's a millionaire and he has a world-famous TV show about exotic animals, which works to my advantage considering the raccoon.*

Reaching up, she gathered her hair and lifted it away from her face, then threw her head back and shook it out, laughing the way she had sometimes heard Arla laugh. Next, she tried to strike a theatrical, seductive pose, pouting into the mirror and squinting to make her eyes look smoky and mysterious, but in the end it just looked like she had a bad stomachache. Worn out, she finally stripped down to her underwear and crawled into bed, wishing she could be someone else—anyone else.

Seven

Hadley left for school one morning and suddenly she was back, sticking her head inside the kitchen door. "Mom, do you know where Grandma is? I forgot to tell her someone called yesterday." She held out a crumpled slip of paper. "I wrote down his name and number, but I forgot to give her the message."

"It's okay," Paulina said, coming downstairs. "He phoned back."

"Sorry, Grandma," Hadley said, and then she disappeared to hurry off to school.

Paulina pulled on her coat and grabbed her car keys.

"Are you working today?" Ellis asked, wiping down the counter.

"No, I'm driving into Missoula," she said. "I'll be staying the night, though, so I won't see you until sometime tomorrow."

Until then, Ellis hadn't noticed the overnight bag she was carrying. "Why do you need to go to Missoula?" she asked.

"I have an appointment there this afternoon, so instead of driving home when I'm done, I'll stay at a hotel tonight, get up early, and be home tomorrow by lunch."

Ellis studied her face. "What kind of appointment? Are you sick? Are you seeing a doctor or something?"

Paulina gave her a half smile that told Ellis it was none of her business. "No, I'm perfectly fine. We'll talk about it some other time, okay?" She glanced at the clock and gave Ellis a quick hug. "I'll see you tomorrow."

Ellis watched her go, thinking, *Who does she know in Missoula?*

The first few weeks at Ellis's new job were relatively routine, although she did learn a lot about her coworkers and everyone she had been assigned to take care of. Mealtimes were exhausting. Louie occupied the same chair in the dining room every day. First, he'd tuck a napkin into his shirt, spread mustard on one half of a whole-wheat roll, horseradish on the other, and then set both to one side for later—"Dessert," he'd say. Then he would mix the rest of his food into a pile—"Trying to make it more edible," he'd explain—and eat slowly, making faces that told you it was an effort to do so, lifting his head and saying things like "I wouldn't feed cattle what they feed us in here" or "Anyone else gagging on these pork chops?"

When it came to the staff, Ellis noticed that Charlene took shortcuts, putting in as little effort as possible to get her job done, whereas Oliver almost always did more than was expected of him, including laundry, which he wasn't any good at. Murphy was a mother hen, overseeing all of the residents when the other aides were busy, shopping for groceries to help out in the kitchen, baking for special occasions, and stocking up on whatever they needed in bulk—toilet paper, cleaning solvents, and so on. And Ben had the unwavering disposition that seemed to keep everyone calm and centered.

Ellis learned that she liked Fran Wilson's family more than she liked Fran. Fran had six grandchildren and was always forgetting their names, so Ellis went out of her way to memorize them, saying, "Hello, Alle," short for Allessandra, or "What's new, Brianna? Are you still beating Matthew and Rayan and Neal at Monopoly? And how's that little Mona?" Ellis's friendliness usually earned her a steely glare from Fran, but she didn't care.

She learned that Joseph had once owned a group of bedding stores, and although they had gone bankrupt years ago, he talked about mattresses all the time, often telling the same stories—maybe eight in total—over and over again. How he had won salesman of the year in 1971; how he had caught his best friend and his neighbor's wife sleeping together on a mattress he'd sold him; how he had once personally delivered a king-size mattress to the governor's residence in Helena.

Vera-Lee was a statuesque woman with bottle-blond hair, and although she was in her seventies she wore low-cut blouses, tight slacks, and lacy push-up bras. She openly flirted with any man in sight. She also had a mannequin in her room, and each week she would dress it up in racy showgirl costumes, primping and fawning until it looked like the truest and most accurate reflection of how Vera-Lee felt she herself had once looked wearing the same outfit.

"I spent ten years working in Las Vegas," she confided to Ellis. "They were the best years of my life." It was a statement that helped explain both the mannequin and the excessive amount of rouge Vera-Lee had a penchant for wearing.

One entire wall in Ed Notton's room was decorated with autographed photos of himself shaking hands with someone famous. There was one of Ed and Steve Martin at a charity event, Ed and Sylvester Stallone at the grand opening of Planet Hollywood in Chicago, Ed and John Candy at a comedy club in Toronto. One day at lunch, Vera-Lee leaned in close to Ellis's ear and whispered, "I heard Ed used to be a big mover and shaker in Florida until his sons robbed him of all his money and shipped him up here."

Nina Ballard, who suffered from Alzheimer's, was the oldest and frailest of Ellis's charges. Every day Nina would rise and dress for a new adventure. After breakfast, come rain or shine or snow, she'd make her way outside to the cedar bench and wait for her husband to pick her up. It was Louie who always carried her suitcase out front for her, and Louie who tucked her arm into his and brought her back inside each day for lunch. Without exception, all the staff and residents at Pleasant View Manor adored Nina. It seemed there was always someone taking her a cup of tea, or a warm blanket, or a glass of lemonade.

For the most part, everyone got along well, other than Louie and Rolly, who acted like two children who'd been forced to share the same toys. Day in and day out, they were constantly arguing.

One afternoon, Ellis found Rolly sitting on the couch in the dayroom, sulking. When she asked if everything was all right, he gestured to Louie. "He keeps tilting all the pictures sideways. Haven't you noticed?"

Louie spread his hands in feigned innocence.

Ellis saw for the first time that every picture was crooked, leaning a few inches to the left or right.

"Every time I turn around, I'm straightening pictures," Rolly complained. "He knows it makes me crazy. Then at lunch today, he made a snarky comment about my hair."

"I asked if he wanted a pear," Louie corrected.

"He says I'm rude."

"I said you've got an attitude."

Rolly gave Louie a murderous glance, and Louie threw a hand in the air in disgust, bringing the argument to an end.

They reminded Ellis of squabbling brothers at their worst, but as she studied them, she realized how lost they'd be without each other, how lacking their lives would be in drama and a sense of purpose, hearts empty of the sheer effort it took each of them to continue their daily one-upmanship.

One day, an hour before her shift was over, Ellis was standing with Louie at the front desk as he sifted through his mail, opening more envelopes and newspapers and packages than she received in a month. After wrapping elastic bands around a handful of envelopes, he clapped his hands together.

"Care to join me outside?" he asked.

Ellis briefly closed her eyes, searching for patience. It had snowed that morning and the last thing she wanted to do was sit outside in a lawn chair, but there was no way in the world she was going to tell Louie that.

"Can't think of anything else I'd rather do," she said, forcing a smile.

Louie played Christmas music all year round. Apparently, there had almost been a full-blown uprising over it three years ago. After a particularly heated exchange between Louie and Rolly—hair was pulled, punches were thrown—Ben had finally taken a hard line over the issue. Discussions were had, meetings were held, and in the end it was decided that other than during the month of December, no one would be allowed to listen to Christmas music inside the nursing home.

So now Louie took his music outside. Some days he listened, others he danced. It all depended on his mood. And even though it was late December, he still stubbornly refused to play his music inside, unwilling to let Rolly think he'd gotten the better of him.

Ellis slipped on her coat and boots and followed him into the cold, carrying his portable boom box and two lawn chairs. Louie squinted up at the sunny afternoon sky and told her he felt like dancing. She unsnapped a chair and sat down with his boom box balanced on her knees. "Go for it," she said, pressing PLAY.

As she watched him, thankful that Ben paid a company to clear away the snow and spread salt so ice wouldn't build up, it occurred to her that those who didn't know Louie probably thought he was drunk or suffering from dementia when they saw him dancing to Christmas music like this, alone, in the middle of the parking lot. This was the fifth time she'd sat outside with him. As visitors walked past frowning, she felt she should explain, but so far she hadn't. If watching over Louie was some kind of test, then she intended to pass it with flying colors.

Mostly Louie danced slowly, eyes closed, one arm bent against his chest and the other swooping through the air in front of him like an elephant's trunk. But if Ellis played "Jingle Bell Rock" or "Feliz Navidad," he became a fireball of energy for a minute or two, moving from a waltz to a two-step and then off into an odd hip-rolling rumba that looked painful for a man his age. His CD collection was extensive, including Bing Crosby, Vince Gill, Dolly Parton, Boney M, even Christina Aguilera. It didn't matter, though. He danced to all of them. From what Ellis could tell, "I'll Be Home for Christmas" was one of his favorites, followed closely by "Winter Wonderland."

What amazed Ellis most was that Louie always had a smile on his face while he danced, even when he was wiping sweat from his brow after he had called it a day. That afternoon, when he said he was ready to go back inside, Ellis tried to make polite conversation. "You sure seem to enjoy this," she said, folding her lawn chair.

Clutching one hand to his chest, he shot her a mile-wide grin. "Dancing gives me the same kind of bliss others spend years popping pills to find. You should try it sometime. It'll change the way you look at life."

EIGHT

On weeks when Anissa was staying in town with her mom, she usually stopped in after school to see Hadley. Often, she would glide across the speckled linoleum of their kitchen floor with an old battery-operated microphone she had bought at a garage sale, singing songs like "Proud Mary" or "I Saw Her Standing There" or her favorite, "Paperback Writer." Now and then she'd bring along her dog, an old basset hound named Lipton with an age-white face. When Anissa sang, Lipton would throw back his head and howl. Hadley would roll her eyes and say, "You're a nut job, Anissa," but Ellis could tell Hadley was secretly thrilled to have her around.

It wasn't only Anissa who began dragging the light back into their lives, though.

Three days before Christmas, Ellis pulled in to the driveway and parked, wishing she could fast-forward to New Year's and skip all the festivities. It had been a tough week. She'd had trouble sleeping, she had no appetite, and she had found it increasingly difficult to focus on her new job. Making matters worse, Hadley had been more quiet and withdrawn than Ellis had seen her in weeks. Late the night before, Ellis had crept down the hallway and leaned against Hadley's bedroom door, certain she'd heard muffled crying.

Ellis's mind suddenly filled with visions from the past, all jumbled together like a ball of string. One year ago, Mark was still alive. By now, he and Hadley would have bought, dragged home, and decorated the tree, the same as always. There would be a box of stocking stuffers underneath Mark's side of the bed filled with tiny, individually wrapped gifts he'd spent months accumulating. Weeks ago, he would have phoned Ellis's mom, asked her to fill two coolers with snowballs, and had them FedExed to Dallas, where he would keep them in the deep freeze until Christmas morning. Then, after all of the gifts were opened, while Ellis cleaned the turkey and made stuffing for dinner, he and Hadley would lug the coolers outside and have a snowball fight. Mark always made everything exciting, as if where they were at that very moment was the best possible place to be.

How can I compete with that? Ellis wondered. *He was always doing something spontaneous that took Hadley's breath away. I can't decide what traditions would be comforting to re-create and which ones would be too painful.*

As she climbed the back porch steps, she could hear music pulsing from inside the kitchen, followed by Anissa's singing and Lipton's low, long howl.

Standing on the porch, Ellis smoothed away a spot of ice fog on the window using the cuff of her jacket, and squinted to look inside. Spread out all over the kitchen—on the table, the countertops, and even on top of the fridge—were dozens of baking trays filled with bell-shaped sugar cookies. Hadley was moving from one tray to the next, shaking candied sprinkles onto each cookie. Lipton was sitting in the corner next to the fridge, and Anissa was standing on a chair with a portable CD player on the table next to her, cradling her microphone and singing "All I Want for Christmas" in a surprisingly lusty voice along with someone on the CD. But it was Paulina who Ellis watched most avidly, in awed silence, as her breath came out in tiny clouds.

Ellis's mom was wearing a Santa hat and a green boa draped around her neck, and she was dancing, shaking her shoulders to the music as Anissa sang. "I just want you for my own . . ." Paulina did a step-kick to the left followed by one to the right before taking a few strides into the middle of the room and spinning around to face the girls.

"More than you could ev-v-v-e-r-r-r-r know . . ."

Paulina stretched her hands high in the air, twisting her wrists this way and that. "Make my wish come trooooo . . ."

She shimmied her shoulders, waiting for Anissa to cue up the final line, and then she and Hadley threw their heads back and joined in together, belting it out as loud as they could. "All I want for Christ-mu-u-u-s-s-s . . . i-z-z-z-z . . . yewwwwww!"

There was a moment of stillness before Anissa hopped down from the chair, pulled a felt-tip marker from her back pocket, and uncapped it with her teeth. "That was wicked," she said, marking a fat number nine under Paulina's name on a piece of paper taped to the fridge. Hadley agreed, grabbing the pen and matching Anissa's score with her own.

Paulina pulled off her Santa hat and smoothed her hair with her hands. A blush crept across her face and she bowed three times, aiming first at Hadley, then Lipton, and last of all Anissa. The boa slid off her shoulders onto the floor. Hadley retrieved it and held it out to her, but Paulina smiled, and wrapped it around her granddaughter's neck twice, giving the tail end a toss. "Why don't *you* try it?" she suggested, running a finger up Hadley's cheek.

Hadley averted her eyes. "I don't think so."

Insistent, Anissa took over, prodding her to pick a song, any song. Moments later, she climbed back up on her chair, singing "Santa Baby" as Hadley stood with her arms slack at her sides. Paulina moved over beside her, slid an arm around her waist, and gently hip checked her into some experimental movement that quickly caught fire. Soon Hadley was galumphing her way through the same moves her grandma was making, mimicking her with a look of fierce determination on her face.

As she watched them, Ellis felt emptied out and filled up all at once. She covered her mouth with one hand, completely absorbed by how Hadley seemed to unwind like a ribbon as she began dancing with her grandmother. Part of Ellis was struck by how much she wanted to join in, but another part worried that if she did, she might shatter the fragile wonder of what she was watching and bring it to a screeching halt.

Just then Paulina looked up and caught sight of her in the window. Ellis was perilously close to tears, and when her mom locked eyes with her, she gave her a quick wink and looked away, pretending not to see her. Ellis felt a small flutter of hope in her chest. Maybe Christmas wouldn't be so bad after all.

The song ended and Anissa jumped off the chair and gave Hadley a high five. She ran over to Lipton, unzipped a big duffel bag on the floor next to him, and lifted out what looked like a miniature propane tank. Grinning, she lugged it over to the kitchen table and set it down on the only corner that wasn't taken up with cookie trays.

Paulina and Hadley crept closer, watching as Anissa reached into her pocket and pulled out a handful of balloons. She clamped the end of one onto a valve, flipped on a switch, and the balloon filled. Just when it looked like it was ready to burst, she turned the switch off and pinched the balloon closed between her thumb and forefinger. Waving a hand at Hadley, she said, "Press play," nodding at her portable CD player.

Hadley did and a voice began singing "Silver Bells." Anissa quickly lifted the balloon to her mouth and inhaled before grabbing her microphone to join in. Her voice came out high and tinny and laughable, her voice immediately altered by the helium. "Soon it will be-e-e-e Christmas day!"

Laughing, Hadley bent over like a jackknife.

Paulina could not hide her delight. “Anissa,” she said, “you’re a modern-day Pippi Longstocking,” to which Hadley and Anissa shared confused looks before bursting into giggles all over again.

Ellis felt the back of her throat tighten. She wasn’t ready to go inside. Instead, she nestled against the wall and continued watching them through the window. She felt as though she’d just stumbled across a glittering diamond in her mom’s kitchen, one of the least likely places she ever dreamed she’d find anything so breathtaking. And as they sang and danced, occasionally bending over with laughter, it occurred to her that this was the second time she’d had to start her life over from scratch in this old house.

Tears quivered in her eyes. Before her dad left, they had been wealthy, that much she knew for sure. He’d owned a statewide trucking company, and their home, a monstrous two-story custom log-and-stone affair with six bedrooms, three baths, two fireplaces, and a three-car garage, had sat high on a hill outside of town, surrounded by breathtaking wilderness. Men tipped their hats with respect when they saw her dad walking down the street after church each Sunday, and women often tittered stupidly when he passed, blushing as they ran their hands over their hair or down their hips.

For the first decade of Ellis's life, her dad had been her safe place to fall.

At six, when she knocked out a tooth on the monkey bars at school, it was her dad who took her by the hand and helped her look for it. At nine, when she accidentally rode her bike into the back of a parked car, he made a temporary splint for her sprained wrist. And in sixth grade, when her teacher lost his patience and yelled at her in front of the class, it was her dad who demanded an apology. As a child, she believed he was invincible, the closest thing to a hero a girl could wish for.

Back then, Ellis also had a brother, who was six years older than she was. Donnie was tall, with broad shoulders and a neck like an ox, and as far as her dad was concerned, he could do no wrong, even when he did.

There was always something with Donnie. Like when he failed seventh grade and Ellis's dad took the principal out for dinner to "set things straight." Or how, at fifteen,

Donnie got drunk with two of his friends and they pulled on black-stocking balaclavas, stole the mayor's truck, and rolled it into a ditch. That time, her dad sent the mayor and his wife on a weeklong golfing trip to Arizona to "smooth things over" so he wouldn't press charges. From Ellis's standpoint, Donnie spent more time avoiding work than he ever did doing any, content to ride on his charm and good looks.

Every winter Ellis's dad would take Donnie to hockey games and Ellis would beg to go with them. Donnie usually lost interest and wandered off with his friends before the first period was over, and she'd scoot over next to her dad and try to be whoever he wanted Donnie to be.

"Think they'll pull the goalie?" she'd ask, resting her elbows on her knees.

"If they don't, they're crazy," he'd say.

"Number eight keeps high sticking," she'd point out.

"I know, but you wait. He'll get a penalty."

And he almost always did.

The year Donnie turned eighteen, Ellis's dad put his foot down, insisting that Donnie take a summer job with a roofing company. Two weeks later, Donnie fell off a building and broke his neck. Apparently, he was acting stupid when it happened. He had taken his roofing gun, which was operated by compressed air, and was shooting nails at the feet of another roofer, a buddy of his. Laughing, Donnie backed up and tripped over a piece of wood nailed to the roof they'd been using as a brace. He fell two stories onto a cement sidewalk.

Seconds later, he was dead.

When Ellis came home from a friend's house that afternoon, her parents were sitting across from each other in the living room, both sobbing. She had seen her mom cry before, but that was the first time she'd seen her dad weep, and it had unnerved her. This wasn't a man she knew. This was not her confident, Donnie-adoring, hockey-loving father.

After Donnie died everything changed. Ellis's dad stopped going to hockey games, taking them out for breakfast after church on Sundays, and hosting his infamous county-wide get-togethers that everyone in town was always talking about. He spoke of Donnie less and less often, and frequently his eyes would glaze over when Ellis hugged him. It was as though he was holding her off instead of pulling her in for one of the trademark bear hugs she loved so much, the ones that left her feeling safe and protected.

Her mom reminded her that he was grieving, not to take it personally. And until he'd packed up and driven away, Ellis hadn't.

The day he left was a day burned into her memory.

That morning, she'd heard her parents arguing when she woke up. Slipping on a pair of jeans and a shirt, Ellis quickly made her way outside, along the brick façade of their house and through the arched passageway that led to their backyard. At first, she pretended to practice cartwheels on the lawn, but then she noticed their bedroom window was open, so she drew closer. There was a rain barrel next to the house; she lifted herself up onto it and peeked inside, entranced by a conversation she wasn't meant to hear.

Her dad was stuffing a suitcase with clothes, heaps of them spilling onto the bed and the floor. He seemed in a hurry, as if he might not have the courage to do this at all if he didn't do it fast, and her mom was sitting on the bed, crying.

"Please don't do this, Dennis!"

He ran his hands over his face and groaned. "Don't make it harder than it already is. I don't want to hurt you."

"Then don't go," she said, reaching for him.

He stepped back and raised his hands. "Damnit, Paulina! What's a man supposed to do when he wakes up one day and realizes he never should've married the woman he did? Stay? Is that what you want? You want me to stay even though I don't love you?"

He snapped the suitcase shut and straightened. "Look, I'm trying to be honest with you here, so let's stop kidding ourselves. We got married because you were pregnant. We agreed it was the right thing to do—the Christian thing to do—and when Donnie was born . . ." His voice choked up and he slammed a closed fist into the open palm of his other hand. "I couldn't have been happier."

Confused, Ellis felt as if someone had just pinched her.

Her dad turned away for a moment, and then he looked back at her mom, shaking his head. "But that was then," he said in a low voice. "And this is now, and if I stay here one more day, I swear I'm going to break apart from the pressure that's building inside me. I'm exhausted, Paulina. Tired of constantly trying to be big man on the hill in Barrow, worn out from the stress of the business and the constant need to be on. I didn't completely realize it until Donnie died, but I'm miserable."

Ellis watched her mom's narrow shoulders drop.

"I don't want this anymore, Paulina. Not any of it."

Her mom looked ruined and beautiful in her anguish. "Please don't go," she whispered, but he was unfazed by her pleas.

"I'll phone," he said. "After I find a job and get settled."

Sobbing, she grabbed the comforter and crumpled it in her fists, shaking her head no.

"I'm sorry," he said again, and then he left, almost running in his haste.

Fear chugged up Ellis's spine. *He's really leaving!*

Brushing hair off her face, she dropped to the ground and ran around the house into the front yard, where she watched him stride down the sidewalk and throw the suitcase into the back of his pickup truck.

"Dad?" she called, hearing her voice wobble.

He stopped and stared at the ground for a moment.

"Where're you going?"

"Go see your mom," he said, and then he hopped into the driver's seat, started the truck, and pulled away.

Running to the garage, Ellis grabbed her bike and jumped on. The sun was hot, pounding down from a clear sky as she followed his truck from their property into Barrow, down streets canopied by lush trees and up the long hill that would take him out of town on the south side. The word "no" beat time in her head with each revolution of her front wheel, and her shirt stuck to her back as she watched her legs moving beneath her.

Halfway up the hill, beads of sweat gathered along her hairline, and she stood on the pedals, pushing hard to keep his truck in sight. Cars arced past her, as did a gravel truck and a school bus, and still she kept going, glancing up in panic as his truck grew smaller and smaller in the distance. Then, just as she was about to give up, she saw him turn left at the top of the hill onto Airport Road, a dead end.

She stopped to catch her breath, relief hitting her as she leaned over the handlebars. Moments later, she continued, pedaling slower than before as she watched out for him. Airport Road was two miles long, and she finally saw his truck parked at the end of it, facing a chain-link fence that lined the table-flat runway of the regional airport. She slowed as she got closer, noticing that the driver's door was open, but her dad wasn't inside. When she drew near, she spotted him lying on his back in the grass, watching a plane rise up into the air.

She set her bike down, wondering what to do next. This whole day suddenly seemed too big and the problems her parents were having too confusing to understand, but that's all they were—problems. Things to be worked out, issues they could solve as a family.

She walked over next to him and sat down cross-legged on the grass. He shot her a quick glance and looked away. Minutes passed in awkward silence, magnifying their separateness as she breathed in the familiar scent of his aftershave.

Another small plane zoomed down the runway and lifted off, bursting through clouds that were now hugging the sky, the roar of its engines filling the space between them. Ellis watched it rise above them, a red banner zipping through the air behind it that read, "Welcome to the Barrow County Fair." She suddenly thought she knew why he had come here. Donnie had always loved the annual county fair, the Ferris wheel rocking to a stop as each car was loaded, girls giggling into their hands when he and his friends walked by, the roller coaster twisting and screeching as it whipped past on a rusty track—"the whole shebang," as her dad liked to say, clapping Donnie on the back as he handed him a wad of bills so he could go enjoy himself.

She lowered her chin to her knees. "You're going because of Donnie, aren't you?"

"Donnie's got nothing to do with it."

"Then why are you leaving?"

There were dark circles under his eyes and his salt-and-pepper beard was messier than she'd ever seen it, evidence that he was tired and hadn't been taking care of himself, that leaving them wasn't as easy as he was making it out to be.

Ellis plucked a blade of grass and rolled it between her palms, then lifted her hands to her nose and breathed in the scent that had been left behind. Inexplicably, she suddenly believed that if she could get him talking, for a few minutes, and then maybe a few more, he might come to his senses and stay. He hadn't answered her question, though, so she knew she had to be cautious, that she had to think about what she was going to say before she said it, or else he might get impatient and storm off.

"Sometimes I wanna run away, too," she admitted.

She saw a muscle jump in his jaw, and in that moment he reminded her of a caged animal with nowhere to go, exactly like the lions and tigers she'd seen at the Oregon Zoo on vacation two years ago.

"I'm not running away," he said. "I'm leaving. There's a big difference. You're just too young to understand."

She took a long swallow and whispered, "What about me?"

"You'll be fine," he said, staring up at the sky. "You're a lot stronger than you think you are, Ellis." Seconds later, he ran a hand over his face, dismissing her needi-ness. "I'm actually doing your mom a favor, you know."

Ellis stared at him, trying to comprehend how this could be true.

"It's time she learned how to stand on her own two feet. Time she took care of herself instead of me always taking care of everything."

Watching another plane lift into the sky and slowly fade to a tiny silver speck in the distance had a hypnotic pull, and as Ellis stared at it, she thought about what he'd just said. The very idea of her mom being in charge and having to take care of things worried her more than she could put into words. She took two quick breaths.

"Couldn't you do it a little longer? Take care of us, I mean."

"No, I can't." His voice was soft, but firm.

"Then take me with you."

"Can't do that, either."

She felt as if something had just hit her in the chest, something hard and unforgiving. And to top it off, she'd just broken her unspoken rule when it came to dealing with him: *Don't let your feelings show. Act tough like a boy. He likes boys better.* Trying a different approach, she stood and brushed dirt off her jeans. "Okay, when will you be back?" Because of his trucking business, she was used to him being away, often for weeks at a time.

Shaking his head, he pushed to his feet and walked over to his truck, where he lifted the lid on a metal compartment in the back marked "Tools." Ellis watched him pull out a road map, unfold it on the hood of his truck, and smooth it out with both hands.

"You'll come home for Thanksgiving, won't you? You wouldn't want to miss the big cabaret at Grosmont Hall."

Frowning, he ran a finger down a highway she couldn't see.

"And what about Christmas?" she pressed. "You'll be back then, right? You know Mom can't chop down a tree by herself and I'm not allowed to use the ax."

"No, I won't be back for Christmas."

Stricken with the full and complete awareness that nothing she said was going to change his mind, Ellis felt her desperation quickly turn to fear. "You better watch your step," she said, assuming a tough-girl stance even though her voice was trembling. "Or you'll mess things up real good . . . "

He closed his eyes and went very still.

". . . and Mom'll never take you back then."

"Ellis, I know this is hard for you to understand—"

"And when you do come home," she said, raising her voice to drown him out, "maybe we won't be here anymore. Then how would you feel?"

His jaw twitched.

"Yup, you just keep it up, mister—"

He took two long strides, then grabbed her arm and gave it a shake. "Stop it! This isn't about you. It's about me and your mom, and you need to understand I'm not the first person on this earth who's ever been unhappy or confused about life. There are lots of people just as screwed up as I am right now, Ellis." He let her arm drop and took a few angry steps back, running his hands through his hair. "Damnit anyhow, life is a huge minefield and it's time someone warned you about it!"

Ellis stared at him. "If you go," she whispered, "I might have to stop loving you."

He squatted in front of her and took in a long, slow breath. "Ellis, I need to sort out my life."

"I could help. I'm real good at sorting."

"No," he said. "I'm not taking you with me." He straightened and walked away.

Ellis stared at her running shoes, scared to push any harder, worried that if she did he'd say something that might hurt even more. When she was little, it was her dad who had always lectured her about being responsible. Unreliability had always disappointed him, and he had wanted it to disappoint her, too.

"Be good for your mom."

He folded the map and climbed into his truck.

Ellis briefly closed her eyes. She felt something climb up inside of her and spread out in small waves, a mixture of fear and sadness so deep she suddenly burst into tears. "Fine then!" she yelled, banging balled-up fists into her hips. "Leave, you coward!"

He flexed his hands on the steering wheel and stared straight ahead out the windshield, but she was sure she saw his chin quiver with the effort it took not to look at her. She was sobbing now, tears running down her face.

"And don't come back, either, because we don't need you!"

Years later, it would be this memory that would be frozen in Ellis's mind: a brazen feeling breaking loose inside her as she spewed profanities at him, saying horrible, hateful things she'd never said before, trying to get a reaction—any reaction—and him putting his truck in gear and driving slowly away.

Her dad had always been her rock, the one person she'd trusted implicitly, and yet he'd let her down in the worst possible way. The words he'd said to her mom often echoed through Ellis's thoughts. *What's a man supposed to do when he wakes up and realizes he never should've married the woman he did? Stay?* It was the only reason he ever gave for leaving. One day he was there, and the next he was stuffing suitcases with things that really mattered to him.

Ellis, of course, hadn't been one of them.

It took her a long time—long after she'd

had Hadley and married Mark—to fully understand that the biggest impact her dad made on her life occurred not during the twelve years she knew him, but in the ten-minute conversation when she realized she didn't. Until the day he left, her life had been safe, secure. Until then, everything had made sense or could be explained, even Donnie's death. And until that moment when he drove away, in her mind, he'd always been perfect.

Nine

One day in January when Paulina was in Missoula—doing what, Ellis didn't know—Ellis slipped home at lunchtime to take out the garbage cans. The truck only picked up once a week, on Wednesday afternoons, and she had forgotten to drag the cans to the curb that morning. It had snowed six inches the night before, and as usual she'd driven Hadley to school on her way to work, so when she pulled into the driveway, there were two sets of telltale footprints leading from the back porch out onto the driveway.

She got out of the car and headed to the

garage, the crunch of her feet muffled by the heavy snow that blanketed the ground and hung from bent tree branches. It was then that she saw another set of footprints leading out of the trees from behind their house to the garage's side door, where they disappeared.

Ellis stopped in her tracks. What was going on?

Grabbing the door handle, she twisted it to the right and pushed the door open. Her heart was racing. When she stuck her head inside, she saw an old baseball bat leaning against the wall. She reached in and grabbed it, worried about coming face-to-face with a homeless hobo or some delinquent who might be trying to rob them. Frowning, she noticed a small pile of snow just inside the door where someone had obviously stomped off boots.

What's this? A polite thief?

Directly across from the door, an untouched wall of spiderwebs was still strung between an old bed frame, a wheelbarrow, and a shelf filled with clay pots and gardening tools. Moving slowly, she stepped inside and looked this way and that, but she couldn't see anyone. Even though it was winter, there was a strong smell of mildew and mold, and it was eerily quiet. It took a moment for her eyes to adjust, and then she noticed the ladder at the far end of the garage leading to the narrow loft. The only time she had ever been up there was to help her mom take down or put away Christmas decorations, which were stored in six large Rubbermaid containers, two with lights for the house, the others filled with tree ornaments and wreaths.

Holding up the bat, Ellis walked to the bottom of the ladder, where she noticed a dusting of snow on several of the rungs.

"Who's up there?" she called out.

She heard rustling, followed by what sounded like mumbled cursing.

"Answer me," she demanded.

There was a long pause. "It's me," Hadley finally said, her voice drifting down.

Ellis's eyebrows shot up.

Dropping the bat, she climbed the ladder and leaned over at the waist to peer around the Rubbermaid containers lined up across the front of the loft. An old mattress that had been pushed into the far corner took up most of the floor space. Next to it was a wooden crate turned upside down with a stack of magazines on it, and on top of the magazines was a can of Coke. Sitting cross-legged on the mattress, covered with at least two sleeping bags, was Hadley, her black Goth hair, almost an inch blond at the roots now, mussed up and sticking out all over.

"What in the world are you doing up here?" Ellis asked.

Hadley pulled a tube of ChapStick out of her pocket and rubbed it across her lips. "Sleeping," she said matter-of-factly.

Ellis blinked in confusion. "Why wouldn't you go inside?"

Hadley lifted one shoulder, let it drop.

"I see." Ellis nodded with sudden realization. "When you're cutting school, I guess it's easier to hide up here than get caught by me or Grandma in your room in the middle of the day, huh?"

Hadley looked sideways at the stack of magazines next to her, but didn't answer.

"How often have you been doing this?" Ellis asked.

"Couple times a week," she admitted.

Ellis stared at her for a long moment. She understood Hadley's secret grief, recognized it immediately. The need to act normal in front of others, the desire to show everyone, maybe even yourself, that you were doing fine. But keeping up that façade could be exhausting. There were often times when you'd feel yourself start to crumble, and when that happened, it was best if you were alone.

On impulse, she lifted herself up into the loft and crawled over onto the mattress. She didn't have the heart to send Hadley back to school. In fact, if she had a choice, she'd probably stay up here with her all afternoon.

Careful not to look at her daughter, Ellis leaned back and stretched out her legs, boots dangling off the edge of the mattress. The toughest part was that she didn't know exactly how to *talk* to Hadley. She couldn't feign similar interests because she had never been anything like her at that age. Where Hadley had self-esteem, she'd had little. Hadley wore low-rise jeans and belly-baring tops without giving it a thought, whereas Ellis never would've had the confidence to do so. She didn't even get her ears pierced until she was seventeen, and only then because she was pregnant and terrified about giving birth, so she decided to measure how much pain she could withstand by having them done.

How am I supposed to build a close relationship with you, she wondered, *when I never had one with my own mom?*

"I wasn't all that happy when I was your age," she finally said.

Hadley's eyebrows shot up. "Why?"

Ellis hesitated, trying to decide how much to tell her. "Well . . . I wasn't popular, for one thing, and I had bad acne, so I got picked on a lot."

Hadley frowned. "Did you have any friends?"

"No one I was really close to."

"Not like Anissa."

"No," Ellis agreed. "Not like Anissa."

"So what'd you do?"

Ellis shrugged. "I bumbled my way through school. I was a loner, which wasn't that bad, and I got good at faking it. I learned to keep my face blank when anyone gave me a rough time. I acted like everything was okay even though it wasn't. Sometimes it actually worked, too. Sometimes pretending everything was okay made it seem so."

Hadley nodded as if this made sense to her.

"And then you met Dad?" she said, sounding hopeful.

"Yes," Ellis said, smiling. "And then I met your dad."

She tilted her head sideways and studied Hadley openly for a moment. She looked much too thin, her shoulder blades sticking out like sharp wings under her long-sleeved shirt, but her eyelashes were still as long and thick as they'd always been, and her breasts, which used to be as flat as drink coasters, now filled out the small B-cup bras Ellis had recently bought her. A leaden feeling suddenly settled in her chest. Her little girl was growing up and Mark would never get to see any of it.

"What're you staring at?" Hadley asked, chewing on a thumbnail.

"You," Ellis said. "I was thinking that I'd give anything for eyelashes like yours."

"Right," Hadley said, looking uncomfortable. "At least you have, like, great hair."

Ellis's eyes widened in surprise. "It's long and straight. What's so great about it?"

"You can do anything with it. Mine's a

mess," she said, running her hands through hers. "Dad would have hated it."

Ellis brushed a renegade strand of hair off Hadley's forehead. "Not a chance. You could've shaved your head bald and your dad would have thought you were beautiful."

Silence pulsed between them. Hadley dropped her gaze, readjusted the sleeping bags around her legs. "I used to be able to close my eyes and picture him," she said in a voice so quiet Ellis had to strain to hear her. "But it's getting harder all the time."

Ellis didn't know what to say. They sat next to each other in silence. "I keep a picture of him under my pillow," she finally said.

Hadley's head snapped up. "You do?"

Ellis nodded. "It's a shot of your dad carrying you on his shoulders. You were five or six, and we were at the annual teddy bear picnic. You're carrying a knapsack and your favorite teddy bear is sticking out the top with one of its arms in a cast. You and your dad have temporary daisy tattoos on your cheeks. I bought you a minibucket of them one year, and every now and then you'd insist that he put one on, too."

Ellis paused, trying to think of other details she could add, and then she noticed that Hadley was crying, without making a sound. "I remember those tattoos," she said, wiping her cheeks with the heels of her palms.

Ellis crawled across the mattress on all fours until her head was almost touching Hadley's. "You used to make everyone who came over for a visit put one on. I still have a dozen of them," she whispered.

"Honest?" Hadley said, biting back a smile.

Ellis nodded. "After you outgrew them and moved on to something else, I put what was left in an envelope and tucked it into your baby book."

"Really?" She seemed delighted by this.

Ellis could hear the screech and roar of the garbage truck outside as it moved past their house and continued on down the street. Sighing, she glanced at her watch. She decided not to give Hadley a lecture about skipping school, choosing instead to see if having gotten caught would be enough to put an end to it.

"I'd better get back to work," she said.

She gave Hadley's hand a quick squeeze before crawling over to the ladder. She turned and gingerly lowered her feet one rung at a time, and when she reached the bottom, she smoothed down her jacket and peered up at the loft.

"Hadley?" she said.

"Uh-huh?" Her voice drifted down.

"If you'd like, when I get home from work today we can go down to the drugstore and buy some hair color to fix your roots."

Hadley peeked down at her with a shy smile. "Okay," she said. "Could you help me put it back the way it was?"

Ellis stared up at her, touched by words she couldn't recall hearing from Hadley since she was a toddler: *Could you help me?* "Of course I can," she said, thrilled to be needed, to be able to put *something* back the way it had once been.

That night after dinner, Hadley was sitting at the table timing the hair color they'd applied when Ellis broached the topic of grief counseling.

"But I don't *need* counseling," Hadley argued.

Ellis stuffed the empty bottle of dye and directions into the box they'd come in, glad that her mom wasn't home yet. She'd been meaning to discuss this idea with Hadley and right now seemed like a good time.

"I think we could both use some," Ellis said. "I've been to three sessions now and it's not that bad. You don't have to say anything if you don't want to. Just come and listen."

"No, thanks," Hadley said. "I'm fine."

Turning away, Ellis tossed the remnants of the Miss Clairol color kit into the garbage. *No, you're not. I've heard you crying at night and I see those dark circles under your eyes.* "Hadley, can I tell you something?"

"Sure," Hadley replied, watching her warily.

"The only time I let myself cry is when I'm in the shower where no one else can hear me." Hadley's chin dropped to her chest, but not before Ellis saw a flash of something cross her face. "And there are days when I either want to sleep all the time or else I can't stay busy enough," she continued. "It's like I'm afraid to give my mind any time to explore memories about your dad, and the minute I find myself alone in a room where it's quiet and still, I feel like I'm suffocating and I need to jump up and get *moving*."

Keeping her eyes on the fruit bowl, Hadley adjusted her grip on the towel around her shoulders.

"There are days when I'm so angry I want to stick my head outside and scream up at the sky."

The room went quiet other than the soft *tick-tick-tick* of the timer.

Drawing in a breath, Ellis reached across the table and squeezed Hadley's hand. "I'm not going to make you go, but I wish you'd think about it."

Hadley slid down in her chair until her fingers slowly dislodged from her mom's. "Sounds like you need it more than I do," she said.

The timer went off and Ellis moved over to the sink to get ready to rinse Hadley's hair. "Maybe," she said. "Then again, I'm not hiding under a pile of sleeping bags in the middle of the day."

One morning, Ellis was walking across the parking lot at work when she thought she heard a noise coming from the storage shed. She slowed to a stop, straining to listen. It was only nine a.m. and her shift didn't officially begin until ten, so she decided to check it out. Carefully touring the perimeter of the shed, she edged up to the door. Half expecting to find a squirrel or some small animal trapped inside, she tugged open the door and looked inside. At first, she didn't notice anything amiss, squinting as her eyes slowly adjusted to the dark. Stacked along one side were a few folding tables and dozens of plastic hard-back chairs. Down the other were dozens of boxes and crates and paint cans, along with a shovel and two rakes hanging neatly from metal hooks.

Opening the door wider, Ellis frowned. A few shards of morning sunlight fell through slats on the right side of the shed, illuminating something so out of place—so unexpected—that she gawked in disbelief, unable to turn away.

There was Ed Notton, one of the elderly

residents she'd been assigned for, casting an anxious glance over his shoulder, pants puddled around his ankles.

I must be seeing things.

Only she wasn't, and that was when it hit her that there were two naked bodies at the back of the shed: one was Ed's, and the other belonged to a woman who was leaning back on the table in front of him, legs spread wide. Her face was hidden in the dark, undistinguishable, but Ed's naked butt flashing back and forth wasn't. Ed quickly turned back to the task at hand, going at it even faster than before as he calmly endured the indignity of being caught in the act.

Ellis's mouth dropped open. Wrenching her eyes away, she backed up and closed the door behind her. She took a few hurried steps away and then circled back, standing with both arms slack at her sides. It occurred to her that the woman inside was probably Vera-Lee, but what was she supposed to *do* about it? Unless one of them was in danger of having a heart attack—and as far as she knew neither of them had heart conditions—weren't they both consenting adults with the right to have sex if they wanted to? After all, it wasn't like she'd seen a vein bulging dangerously on Ed's forehead, signaling an oncoming stroke.

Tucking her hands in her pockets, Ellis worked her way back along the path that led through the garden to the front of the nursing home. *What am I going to say the next time I see either of them? I'll find it impossible to look them in the eye.*

Grabbing a seat on Nina's favorite bench, she threw her head back and laughed out loud at the sheer absurdity of it, because it really was none of her business. Moments later, she pushed off the bench and went inside, deciding to pretend it had never happened. Yes, they were both acting like teenagers, but why should they be embarrassed or ashamed about having sex simply because they were old?

She was pouring coffee in the staff lounge a few minutes later when Murphy stuck her head inside. "Morning, Ellis," she said. "I'm leaving in five minutes and won't be back until after lunch. You should check in on Vera-Lee first thing this morning. She was up with the flu most of the night. Poor thing is flat on her back in bed. Try to keep her fluids up, all right? She puked so much I'm worried about her getting dehydrated."

Ellis slowly set her coffee mug down.

Hurrying down the hallway, she made a beeline for Vera-Lee's room, and as she passed through the lobby, Ed came shuffling in through the front doors, hair askew and wire-rimmed glasses tilted on the end of his nose.

"Morning," Ellis said, giving him a brisk, all-business nod.

She found Vera-Lee perched on the edge of her bed, legs crossed at the ankles and face pale as a ghost's.

"Morning, love," Vera-Lee said, managing a weak smile. Hands trembling, she slipped a luminous rope of plain white pearls over her head and adjusted her matching drop earrings. Then she gestured weakly for Ellis's help. "Give me a hand to the bathroom, will you? I really need to fix up my face before breakfast. Can't disappoint all of my male fans now, can I?"

Ellis gently took her by the elbow, and Vera-Lee lowered her feet to the floor and slid them into a pair of high-heeled shoes. "Why don't we put on a pair of slippers today?" Ellis suggested. "Something soft and warm and easy to get around in."

Vera-Lee took Ellis's face between both of her hands, laughing softly. "That's never gonna happen, love," she said. "'Cause when the good Lord handed out everything that was needed to make it through this crazy life, I skipped the essentials aisle and headed straight for the one that sparkled with ribbons and bows and rhinestones. There's no going back, you know, not for an old woman like me anyhow."

TEN

Rolly was squaring off with Louie in the dining room over his eating habits. Ellis could hear their voices escalating, but she couldn't do anything about it because she was busy guiding Joseph back to his room. For the second time in the last week, he had shown up for breakfast without his trousers.

On their way past her room, Fran Wilson emerged clutching her Bible in one hand and her cane in the other. "Good God," she said when she saw Joseph. "Not again!"

"Please, Fran," Ellis said, meaning, *That's enough*.

Fran marched by them, as much as someone like Fran could march using a cane, presumably to spread the word about Joseph's flagrant indecency, unaware that his appearance in the dining room had already stirred everyone up.

Joseph peered down at his putty-colored legs. "Who took my pants?" he asked.

"You forgot to put them on," Ellis said.

He shot her an accusatory look. "Good try, missy."

Ellis reached out to steady his elbow. "Why don't we get you back to your room?" She was determined to remain professional, especially given the indignity he was now having to suffer after wandering into a packed dining room in his Fruit of the Looms.

Joseph yanked his arm away, waving his half stump of a finger in the air between them. "I know what you're up to. I wasn't born yesterday." He cocked an eyebrow for emphasis. "Are you one of them hussies who likes to take advantage?"

A blush prickled up the back of Ellis's

neck, but her face assumed a deferential expression. "No," she said. "Now let's get some pants on. You must be freezing."

"Damn right I am," he muttered, grabbing hold of his walker. "You would be too if you were in your skivvies!"

He lifted his walker, took two steps forward, and then plunked it back down again. Ellis inched along behind him, ready to grab him if he fell. Halfway to his room, he slowed down. Then, all at once, his confidence and bluster seemed to fall apart. He stopped and stared off into the distance. Except for his knobby hands wrapped around the padded handles of his walker, he didn't move a muscle.

"When did I get so old?" he said in a half whisper.

Ellis stared at him for a long moment. "I ask myself that same question all the time," she said, giving him a pat on the back.

When they got to his room, she grabbed his pants, which were folded neatly over the back of a chair, and held them out to him, but he moved past her and lowered himself onto the bed. He looked tired and worn out.

Ellis hung the pants back where she'd

found them. "Why don't I go get you a muffin and a glass of orange juice and you can rest for a bit?"

Joseph paused for a moment and then nodded his agreement.

"Would you like blueberry or bran?"

He slowly lifted his gaze. "Sometimes," he said, "my hands shake so bad I can't hold a spoon or a knife." He looked perplexed, as though the thought of his hands betraying him wasn't only unfair, it made no sense.

"I'll bring blueberry," Ellis said. "They have more flavor and they break apart so easily you won't need any utensils."

There was another pause, longer this time. Joseph leaned forward and squinted to read her name tag. For weeks now, he had called her Emma, Erica, Eileen, and Evelyn—every name but her own.

"Ellis?" he said.

"Yes?" she said.

His eyes misted. "I miss my wife," he said softly.

Ellis reached over and straightened the edge of his bedspread, feeling an unexpected chink in her all-business manner, a soft spot for this man who shared more with her than he realized. "I know you do," she said, and then she left the room, discreetly ignoring the tears he could no longer hold back.

On her way back to the dining room, she knocked on Ben's office door and stuck her head inside. "Joseph's getting worse," she said.

"Has he been forgetting to put his teeth in?" Ben asked.

"No, he keeps forgetting to get dressed. Last Sunday, Fran Wilson's family came to visit, and when they were hanging up their jackets in the lobby, Joseph wandered down the hallway wearing a tie and his old fedora, but that's it. Fran's eight-year-old granddaughter screamed, which startled Joseph and made him scream, and by the time Fran made it out of her room, all hell had broken loose."

Ben swiveled in his chair and opened the filing cabinet behind him. "I don't want to move him to another facility until I absolutely have to," he said, half to himself. He reached into the back and pulled out a large ziplock bag.

"Would you do something?" he asked. "As a favor to me?"

"Sure," Ellis said, curious.

He upended the bag onto his desk and a jumble of rubber wristbands fell out. They looked like the LIVESTRONG wristbands Lance Armstrong's foundation sold to unite people living with cancer, only these weren't yellow. They were coral, ice blue, even black. Ben sifted through them and pulled out a navy band with "Get dressed" printed on it.

"See if you can get him to wear this," he said.

Ellis took it from him. "Interesting idea," she said.

Ben cocked his head and smiled. "Well, it's not like we haven't seen this here before. The bigger issue is getting them to admit wearing one is necessary. We once had an old guy who refused, said it was humiliating."

"But wandering around naked isn't?" Ellis said.

"Exactly," Ben said, shrugging. "Wait until Joseph is having one of his more lucid days and then explain how if he wears it, he'll be less apt to forget his clothes every morning. Appeal to the gentleman in him," he suggested.

"I'll do that," Ellis said, pocketing the band on her way out.

In the dining room, Charlene was trying to calm a red-faced Rolly. "I won't sit with him anymore," he said. "The man has no table manners."

Charlene moved behind Rolly's wheelchair and released the brake, clucking sympathetically. "Okay, okay," she said. "Let me talk to Murphy. She does the dining room seating assignments." Before he could respond, she backed the chair up, swung it around, and wheeled him out into the hallway.

Louie was reading the newspaper, seemingly oblivious of Rolly's dramatics.

"What happened at breakfast?" Ellis asked, crossing her arms.

"Eh?" Louie said, dragging his eyes away from the paper.

"What went on here?" Ellis asked, waving a hand at the table.

Louie lifted his grizzled chin and frowned, as though trying to remember. "I don't know," he said.

"Honestly," she said, "I feel like I'm dealing with two children."

"I think Rolly's head got a little muddied,"

Louie said, twirling a gnarled finger next to his ear. "That's all. He needs to put in his hearing aid, and do a few knee bends when he wakes up before he does anything else. Doesn't seem fair he should get wheeled in here half asleep when I'm eating my egg whites."

At the far end of the table, Vera-Lee was finishing up her breakfast. Ellis noticed her eyelashes were too long to be real and her bra looked lumpy, as though she had stuffed it with paper towels. "Morning, love," she said to Ellis as she got to her feet, and then, to Louie, "Would you like to join a group of us for bingo tonight?"

"Depends," Louie said. "What's the pot?"

"Maybe I'm the pot," she said, winking at him.

Louie looked her over from head to toe. "Vera-Lee, you have to stop talking garbage like that and disrespecting yourself. One of these days someone's going to take you seriously, and then what'll you do?"

"Ellis?" Oliver said, sticking his head into the room. "Could you give me a hand in the dayroom? I can't find Charlene again." He was holding a kidney-shaped dish that needed emptying and he looked irritated.

"Sure," Ellis said.

"It's Vern Heeley," he said, lowering his voice.

Vern was eighty-seven, a tall, gaunt man with deeply creased cheeks. A diabetic, he required daily shots of insulin. Ben had brought him up in the last staff meeting, trying to determine when would be the best time to move him into another facility.

Charlene had shrugged, unconcerned. "He's really not much trouble."

"Maybe not," Ben had replied, "but I need to evaluate what's best for him, not you."

Now, Ellis assessed the situation. There were almost a dozen people spread out around the dayroom, most of them settling in to watch a few morning game shows. Vern was parked next to the sofa in his wheelchair, and from the tilt of his head, Ellis could tell he'd nodded off to sleep.

Huffing with apparent frustration, Fran moved to the far end of the sofa. "Oh, good," she said, adjusting the blanket tucked around her legs. "Here's someone who can help! Charlene went outside for a cigarette," she said, making no attempt to hide her disdain. "Someone needs to have a talk with that girl, and this one here"—she scrunched up her face and pointed at Vern—"should be wearing Depends."

Ellis moved closer. A dark stain had spread across Vern's lap and there was the unmistakable odor of urine. Feeling sick for him, she moved behind his chair and gently released the brake.

Vern startled awake and sat up, trying to get his bearings. "Wha . . . what?"

"You're okay, Mr. Heeley," Ellis assured him.

He twisted around and looked up at her, blinking uncertainly. The room went quiet, and then his face froze and he looked down at himself.

Ellis searched for a dignified exit. She'd been through enough humiliation to know how he was feeling. Instead of discreetly averting her gaze like everyone else, Fran stared straight at Vern, shaking her head with undisguised disgust. "Better not forget your book," she said, pointing to a paperback on the table.

Vern darted a look at Ellis, his face hollow and eyes desperate.

"We won't," Ellis said, raising her voice as she snatched it up. "Oh, and Mr. Heeley, I hope you don't mind"—she grabbed the blanket covering Fran's legs and yanked it away from her—"but on our way to your room for your French lesson we need to stop and toss this in the laundry." She draped it over his lap, covering the offending stain. "Murphy mentioned someone had thrown up on it yesterday and I forgot to take it away."

Fran's face recoiled in a grimace.

Ellis turned the chair around and wheeled Vern out of the room, almost colliding with Charlene on her way in. "Everything okay?" Charlene asked.

"Yes," Ellis said, giving Vern's shoulder a squeeze. "Everything's fine."

Charlene frowned. "Did you, um, need my help with something?"

"That'd be great," Ellis said, motioning for her to follow as she pushed Vern into the hallway. Charlene did, and as soon as they were out of earshot of those in the dayroom, Ellis said, "Mr. Heeley needs a nice hot bath."

"Now?" Charlene asked.

"Yes, now."

Shrugging, Charlene grabbed hold of the chair. Ellis turned away. "Miss Ellis?" Vern said in a halting voice.

She looked back at him. "Yes?"

"Thank you."

"You're welcome," she said, giving him a wink.

Later that night at home, Paulina came through the back door laden down with groceries after another mysterious trip into Missoula. Hadley was doing homework in her room and Ellis was pulling a pan of homemade lasagna out of the oven. Sniffing the air with appreciation, Paulina slipped off her coat and hung it on the back of a chair.

"How was your day?" she asked.

Ellis straightened. The kitchen was tidy, the fireplace was roaring, the radio was playing low, and for the first time in longer than she cared to remember, she felt as though she had contributed something worthwhile to the world. Her job was hectic and busy, but satisfying, and she was quickly becoming adept at solving crises she never would've had the confidence to address six months ago. She was becoming the person she'd always imagined she might become, handling situations like those thrown at her today with a relaxed and instinctive calm.

"It was good," Ellis said. "How about yours?"

Distracted, Paulina picked up the mail and flipped through it. "It was fine, thanks."

As usual, her words were a wall, and Ellis felt the immediate pull of curiosity. Paulina's once restricted, solitary life had been positively transformed in the time since Ellis had first left town, and yet there was something more going on here, something that obviously gave Paulina quiet pleasure and financial stability, neither of which she'd had years ago. Ellis grabbed plates from the cupboard and set the table, determined to begin bridging the distance between them, a distance she felt she herself had contributed to.

She slipped the loaf of garlic bread she'd prepared earlier into the oven and turned on the timer for two minutes so she didn't burn it. "Would you like wine with dinner?" she asked.

Paulina sliced open an envelope and waved her hand, indicating that she didn't.

Ellis watched her from the corner of her eye. Had her mom felt like she did now, frustrated and closed out, when Ellis was living at home? Recalling how independent she'd become after Hadley was born, insisting that she didn't need help, that she could handle bathing and feeding Hadley on her own, Ellis realized that Paulina must have.

Setting a shaker of parmesan cheese on the table, Ellis suddenly understood her mom differently than she had before. The constant worry after her husband left, the willingness to face obstacles she had never had to face before—paying bills, balancing a budget, making sure Ellis had what she needed for school—all of these were, in their own way, expressions of love and devotion.

The only difference, Ellis thought, *was that it took you longer than it took me to grow strong after Dad left.*

"Can I talk to you before you call Hadley down for dinner?" Paulina asked, taking a seat at the table.

"Sure," Ellis said, startled back to the present.

Paulina pushed the mail to one side and folded her hands together. All at once she looked more serious and intent than Ellis had seen her in weeks. Oh, no. Was she sick? Or was she finally going to admit that she was seeing someone in Missoula? Maybe that she loved this man and was thinking of marrying him?

"I've had a few conversations with your father over the last month," Paulina said.

Ellis slid into an empty chair, her expression utterly blank. She was conscious of her lungs moving, of Hadley's footsteps upstairs, of the timer going off on the oven telling her the bread was ready.

What had her mom said?

After a long, hesitant moment, Paulina spoke again. "He's still living in Canada," she said. "But he's staying in a motel right now because his house burned down. It wasn't insured and he has no way to rebuild it. . . ."

Ellis sat back and crossed her arms. What was her mother saying?

"I suggested he come here," Paulina said, lifting her gaze. "That he can stay with us for a few months until he figures out what he wants to do."

Speechless, Ellis stared at her. "But we haven't heard from him in years," she finally said. "Why would you offer to help him now?" She got up and pulled the bread out of the oven. Whatever love she'd had for her dad had been so deeply woven with resentment for so many years that she couldn't even begin to untangle the two.

And now he's coming here to live?

"He has no one else," Paulina said.

"And whose fault is that?" Ellis asked, bringing the lasagna to the table. "Hadley, dinner!" she called, determined to ignore this bombshell until she was alone and calm. "When is he coming?"

"Ten days," Paulina replied. "He's got to make some arrangements."

Ten days, Ellis thought. Ten years would be too soon as far as she was concerned.

ELEVEN

After Ellis's dad had left when she was twelve, it hadn't taken long for the realities of life to demand their attention. Bills began arriving with "Past Due" and "Final Notice" stamped in bold letters, and within weeks the phone began ringing off the hook. Paulina refused to talk to anyone. One afternoon, frustrated by all the envelopes and unanswered messages, Ellis scooped them up, took them into her mom's room, which she now rarely left, and set them on the bed.

"Come on, Mom," she said gently. "I can help you go through these."

Paulina rolled over. "There's no way to pay them," she said quietly.

"We don't have any money?"

"No."

"Nothing?"

Her mom shook her head. "I have ninety dollars in the bank, but we need that for food." She looked past Ellis to the other side of the room. "When you were in school yesterday the bank manager stopped by. We're four months behind on our mortgage payments and there's no way to pay them. They have no choice but to foreclose."

"Mortgage?" Ellis said. "Foreclose?"

"It means we won't be able to live here anymore."

Ellis had been so busy waiting for her dad to come back that she hadn't bothered to consider the more obvious problems caused by his desertion. Wondering who would take care of them had come to mind, since her mom had always been so dependent on him, but that they would have to move hadn't occurred to her. Until then, she'd assumed they would always live here. It was the only home she'd ever known.

Ellis had run out of her mom's room.

Moments later, she was barreling across the lawn and into the stream that ran through their backyard, leaping over stumps and rocks up the hill on the other side, past trees and undergrowth so thick she had to dodge left and right. She didn't stop until she stumbled into a fence marking the end of their property. Then all the wind seemed to leave her and she dropped to her knees and prayed.

"Our Father who art in heaven, hallowed be thy name."

Please, God, hear me. . . .

"Thy kingdom come, thy will be done on earth as it is in heaven."

Please, make my dad come back. . . .

"Give us this day our daily bread, and forgive us our trespasses . . ."

But God must not have been on duty that day because her dad never did come home.

The morning they moved into the welfare rental house in town, a heavyset woman with bad breath met them at the front door. She was from the regional welfare office and Ellis could tell by the way her mom's hands trembled that Paulina was intimidated by her. Even from the outside, the house was a run-down mess.

The woman unlocked the door and pushed it open with her shoulder. She handed Paulina the keys and motioned them inside. Holding a clipboard, she quickly led them through the rooms, checking off items on her list as they followed her.

"Toilet works," she said, flushing it. *Check.* "You've got a washing machine." *Check.* "There's no dryer, so you'll have to use that for now." She pointed to the clothesline through the kitchen window. "Or else take your clothes to the Laundromat."

Paulina nodded, looking pale and overwhelmed.

"Kitchen's equipped with a stove," the woman said. *Check.* "Floor seems solid and there are no broken windows," she added. *Check. Check.*

She opened the refrigerator, which had a foot-sized dent in the door, as though someone had given it a swift kick, and pronounced it in good working condition when the light came on. *Check.* "Place is spit clean," she said, sounding impressed. *Check*.

Looking efficient and in a hurry, she flipped through her paperwork, telling Paulina that the house had been built in 1942. Ellis thought it looked older. Sure, it was clean, but a strip of linoleum was missing in front of the sink and an even bigger one in front of the fridge. A rectangular table was pushed up against the wall that ran parallel to the staircase leading upstairs; a chunk of cardboard tucked under one leg kept the table level. A stone fireplace and mantel, both stained black, took up one corner, with bare patches where stones had broken away. The screen door leading into the kitchen from the porch had no screen, and the kitchen light consisted of a bare bulb hanging from the middle of the ceiling. Turning in a full circle to take in everything, Ellis noticed a ceramic plaque hanging next to the sink that read: NO, THIS ISN'T HOME SWEET HOME—ADJUST.

She followed her mom and the woman upstairs. A creaking narrow staircase led to four rooms with steep, sloped ceilings. Three were bedrooms with closets, and the fourth looked like it was meant to be a storage room, although someone had crammed a wrought-iron bed into it, leaving no more than two feet of space down one side. A hole had been punched in the wall at the top of the stairs and there were notes posted all over: *Latch on this window sticks—yank hard. Twist dial halfway back and once forward to turn radiator on. If you hear odd noises coming from the attic, bats have probably moved in again—call me. This door opens to a fold-down ironing board—don't get smucked in the head.*

The main floor consisted of a living room, a screened-in porch, a kitchen, a tiny laundry room, and the house's only bathroom, which had a huge concrete bathtub. As soon as Ellis saw it, her eyes widened. She couldn't help herself; she climbed right in and sat down, stretching her legs out in front of her as far as they would go. Whoever had built the house had poured cement into an eight-foot-long mold to create the biggest and deepest bathtub she'd ever seen. On the walls behind and around it were hundreds of tiny ceramic tiles with seahorses on them. Despite herself, she smiled, because it truly was a thing of beauty in the middle of this horribly ugly house.

The woman continued going from room to room, flicking on light switches to make sure they worked. "I don't know if you noticed, but you're going to have to hang a few blankets over the bedroom doors for now," she called out over her shoulder. "Makes no earthly sense to me why someone would steal doors, though. . . ."

They probably burned them to stay warm, Ellis thought, climbing out of the tub.

The living room came equipped with dirty orange shag carpeting. Someone had left a plaid pull-out sofa, and there was a horseshoe nailed above the front door, although one of the nails had fallen out and it had flipped upside down, dumping out all of its luck.

From the kitchen, Ellis could hear the welfare woman talking to her mom, asking her to sign her name here and there, going through a list of items she'd be held accountable for as the renter of this humble abode. "Rent must be paid by the first of each month. You'll be responsible for the utilities, the phone, cutting the grass, and clearing snow from the sidewalk out front. The home is currently in good repair and will have to be kept that way. . . ."

It wasn't until after the woman left that Ellis and her mom discovered that only two of the burners on the stove worked, the hot water tank barely had enough oooomph to heat water past warm, and the fridge freezer was broken.

"Mom, you should call that lady and tell her," Ellis said.

Paulina went to the kitchen window and stared outside. "No," she said softly. "There's nothing else available in town, and welfare made it clear up front that this place barely makes the grade, so if I do that, if I call and complain and say that we need something they can't give us, we'll have to leave Barrow and move to another town, and I don't want that, do you?"

Ellis pried a yellowed piece of tape off the table. "No," she whispered, thinking about everything they'd been through. "I don't."

And so they stayed, and made the best of it.

The day after Ellis turned thirteen, she awoke with a start. She'd been having the same bad dream again and again. She was stuck in the middle of a huge crowd with no beginning or end in sight. There were thousands of people everywhere, all different sizes and shapes, preoccupied as they jostled past, laughing and calling out to each other. Nervous, she reached out for her dad's hand, but somehow, in the steady ebb and flow of people, he'd disappeared, and now she was standing alone, waiting for him to reappear and claim her, feeling dizzy and misplaced.

That morning, the dream left her more disoriented than usual.

At first, she wondered where she was, and then it hit her, hard and fast like always. She grabbed a sweatshirt and tugged it on over her head. It'd been almost a year since her dad had left, and she and her mom had been living in this drafty old house for seven months. The walls of her room were a pale celery color, and she couldn't stand looking at them for another second. Quiet as a cat, she sneaked past her mom's bedroom door, down the stairs into the kitchen, and outside across the porch onto the back steps.

Months ago, after she'd gotten sick and

tired of hearing her mom crying in her room one night, Ellis had burned a handful of photographs in their fire pit. She threw in a shot of her dad mugging for the camera, holding up a record-breaking fish he'd caught. *Phsst*, it went up in flames. She threw in one of him as a young man, posing in his hockey gear; a few of her parents on their wedding day; another of him at his annual company picnic, handing out gift certificates for dinner at their local steak house. *Phsst. Phsst. Phsst.*

The flames danced around the outer edges of every picture, slowly consuming them as the wind whipped sparks up into the treetops, making each carefully captured memory disappear. Ellis tossed in a photo of him unwrapping Christmas presents and one of him standing next to a long row of brand-new semitrailer trucks, one arm pushed up into the air as though he'd just conquered a mountain. *Phsst. Phsst.* And when she was done, she was so tired, she crawled into bed and slept like she hadn't slept in months.

Sitting with her back pressed against the railing on the porch steps, Ellis surveyed Louie Johnson's yard next door, filled with dried-up sunflowers that had bent under their own weight. Louie refused to grow a lawn. Instead, every year he would plant sunflowers in precise rows across his entire backyard. "Gives me something wondrous to look at every day," he explained. "Think about it. There's nothing special about grass if everyone else in town has it."

Ellis hadn't bothered to put on a coat. Maybe if she got sick, really sick, her dad would come back, although that seemed less likely with each passing day. For almost a year now, she'd gone from shock to despair to a deep-rooted sadness she couldn't seem to shake. The worse part was that until her dad had left, the thought hadn't occurred to her that he ever might. She'd turned thirteen the day before and she'd been distracted all afternoon, getting up every few minutes to look out the living room window, straining to listen for the phone, hoping he'd call or walk through the door or have the local flower shop deliver a fancy bouquet with her name on it.

But there'd been nothing. No phone call, no card. Nothing.

For the longest time now, Ellis had clung to the hope that her dad had only temporarily lost his grip, that any day now he would return and change her world back into the kind of mind-numbing ordinary she used to hate, but now craved. For the last few weeks, she'd fantasized he might come on her birthday, all apologetic and sorry but completely content now that he'd sorted out his life and realized he wanted to be with her and her mom.

"Where've you been?" she'd say, tears stinging her eyes.

"The Grand Canyon," he'd say, grinning as he picked her mom up and twirled her around the kitchen. "Alaska. Paris. The moon." All said with a big sweep of his hand, face alive and voice breathless. "I watched the sun set over the Rocky Mountains. . . ."

"Wow," Ellis would say.

"I paddled a canoe down the Mississippi River. I stood at the top of the Eiffel Tower. I took a cruise down the Rhine River in Germany. . . ."

Like her mom, Ellis would nod and smile and wait patiently for him to finish, knowing from experience that it was best to let him go on until he was done, not wanting to say anything that might upset him or make him change his mind. And then suddenly his eyes would tear up and he'd stop talking and shake his head in silent remembrance. "But, I swear, none of it made me feel the way being here in Barrow does."

For a second, Ellis would want to cry, but she'd hold back.

Instead, to be on the safe side, she'd go straight to the corner cupboard and pull his favorite coffee mug down from the top shelf, where she'd hidden it behind the sugar canister. And then she'd say, "I'm glad you're home, Dad," biting her tongue to all the rest.

It was a silly thing to daydream about; it made no rational sense. It was a thirteen-year-old girl's secret fantasy, and yet each time Ellis closed her eyes to imagine his return, she felt warm and safe.

A stray cat bounded up the steps, startling her. Ellis watched as he began playing with a piece of string tied around a small parcel she hadn't noticed until then. It had been set on the far side of the top step next to the dirty rubber boots her mom used when she worked on her flower beds.

Ellis slid over next to the parcel. Upon

closer inspection, she saw that it was wrapped in brown paper. Taped to the top, underneath the string, a note said: *Happy Birthday, Ellis*. Confused, she picked up the small parcel and turned it over, and as she touched it, she began to comprehend its significance.

He didn't forget, she thought, heart pounding.

Ripping open the paper, she pulled out a small hinged case. She stared at the perfect roundness of it, at the tortoise frame that surrounded the lid.

He remembered!

Inside, a piece of parchment paper lay on top of a tiny silver compass with a preprinted message:

HOPEFUL AND UPLIFTING, YOUR SILVER COMPASS IS MEANT TO HELP STEER YOU IN THE RIGHT DIRECTION ON YOUR JOURNEY THROUGH LIFE. IT WAS PRE-ORDERED AND HAS BEEN ENGRAVED WITH A UNIQUE INSCRIPTION CHOSEN ESPECIALLY FOR YOU BY SOMEONE YOU LOVE. WE HOPE YOU'LL TREASURE IT FOR YEARS TO COME.

Ellis picked up the compass and turned it over, squinting at the words inscribed on the back: *Promise me you'll always remember: You're braver than you believe, and stronger than you seem, and smarter than you think.*

Her eyes filled with tears as she recalled what her dad had said before he'd driven away that afternoon on Airport Road. *You'll be fine, Ellis. You're stronger than you think you are.*

She stared at her name written in precise script on the note stuck to the box.

Why couldn't you give it to me in person? she thought. *Why didn't you come inside and say hello? Were you afraid I might make a scene? Scared I'd tell you how I've been stealing clothes from the lost-and-found box at school so Mom doesn't have to buy them new? Embarrassed to see how we make a game of not knowing what's inside the cans of food we open from the food bank that no longer have labels on them?*

All at once, she felt numb. Ellis closed her eyes and pictured her dad, grinning all big and foolish because he'd given her something so fine, something so unique and thoughtful. She turned the compass over and stared at the inscription in pained confusion, disliking him for leaving more than she ever imagined she could, and yet feeling, in that moment, the greatest intimacy she'd ever felt with another person.

At breakfast, she was distracted.

"Look at the present Dad left on the back steps for me," she said, nudging the box across the table to her mom.

Paulina's spoon froze halfway to her mouth. "Your dad?"

Her threadbare nightgown was wrinkled, and in the soft morning light her skin looked pale and drawn, but at least today she was up and eating breakfast, and for this one small thing, Ellis was relieved. For months now, her mom had spent a lot of time in bed, although she no longer stayed curled in the fetal position for days on end the way she had right after her dad left. Now she kept the curtains shut and she would sit propped against her pillows, the light from the TV flickering across her face as she sipped tea.

Ellis smoothed out the note with her name on it and lay it on the table. "It was on the back steps with this taped to the top."

Paulina glanced at it, then opened the hinged case and took out the silver compass. After reading the parchment paper, she slowly turned the compass over and examined the inscription on the back, her expression unreadable. Eventually, her mouth opened and she pressed her fingers against her chest.

"Well," she said. "Isn't this nice?"

"Nice?" Ellis shot her a dirty look. "I can't believe you aren't mad. Mom, he left it outside! He didn't even have the courage to give it to me himself."

Paulina's face remained impassive. "Maybe not, but the right thing to do isn't always the easiest thing to do." She carefully put the compass back into the box and shut the lid. "Your father's going through a hard time right now, but I do know he loves you, Ellis."

"He does?" Ellis said, dumbstruck by her own need to believe.

"Of course he does."

"Well, I think he's a coward."

"Maybe so." Paulina shrugged. "But at least he remembered."

Later that night, when her mom was asleep, Ellis dragged an entire box of photo albums outside, *thump, thumping* down the steps and across the wet grass to the fire pit. After lighting a fire, she opened each album and set to work, once again tossing photos of her dad into the flames, only this time she didn't stop until they were all gone. The air smelled acrid as they curled and burned, turning to ash and floating up into the impenetrable darkness, and when she was finally done, her stomach twisted into a fresh ache.

TWELVE

Anissa was bold and theatrical and undeniably likable, but better yet, she knew exactly how to draw Hadley out of her funk by appealing to her competitive spirit. Early one March morning, Anissa had knocked on the door at six thirty wearing stretch mitts, a long-sleeved shirt, orange shorts over black leggings, and a big grin.

"Morning, Mrs. Semple," she said, jogging in place on the porch. "I was wondering if Hadley wanted to go for a run with me."

"Not a chance," Hadley said, yawning as she came downstairs.

"Why not?" Anissa said. "Scared I'll beat ya?"

She dodged and feinted in circles around the porch, pretending she was boxing against an invisible foe. Hadley watched from the corner of her eye, shaking her head as she grabbed a box of Cheerios from the cupboard.

"It's totally okay if you are," Anissa said, doing a few side lunges. "I mean, I can outrun everyone else in our class, so why not you, right? The indoor track meet's coming up in April, but I guess it's up to you if you don't want to get ready for it. . . ." She let her voice trail away, then turned to Ellis and cracked her knuckles. "I don't know if Hadley's ever told you, but I run like I'm the Bionic Woman. My dad thinks it's probably from all the maraschino cherries I eat," she said. "Gives me lots of extra energy."

Hadley rolled her eyes as she poured milk on her Cheerios.

"Anyhow," Anissa said, carrying on for Ellis's benefit, "in the original TV show the main character, like, almost dies in this skydiving accident?" She smacked her hands together, making Ellis jump. "*Splat!*

But then they completely rebuilt her with super-amplified hearing, a bionic arm, and legs that let her run faster than a speeding car."

Hadley peered past her mom, eyes widening as she looked Anissa over more carefully. "I'm *so* not going with you," she said.

"Okay." Anissa lifted a shoulder and let it drop. "Just thought I'd ask."

She ran down the steps to the sidewalk. Dropping into a crouch, supporting her weight on the tips of her fingers, she lifted her butt in the air and struck a pose, as though waiting for a gun to go off at the starting line. Then off she went, down the side of the house and onto the street, dragging her words out behind her as she called over her shoulder, "E-a-t . . . m-y . . . d-u-s-t . . . e-a-r-t-h-l-i-n-g-s!"

Hadley carried her cereal bowl to the living room window. "Sometimes she can be totally whacked," she said under her breath, watching Anissa disappear at the end of the street.

Ellis stood behind her, smiling. "Maybe, but she really is fast, isn't she?"

For the rest of the week, Anissa had

stopped by every morning, revved up with energy and determined to goad Hadley into joining her. "You're, like, totally becoming a couch potato," she complained.

Finally, Ellis came downstairs for breakfast to find Hadley putting on her running shoes. "If I don't go with her," she said, "she'll never leave me alone."

For weeks afterward, they ran for almost an hour every morning, looping up around the hospital, past Pleasant View Manor, and then back down the hill into town. It was now Saturday morning, the day after Paulina had told Ellis that Dennis would soon be moving in with them. As Ellis pulled in to the parking lot at work, she saw the two girls on their way up the hill, arms and legs flashing. As they drew near, she waved, then stood watching until they became pinpricks in the distance.

Ellis hadn't even hung up her jacket before Ben waved her into his office. Charlene was three hours late for her shift and he was busy trying to track her down. "I keep calling her apartment, but there's no answer," he said, running a hand through his hair. "This is getting ridiculous! I need people I can depend on. She knew Murphy was taking this weekend off. Now what am I supposed to do?"

When approached by Murphy the week before, Charlene had confessed that she was distracted. She had a new boyfriend. He worked at a motorcycle refit shop in Kalispell, and she'd been spending most of her weekends at his apartment. As their relationship intensified, she'd been taking her job a lot less seriously.

"It's okay," Ellis assured Ben. "I can handle everything until Charlene gets here, and if she doesn't show up, we'll survive that, too."

Most of the residents were in their rooms, on weekend outings with family, or gathered in the dayroom for the weekly bingo game. Ellis decided to stroll down the hall to make sure everyone was okay.

She passed several open doors, and as she did she glimpsed Fran Wilson pulling the sheets taut on her bed, sharp, military folds at each corner, a no-nonsense look on her face; Nina Ballard, head bobbing forward, on the cusp of sleep now that she'd eaten breakfast; Vera-Lee gazing at her fully dressed mannequin with a melancholy look on her face; Vern Heeley, flipping through a book, face cast in shadows; and Louie, dressed in a crisp button-down shirt and bow tie. The moment Ellis saw him, she knew something was up. He was standing in front of his dresser and there was something in his stance—a quiet reflectiveness—that she cued in on right away. She paused in his doorway.

"Louie?" she said. "Are you okay?"

"Eh?" He turned and blinked at her, as startled by her presence as if a hole had just appeared in the floor at his feet. "Uh . . . yes, I'm fine."

"Going somewhere special?" she asked.

"Over to the church," he said, removing his hat. "To light a candle."

"Who's taking you?" she asked, realizing the moment the words were out that he'd been planning to go alone.

The United Church was only two blocks away. Often when the weather was good, staff members would take residents over in their wheelchairs. Today, snow from an April storm was melting, dripping from the gutters outside, making the sidewalks relatively clear, yet letting Louie walk there on his own wasn't standard procedure.

Without answering, Louie dropped his

gaze to his hand holding a photograph in a pewter frame. He lifted it in the air, motioned for Ellis to come see. "Today would've been our fiftieth wedding anniversary," he said. Ellis moved closer to take a look. "You never knew her, but my wife, Ruby, was a beautiful woman," he said.

Ellis studied the photo and decided he was right. Ruby Johnson's eyes were luminous and soulful, her hair swept back in an elegant chignon, slender hands folded in her lap; behind her a chandelier with graceful sickles of gold caught the light.

"I took this picture at the Performing Arts Center in Butte," Louie explained. "It was our tenth anniversary. I wanted to surprise her so I hired a babysitter for Arla and then I took her to this play she'd been talking about for months. I don't think I've ever seen her more excited, getting all dressed up like that."

His voice was wistful and sad, and as Ellis listened to him, she felt a sudden tightness in her throat. What had losing his wife cost him? What did it cost him now to move through each day without her?

"She was the love of my life," Louie said with quiet adoration.

Ellis thought back. In all the years she

had lived next door to him, she couldn't recall Louie ever talking about his wife. "What was she like?" she asked.

Louie set the frame on top of his dresser. "She was shy and awkward, and not much of a social butterfly. I'd have to say Ruby was probably happiest observing and watching rather than taking part." He tilted his head sideways, giving Ellis a long, intent look. "I guess she was like you that way," he said, with a flash of sudden mischief. "Only she didn't try to blend in to the trees like a Sasquatch."

Ellis's eyes widened, surprised he had remembered.

She gathered her thoughts and was about to say something, but by then he'd turned away. He was gazing out the window, as though seeing all of his old memories coming to life outside in the frozen grass. "She once told me that I was the most dependable person she knew on this earth," he confessed, sounding proud.

Hearing this, Ellis suddenly thought about her dad. How, the year she had turned nine, he'd driven straight through the night on one of his long-haul trucking trips so he could make it to her birthday party the next afternoon. Then, a year later, how he'd forgotten it altogether.

"Dependable is good," she said.

Distantly, Ellis heard the buzzer for the main lobby doors, signaling someone's entrance. Moving in front of Louie, she tugged at the edges of his bow tie, stood back, and cocked her head. "Looks good," she said, nodding in approval. "If your wife were here, she'd be proud of you."

Louie placed his hat back on his head and rubbed his chin.

"Tell you what?" Ellis said on her way out of his room. "Meet me up front in ten minutes and I'll walk you over to the church, all right?"

Not waiting for an answer, she hurried off to the lobby.

Standing next to the reception desk was a statuesque woman in her late forties, carrying a Hermès bag and dressed in a navy blazer with a mango-colored silk scarf draped over her shoulders. "Oh, hello," she said, giving Ellis an all-business nod. "I'm here to see my mother, Vera-Lee Dale."

"Your mother?" Ellis said. Vera-Lee had never mentioned having children, so this was a surprise.

The woman glanced at her watch. "Yes, I was in Helena this week on business and decided to drive up and surprise her."

"Please grab a seat," Ellis said. "I'll go get her."

In Vera-Lee's room, Ellis found her stuffing Kleenex into a full-piece bustier her mannequin was wearing. The mannequin's hair was tucked into a feathered headdress and she had a beauty spot painted next to pouty red lips. She also wore a pair of tight-fitting elbow-length black gloves and matching feathered mules, her long legs and full hips accentuated by the high cut of the bustier.

"Vera-Lee?" Ellis said, knocking on the door. "Your daughter's here to see you."

Vera-Lee's hand froze in midair and she turned to Ellis, panic spreading across her face. "My daughter?" she said.

"Yes," Ellis said. "She wanted to surprise you."

Vera-Lee lowered herself onto her bed, cradling the box of Kleenex. She glanced from the mannequin to Ellis and back again. "Oh, my," she said, running a hand over her hair. Pulling herself together, she stood and smoothed down the front of her blouse. "Ellis, love, could you do me a favor?" she asked, never meeting her eyes.

"Sure," Ellis said. "What would you like?"

Vera-Lee grabbed a tube of lipstick off her dresser and moved in front of the mirror to apply it to her lips. "While I take my daughter into the dayroom for a cup of tea, could you stuff my mannequin in the storage closet in the hallway?"

"The storage closet?" Ellis repeated.

"Please," Vera-Lee said. "It would mean the world to me. My daughter might want to come to my room and I don't want her seeing this—" She waved a hand toward the mannequin. "You see, it reminds her of a time in my life that she's always greatly resented." She reached into her closet, pulled out a beige cardigan Ellis had never seen before, and slipped it on. From her bottom dresser drawer she took out a pair of sensible-looking shoes.

"Better hurry, love," she said to Ellis, waving at the mannequin.

Moments later, Vera-Lee was on her way to the lobby and Ellis was tugging her mannequin out into the hallway. When she opened the storage closet, she groaned at how full it was. How was she supposed to fit this in there?

“Need a hand?”

She found Louie standing behind her, hat in hand as he watched her struggling to stuff the mannequin into the already overflowing closet. “Actually, I might,” she said, setting her hands on her hips. “Vera-Lee’s daughter showed up and Vera-Lee wants me to hide this in here so she doesn’t see it.”

Louie jerked a thumb over his shoulder. “Why don’t you drag it into my room until she leaves? That’d be easier, wouldn’t it?”

“It would,” she agreed.

Lifting the mannequin around the middle, she tilted it sideways against her hip. Louie held his door open as she maneuvered inside and set the mannequin down next to his bed. “I don’t see why this is such a big deal to Vera-Lee,” she complained. “I mean, heavens, it’s just a mannequin.”

Louie was laughing as he put his hat back on. “It’s a big deal ’cause Vera-Lee was never a showgirl,” he explained. “When her daughter showed up for a visit last year she had a fit when she walked in and saw her mom all gussied up, wearing a tight blouse and one of them push-up bras."

"You mean she never worked in Las Vegas?" Ellis said.

Louie shook his head.

Ellis stared at him, speechless. Vera-Lee was seventy-seven. She'd lived the bulk of her life and had obviously raised a child, and yet here she was perpetuating a falsehood every day that made people believe she was someone else entirely.

"Everyone has a few secrets," Louie said, shrugging. "This is hers."

Yes, Ellis thought. *But how sad is that?*

In some ways, she wished Louie hadn't told her, that she could go back to believing Vera-Lee was who she'd been since Ellis had first met her.

By the time they made it out to the lobby, Vera-Lee and her daughter were gone. Oliver stuck his head out of a room and waved at Ellis, popping the fastener up and down on his clipboard. "Think you could give me a hand here for two minutes?"

Glancing outside, Ellis saw Hadley and Anissa running in the distance. They had turned around and were now on their way back, drawing nearer. "Give me a minute," she called out, then she hurried outside and waved the girls down.

Once they reached her, they bent over with their hands on their knees, dragging deep breaths into their lungs. "Girls, could you walk Louie Johnson over to the church? We're short-staffed today and I don't want him going on his own."

"Sure," Hadley said, straightening.

Louie walked up behind them. "Found two pretty escorts for me, did you?" Ellis nodded. "Well now, a feebleminded old man couldn't ask for more, could he?" he said, holding an arm out to Hadley and Anissa. "Either of you girls like dancing?"

Watching them walk away—Hadley laughing as Louie showed her how to do a quick two-step—Ellis suddenly could not seem to find her voice. There was her daughter, arms linked with the man who'd saved both of their lives years ago, unfolding like a flower that had finally been given a slice of sunshine.

The night before, Ellis had taken a long bath, and for the second time since they'd moved to Barrow she'd found Hadley waiting for her on her bed when she went upstairs. "We're having career counseling at school tomorrow," Hadley said, "and I wanted to ask you something, but I don't want you getting all deep-thoughty on me, okay?"

"Okay," Ellis said, sitting next to her.

Hadley pulled a pillow into her lap. "When you were my age, did you know what you wanted to be when you were older?"

Ellis played with the piping on the bedspread. "No, but I always believed my life wouldn't be ordinary. That a moment would come—I would know it when I saw it—and everything would change from that point forward. I used to dream that I'd be a famous painter, but by sixth grade it was obvious that I could barely draw stick figures, let alone fiery landscapes."

Hadley stared at her, transfixed.

"By ninth grade, it had all changed again," Ellis admitted, blushing. "By then I had decided I wanted to be a professional dancer, the kind that headline Broadway shows in New York, but that didn't last long either because I didn't have an ounce of rhythm—still don't—and I was very self-conscious about it."

"Did it ever happen?" Hadley asked.

"Did what happen?" Ellis said, momentarily confused.

"That moment you were talking about," she said, splaying her hands against the bedspread. "A moment that changed your life and made it not ordinary?"

At first, Ellis didn't trust herself to do more than nod. When Hadley was a baby, she had often watched her as she slept. In those precious minutes every painful loss and disappointment of Ellis's life had become utterly unimportant. In the deep flutter of Hadley's eyelids, the tiny ski slope of her nose, the even movement of her chest as it rose and fell lay what truly mattered.

Downstairs, the furnace clicked off, and Ellis could hear wind rushing through the trees outside in the distance. She reached out one finger, halfway across the bed, and touched it to one of Hadley's.

"Yes, it did," she finally said. "The moment you arrived."

THIRTEEN

Ellis happened to be walking past the lobby early the next week when the glass doors opened and Anissa and Hadley walked in, shaking rain from their hair. Their sudden presence startled Ellis and she slowed to a stop, arching her eyebrows.

"Hey, what are you guys doing here?"

"We came to see my grandpa," Anissa announced.

Ellis blinked at her in confusion. "Your grandpa lives here?"

"Has for five years. After my grandma died, he had a stroke and couldn't take care of himself anymore."

Ellis studied Anissa's shoe-polish black hair, her small, close-set eyes. "You're Joseph's granddaughter?"

"Every inch of me," Anissa said, doing an impromptu pirouette that sent her smashing sideways into Hadley. They were righting themselves, laughing at each other, when Oliver came around the corner.

"Anissa!" he said, giving her a smile. "Your granddad's been wondering where you've been. Did you bring anything for him?"

She blushed as she opened her knapsack. "Yup, I did. I got a brochure about that new Tempur-Pedic mattress made from memory foam, a few others promoting those adjustable his-and-hers mattresses, and a catalogue from the distributor of Mattress World in New Jersey. They carry King Koil, Sealy, Serta, Simmons . . ."

Minutes later, Ellis was rolling Nina Ballard's wheelchair into the dayroom when she saw Joseph raise his milky eyes from where he was sitting, stand, and pull Anissa against him in an almost violent embrace.

"Collette," he said gruffly.

Having read Joseph's file, Ellis knew that Collette was his daughter, and yet Anissa didn't miss a beat, patting him on the back and helping him sit down again before waving Hadley into an empty chair. She handed him a pamphlet on Tempur-Pedic mattresses and leaned in so close that their foreheads were nearly touching.

"Look at this, Grandpa," she said.

"Foam mattresses have been around for years," he said, unimpressed.

"Not memory foam," Anissa said, oozing confidence as she pointed to a list of the product's strengths.

Joseph squinted as he took a few moments to read the pamphlet. "Are you serious?" he said, lifting his gaze to hers. Anissa nodded, giving him a gleeful smile, and he shook his head, amazed. "This is revolutionary," he said, thumping a hand against the table. Joseph expounded the virtues of investing in a good mattress, Anissa raptly attentive to everything he had to say.

"And when you do buy a new mattress, for God sakes buy the matching box spring!

Anyone who buys a new mattress and puts it on top of an old box spring is just throwing good money out the window."

Finally, Joseph sat back and ran a hand through his thinning hair. He looked tired, but he wasn't ready to stop yet. "Have I ever told you where the saying 'sleep tight' comes from?" he asked Hadley.

She shot a nervous look at Anissa. "No," Hadley said politely. "You haven't."

Joseph rubbed his hands together. "It comes from the seventeenth century, when mattresses used to be placed on top of ropes that were regularly tightened." Anissa and Hadley leaned forward, listening. "And did you know," he continued dramatically, "that today the average mattress will double its weight in ten years as a result of being filled with dust mites? There have been many studies." He lowered his voice. "Experts have reported that a typical used mattress can have anywhere from a hundred thousand to ten million dust mites inside it. . . ."

Hadley's face twisted into a grimace.

Trying to change the topic, Anissa fished in her knapsack and handed him the catalogue she'd brought. Joseph took it from her, but carried on with his lecturelike rant. "The average person spends one-third of their lifetime on a mattress," he said, raising his voice to address everyone in the room. "And every child does sixty percent of his or her growing nocturnally, so people need to understand that a good mattress will help produce a lifetime of good posture. You need to think about the quality of the product you're buying," he insisted, waving a pamphlet in the air. "Unlike whoever bought the mattresses for this place." His voice went up at the end, his face flushed with exasperation.

"Oh, Joseph, they aren't that bad," Fran said and clucked from across the room.

He lifted his grizzled chin. "You, my dear, are sadly misinformed. I spent forty years selling mattresses all over this state, so I think I know what I'm talking about."

Fran rolled her eyes and went back to the puzzle she was working on.

"Collette agrees with me," he said, studying the pamphlet Anissa had given him. "Don't you, Collette?"

There was an awkward silence before Anissa nodded.

Hadley went perfectly still, watching as

Anissa flipped through a few more brochures with him, talking about daybeds and sofa beds and bunk beds. Finally she stuffed everything back into her bag and leaned over to kiss his forehead.

"I love you, Gramps. Let's talk more next week, okay?"

Joseph lifted his gaze, eyes shining and hopeful. "That'd be nice."

That night after dinner, Hadley was cuddled up on the couch watching TV when she called out to Ellis on a commercial break, "Mom, guess what. Mr. Muldoon offered me and Anissa part-time jobs at the nursing home."

Ellis rinsed her coffee cup in the sink, and then backed up a few steps to poke her head around the corner. "Sorry, what'd you say?"

"Ben wants to hire me and Anissa part-time. He said he needs someone to do yard work. You know, cutting the lawn, things like that. But he also wants us to help out with small things that take up too much of everyone's time."

"What sort of things?" Ellis asked.

"Like reading to residents, or helping

them write letters, or playing cards with them to keep them company, that sort of stuff. He said he'd like us to work two days a week after school and maybe the odd weekend too."

Ellis stared at the ceiling, letting this sink in. "What about homework? You've got a heavy load this year."

Hadley shrugged. "He said he'd work around us. He wants us to start the day after tomorrow."

For weeks now, Hadley had been talking about finding a job to earn her own money, but Ellis assumed she would end up working at the pool or bagging groceries at Save-On-Foods or taking orders and artfully balancing trays at the local Steak 'N Egger. Never had she considered that she might want to work at the nursing home, and yet she could tell Hadley had made up her mind.

Ellis suddenly got interested in a hangnail. "Are you sure this is the kind of job you'll enjoy?" she asked.

"I don't know," Hadley said, shrugging. "But I guess I won't know if I don't give it a try, right?" She turned her attention back to her program.

Ellis stood in the doorway watching her, lost in thought. Hadley was the kind of girl who stood out in a crowd, and yet if you had asked Ellis to describe her a year ago, her looks wouldn't have been the first thing that came to mind. Instead, she would have said Hadley was old enough to wear makeup and young enough not to care that she does. That she sleeps with a four-leaf clover under her pillow, wears a quarter on a chain around her neck, and swims like a dolphin—an irony that wasn't lost on Ellis, who had never learned how and remained terrified of water. That she hates apricot jam, pepper on her eggs, and any kind of shellfish. Her favorite color is blue, her lucky number is ten, and nothing relaxes her more than painting her nails.

Resting her fingers against her mouth, Ellis studied Hadley as she hadn't in months. When had Hadley begun wearing makeup? When was the last time she'd found a four-leaf clover tucked under her daughter's pillow, or seen that old quarter hanging from a chain around her neck? The little girl she had once been was fading fast, and these days Ellis's heart didn't know which way to turn. She caught herself wishing she could stop her from growing up. *Lord, please let her stay innocent and naïve. Let her dream big and love easily and trust completely.*

Then, seconds later, her throat tightened as she recalled standing on a bridge at seventeen, preparing to jump—the sharp reality of what had brought her there, how raw and real and painful her decision had been—and she immediately hardened inside, wishing nothing more than to see Hadley grow into a strong, confident woman who only trusted those who'd earned the right.

Hadley twisted sideways on the couch. "Think it sounds like an okay job?"

"It sounds great," Ellis said, and realized that she meant it.

At Paulina's urging—"Hadley's been through so much already this year"—Ellis agreed to show a united front and tell Hadley on Saturday over lunch that they'd soon have a long-term houseguest: her grandfather. Ellis made soup and sandwiches and Hadley took bowls down from the cupboard. Paulina shook out the tablecloth and lifted her arms high, watching it float for an instant in midair before gently draping it over the table.

"Hadley?" Paulina said, glancing sideways at her.

"Uh-huh?"

"Your mom and I wanted to talk to you about something."

Hadley shot Ellis a surprised look. "About what?"

Ellis had decided that if she acted as if it were no big deal, it wouldn't be, and yet she wasn't comfortable meeting Hadley's gaze, busying herself instead with dishing up their soup, determined not to impose her negative thoughts on her daughter.

Paulina paused as she smoothed a crease on the tablecloth. "Your grandfather is coming to live with us for a while."

Silence pulsed across the kitchen.

"Here?" Hadley asked skeptically.

"Yes," Paulina said. "He'll be arriving next week. His house burned down so he's going to move in until he can get his life back on track. I cleaned out the storage room upstairs and made it into a small bedroom for him."

Hadley's gaze shot straight to Ellis. "How long will he be staying?"

"For a few months," Paulina said. "Until he can make other arrangements."

Hadley slid into a chair, and appeared to be pondering this information. "But, Grandma, you haven't seen him in, like, what, almost twenty years?"

"That's right," Paulina said.

"Doesn't that make you feel . . . weird?"

"Not really," Paulina said, shrugging. "It's not like we're getting back together," she pointed out. "It's just, well, he's family, Hadley, and he needs us right now. We've been divorced for a long time, but we've always kept in touch. Your grandfather still phones every now and then to see how I'm doing and to ask after your mom."

Hadley folded one leg under the other. "Where's he been living all these years?"

Ellis carried their soup bowls to the table. *Probably in one of those intentional communities where they all pitch in and pay the bills together, the kind that has some ridiculous name like* the Acorn House.

"In a rural community in Canada," Paulina said. "About five hours north of here."

"Huh." Hadley blew on her soup. "It's unreal that his house burned down!"

I know, Ellis thought. *Just our luck, huh?*

"I wonder how it happened," Hadley continued.

Ellis almost caught herself saying, *Who knows? Maybe he left candles burning after a séance with his Acorn House friends*.

"The fire department thinks it was electrical wiring," Paulina said. "Anyhow, I hope you'll look at this as an opportunity to get to know him. Keep in mind, honey, that other than me, he's the only other living grandparent you've got."

Ellis bit her tongue as she slid into the chair across from Hadley. Obviously it hadn't occurred to her mom that Dennis might not be any more interested in his granddaughter than he'd been in his daughter.

"Grandma, can I ask something?" Hadley said.

"Ask away."

"Why did Grandpa leave?"

Ellis had given Hadley a watered-down version of events years ago. How her dad had left when she was twelve, how she barely remembered him, how she had long ago accepted that she would probably never see him again.

"I don't know," Paulina said. "You'd have to ask him that."

"Yes," Ellis said, trying to keep her voice level. "And when you do, I'd love to hear his answer too."

Hadley froze with a spoonful of soup halfway to her mouth, eyes wide as she looked from her mom to her grandmother and then back again.

Later that afternoon, Ellis dug through her nightstand and pulled out her yellow notepad, then went over the list she'd updated weeks ago. "Grief counseling" had been scratched off, as had "Save money"—she'd been putting half of her paychecks away and planned to continue doing so. "Go through Mark's things" still remained on the list, something she wasn't ready to do yet, as did "Get our own place." Now she scribbled "Top priority" next to it.

She imagined Mark gently lecturing her, saying, *I understand why moving out on your own with Hadley is important to you, but what's the rush? And maybe you shouldn't be so quick to decide how you feel about your dad.*

Thinking of Mark made a deep sense of loss rise up in Ellis, so forceful she had to briefly close her eyes and make herself list everything she had accomplished without him so far, imagining the tender, supportive touch of his hand against her back as she tackled each new challenge, knowing her and Hadley's lives would be forever shaped around his absence. And now her dad was coming to live with them, and the very real possibility that Hadley might actually like him, or worse yet, develop some sort of relationship with him, filled Ellis with a rush of emotion she wasn't ready to identify or address.

There was a knock on her door. "Mom?"

"Yes?"

Hadley stuck her head inside. "Can I talk to you for a minute?"

"Of course."

Ellis patted the bed, but Hadley walked over and wiped at the window with the cuff of her favorite sweatshirt, peering outside at the fresh beginnings of grass in the yard, at the wall of daffodils that were starting to spring up along the fence. Ellis couldn't read her expression, so she sat back on the bed and watched her, waiting.

Hadley pushed a strand of hair behind her ear. "I'll go to a few grief counseling sessions if it'll make you feel better."

Her calm statement so startled Ellis that she couldn't speak for a moment. A flicker of pleasure pulsed through her, yet she willed herself to stillness, sensing Hadley wouldn't want to get all "deep-thoughty" at this point. She marveled at the young woman Hadley was becoming—reading to Nina at the nursing home earlier that week, playing cards with Joseph, laughing when Louie teased her—all wondrous, astonishing developments on her way back to a normal life. And running had become the biggest gift of all. Even when Anissa was staying with her dad outside of town, off Hadley would go every morning. Ellis would watch for her return, standing back from the living room window. She liked the way Hadley stopped out front on the sidewalk, walking in circles to slow her breathing before coming inside, the way her cheeks pinked up, how her eyes danced with energy when she left for school.

"I'd like that a lot," Ellis said.

Hadley nodded, jammed her hands into the pockets of her jeans. "I'm doing it for you," she clarified. "I'll go twice, and then if I think it's a total waste of time, I won't go anymore." She sounded firm on that point, but even so, nothing could dampen Ellis's pleasure.

Fourteen

On Wednesday night Hadley attended her first grief counseling session. Ellis was more nervous than her daughter seemed to be. On the drive there, Hadley was a silent, sulking presence. She kicked off her UGG boots and rested her feet on the dashboard, a habit that got on Ellis's nerves. Looking bored, she ripped open a Snickers bar, took a bite, and began flipping through a copy of the National Enquirer she'd grabbed on her way out the door.

"God, Britney Spears is such a freak show," she said to herself.

"You can't believe everything you read," Ellis said.

"What*ever*. All I'm doing is looking at the pictures."

She had been in a foul mood since dinner, and the closer they got to Great Falls the worse she seemed to get. The brake lights of the car ahead of them flared and Ellis slowed down, then reached into her purse and handed Hadley a journal she had bought for her, a field of daisies on the front.

"What's this for?" Hadley asked.

"Our grief counselor often asks us to write things down," Ellis explained.

"Why?" Hadley frowned.

"To help us feel better."

Hadley's feet dropped to the floor and she seemed to be trying to decide whether explaining one more time would be worth the hassle. "Mom, I already told you, I feel fine," she said in a prim, grown-up tone. "I'm doing this for you." She had a smudge of chocolate on her chin and Ellis had to resist the impulse to reach over and rub it off. "I said I'd give it a try, and I will, but please don't expect me to win some kind of grief group gold star, because that is *so* not going to happen."

"Okay," Ellis said, sinking her teeth into her lower lip. "Fair enough."

It had been a stressful day at work and Ellis was tired. For the second time in a week, Charlene had gone home sick after lunch and Ellis had had to take care of all of her charges along with her own. Ed Notton had gone missing around two and then the fire alarm went off, causing complete chaos. By the time the alarm had been turned off—Louie had been smoking in his room again—Ed had suddenly reappeared, face flushed. "Decided to take a little walk," he said, straightening his pants. Other than Joseph finally agreeing to wear the "Get dressed" reminder bracelet Ellis had given him, the day had pretty much been a bust.

"I've got an idea for next weekend," Ellis said, keeping her eyes on the road.

Hadley's eyes brightened. "What's that?" She took off her jacket and tossed it in the backseat. She was wearing low-rise jeans and a giant hooded Calgary Flames sweatshirt that had once belonged to her dad.

"Instead of our regular movie night on Friday when you and Anissa pick a DVD to watch, I thought I'd rent *Doctor Zhivago* and we'd all watch it together."

Hadley gave her a blank look. "Doctor *who*?"

"*Doctor Zhivago*. It's a classic."

"What's it about?"

"It's set against the backdrop of the Russian Revolution of 1917."

"Sounds like a real winner," Hadley said.

"It's about Yuri Zhivago, a medical doctor and a poet who's torn between his love for two women. After he marries and has a son, he falls in love with this other woman, Lara, and they have an affair. Eventually, he leaves. Actually, he gets caught and taken away by the army or something, so his wife has to raise their son alone. On a much deeper level, though, it's all about Yuri's life slowly being destroyed by the violence of the revolution."

"Ugh!" Hadley's head lolled back on her neck and her arms flopped at her sides like she'd been struck dead.

"Come on," Ellis said. "It's a good movie. I've never seen it, but I've read all about it."

"Can't believe everything you read."

Ellis pulled in to the parking lot. Hadley climbed out and waited for her on the sidewalk, hopping up and down to keep warm, hands tucked into her armpits. Around them, visible in the cones of light cast by the streetlights, snow fell quietly. Ellis locked the car, knowing that within an hour it would be a soft white hill, the world subdued and hidden beneath white flakes that had billowed, swirled, and then drifted to the ground.

"Ready?" she said, opening the glass doors of the health clinic.

"I guess," Hadley said, shrugging.

A thin vertical line had formed between her eyes, as it did whenever Hadley was worried or nervous about something. Despite Hadley's bravado, Ellis knew her fear was real, and she shared it.

Roma was over-the-top pleased to have Hadley join them. "How nice to meet you," she said, clamping Hadley's hands between her own.

Ellis bit her lip, praying her daughter wouldn't say, "What*ever*!"

"Nice to meet you, too," Hadley said.

They were saved from having to converse any further when the door opened and Gregory walked in. He'd joined the group right after Ellis had. He was tall and thin and slightly effeminate. His partner had died six months ago after a long illness, and Gregory had told the group he didn't know what he was going to do with the rest of his life. Today, he was carrying a cardboard box; the flaps lifted and fell with his every step.

"I made Nanaimo bars," he said, setting the box on the table and carefully taking out a plate covered in tin foil.

"Well, aren't you a peach?" Roma said loud enough that everyone else looked up.

Above them, thundering footsteps echoed through the ceiling from the aerobics class that hadn't quite finished yet. Roma pulled out a chair for Hadley and waved Ellis into an empty one next to it. After Roma had introduced Hadley to everyone and Gregory had personally handed out napkins and Nanaimo bars, the noise upstairs stopped and the conference room took on an expectant hush.

"Welcome, everyone," Roma said. "This week, I'd like to open our session by talking about our fears. Things we find ourselves avoiding. Things we don't look forward to now that we've lost our loved one."

"Like eating at our favorite restaurant?" Gregory asked. He had kept his jacket on and was slumped next to Ellis, looking tired.

"Exactly," Roma said. "That one's always difficult."

"Holidays are bad for me," one woman said. "I don't think I would've made it through Christmas if I hadn't been medicated."

"For me, it's birthdays," an older man with a goatee said. He'd lost his wife to ovarian cancer a year ago. "We used to make a big deal about them. My wife's sixty-third is coming up and I'm dreading it."

Roma leaned forward at her end of the table and gave everyone an encouraging smile. "This is all very helpful." She got up and went to the blackboard. "Please keep talking. I'll jot everything down."

Ellis almost offered to do it for her, but caught herself in time. *Where's my head? I might be good at lists, but staying unnoticed and invisible on the far side of the room is what I'm known for here. No need to shock anyone.*

Still slumped in his chair, Gregory tilted

his head back and talked to the ceiling. "Better add going to work. For those who *have* a job, that is."

Roma shot him a pitying look. "Oh, no. You lost your job?"

"More like a forced leave of absence," he clarified, dropping his hands at his sides and dangling his fingers against the floor. "I guess it would have helped if I'd shown up dressed appropriately. Apparently it's frowned upon when X-ray technicians wear flannel pajamas. Clogs are okay, though," he added.

Hadley frowned. "That's totally not fair," she said. "I mean, if you're an X-ray technician you work in a *lab*, right? Everyone who comes in there is sick or else they have broken bones or something, so who *cares* what you wear?"

"My thoughts exactly," Gregory said, sitting up.

The woman across the table from Ellis raised her hand. "Can I ask something a little off topic?" she asked, twisting a Kleenex.

"Of course," Roma said.

"My sister died a year ago and my parents are still trying to come to terms with it." As she talked, a string of pearls glimmered against her throat. "She never got married and she was still living at home when she died. . . ." Her voiced trailed away and she glanced around the room, looking nervous.

"Yes?" Roma leaned forward, prompting her to continue.

"Anyhow, I'm not having any trouble with fear, but I'm angry all the time." She said this softly, as though embarrassed to admit it. "I check on my parents every day after work. I have them over for Sunday dinner. I pick up their medication. I take them grocery shopping. I drive them to doctor appointments, the bank, even the movie store when they want to rent a DVD." She was talking faster and faster, her face flushed.

"Wow. If I had to do all that," Hadley mumbled, "I'd be mad, too."

"But they're my *parents*," the woman said. "It's not fair to be angry with them."

"Maybe not," Roma interjected. "But it's natural given the adjustments you've had to make for them. Grief-related anger is often misdirected."

"I think she's probably right," Hadley

said, nodding sagely. "Ask my mom. She beat up her boss a few months ago. *Kaboom!*" Hadley smacked her fist into the open palm of her hand for effect. "She kneed him hard right in his privates, and trust me, until my dad died, she was totally *not* a violent person."

Ellis's eyes flew open and she gaped at her daughter.

Next to her, Gregory grimaced. "Oooh!" he said, leaning away from Ellis. "Did she get fired?"

"No," Hadley answered, glancing around the room. "She wasn't actually working for him yet. He hired her a few days later."

All at once the room went still, fluorescent lights humming against the ceiling. The distant sounds of snow plows could be heard outside clearing the roads. Everyone's eyes were on Ellis and she felt herself slowly sink back against her chair.

Who invited this chatty kid?

"It seems it all worked out then, didn't it?" Roma asked.

Ellis didn't trust herself to do more than nod.

"All right then," Roma said, clearing her throat. "Let's get back to our fears, shall we?" The older man with the goatee shot Ellis a nervous look, shifting in his chair. "Anyone else?" Roma asked.

A tiny elderly woman whose husband had died of a heart attack said she wasn't looking forward to the summer, that she wanted to sell their family cabin, but her sons were against it. "Harold died in our cabin last July," she said, lowering her cottony head. "I don't ever want to go back there."

Ellis felt a welling up of tenderness for the woman. She wanted to reach across the table, gently squeeze her hand, and reassure her that she didn't have to. She wanted to say, *I understand. Some people might need to go back to a place where something horrible happened, but I'm like you. I'd stay far away.*

The man who'd lost his wife in a river rafting accident said he'd sold his house and was moving back to Vermont, where he'd grown up. "I can't live here anymore. We moved here because of my wife's work with the forestry service. We planned to grow old here, and now everything reminds me of her. Absolutely everything." He dropped his gaze. "Lately, I've been pretending she didn't die, that she left me for someone else instead. I know it's not true, but I wish it were. I can't stand the thought of never seeing her again, of never hearing her voice. At least that way I'd be able to drive by her new home and see her being happy with someone else." His voice grew louder, halfway to a sob. "I'd want her to be happy, you know?"

Hadley was staring straight at him, hands balled into fists under her trembling chin. The bowl of peppermints in the middle of the table suddenly grabbed Ellis's attention, but this time she wasn't thinking about Mark; she was thinking about her dad. About how unhappy he must have been when he'd left her mom all those years ago.

By the time Ellis had turned sixteen she had stopped missing her dad. Every six months or so he would mail her mom a batch of postdated checks for alimony and child support, and this, along with what Paulina earned part-time at Bianca's Café, eventually helped get them off welfare. Still, it seemed as though they were forever scrimping and saving to get by.

Now and then her dad also sent letters, and her mom would leave them on the counter for Ellis to read. He hadn't remarried, although he was living with a woman he'd met while managing a fish hatchery in Jasper, Alberta. Her mom encouraged Ellis to contact him, giving her his address and phone number, but Ellis refused.

Why should I? He should be calling me.

Then in June of eleventh grade, Ellis's environmental studies class went on a five-day field trip to Alberta. They took one day to travel there by bus, another to return, and three more exploring areas Ellis knew she would never forget. First, they stopped at the Columbia Icefields, where they rode tractorlike snow machines up a glacier and cupped their hands to drink from the tiny streams that flowed from it. They hiked through Maligne Canyon, one of the most spectacular gorges in the Canadian Rockies, with sheer limestone walls that plunged to depths of over one hundred and sixty feet. Last of all, they spent a day at Miette Hot Springs, the hottest mineral springs in the Rockies, where on another hike they snapped pictures of mountain goats and a black bear.

After arriving at the hot springs, Ellis became preoccupied with the weirdness of the situation. Her dad lived only miles from where she was sitting in this restaurant. If she wanted, she could call him, but maybe she wouldn't have to. Maybe she'd run into him by accident when the group wandered around downtown Jasper after lunch. *Maybe when I'm done eating, I'll get up to leave this restaurant, turn around, and there he'll be, sitting on the other side of the room.*

Despite her determination not to care what he was doing with his life anymore, Ellis caught herself wondering if he still sang those roof-raising country songs he used to love, if he'd ever bought himself a new guitar—he had left his old one behind—if he still liked building things with his hands.

"You okay?" one of her friends asked.

Nodding, she dropped her gaze to her lap.

When everyone else was preoccupied, she excused herself from the table, took a deep breath, and did one of the hardest things she'd ever done. She walked to the lobby, stepped into a phone booth in the far corner, and dialed the number her mom had given her before leaving on the trip.

It's probably not in service, she thought, leaning against the door. The line clicked and began to ring. *Or else someone will answer and say he doesn't live there.* She ran a trembling finger around a heart someone had scratched into the Plexiglas with "JULIE LOVES BRENT" carved inside.

Her dad answered on the third ring. "Hello."

Startled, Ellis opened her mouth, but nothing came out. There was so much she wanted to ask him, so many things she needed to say. Was his life better now? Was he happier than when he'd lived with them? Did he ever think about her?

"Who's there?"

The unmistakable sound of his voice caused a sudden fullness in her, choking her throat and making it hard to breathe. And then all at once her mind began spinning with a burst of accusatory thoughts. *Why did you leave like that? How come you've never phoned me? What kind of man walks away from his wife and child?*

"Who's there?" His voice sounded hard and precise.

Ellis noticed her friends watching and turned her back on them. *Did you ever love me? When I was first born, when I used to toddle across the grass with my arms stretched out to you—did you love me then? When I sat at your feet watching all those stupid hockey games—did you love me then?* She clamped a hand over her mouth, biting back a strangled sob, her eyes burning with the effort it took not to cry.

"Hello?" he said, irritated.

She opened her mouth to tell him that she took her silver compass everywhere, but then she turned around and the restaurant was spinning with a steady whir of normalcy that made her hesitate. A family was waiting to be seated, waitresses were taking orders, bursts of laughter shot from a group seated somewhere in the back.

"Who is this?!"

Reaching into her pocket, she fingered her silver compass. In the silence that followed, she sensed a blossoming realization at his end.

"Ellis?" he said, his voice cracking. "Is that you?"

She stared at her shoes and a strange feeling came over her, a memory pushing to the surface, hard and insistent and unforgiving. She let it come, remembering what he had said to her the last time she'd seen him: *You'll be fine, Ellis. You're a lot stronger than you think you are.* The line between wanting to talk to him and wanting to hurt him became blurred. She was tired of waiting for him to come back, tired of loving someone who didn't love her in return, and she suddenly realized that the last thing she wanted to do was let him know how much his leaving had devastated her.

"Ellis?" he said, softer now, almost pleading.

Swallowing, she pulled the receiver away from her ear and slowly hung up, figuring that was the only answer he deserved.

FIFTEEN

Ellis came up the back steps after work juggling her purse and three bags of groceries. Making her way across the porch, she reached down and fumbled for the knob to the kitchen door.

"Mom?" she called out, kicking off her boots. "You home?"

"Yes, I'm right here."

Ellis set the bags on the counter with a thump. Her hair, which had been pulled back in a clip, had fallen loose. Frustrated, she tucked a few strands behind one ear and straightened. Paulina was standing at the stove, stirring spaghetti sauce in slow, wide circles. She set her spoon down before she spoke.

"Look who's here," she said.

Ellis glanced sideways, startled to see someone at the table, an older man turned in profile to her, his right elbow hooked over the chair back, his legs crossed at the knees. The moment their eyes met, she knew him, and her stomach went through a series of drops and lurches as she tried to reconcile this man with the one she'd known almost twenty years ago. He was smaller than she remembered, thin and washed out, the sleeve of his shirt torn, his tinsel gray hair in need of a trim. As a kid, she'd believed she couldn't live without him, although for years she'd done exactly that—a huge chunk of her life decided for her when he left—and now here he was, sitting at their kitchen table.

Earlier, her mom had said he'd be arriving this week. She'd even put fresh linens on the bed upstairs, so Ellis shouldn't have been surprised, and yet the reality that he was sitting in front of her was unsettling. For days now, she'd tried to imagine walking past that room each morning, hearing his snores, seeing his feet sticking out from under the blankets. This man who had once been her father, someone she hadn't seen in two decades, was now going to be living with them.

"Ellis," he said, and then lapsed into silence.

Gone was any hint of the confident, charismatic man he had once been, the trademark take-charge twinkle in his eye replaced with a deep flush that crept up his neck as she studied him. Ellis heard herself say, "Hello."

Paulina crossed the room and touched her shoulder. "Why don't you pour us each a fresh cup of coffee?" she suggested.

Ellis shook her head. "No. I'm not feeling all that conciliatory, and if he's staying with us, he'll have to get used to serving himself, won't he?"

Paulina shot her a look, but Dennis rose from his chair, empty cup in hand. "No, she's right," he said. "I can get it myself." He limped over to the counter, favoring his left leg. Gone was his old kick-down-the-door walk; now he had the awkward gait of a man who'd once been seriously hurt.

Paulina put lasagna noodles on to boil and grated a brick of cheese, asking her ex-husband how long he'd owned the old car parked out front ("Twelve years"), if he had liked living in Canada ("Yes"), what kind of work he'd been doing ("Carpentry"). Then Dennis asked if she still worked part-time at Bianca's Café ("Yes, although I've gone from an employee to part owner"), when she'd gotten her driver's license ("Ten years ago"), if he could help make dinner ("Thanks, but there's no need"). He didn't talk to Ellis directly, didn't try to explain himself, didn't attempt to apologize.

Taking her time, Ellis put the groceries away and wiped out the sink, even though it didn't need cleaning. She was reluctant to look at her dad and amazed by her mom's calm and pragmatic approach to his arrival. Outside, the sky darkened, and then it started to rain, coming down hard and fast, soaking everything in sight. Every now and then pitchfork lightning shot across the sky, illuminating everything for a few seconds. Ellis stared out the window at an old birdhouse swinging from a chain on the neighbor's porch, at dollops of bird shit that had accumulated on the steps below, the rain now smearing them into the crevices of the wood, making them disappear.

She stood with her back to her parents, tuning them out as she stared out the window, recalling the day she had found her silver compass on the back steps. Listening to them make idle and pointless conversation threw her off center so badly, she suddenly felt dizzy and had to touch the wall to make everything go still again. *There are bigger topics to be discussed here,* she thought.

Hadley came pounding up the back steps and across the porch into the kitchen, dropping her knapsack on the floor. Paulina walked over and kissed the top of her head. "Dennis, meet your granddaughter, a true force of nature."

In the window's reflection, Ellis saw Dennis's face open up with a quick flash of joy, wonderstruck by Hadley, and then it closed as he struggled to hide his sadness. "My granddaughter," he repeated with a look of total astonishment.

Ellis's breath snagged in her throat. This was too much for her.

Clearing her own throat, Paulina motioned at Hadley. "Come on. Let's run you a bath so you can get out of those wet clothes."

As soon as the bathroom door had shut behind them, Ellis turned and gave her dad a hard, steady look. His leaving had changed her, in ways both large and small, and maybe her mom was able to forgive him, but she couldn't. "I want you to know I don't need you in my life anymore and neither does my daughter." It wasn't an appropriate thing to say, but she said it before she could stop herself, her voice charged with emotion.

"I can see that," Dennis said. "You seem to be doing well."

Ellis didn't look away until she felt some sort of understanding had passed between them. *That you came back doesn't change the fact that you left,* her eyes said. He nodded slowly, as though he understood. Then he dropped his gaze, slipped his fingers under his glasses, and rubbed his eyes.

Later, after they had all eaten and everyone was in bed, Ellis stared at the ceiling, thinking. The child in her wanted to storm out and tell him what it'd been like after he'd left. How her mom had barely eaten for two months. How the owners of the local mini-mart had let them keep their food in a cardboard box at the back of one of their store fridges because their fridge at home didn't work. How they ate so many tuna casseroles those first few winters Ellis couldn't stomach the smell of it anymore. How their power had been cut off and they'd had to burn candles until they could afford to pay the electric bill. How her mom had gone from sheeplike docility when Dennis was married to her to the independent woman she was today.

Unable to sleep, Ellis slipped downstairs to get a glass of water.

Her mom was sitting at the table, her slim bare feet propped on a chair rung as she flipped through a catalogue. Ellis poured herself the water and sat down. It was a while before either of them spoke. Her mom eventually broke the silence.

"He has nowhere else to go."

"You told me that," Ellis replied.

Paulina stared at her for a moment and a sad smile trembled on her lips. "Ellis, he's your father and right now he needs us. I wouldn't turn him away any more than I would you." The expression on her face told Ellis that arguing would be as futile as trying to stop a boulder from rolling down a hill.

Ellis was determined not to warm to her dad, but as the days slid into weeks, she didn't count on the persistent lure of the past, or on how it would feel to watch a new relationship form between her parents: a respectful friendship born of loss and grief, stemming from years when life had been good to them, and some when it hadn't. As that happened, it occurred to Ellis that her parents' roles were now reversed: her mom the strong one, her dad in need of someone to lean on.

Late one night, Ellis went upstairs to bed and found Hadley sitting in the middle of her mattress with her knees pulled to her chest beneath her nightgown. "Grandpa told me Uncle Donnie locked him inside a shed once."

Ellis raised her eyebrows, surprised that he had shared this with her.

Hadley continued. "He said he was inside when Uncle Donnie slammed the door shut and stuck a nail in the hasp. That after five minutes of yelling and pounding, you came along and pulled the nail out, but he was so mad he wouldn't listen when you said you didn't lock him in there. He said he didn't believe you, that it was a 'shoot the messenger' kind of mistake and that you got in trouble instead of Uncle Donnie."

That's one way to put it, Ellis thought, recalling how Donnie had set her up that day.

At the time, Donnie was always trying to trick her. He'd come running down the hill to the frog pond, where she was crouched on a rock. She'd glared up at him, ready to be annoyed before he opened his mouth.

"Thank God I found you!" he said. "Something's wrong. I can hear Dad yelling for us, but I can't find him."

Ellis was suspicious.

"I'm not kidding," he said, turning to sprint back up the hill. "He needs our help!"

At that, she dropped her pail and hit the ground running, arms and legs pumping. "You go that way," Donnie said, pointing to the shed. "I'll check the backyard."

Immediately, Ellis heard her dad yelling from inside the shed, the door shaking on its hinges as he threw his weight against it.

"Dad?" she called out.

She reached up and lifted the nail out from the fold-over hasp, then pulled the door open. Standing to one side, she dangled the nail in the air between them with a triumphant smile. She'd just rescued her dad. How much better could the day get?

He stepped outside, his face red, hair drenched with sweat. In one single motion, he lifted her by the waist and hoisted her over his shoulder, the palms of her hands bouncing against the flat of his back as he held on to her knees.

"Think that's funny, huh? Locking me in the shed?"

A shiver crawled across Ellis's skin when she realized he thought she had locked him inside. Out of the corner of her eye, she spotted Donnie poking his head around the corner of the house.

"Dad, it wasn't me," she said, blowing her bangs off her forehead. "I didn't do it!"

But her dad ignored her protests. He

stormed across the yard and unceremoniously dropped her feetfirst into an old barrel they used to burn garbage. Thankfully, it had recently been emptied, but even so, when Ellis's feet hit the bottom she found herself standing neck-deep in a filthy barrel with a cloud of ash rushing up, coating the skin on her arms and legs with a layer of grime. Sputtering, she plugged her nose with one hand and waved the other in front of her to clear the air. She grabbed the top of the barrel and tried to lift herself out, but she was too small to raise herself up or tip the barrel over without help.

Her dad's gaze sliced straight through her, hard and unflinching. "You want to be a smart aleck?" he said, pointing at her. "Then you figure out how you're going to get out of there on your own."

"It wasn't me," she said, her voice thin. He turned away, smoothing his hair back as he walked into the house.

Her bottom lip trembled as she slid down inside where it was dark and quiet, pulling her knees to her chest. She leaned forward into her hands and started to cry, ignoring Donnie when he reached in to lift her out by her armpits, saying, "It's okay, you'll be fine. It's okay, you'll be fine. It's okay . . ."

"Is that true?" Hadley asked, bringing Ellis back to the present. "Did you really get in trouble instead of Uncle Donnie?"

"Yes," Ellis said, trying to sort out how she felt about her dad sharing stories with her daughter. "It is." She hadn't realized how many memories she'd conveniently erased. Now that her dad was back, Hadley seemed as interested in him as he was in her, and Ellis wasn't sure how to feel about that.

"Mom? Why don't you talk to Grandpa?"

Because a man who leaves his family behind is no kind of man. Because I loved him more than he ever loved me. Because parents should never be allowed to have favorites.

"That's between me and your grandfather," she finally said.

Hadley crawled across the bed and leaned against her. Startled by this unusual show of affection, Ellis pulled her in closer.

"Did Grandpa ever meet Dad?"

Ellis buried her face in her hair. "No, he didn't."

"I think he would've liked him."

"I've no doubt."

"God, Mom, I miss him," Hadley whispered.

Ellis could have said, *I know*. She could have said, *I miss him, too*, but Hadley already knew that, so in the end, she just closed her eyes and held her daughter a little tighter, silently nodding her agreement.

Moments later, Hadley sat up and pulled away. She splayed her hands across the nubby fabric of Ellis's bedspread, the way she often did now when she stopped in to talk. "You know what?" she finally said. "I don't think Dad ever would have thrown me in an old barrel no matter how mad he got at me." She looked up at Ellis, her expression utterly open, washed with a stab of fresh loss.

"Never," Ellis agreed.

It began to rain, softly at first and then drumming as it cascaded from the gutters and the downspouts. And as it did, Ellis thought of Mark, feeling something open up in her heart, a rush of emotion that made it impossible for her to speak. *No,* she thought. *Your dad was always our protector. My protector. Except for the one time when he wasn't able to be.*

SIXTEEN

Ellis heard about Mark Semple long before she ever met him. At twenty, he was three years older than she was, a Canadian who had been hired with six other guys to work for an oil exploration company five miles south of Barrow. Rumor had it that they worked hard and played with equal zest. Ellis often listened to other girls at school plotting and planning ways to meet them, although no one seemed to have any success.

"Why don't we drive out there and pretend our car broke down?" one of them said.

"Or maybe when they come into town to use the Laundromat, we could wander in and ask for quarters for the pay phone," another suggested.

Ellis was working part-time after school at the Hillside Motel that winter, running the switchboard and taking reservations. It was one of only three motels in town, but most people considered it last on the list because it was so old. It had fifteen rooms, each with a double bed, two hard-back chairs, a small table, and a TV. The walls had been papered in the late '80s, the rugs were threadbare, and the bathrooms came equipped with showers, no tubs. The front desk was an old wooden one someone had bought years before, and when you phoned to speak to anyone, you were put through to their room using an antiquated switchboard system.

Other than Ellis, few people in town knew that the Tesco Oil crew was temporarily staying at the Hillside Motel until a bunkhouse could be built on their job site. Mark walked into the office at the end of each day to check for messages. He was tall and blond, with a dimple in his left cheek. Every time he came through the door, he caused a small jump in Ellis's chest, a split second when her day slammed to a stop and went breathtakingly still.

At first, his visits were brief, punctuated with polite comments, but soon he began to linger, asking Ellis questions about the town, if Barrow had a hockey team, what everyone did on weekends to relax. Eventually, she too came out of her shell, and seeing Mark's smiling face became the highlight of her days.

"How was work?" she asked one afternoon.

"Not too bad. If I play my cards right, it looks like they might offer me a management job soon."

"That's what you want?" she said. "To manage a rig?"

"No. I want to move to Dallas and work where all the big decisions get made, where there's a chance for me to really move ahead."

Ellis was impressed with his drive, but saddened at the thought of him leaving. Then one weekend she ran into him at the town WELCOME sign, where local teenagers often congregated to party. Ellis didn't usually go out on weekends, mostly because she rarely got asked, but that night a girl she had helped tutor that semester had invited her to join a group of them, and at the last minute she said yes.

Everyone was keyed up, primped and primed for a good time as they huddled around a roaring fire, drinking and laughing. The arrival of two Tesco pickup trucks caused a stir. Ellis heard an excited murmur shoot through the crowd and turned to see Mark and three other guys walking toward them. Their eyes met and Mark's face gentled with emotion.

Without exchanging a word, Ellis suddenly understood that they were not destined to remain passing acquaintances. It seemed that she already knew him—that they knew each other—in a profound and unique way. Mark moved closer, touched her elbow. No one else around them existed; it was a moment of such intimacy and magnitude that Ellis stood motionless, transfixed. All at once, pieces of her life that had never completely fit together did fit, and every past sadness and disappointment fell away, unimportant now that Mark was here.

"I keep meaning to ask, how often do

you cut this?" he asked. He lifted a handful of her waist-length hair and let it cascade slowly through his fingers, never taking his eyes off her face.

Caught off guard, Ellis reddened. Before she could answer, one of his friends grabbed him by the arm and dragged him away. Looking back over his shoulder, Mark winked at her and grinned.

Within weeks, they were spending all of their free time together. As each day passed, Ellis's anticipation of what might happen next was so great, she found it difficult to concentrate at school or at work. Mark took her to the movies in Great Falls, to a friend's cabin at Flathead Lake, hiking in Glacier National Park when the weather warmed up. Through it all, she kept their relationship a secret, the closest she'd ever come to being wild. Then one night on their way back to Barrow in the pouring rain, they came across a middle-aged woman with a flat tire and Mark immediately pulled over to help her change it. It was then that Ellis fell in love with him, for his goodness, his infinite capacity for kindness.

Weeks later, they spread a blanket on a circle of tamped-down grass next to the river and made love. As they lay curled together afterward, Mark told her stories about his family, how he missed them, how he couldn't wait to have one of his own. Ellis loved listening to him convince her that she deserved better, that one day they'd travel the world together. They would take pictures of the Grand Canyon, swim in the Pacific Ocean, watch the sun set from a hot air balloon. "God, you're beautiful," he said, running a hand down the side of her face. His compliments were like a row of jarred raspberries, her favorite fruit, lined up in a window, gleaming jewellike; each one made her a little stronger and more certain about who she was and where she was going in life.

Then, four months later, during lunch at Plaza Pizza in Great Falls, Mark pushed his plate to one side and brushed off his hands. "I need to tell you something."

Ellis froze, a slice of pizza halfway to her mouth. "Okay. Go ahead."

His smile had a peculiar nervous tilt to it and he seemed to be having trouble meeting her gaze. "Tesco offered me a promotion." He straightened the salt and pepper shakers. "I applied for it long before I was sent to Barrow." For a moment when he stopped talking, it seemed as if the entire restaurant had quit breathing along with her.

Ellis studied him, sensing there was more.

"It's in Dallas," he finished.

"Oh," she said.

He looked down. "I start next week."

It took her a moment to realize what he was saying, and then her voice got shaky. "So, are you saying we're done?"

"No, but I also can't turn this job down. I'll never get an opportunity like it, working in the field the way I do. It's the right job at the wrong time, and I know it won't be easy, but I really think we'll be fine."

Ellis felt the back of her throat tighten.

"A year goes by faster than you think," he said, "and by then you'll have graduated and we'll be ready to take our relationship to a new level. That I'm going to Dallas is only a temporary setback."

She nodded, telling herself not to make a scene, to act like an adult.

"I'm not sure I can come back for Christmas," he rattled on. "But I should be able to fly out and see you for a few days in January or maybe February. . . ."

Ellis was only half listening. She wanted to believe what he was saying, that their four-month-old relationship could survive a twelve-month separation, but the truth was, in that moment of stillness before she congratulated him, she felt a piece of her heart harden and close itself off. Other than her dad, Mark was the first person in the world she had ever trusted, and now he was leaving her, too.

The day of his departure was an emotional one. "I love you, Ellis," he said, hugging her the way he always did, with an extra little squeeze at the end.

Then why are you leaving? she wanted to say.

That year's high school graduation party was held three miles north of Barrow on a classmate's property. When Ward Murdock asked Ellis if she wanted to go with him, she said yes. Ward wasn't good-looking or smart or funny, but going to the year-end grad party alone was unheard of, and now that Mark had moved to Dallas, Ellis had decided to stop being so reclusive and start socializing more.

She'd known Ward since grade school

and felt a certain kinship to him, mostly because he, too, had never fit into the mainstream. He lived in an old trailer with "Eminem Rocks" spray-painted down one side, and his parents were rumored to be heavy drinkers. One legendary fall day in third grade he'd come to school wearing only rubber boots and a bathing suit, and the teacher had had to call home and have someone drive into town and pick him up.

Grad parties in Barrow usually drew large crowds, and when Ellis and Ward arrived, thirty cars were already lined up and down both sides of the quarter-mile-long driveway that led from the highway to a well-lit two-story house. Tall hedges surrounded the house and there were chairs and tables and even two old sofas set up on the grass outside. Watching vehicles pull in behind them, Ellis began second-guessing her decision to come. Where was her head? She wouldn't fit in here.

Ward parked, reached into the backseat and grabbed a case of beer. He twisted the cap off a bottle and handed it to her. "If we get separated, meet me back here, okay?" His eyes were dancing with anticipation.

"Sure," Ellis said, a knot forming in her

stomach. She hadn't wanted to hang on to his arm all night long, but she also hadn't considered that she might be left on her own.

Within an hour, she'd lost Ward altogether.

Clutching herself with folded arms, Ellis stepped through the front doors and made her way into the crowd, looking for familiar faces. This was the first grad party she had attended and she was nervous. People were everywhere, chatting in the hallways with drinks in hand, smoking on the stairs, leaning against doorways. She passed a group in the kitchen that was rolling joints at the table, and although she recognized two of them, they were older than she was and didn't acknowledge her. She mingled, talked to a few people, saw a guy from physics class busy necking with his girlfriend. In the front room, a girl she vaguely recognized was having her tarot cards read; Ellis couldn't place her name. She listened for a long while, then got bored and moved on.

Much later, when Ellis went back outside, two girls came walking down the driveway toward her. Their arms were linked and they kept stopping every now and then to throw their heads back and laugh at something one of them said. They had been friends for years and both of them liked giving Ellis a hard time at school. They were obviously drunk, and when they saw her, the taller one pointed and said, "Hey! What're you doing here?"

Ellis tried to walk around them.

The shorter one blocked her path. "Ooooh, I like your jacket," she said, fingering Ellis's arm. "Didn't I see you pick it out of the lost-and-found bin at school the other day? That is where you get most of your clothes, right? There and at the local Salvation Army drop-off box?" This comment sent the taller girl into gales of laughter.

Face burning, Ellis pushed past them.

Halfway down the driveway, they were still laughing and pointing at her. She considered pretending her hand was a gun, so she could spin around and shoot at them in a theatrical who-gives-a-damn way—*bang, pop, boom*—and then blow on her fingertip, giving them a cocky wink. But she didn't. Instead, she kept walking, acting like they hadn't gotten under her skin, not wanting to give them the satisfaction of knowing they had.

Where Ward's car had been parked there was now an empty hole.

Oh, my God! she thought, spinning around to look up and down the driveway. *He left me here?* She threw up her hands, determined to tell him off the next time she saw him. She zipped up her jacket and stuck her hands in the pockets, and fingered her silver compass. *Who needs this abuse?* she thought, feeling the back of her throat tremble.

She started walking down the driveway to the road that would eventually take her into town.

The wind had picked up in sharp gusts. She could hear the distant sound of a dog barking, the tinny thrum of music from the party leaking through the oily night air, and then a vehicle approaching before she was illuminated in its headlights. Wind-driven eddies of dust and grass swirled around her legs; lightning flashed across the sky above the tree line.

A pickup truck pulled up alongside her and a guy leaned over, unrolled the window, and called out to her, "It's gonna pour rain any minute. Need a ride?"

Ellis pulled her chin out of her zipped-up jacket. Had he been at the party, too? Had he seen what had happened between her and those girls?

"Are you heading into town?" she asked.

"That was the plan," he said, smiling. She hesitated, chewing her lip. "I've got lots of room," he prodded gently. "And I promise I won't bite."

Ellis glanced over her shoulder, still a little uncertain. Then she climbed in, relieved to be out of the wind.

"I hope I didn't startle you," he said.

"It's all right," she said. "You didn't."

After he'd pulled back onto the highway, she noticed that he drove with one hand and kept checking his mirrors every few seconds.

"Do you know what time it is?" she asked.

"Late," he answered. In a little while he said, "Aren't you warm? Why don't you take your coat off?"

"I'm okay," Ellis said.

After that he said, "You sure have nice hair."

Ellis saw that he had a bottle of rum in

his other hand. Tilting it up, he took a swig. There were two secondary roads he could have taken into town. Both were clearly marked, and when he drove past the first one, Ellis felt her insides clench. She shot him a sideways look, and then she began talking fast so she wouldn't have to take in the sudden knowledge that she knew nothing about him or where he was from.

"Do you live around Barrow?"

"Nope," he said.

"Were you at the party, too?"

He shook his head.

The second turnoff was coming up, but when Ellis pointed it out to him, he ignored her, keeping his eyes on the road. "What's your hurry? I was thinking maybe we could do some partying ourselves, just the two of us."

He put his hand on her leg just above her knee and Ellis froze, staring straight ahead. "I can't," she said. "I have to get home."

He removed his hand and turned left down an old service road. He drove two hundred feet, pulled over, and parked. He turned off the truck, pulled the keys out of the ignition, and looped his index finger through the ring, dangling it in front of her.

“Is that so?” he said.

Ellis stared out the window, trying to figure out her options. “Could you please drive me to town?” she asked, hearing the quaver in her voice as easily as he must have.

He laughed and took another long pull from the bottle of rum.

“I mean it,” she said, raising her voice. “I need to get home *right now*!”

“Well, that was certainly”—he paused, searching for a word—“abrupt.” He smiled, but underneath it, Ellis could sense he was angry.

She reached for the door, and he snaked one long arm across her and caught hold of her hand. She let out a short, sharp scream, and then he got really mad. He kicked open his door and dragged her by the wrist across the front seat behind him, cussing under his breath. He stepped out of the truck, jerked her forward hard, and let go.

Ellis slid off the seat onto the gravel, smacking her head against the running board on her way down. She pushed herself up with both arms as pain bloomed in searing waves inside her head. He took another long swig from the bottle, wiped his mouth on his sleeve, and pitched the bottle in the back of his truck.

"What's with you?" he said, throwing his arms in the air. "I offer to drive you home and you can't even party with me first?"

For the first time since she'd gotten in the truck, Ellis noticed that he was a lot older than she'd realized. He was a compact guy, with muscular arms and dark hair, wearing faded jeans and work boots, definitely in his late twenties and probably not someone who'd been at the party.

"Here I am, visiting the great state of Montana, and here you are being a completely inhospitable little shit!" His voice was conversational, jokey even, but his eyes remained flat and dull. He looked her up and down as though he owned her. It had the desired effect. Ellis struggled to her feet and edged backward.

"Please," she said. "I just want to go home."

"Where do you think you're going?" he said, cocking one eyebrow in a self-important way. "It's after midnight and we're a mile from that hick town of yours."

He followed her, step for step. "There's nowhere for you to go."

He stumbled forward and slung an arm over her shoulder to steady himself. "Hold on now! Slow down, all right?" He leaned in close and ran the back of one hand down the side of her face. He smelled like machinery grease and sweat and rum; his eyes bored into hers with an almost manic glint.

Ellis wrenched away from him and started to run, but he quickly caught up to her. He grabbed her from behind and pinned her arms to her sides with his right arm, covering her mouth with his left.

"Don't scream," he hissed into her ear. "Not one word, you hear?"

She went immediately still, shocked into silence.

"I mean it. You scream, you're dead."

She remained motionless.

Lifting her half off the ground, he dragged her backward into the ditch. She twisted and struggled and tried to land a few wild kicks with her feet, hoping to hit him in the crotch. Laughing, he grabbed her by her long hair and wrapped it around his hand, throwing her off balance and making her stagger as he yanked hard and brought her to her knees.

Fighting back a sob, she tried to get up, but he kneed her in the back of the legs and she fell down again. "Lay down," he said.

"On the ground?" she asked, stupidly, hopelessly.

She did, and then a wild rush of fear rippled through her when he straddled her and pinned her down with his weight. She struggled, but fending him off was impossible. She began babbling, begging him not to hurt her, promising that if he let her go, she'd never say anything to anyone. He slapped her with a backhand and her stomach heaved, the metallic taste of blood undeniable in her mouth. She looked up into his face, convinced she wouldn't survive this, trembling with the sudden belief that he planned to kill her.

He tugged on her belt. After yanking her jeans and underpants off her, he ripped open her blouse and unsnapped the front of her bra. Then he raised himself up to look at her lying there between his legs.

"You're pretty," he said, without any expression on his face.

"Please don't do this," she said. "Please . . ."

The headlights of his truck were blinding her in their glare. Ellis heard him unzip his pants. "You're gonna enjoy this," he said against the side of her face, his voice flat and colorless. She turned her head and went deep inside of herself, where her mind locked itself away from her body. Maybe if she made herself invisible, it would stop sooner. She felt his belly slapping against hers over and over as he did his business, panting and grunting. The base of her spine was crushed into the ground; gravel cut into the skin of her back and behind. Tears leaked out of her eyes, sliding down her cheeks. In her mind, she turned herself into a Sasquatch, moving over the mossy ground next to the river, unnoticed as she made her way through the trees, ducking beneath intricate, glassy spiderwebs that had been spun between the branches, up the side of a rocky, cavernous mountain, higher and higher, searching for a slice of sunshine.

He finished and slumped against her.

Afraid to antagonize him, Ellis lay motionless.

He pushed to his feet, jerked up his jeans, and stuffed himself back into his pants. Then he staggered sideways and the world suddenly went still and quiet, as though everything and everyone had died.

Ellis ran the back of a trembling hand across her mouth, wiping away his touch, knowing that everything would forever be different for her now.

"You gonna keep your mouth shut?" he asked, all matter-of-fact.

Staring past him, she nodded. She refused to look him in the eye; that would have only sweetened the moment for him. After he left, weaving his way up to where his truck was parked, she rolled onto her side and curled into a ball. A mile away, people were streaming in and out of the annual party, oblivious of what had just unfolded on this old service road. She lay in the ditch with her face turned sideways, gravel denting the skin of her cheek. She heard the distinctive *ding-ding-ding* signaling an open door, and then the hard slam of it closing after he had climbed inside.

She turned her head and saw a set of Oregon license plates on the front of his truck. He pulled away, slowed down beside her, and leaned out his window.

"Not a word about this, you hear?"

She nodded.

"Don't even think of moving 'til you can't hear my truck anymore." And then he was gone, the sound of gravel spitting up behind his tires as he gunned it on the highway.

Ellis cradled her head in her hands and burst into a flurry of short, racking sobs. All around her it was dark. It seemed as if the night had a distant heartbeat, as though it was a living, breathing thing that had been watching the entire time. Terrified he might come back, she waited until she couldn't hear his truck anymore; then she rolled over and lifted herself up onto all fours. A different vehicle drove by on the main road, a chorus of voices screeching out the lyrics to Tom Cochrane's "Life Is a Highway." The world rushed past, ordinary and yet utterly changed.

She wanted to hurry, but her battered body wouldn't cooperate. Her knees felt rubbery. She crawled over to where he'd thrown her clothes, pulled on her underpants, then stood and inched her jeans up over her hips. Twice, dizzy, she put her hands on her head to stop from swaying back and forth. She fastened her bra and gathered her shirt against her chest where he'd torn it, feeling soiled and sore.

Somewhere deep inside, part of her raged. She wanted to run after him down the middle of the highway, screaming profanities into the thick night air. She considered calling her mom, but that would mean using a phone, which would mean going back to the party, and she couldn't bring herself to do that.

I need to get home.

Shaking, she pulled her silver compass out of her pocket and clutched it between her hands. *I need to get away from here.*

She stumbled through the trees that bordered the highway, staying far enough back that no one would see her. Now and then, when headlights from oncoming vehicles illuminated everything, she would move behind a tree and wait until they had passed. Taking shallow breaths, she tried to remain calm, focused on how sore she was. The walk back to Barrow seemed to take forever, but eventually she found the alley behind her house and sneaked inside through the back porch.

She kicked off her shoes and went into the bathroom. Standing in front of the mirror, she slowly lifted her gaze. Her hair was matted with dirt and leaves, and there was a small cut on her upper lip from where he'd hit her. She stripped and dropped her clothes on the floor. She would never wear them again.

Then she climbed into the bathtub and wept until her face became mottled and swollen, rocking back and forth as she let the hot water run and run until the super-sized tub was ready to overflow—knowing even as she did that her mom would have taken her customary sleeping pill and would never hear her. She was aware of her body, and yet in some ways she felt separated from it. She took a washcloth, lathered it with soap, and scrubbed her skin until it was beet red and raw. She climbed out like a wobbly old lady and dried herself off. She pulled on a T-shirt and a sweater and a thick pair of sweatpants, and then she curled up on her bed, shaking. She was cold all over.

It felt as if her heart and soul had both been frozen and now she had to wait for them to thaw out before she could get on with her life. The sun and moon seemed to have switched places and nothing would ever look the same again.

Under the shock, her humiliation and shame were huge.

Who could possibly understand what she was going through? Certainly not her mom. It would tear her already fragile world apart. Ellis bent forward and cradled her head in her hands. She didn't come from a background where people talked about their problems; she came from a family that ran away from them—her mom with pills and her dad with selfishness. Thinking of Mark, she felt tears burn the back of her eyes. He had made her happier than ever before. He had made her look at herself in a new light, giving her hope for the future, and now a stranger had come along and changed everything.

"I was raped," she whispered, feeling the need to say it out loud, and then feeling worse for having said it.

It was a night filled with sharp edges, a night she would spend years trying to forget, but by morning she had decided to tell no one. She would keep to herself over the summer and pretend to be unbroken, and the longer she did so, the easier it would become. *I'll handle this alone,* she thought. *I'll get through it by myself.*

What she didn't know then was that four long months later she would find herself wedged between two steel posts on the town bridge, pregnant and unsure who the father was. And as she stood there, she would pull out her silver compass, rub her thumb in circles against the inscription on the back, and jump.

Seventeen

Trees flashed past as Ellis drove over a narrow bridge and headed down into a valley. She couldn't believe spring was already moving toward summer. She also couldn't believe Hadley was now fifteen. They'd celebrated her birthday weeks ago, before Ellis's dad had arrived. Hadley, Anissa, Ellis, and her mom had gone into Great Falls, where Paulina had reserved connecting hotel rooms at the Best Western. They went out for dinner, then the next morning, after the girls went swimming in the hotel pool, Ellis took Hadley to Target and bought her the iPod nano she'd been wanting for months. Now, as they drove to their second grief counseling session together, Hadley was listening to it, feet resting on the dashboard.

After their first session, Hadley had surprised Ellis by talking nonstop all the way home. She said she felt sorry for the elderly lady whose husband had died in their family cabin; that Roma was nice, but seemed a bit hard-core when it came to following a "grieving path"; and that she liked Gregory's dramatic personality.

Ellis shot her a sidelong glance. Hadley's eyes were closed and she was singing along to Justin Timberlake's "Lovestoned" under her breath, a song Ellis knew all the words to, along with Hadley's other favorite, "Teenagers" by My Chemical Romance. For several weeks, she'd cranked up the volume on the portable CD player in her room every night, driving Ellis crazy, but now that she had an iPod their evenings had gone back to a blessed level of silence that even Paulina had commented on.

In some ways, Ellis wished Hadley had left her iPod at home tonight because she'd been looking forward to talking to her on the drive into Great Falls. Whenever they used to drive anywhere, Mark would entertain Hadley and Ellis would sit back and listen. He was a natural at it, spontaneous and funny. As a little kid, Hadley would point to a field covered in yellow and ask what it was. Without hesitation Mark would say, "Mustard. They put it in a huge barrel and stomp it down into that yellow mush we put on our hot dogs."

Ellis would swivel around to the backseat and correct him, saying, "It's actually canola, honey," but Hadley seemed to prefer her dad's more whimsical explanation.

By the time Hadley was thirteen, when she'd begun going through a roller coaster of daily mood swings and was less approachable, Mark still managed to work his magic on her. Flipping on the radio, he'd find a song like "Smoke Gets in Your Eyes" by the Platters and off he'd go, ad-libbing the lyrics, singing "Soap gets in your eyes." Hadley would stare out her window, fighting a smile, but she'd eventually give in and grin.

Keeping one hand on the wheel, Ellis reached into her purse and fingered the small hinged box that held her silver compass. Back in January, when she'd found Hadley up in the garage loft skipping school, she had considered giving the compass to her, thinking she might draw strength from it, but for days afterward it seemed as if they were never alone and then Ellis forgot about it. Watching Hadley now, though, Ellis realized that her daughter didn't need the compass. She had come a long way since they'd moved to Barrow, maybe more than Ellis had herself.

Hadley dropped her feet and yanked out her ear buds, startling Ellis. "You know what Louie Johnson said yesterday?" she said. "That youth is overrated."

Ellis's eyebrows shot up. "Really? Well, in some ways he's probably right."

"He also said, 'Christmas music opens the chambers of a person's heart reserved for the very best of themselves, coaxing out all their goodness.' Isn't that funny? The way he talks, I mean. He's, like, totally poetic and good with words."

The week before, Charlene had quit her job without bothering to give notice, so Ben had told Hadley she could work as many hours as she wanted; that he could use the extra help until he hired another aide. Since then, Hadley had shown up at the nursing home every day after school and yet still managed to get her homework done. Ellis had noticed a growing self-confidence and a fresh sense of purpose in Hadley. Twice she'd given Oliver a hand with laundry. She'd started an impromptu game of canasta in the dayroom when she'd noticed everyone looking bored, and she'd offered to watch Louie dance outside so Ellis could deal with the other residents Ben had temporarily assigned to her.

"Know what else Louie said?" Hadley said, rubbing her chin against the seatbelt.

"What's that?" Ellis said.

"He told me he has no time for pretentious people who believe they are better than others, that when he was the janitor at the high school he once caught the mayor's son peeing on a teacher's car and he made him walk up and down the parking lot for an hour after school wearing a placard that said, 'I will not urinate in public.'

"The principal backed Louie up but the mayor, like, totally freaked out. He demanded an apology from Louie, but Louie refused. He said he would go before the school board if necessary, that if he had urinated on a teacher's car, no one would make an exception for him; that if you're gonna disrespect someone, no matter who you are, then you'd better be willing to live with the consequences."

Ellis's gaze stayed fixed on the road. She caught herself thinking how her dad once used his money and power and position to bend the rules for Donnie, even though it hadn't done Donnie any favors. Back then Dennis had been the kind of man Louie had described to Hadley—pretentious. Ellis just hadn't seen it until now.

And unhappy, she thought. *Unfulfilled and deeply unhappy.*

If she were honest with herself, she'd have to admit that she'd sensed problems between her parents without understanding what they were; had known deep inside that her dad wasn't content. In her mind, over the years, he had remained the same, and yet now that he was back, Ellis could see that he was vastly changed. From what she had observed, it seemed he'd traded all the pomp of his old life for one that put him on an equal footing with the rest of society. For twenty years, he'd lived a whole other life without her and her mom, and now he was quiet and reflective, someone she hardly recognized.

"Cool story, huh?" Hadley said.

"Yes," Ellis said, pulling herself back to their conversation.

"That must have been hard for Louie," Hadley said. "I mean, standing up to the mayor like that, especially because he was black *and* a janitor."

Ellis slipped on sunglasses to shade her eyes from the setting sun. "Whether you're black or white has always been a cosmetic issue to him—as it should be—and what you do for a living is completely irrelevant when it comes down to right or wrong. Louie measures a person's character based on how they treat others. He can be a bit eccentric, but his personal standards are high."

"As they should be," Hadley said, parroting her.

Ellis smiled. "Right."

She pulled in to the health clinic's parking lot. Then briefly, lightly, she passed her hand over Hadley's hair, mussing it up. Ducking away, Hadley fished inside her knapsack and grabbed her daisy-covered journal. Flipping it open, she pulled out a picture and held it up between them. "Look at this," she said. "Anissa took a shot of me and Louie last week. Her dad gave her this old thirty-five millimeter and now she won't stop snapping pictures."

Ellis took the photo from Hadley and went very still.

There was her daughter standing next to Louie, and there was Louie holding his hat to his chest, a definite twinkle in his eye, wearing a green shirt with a pink tie. One heartbeat passed, then two and three as Ellis stared at them, a lump in her throat. Hadley had one foot behind the other, and she was laughing, but the camera had also caught a flash of awkward unease on her face: a young girl who both liked and felt slightly uncomfortable around this old guy—a man whose modest heroism had made it possible for her to be here today.

For a few seconds, Ellis couldn't speak. Her life as Hadley's mom was rich and full and complicated. Whether arguing with her about the way she dressed—"Oh, fine," Ellis would say, waving one hand. "Go then or you'll be late for school"—or sneaking into her room late at night to check on her, the way she used to when she was a baby, Hadley's mouth working around unspoken words the way it still did now and then when she was dreaming, Ellis was filled with pleasure.

It suddenly seemed right that Hadley and Louie had finally met and were sharing the beginnings of what Hadley must consider an inexplicable connection. All unknowing, Louie had given her the gift of life, and now Hadley was giving back the gift of her youthful, exuberant company.

Hadley tucked the photo back into her journal. "Did I tell you Louie's gonna help me with my nature exhibit for the year-end school fair?"

"He is?" Ellis said, unsnapping her seatbelt.

Hadley nodded. "I've decided to do bald eagles. He said he knows a ton about them."

"Yes," Ellis said with a grin. "That he does."

The conference room where Roma held their weekly sessions was a riot of food and color. Gregory was setting colored napkins around the table. Plates of finger sandwiches and dainties were spread from one end to the other—shortbread cookies, cupcakes decorated with M&M candy bits, chocolate truffles sprinkled with coconut.

"When I'm upset I bake," he said to Ellis and Hadley by way of explanation. "And since tonight is my last night, I thought I'd share with everyone."

"Why is it your last night?" Hadley asked, tasting a truffle.

He took off his jacket, folded it, and held it in front of him. "Well," he said, heaving a sigh, "since I don't have a job anymore, I've decided it's time to leave. Nathan would've hated seeing me this miserable."

"Where are you going?" Hadley asked.

He shrugged. "I'm not sure yet. At first I considered moving to New York so I could test out a big city, but I gave it some thought and realized I'm not a New York kind of guy. I grew up in a small town in North Dakota—a lot smaller than Great Falls—and I always felt safe there. I liked that I knew the name of the butcher and that the town dentist coached soccer and I could always count on the principal to put one of those orange vests on at the end of each day to direct school buses through the parking lot." He scrunched up his nose. "I'd be miserable in New York."

Ellis stared at him, listening as a difficult truth of her own struggled to surface.

When she'd moved to Dallas years ago, everything had been so radically different from Barrow. The huge, looming buildings, the fancy cars, the expensive houses. There were no mountains or narrow country roads snaking over wooden bridges. People moved fast and with a purpose. As she walked around downtown, it seemed that everyone was carrying ticking bombs in their pockets, they all moved in such a hurry. It was exciting and stimulating, and exactly the sort of place you could lose yourself in without any trouble at all, but what she'd failed to realize was that you couldn't run away from your past; it followed you. The same gnawing anxieties that had crawled across her skin in Barrow whenever a strange man said hello or approached her to ask directions or, worse yet, walked up behind her and touched her arm to get her attention showed up full force when she moved to Dallas.

Roma clapped her hands to get everyone's attention. "All right, let's do some journal work," she said. "Last week I asked you to think about the relationship you shared with the loved one you lost and to jot down a few things about yourself that your loved one didn't know. Habits, dreams, fears. Anything like that. Did everyone manage to write a few paragraphs?"

Hadley raised her hand. "I did," she said, scootching forward on her chair.

"You did?" Ellis said, taken aback.

"Well, yeah," Hadley said, scrunching up her face. "It was assigned, Mom."

The man sitting across from Ellis smiled and ducked his head. Maybe he was thinking what she was: how cute it was that Hadley had taken Roma's instructions to heart, as though this were a class.

"Please, go ahead," Roma said, lighting up. "Read to us."

"All of it?" Hadley asked.

"Whatever you feel comfortable sharing."

Ellis sat very still, almost holding her breath as she listened to her daughter read out her innermost thoughts to this roomful of strangers.

"Things my dad didn't know," Hadley began, speaking so softly at first that Ellis almost couldn't hear. "My dad and I were really close, but I was glad he and Mom never had other kids 'cause I wouldn't have wanted to share him with anyone other than my mom. I never told him that."

A shiver climbed Ellis's spine as she recalled a conversation she'd had with Mark when Hadley was six or seven. They'd been out to dinner, the three of them, and as they walked to the car, Hadley ran ahead, playing with a yo-yo. Ellis glanced up at Mark and saw a look of such adoration on his face that she impulsively asked if he wanted another child. "Not really," he said, surprising her, and when she asked why not, he said, "Because I wouldn't want to share Hadley with anyone else. I like that it's just you and me and her."

Hadley paused to scratch her nose. "My dad also used to think that he could make, like, this world-class chili, but it actually sucked and I never had the guts to tell him how much I hated it."

Ellis smiled. Somehow she'd known this was true, had sensed it whenever she'd watched Hadley eating Mark's chili. She was suddenly aware of her lower back pinching, but she couldn't bring herself to move, not even an inch, while Hadley was reading. Instead, she focused on a tear in the wallpaper behind Roma's head.

"My dad didn't know that caterpillars freak me out, or that I actually like wearing skirts, and we *never* talked about guys." She looked up at Roma and paused for a moment. "Oh, and he also didn't know I was afraid of heights," she added.

Ellis stared at her, stunned. "You're scared of heights?"

Hadley nodded. "Big-time."

"But, Hadley, you went bungee jumping with your dad," Ellis said. "You went rock climbing. God, you even jumped out of a plane last year when he took you parachuting. How can you be afraid of heights?"

"I didn't want him to think I was a wimp," she whispered.

Ellis stared at her, transfixed. "You never told me," she said.

"I'm telling you now."

Roma's eyes fell shut for a moment as though she were pondering this disconnect in their relationship. "Actually, this is healthy and typical, and exactly what I was hoping you'd come up with," she said, praising Hadley. "Good work. Wonderful, really. The whole point of this exercise is to show you that you are an individual, and although your relationship with your loved one may have enhanced your life, it didn't completely define it. You are, and will continue to be, okay on your own now that this person is gone."

Hadley squared her shoulders and sat back in her chair. Ellis could almost sense her thinking, *Could someone please pass me the grief group gold star?*

"Would anyone else like to read their thoughts?" Roma asked, clasping her hands together with fresh enthusiasm.

As she looked around the table, Ellis felt herself sink in her chair. She hadn't written one word, hadn't had time all week, especially now that Charlene had quit and she'd taken on extra shifts to help out.

An elderly woman with cottony hair pulled out her spiral notebook. She began reading, haltingly at first and then with a quiet pride, telling everyone how, for fifty-two years, she had tucked money away in coffee cans she kept buried in her garden. Her husband would give her grocery money every two weeks, and each time she would put a little aside and stash it away, never telling him. She explained that she hated being dependent on him, that she felt better—safer somehow—knowing she had money if she ever needed it; that doing so had kept her marriage truer, that she didn't stay married all those years because she had to, but because she'd wanted to.

"Wow," Hadley said, impressed. "That's a lot of coffee cans."

Ellis's thoughts kept slipping back to what Hadley had said earlier. Illogical though she knew it was, she felt a sudden compulsion to know everything about her daughter. Studying Hadley's profile, Ellis remembered her as she'd been in the weeks following Mark's death: withdrawn, broken, and angry. Where had that girl gone? This one was focused and determined and brimming with life, wiping icing off her hands as she methodically tasted each of Gregory's treats.

At the end of the session, Gregory went around the room saying good-bye. "Thank you for everything," he said, giving Roma a warm hug. "Take care of yourself," he told one elderly woman, helping her on with her coat. "Keep up the good work, kiddo," he said to Hadley, chucking her lightly under the chin.

Watching him, Ellis's heart caught. He seemed like such a genuinely caring man.

"I hope you like wherever you decide to move," Hadley said.

"I'm sure I will," Gregory replied.

An idea blossomed as Ellis watched him move around the room, cleaning up. Gregory needed a job and a fresh start. *Why not Barrow? Why not Pleasant View Manor? Ben would love him. He's empathetic and thoughtful and sensitive.*

Hadley pulled on her jacket. "Mom?"

"Uh-huh," Ellis said, distracted.

"Know what else Louie said yesterday?"

"No, what?"

"He said what goes around comes around, that you get back what you put out in your life. And he believes in fate. That we're in each other's lives exactly when we need each other the most and there's no such thing as coincidence."

Ellis gave Hadley her full, startled attention.

"Do you believe that?" Hadley asked.

Across the room, Gregory lifted a hand. "Don't leave yet, ladies," he called out. "I have a care package of sweets for you to take home."

"Yes," Ellis said, curling her arm around Hadley's shoulders. "I think I do."

Eighteen

Ellis moved through the summer of her rape on autopilot. She ate, she slept, she worked as many hours as she could at the Hillside Motel, but for the most part, that time in her life would remain a blur. At first, the full-on hate she felt for the man who'd assaulted her often left her trembling with her head in her hands. She was sore for days afterward, horrified by the delicate purple bruises that appeared everywhere—across her back, on the underside of her arms, even on her collarbone. She dreaded getting undressed and could not look at herself naked, preferring to stay covered in long-sleeved shirts and overly large sweatshirts, hiding under her clothes. She bathed two, sometimes three times a day, until she finally faced an undeniable truth: no amount of soap and water would ever wipe away what she'd endured.

Thank God, school had let out the day before the graduation party, so for two months she could stay under the radar. She was consumed with thoughts of Mark, who'd been calling every two weeks, and guilt over what had happened. She had no appetite and was tired all the time. All she wanted to do was sleep.

One morning in late August, as she slept in, her mom stuck her head inside her room. "Ellis?" Her voice was soft, afraid even. Usually her mom stayed hidden behind her bedroom door and Ellis would slip inside to say good-bye before leaving for her summer job at the motel.

"Yes?" she said, sitting up.

"Are you okay?"

Ellis tried to think of what she could tell her, some story that would explain why she was so tired, quiet, and withdrawn—a fabrication that would protect her mom from ever having to know what had happened to her. She was on the other side of something she didn't understand herself. How could she dump this on her fragile mother? As she looked up at Paulina's pale, drawn face staring back at her, Ellis felt a quaver in her throat and she had to fight the sudden urge to yell at her. *Why aren't you more vibrant? Why don't you take better care of me?*

"I think I have a touch of the flu," she said, dropping her gaze.

Paulina moved closer to the bed, bringing a hand to her chest. "Do you want me to call in sick for you?" She was trying to get Ellis to look at her, really look at her.

"No," Ellis said, thinking of Mrs. Ferguson, her elderly boss, who had no one else to help out at the motel. Her husband was in the hospital, having just had an operation, and if Ellis called in sick it would turn Mrs. Ferguson's day upside down. "I'll get going."

It was quiet at work that day and the vague nausea Ellis had felt when she first woke up soon got worse. By late afternoon, it still hadn't subsided. She slid down onto the floor next to the front desk and sat with her back against the wall, leaning her cheek against the cool cinder block, counting down the hours until she could go home to bed.

When it finally hit her, her eyes flew open. *When was my last period?*

A tremor of fear went through her.

Oh, no. Please, no . . .

After Mrs. Ferguson returned from the hospital, Ellis pulled on her bulky cable-knit sweater and counted the money in her wallet. Then she walked down to the drugstore and bought a magazine and two packages of sanitary napkins, hiding a home pregnancy test underneath them in her basket, flushing when the woman at the till, whom she thankfully didn't know, gave her a pinched look of disapproval.

When she got home, she locked herself in the bathroom and sat on the edge of the tub to read the instructions. Her hands were shaking so badly, she had to put the box down and take a few deep breaths. Maybe her system was messed up from the emotional trauma she'd suffered. Maybe that was what was wrong.

After carefully holding the dipstick in her urine stream, she set it on the edge of the sink and slid down to the floor to wait. Two minutes passed. Then three, then four. The directions said to wait five minutes, and if the window on the dipstick had changed from white to pink, she was pregnant; if it remained white, she wasn't.

"Please, God," she whispered, her chin wobbling. "Don't do this to me."

Pushing to her feet, she turned the dipstick over and blanched. It was Pepto-Bismol pink.

Dropping it into the box, she grabbed on to the sink with both hands. "No, no, no! This isn't fair." She closed her eyes. She felt switches being thrown, gears shifting as a piece of her fell away. It made her sick, the way these awful things kept happening to her, the way she was becoming a victim of her own life.

Over the days that followed, her mind shut down even as she tried to gather her energy. The implications of this pregnancy were overwhelming, and Ellis slipped into a dark depression unlike any she had experienced in her young life. If not telling her mom about the rape had been an obvious choice, then this new development made her pull away further from everyone around her. She didn't want to share her news with anyone, could not imagine sharing it. Since there was no one who could help her, she would have to handle it herself.

Being pregnant terrified her. Her breasts became swollen and tender, her exhaustion intensified. She considered an abortion, but quickly realized she could never go through with it. Even if this baby wasn't Mark's, half of this child came from her. Until then, she'd believed that by not telling anyone about the rape she could contain what had happened to her, maybe even obliterate it, but now it couldn't be ignored.

For a while, though, denial worked well.

Ellis began disassociating herself from the idea that she was carrying a child. Then, in early September, a week after school started up again, she went outside one night to sit on the back steps after her mom was asleep and burst into tears. The night had an end-of-summer feel to it, a sharp breeze blowing through the trees. Kicking off her shoes, Ellis walked across the grass barefoot and lay down, staring up at the inky black sky.

She was tired of trying to look and act normal when she was in the middle of the worst possible nightmare. Swallowing tears, she reached into her pocket and pulled out her silver compass, reading the inscription on the back: *You're braver than you believe, and stronger than you seem, and smarter than you think.*

Not really, Ellis thought. *Being brave is about standing up to what scares you, and that's not what I want to do right now. Being strong means that you don't run away from your problems, and that's exactly what I want to do. And if I were smart, I guess I wouldn't be where I am right now, would I?*

Over the next month, Ellis had trouble concentrating at school. Her mind wandered, she lost track of what assignments were due when, and her marks began to slide as they never had before. One afternoon during science class she listened in on a conversation between two girls sitting across from her. They were drawing on the back of their jean jackets with Magic Markers, complaining about their curfews, when one said, "I'll let you in on a little secret. Being a parent isn't so hard."

Ellis couldn't help herself. "Really?" she said. "I think it is."

The shorter one glared at her. "Who asked you?"

"Yeah?" the other one echoed.

Until then, Ellis hadn't understood that the possibility of repeating her parents' failures was one of her worst fears, which made being pregnant that much more terrifying. She suddenly felt hollow and washed out. She had a beaker in one hand and a list of the organs that made up a frog in the other. They were supposed to be dissecting one in a few minutes and their teacher had asked them to get ready.

"I didn't mean—I just wanted to say—" She stopped and stared at her feet for a moment, took a deep breath. "I don't think being a parent looks easy, that's all," she said. "At least not from what I've seen."

Both girls stared at her with blank expressions, then they walked away. Before they were across the room, they erupted in laughter.

Ellis set her beaker down, trembling from embarrassment. Why had she said anything? And if this was what it was like now, how would it be when she started to show? Then it wouldn't be the usual problem of bullies throwing garbage at her while she gave them the finger all heroically. It would be about public humiliation—whispers, finger-pointing, speculative gossip—and the thought of it, the inevitability of it, made her want to curl inward. She *liked* being invisible, and soon she wouldn't be. Soon she was going to be the talk of the town.

Her thoughts took her in never-ending circles where there were no easy answers. When she had the baby, she could keep it or give it up for adoption. If she kept it, she would need to know who the father was: Mark or the man who had assaulted her. Either way, she'd have to tell Mark soon, especially if he returned to Barrow as he'd promised. But if the baby was Mark's, would he think she was trying to trap him into marriage? And if the father was the man who'd assaulted her, what then?

Such emotional issues didn't even begin to touch the list of more practical problems. Would her part-time job at the motel pay enough to buy diapers, clothes, food? How much did day care cost? Would she be able to finish high school or would she have to opt for correspondence classes and a GED? Worse yet, would this baby and all of the responsibility that came with it destroy her mom's fragile world?

Each night Ellis wrote in the Sasquatch journal her mom had given her, trying to make sense of her thoughts by writing them down. The cover was decorated with lifelike drawings of Sasquatches that Ellis loved running her fingers over. Years ago, her mom had found a specialty company in New Jersey that sold all kinds of Sasquatch paraphernalia, and since then it had become her fallback for gifts, starting with a life-size cardboard cutout of a Sasquatch Paulina had bought for Ellis the year she'd turned thirteen.

It became exhausting writing everything down. It was easier for Ellis to close her eyes and wish herself away, returning to the inner safety of the hardened shell she had developed. As the weeks went by, the one conclusion she kept coming back to time and time again was that this Pandora's box must stay closed.

Late that summer Paulina's doctor switched her medication and Ellis's mother experienced a series of physical and mental adjustments, including nausea and increased lethargy. She became worse than she'd been before, more distant and sad. One afternoon when Ellis got home from school, her mom was on her way upstairs to her room, looking pale and drawn.

"Did you make dinner?" Ellis asked.

Paulina waved a hand as if to say she'd tried her best. On the counter was a half-thawed loaf of bread she'd taken out of the freezer, peanut butter, and a mason jar of strawberry jam.

Ellis had watched other kids with envy, knowing most of them had the privilege of looking at themselves through at least one parent's loving eyes, whereas she could only see herself through her own eyes, and these days she could barely stand to look. Young as she was, she had already learned that relationships were vulnerable and that you'd better be prepared to get hurt before you gave one hundred percent of your heart to anyone.

The week before Ellis decided to jump off the town bridge, she tried to get out of participating in gym class, claiming that she had a stomachache, but the teacher would have nothing of it and insisted that she change and join them outside on the track.

As she ran the required laps, falling far

behind everyone else with a lumpish gait that drew even more attention, she felt her spirits slide. When she was finished, she leaned against the outside cinder-block wall of the school to catch her breath, realizing that her life was moving in slow motion, a headlong and irreversible fall that wasn't going to end well, no matter what choices she made.

That night after dinner, Paulina hugged Ellis longer than usual, and all the words that had gone unsaid between them, words that were now unsayable—accusations, guilts, fears—rose up inside Ellis like a fog.

"Go, Mom," she said, fighting a lump in her throat as she waved at the stairs. "I'll do the dishes. You need your sleep."

Later in her bedroom, Ellis had stood at the window, palms pressed against the glass, staring out at the ridge of trees separating her from the tea-colored river she'd spent so many summers exploring. Because she couldn't swim, the river scared her in many ways, but she also loved the quiet of it, the way dawn came up glassy orange in the distance, the pencil-long shadows from the trees that stretched along its banks.

Dropping onto her bed, she pulled out her journal and wrote "I can't do this anymore" over and over until she suddenly knew what she needed to do to end the relentless and tormenting ache inside her.

After Louie Johnson pulled Ellis out of the river that morning, she sneaked back into the kitchen and was relieved to find her mom still asleep, her suicide note propped against the toaster exactly where she had left it. Tearing it into pieces, Ellis pushed them to the bottom of the garbage, and then took a bath, thinking about everything that had happened, agonizing over how to tell her mom she was pregnant. She'd learned from experience that it was always best to warn her about bad news before breaking it, so that night at dinner, when Paulina asked her to pass the potatoes, Ellis handed her the steaming bowl and plunged in.

"Mom? I need to tell you something, but you aren't going to like it."

Paulina grew wary. "Then don't tell me."

"You sure you don't want to know?"

"No." She shifted in her chair, rearranged the salt and pepper shakers. "Yes. No."

Ellis folded her hands and waited. Paulina got up and started out of the room, then circled back. "Okay. Tell me," she said, gripping the back of a chair for support.

Ellis looked her right in the eye. "I'm pregnant."

A full minute passed before her mom sat down again, and in that brief time, Ellis watched an emotional struggle take place on her mother's face. "But you don't have a boyfriend," she finally said.

Ellis tightened the lid on the pickle jar with unnecessary force. "Not technically, no."

Paulina looked scared, and because of this, Ellis suddenly wasn't. Whatever the outcome, she would not let the man who had assaulted her haunt the rest of her life.

"Everything's going to be fine, Mom. I'm keeping the baby." She said this with authority, trying to recover some of the false confidence she'd worked up earlier. "I'm due in late March, so I figure I can go to school until February and then take correspondence courses to finish out the year."

"Okay," Paulina said, her voice expressionless. "It will all work out." And Ellis, relieved not to be entirely on her own any longer, half believed her.

Ellis was known for her secrecy, the sort of girl who had hugged her books against her chest even when she wasn't pregnant, so as her pregnancy became obvious, gossip whipped through the high school. *Ellis Williams is pregnant! Ellis, who doesn't have a boyfriend. Ellis, who is straight-down-the-middle average, other than all that long red hair.*

Ignoring the whispers, Ellis worked hard to stay focused, but now and then her thoughts wandered, and when they did, she would doodle Sasquatches on all her notebooks, staring at the bent heads of her classmates, wondering how many of them would have kids, how many would see their dreams come true, how many would be happy.

A month after Ellis broke the news to her mom, a reinvigorated Paulina presented Ellis with a full-length winter coat she'd bought for her at the Salvation Army thrift store. It was beige and quiltlike, with pillowy squares from top to bottom, and Ellis cringed whenever she put it on. Each morning, she would trudge up the hill to the high school, and at the end of the day she would carefully *clomp, clomp, clomp* along the sidewalk as she made her way back down again, keeping an eye out for icy spots. Kids she knew would wave as their buses went by, and she would wave back, feeling like a poster-girl for Charmin toilet paper.

Her mom also bought her a box of secondhand maternity clothes: jeans with wide swatches of elastic built in to accommodate her ever-expanding stomach; a gauzy blouse with ladybugs splashed across the front; an empire-waist shirt that fell to mid-thigh; an extra-large bottle-green cable-knit sweater. At first, there were mean-spirited snickers and kids at school stared when they thought she wasn't looking. Then one morning on her way out of the auditorium after an assembly, she heard someone behind her whisper, "If she keeps this baby, it's going to ruin her life."

Ellis turned around to face them, narrowing her eyes. "Pardon me?"

The students behind her skidded to a stop. Startled, one guy raised both hands, as if to say, *It wasn't me.* Heart pounding, Ellis met each of their gazes before finally stepping to one side and letting everyone pass.

Her English teacher, Mrs. Olson, took her hand and gave it a squeeze, as though declaring war against all of this stupidity. "Ignore them," she whispered. "You're going to be fine."

How do you know for sure? Ellis wanted to whisper back.

For the most part, the teachers and administrative staff were kinder and less judgmental than her fellow students. Mr. Tannas, the drama teacher, brought in an armchair from home and insisted Ellis sit in it as she grew bigger and less comfortable. Mrs. Fedoretz, the school administrator, often gave her an apple or cookie midway through each day. And Joan Martyniuk, the school's part-time nurse, went out of her way to check on Ellis.

Ellis's pregnancy kept the neighbors talking, too.

Most days when she got home from school that winter her mom was working at Bianca's Café, where she'd taken a job not long after Ellis told her she was pregnant.

Ellis would carefully make her way down the sidewalk and Mrs. Dixon, who was almost as wide as she was tall, would step outside and wave, trying to get her attention. At first, Ellis was polite. She'd wave back and Mrs. Dixon would hurry across the street and pepper her with questions that grew increasingly personal. When this behavior continued week after week, Ellis stopped being well-mannered. Ignoring Mrs. Dixon, she began ducking inside the house, locking the door, and pulling the curtains.

The reedy chime of the doorbell would follow. "Ellis?" Mrs. Dixon would call out in a singsong voice. "Are you all right?"

I'm fine, she thought, kneading her lower back.

"Would you like some hot chocolate?"

No, Ellis thought, lowering herself onto the couch.

"Is there anything I can do for you, dear?"

Yes. Go away and leave me alone. Go boss that poor husband of yours who's always washing your windows or vacuuming your car or hauling in all those groceries you eat. I've had as much as I can take today.

There would be a brief pause, and then Mrs. Dixon would start up all over again, rattling the knob. "Ellis, it's not good to lock yourself away from everyone like this. You need to talk and get your feelings out. . . ."

Ellis imagined Mr. Dixon, an Albert Einstein look-alike, standing in his driveway, legs spread for balance as he squeezed the throttle on his snow blower, blasting his wife with ice and snow as she walked up their sidewalk on her way home; taking aim at the Velcro curlers in her hair, at the fuzzy pink jacket she insisted on wearing in public, at her Sorel winter boots; refusing to stop until she had toppled onto her back like a turtle and begged for mercy.

No, Ellis thought. *What I* need *is a big red ejection button like they have in cartoons, the kind the Road Runner uses to shoot Wile E. Coyote into space like a rocket when he won't leave him alone.*

One night that winter, Ellis's mom knocked on her bedroom door and came in smiling. The conversation that followed confirmed what Ellis had suspected for a while, that Paulina was secretly delighted with this new development in their lives. It was as though she'd been given a chance to redeem herself with Ellis's baby, an opportunity to right all of the wrongs she'd made raising her own daughter.

"Have you picked out any names yet?" she asked shyly.

Her mom had always been fascinated with names, saying things like, "Geraldo doesn't suit him, does it?" or "Isn't Marcene an adorable name?" Where Ellis's name came from was one of her favorite stories, something her mom had typed out from a history book long ago and glued inside her baby album, so she'd never forget:

> **From 1892 to 1954, approximately twelve million steamship passengers entered the U.S. through the Port of New York at Ellis Island, just minutes off the southern tip of Manhattan Island. They came from all over the world in their search of freedom of speech and religion and economic opportunity, and then, after their arrival, they anxiously waited for legal and medical processing before entering the country.**

"Twelve million people. Can you imagine?" Paulina used to say. "It says here nearly half of all Americans today can trace their family history to at least one person who passed through Ellis Island. Your great-grandmother came through in 1907. She was alone, having been widowed the year before, and had been waiting to be processed for six days when she gave birth to her son in the main building at Ellis Island. Days later, she died from complications, leaving him an orphan, although he was eventually adopted and raised in Montana.

"My father was seventy when you were born," she went on. "And the moment he saw you he said you weren't a Mary, or a Jean, or even an Annabelle. You were Ellis, plain as the nose on his face."

Ellis hadn't put much thought into naming her own baby.

"I jotted two down for you," Paulina said, setting a slip of paper on the bed.

Ellis leaned over and read: *Marcus for a boy and Hadley for a girl.*

"I've always thought Marcus would be such a good, solid name for a boy," Paulina said. "And, of course, Hadley was the name of Ernest Hemingway's first wife, whom he once said was 'the best and truest and loveliest person I have ever known.'"

Paulina bent over and kissed Ellis on the forehead. A tentative smile split Ellis's face. She took in her mom's new haircut, curled in soft layers around her face, at her hands hugging her elbows like a child. She thought about all the other mothers she knew: women who stood with their hands on their hips, barking orders to their kids; women who ran their homes with the precision of world-class jugglers; confident women who cuddled, nurtured, instructed, and loved their children as though they had been born to the role. Her mom wasn't like those women, but in that moment, Ellis wouldn't have traded her for anyone else in the world.

When Ellis was six months pregnant, Mark showed up in Barrow to surprise her. He had been phoning once or twice a month, and yet she still hadn't worked up the courage to tell him about the baby. She'd been spending most of her free time reading in the town library in an attempt to recover emotionally (*Your Journey Back from Rape*; *Sexual Assault: Will I Ever Feel*

Okay Again?; *Surviving Rape*). According to everything she had read, healing could only begin after you had forgiven yourself, after you accepted that it wasn't your fault.

Mark had called on Christmas Eve and she'd talked to him briefly, begging off after a few minutes, telling him they had company and were in the middle of dinner. So much had happened since he'd left. What she'd been through had changed her and she was no longer sure about anything. Did he still believe they would get together after she'd graduated, or was that simply wishful thinking on both their parts? Worse yet, how was he going to feel when he learned she was pregnant? She'd been steeling herself to tell him the truth, knowing full well that she'd probably lose him the moment she did.

"Was that him again?" her mom asked when she'd hung up. Ellis had finally admitted that he was the guy she'd been dating the summer before, so her mom assumed he was the father of her child.

"Yes," Ellis said. "It was."

The doorbell rang on New Year's Eve just after lunch. Paulina was working until four that afternoon, and Ellis had curled up on the couch with a blanket and fallen asleep. Startled awake, she pushed to her feet and waddled over to answer the door. She stood on tiptoe to look through the high window and there was Mark, holding a bouquet of tiger lilies. *What was he doing here?*

She rested her forehead against the wood. Then, smoothing down her hair, she unlocked the dead bolt and pulled the door open wide.

"I know, I know," he said, bursting into a grin when he saw her. "When I left I told you I'd try to fly out in January or February and this is a little early. . . ."

His voice trailed away and his words hung between them. Shocked into silence, he took a quick step back, looking her over from top to bottom. "What's going on?" he asked.

Ellis dropped her gaze, unable to look at him. She pulled her sweater tight over her big belly. When she looked up, he'd gone pale. "I've been meaning to tell you," she said.

"Really?" he said. He seemed dazed, his face paralyzed with disbelief.

"Yes," she said. "I just didn't know . . . I wasn't sure how to say it."

He gave her a long look. "You could have tried, 'I'm pregnant, Mark. We're having a baby.' I'm pretty sure I would've understood that loud and clear."

Ellis's stomach fell. He assumed he was the father, hadn't even questioned it.

"It's not actually that simple," she said, the last word squeaking out.

"Looks pretty straightforward to me."

Ellis's feelings were jumbled, but her relief at seeing him in Barrow was so huge that she started to cry. "Oh, Mark. It was awful," she sobbed. "You have no idea."

He frowned, caught between anger and frustration. He didn't seem to know what she meant; he hesitated before responding. "What was awful? Not telling me?"

She waved him inside and sat down on the couch, clutching herself with folded arms. Mark shut the door and took up a position across from her in an armchair, setting the flowers on the coffee table between them.

Ellis told him everything, starting from the beginning, when she and Ward arrived at the party. At first while she talked, Mark listened. It was the hardest thing Ellis had ever done, telling him what happened later on that deserted service road, living it all over again so he would understand what she was dealing with—that it had happened only one week after he'd left and now she wasn't sure who the father of her baby was.

Mark's mouth opened and closed a couple of times, then tears began running down his cheeks. He got up and crossed the room, taking her gently in his arms. It was the first time Ellis had been touched by a man since the rape, and for a few seconds she stiffened, unable to hug him back.

"Did you call the police?" he asked.

"No. I was so ashamed. I wanted to put it behind me."

"You never told your mom?"

"I just . . . I couldn't."

He had never met Paulina. How could Ellis explain what her mom had been like for years? She was either wrapped in depression or suffering mild to extreme panic attacks that left her with her head between her knees, rubbing her breastbone to soothe her pounding heart. Her mom's problems had dominated their lives, and as she'd gotten worse, Ellis had compensated by becoming the caretaker in their relationship. Only now that Ellis was pregnant had her mom begun to come out of her shell, getting a job and growing stronger and more vibrant with each passing day.

"God, Ellis, I'm sorry."

She suddenly felt like a bird trapped in a cage.

There, she wanted to say. *I told you. Now go and leave me alone, okay? I can't stand to look in your eyes and see you judging me, wondering how soon you can get out of here. I can't deal with your pain and confusion. I'm having enough trouble with my own.*

He rested his forehead on top of her head. "You're seeing a doctor?"

"A gynecologist," she said.

Pause. "Did they give you a due date?"

"Yes," she said. "The end of March."

He sat back, brushed a stray strand of hair off her face. "It'll be okay."

Ellis wiped her nose with the back of her hand. His presence was a comfort, and although part of her prayed he wouldn't leave, another was braced for it. She stood and took the flowers into the kitchen, busying herself with putting them in water.

"Thank you for the flowers," she said, hearing him come into the room behind her.

"You're welcome."

For a few moments, she stood at the sink with her back to him. Then she carried the vase over to the table and set it down. After she slid into a chair and pushed it back to make room for her belly, he did, too, sitting across from her.

Deciding it was time, she lifted her gaze and stared straight into his eyes. "This changes everything, doesn't it?" she said.

What could he say? Of course it did. She watched for him to pull away from her, for his posture to grow more erect and uncomfortable, but he did neither. This problem had stormed into both of their lives uninvited, and yet Mark reached one hand across the table and gently covered hers.

"Not for me," he said.

Ellis swallowed, trying not to cry. How she had hated hiding what had happened, the hush-hush of that horrible night bouncing around inside of her and pressing up against her heart until it had hardened and shriveled with each passing month, even as her stomach had grown bigger.

"It'll be okay," Mark assured her. "We'll figure it out."

Really? she thought, desperate in her need to believe.

He sat back and spread his hands on the kitchen table, as if he were flattening a newspaper. "I'll be with you all the way through this," he said. "Whatever you need."

Ellis stared at him, dumbfounded. At that moment, he seemed strong and mature and dependable, although inside he must have been as scared as she was. Still, all of her old feelings came tearing back. Her insides turned to liquid and she felt her chin tremble with the effort it took not to cry all over again.

"Don't make promises you can't keep," she warned.

"Never," he said, running the back of one hand down her cheek.

For the next three months, until Ellis gave birth to Hadley at the end of March, Mark flew from Dallas every second weekend, spending three days with Ellis and her mom. Paulina was immediately won over, as entranced by him as Ellis was and thrilled to have him in the picture now that Ellis's due date was rapidly approaching.

In the end, he missed the delivery, arriving an hour after Hadley was born, but Ellis would never forget the look on his face when he came through the door.

The nurse had swaddled Hadley in a receiving blanket and Paulina was cradling her in a rocking chair next to the window. Ellis watched, light-headed and overwhelmed, a deep sense of responsibility flooding through her.

Mark slipped inside the room. He looked serious but charged with nervous excitement. “Everything okay?” he asked.

“We’re both fine,” Ellis said, reaching out one finger, halfway across the bed.

Mark touched it with one of his own, then gently leaned over, took her face in his hands, and kissed her.

“Come hold your daughter,” Paulina said.

“My daughter?” he said. “We have a girl?”

In his eyes, wonder and amazement opened the floodgates of Ellis’s heart, and for one shimmering moment she let herself believe it to be true and irrefutable: Mark was this baby’s father, no doubt about it.

"Yes, you have a daughter," Paulina said. "And she's a beauty."

The next day, Mark arrived with flowers. He wouldn't put Hadley down and he kept asking all kinds of questions, marveling in her fingers and toes, the tiny arc of her eyebrows. Beaming the day they brought Hadley home, he hung a banner across Paulina's living room window that read *It's a Girl.* He walked up and down the street handing out pink cigars to Louie Johnson, Mr. and Mrs. Dixon, even the postman.

When Hadley was a month old, Mark made arrangements to have Paulina babysit for a weekend and he took Ellis to a tiny lodge tucked away in the wilderness north of Kalispell. They stayed two nights, and on the second morning they hiked to the foot of a waterfall that curled over an outcrop of rocks thirty feet above them. Rockets of spray dampened the air as Mark turned to Ellis, took her hands in his, and said, "Marry me."

She looked at him, then across the rocks to the waterfall. Silence pulsed between them.

In many ways, she had dreamed of this moment. Watching Mark with Hadley filled her with uncomplicated joy. He fed her and changed her diaper and took her for long walks in her stroller, the adoration in his eyes unmistakable.

Taking Ellis by the shoulders, Mark turned her gently to face him. "It doesn't matter," he said, cupping his hands around her face. "It never will, Ellis. I love her. She's my daughter and I won't ever let anyone take her away from me." He opened his arms and Ellis grabbed him in a powerful, wordless hug.

That was when the true healing began.

She said yes, and they were married two months later. They rented a two-bedroom apartment in Dallas across the street from the city's light rail transit line. Each time a train went by, their windows rattled and they would have to stop talking for a few seconds until it passed. Over the years, Mark did well, moving into more senior roles with the company, and eventually they bought a two-story house with a big backyard, four bedrooms, and a three-car garage to satisfy his love of sports cars. Mark chose the house, but Ellis didn't care. She wanted whatever he did.

Mark began taking them on weekend

trips. A friend of his owned a ranch east of Dallas and they went there often. Even as a toddler, Hadley loved riding around the ranch standing on the seat of Mark's truck, her arm slung around his neck. And as Ellis watched them, she always felt her heart in her throat, thankful and amazed that she and Mark had found each other and that Hadley had two loving parents.

Nineteen

One Saturday afternoon in mid-May, Anissa's mom took the girls to a movie and Paulina decided to take in a yoga class at the community center. Ellis spent much of her day at work showing Gregory the ropes of his new job as an aide, and although it was rewarding—everyone who'd met him so far, including Ben, adored him—she came home exhausted.

Juggling her purse and two bags of groceries, she walked around the corner of the house and came to a sudden stop. Her dad was standing next to a ladder that was leaning against the garage. An open toolbox was set at his feet and he was stooped over with his hands on his knees, gasping for breath.

Ellis set everything down and ran to him. "What's wrong?"

He looked up, his eyes wide and terrified. "C-can't . . . breathe."

She slid an arm around his waist and tried to prop him up, but the moment she did, his body seemed to collapse and he sank to his knees on the grass. His face was flushed and his forehead beaded with sweat.

"What happened?" Ellis asked. "Did you fall?"

He shook his head and pointed up at the gutter. Ellis lifted a hand to shade her eyes from the late-afternoon sun. The ladder was leaning against the roof, and above it was what looked like a swarm of wasps.

"Nest," he managed.

"Oh, my God! You got stung?" He rubbed the back of his neck, which looked thick with swelling. "Can you walk to the house?" Ellis asked, trying to keep her voice even.

He coughed and wheezed, shaking his head no.

Ellis's mind went unnaturally calm. She ran across the yard. "I'm calling an ambulance," she yelled back over her shoulder, immediately reverting to nurse mode: phone 911, describe the patient's symptoms, request immediate assistance.

"He's having trouble breathing," she explained to the paramedics, who arrived in minutes. By then her dad's face was ashen, his breathing shallow. After examining his neck, one of the attendants unbuttoned her dad's shirt to check his heart rate. Ellis was startled to see freckles beneath the silver tuft of her dad's chest hair, the same dusting of freckles she had on her chest, a reminder of their Irish ancestry. She couldn't remember noticing this detail before, even as a child, and for some reason it suddenly mattered.

"What's his name?"

"Dennis Williams."

"Friend or family member?"

"He's my dad."

"How old is he?" the man asked, slipping an oxygen mask over Dennis's face.

Ellis drew a blank. Her mom was sixty-three and he was five years older, so that made him . . . "Sixty-eight," she confirmed.

"He's having a serious allergic reaction," the paramedic said. He and his partner gently lifted Dennis onto a stretcher. "Any history of heart disease?"

She chewed on her thumbnail. "I don't know."

"Has he ever had a heart attack before?"

Another pause. "I'm not sure."

They lifted the stretcher in one fluid movement and walked to the ambulance, parked behind Ellis's car, its bright light flashing in quick, repetitive revolutions. Ellis followed, stopping at the back steps to grab her purse and car keys.

On the stretcher, her dad pulled at the oxygen mask, yanking it off. "Can my daughter come?" he asked in a thick voice.

"Not in the ambulance," one of the paramedics replied. "But she can follow us." He looked at Ellis for confirmation and she quickly nodded.

"I'll be right behind you."

When Ellis climbed into her car, her hands were shaking, and as she followed the ambulance through town and up the hill to the hospital, she caught herself thinking, *Please, let him be all right.*

Years ago, as a kid, when she had finally realized that her dad wasn't coming back, she'd secretly hoped someone else might fill the void he'd left, that her mom might meet a nice man and remarry. And yet, no matter how much she believed that she had left her dad behind long ago, that her heart had emptied out every speck of him and made room for others, she now understood that he couldn't be erased that easily.

She used to wish he would come pounding through their front door, but now she realized that wishes can wear out—that given enough time, the very thing you may have spent years wishing for no longer mattered; that everything pure and good and sound remained in the wish itself, not in its late and untimely fulfillment. But the terrible thing, the really terrible thing, was that even as Ellis pulled into the hospital parking lot and hurried inside, she still couldn't seem to find the place inside her that was willing to forgive.

"Is he taking any medication?" the admitting nurse asked as the ambulance attendants brought her dad inside on the stretcher.

Ellis blinked at her. "I'm sorry," she said, "I don't know."

For weeks, Gregory had been giving back massages at the end of his shifts to anyone at Pleasant View Manor who wanted one. "I've got nothing else to do," he said, shrugging. "So why not?" Before getting his degree as an X-ray technician, he had been a licensed massage therapist, so with Ben's approval, he'd brought in a portable massage table and set it up in a spare room. At first, he insisted his massages were complimentary, but demand had risen to where residents were now scheduling massages through Hadley, who happily kept track of them in a binder. After a unanimous vote at lunch one day, it was agreed that Gregory would, in future, be paid twenty-five dollars for a half-hour massage and forty for an hour.

"Weekly massages should be mandatory," Louie said, slurping the last of his soup.

"Speak for yourself," Rolly said, shooting him a look of disgust. "I don't need anyone pushing or prodding on my backside."

Ellis glanced at her watch. It was almost

one and Hadley would be here soon to go over her bald eagle school project with Louie. Ellis's dad was dropping her off on his way to an appointment at the clinic. He had recovered from the severe allergic reaction he'd had to what they'd later learned were eight wasp bites across the back of his neck—he'd been trying to remove a nest from the gutter on the garage—but the epinephrine they'd pumped into him had raised the risk of a heart attack, so he'd been hospitalized for two days and put on observation. This afternoon they were running additional tests to see if he was allergic to anything else.

"Louie?" Ellis said. "Could you meet me at the front desk when you're done? Hadley should be here any minute."

"Eh?" Louie frowned up at her.

"For her school project?" Ellis gently reminded him.

After a brief pause, his face lit up. "Oh, yeah. I almost forgot."

Oliver stuck his head inside the doorway. "Ellis, do you know where Ed Notton is? He borrowed a CD from me and I'd like it back."

Ellis glanced around the dining room. Had she seen Ed during lunch? She had stopped by his room earlier for his daily blood pressure check. Impatient, he'd rolled his eyes when she wrapped the cuff around his arm and inflated it, telling her he wished she'd hurry because he had better things to do with his time.

The buzzer for the lobby doors went off long and low, signaling someone's entrance. "Never mind," Oliver said, waving a hand. "I'll go see who's here. I can catch Ed later today."

Ellis followed him, certain Hadley had arrived.

The weather had been so warm that many people were slipping outside to enjoy the fresh air whenever they could. The walkway that led to the main doors also branched off to the left and the right, looping around the outside of the building on both sides before coming together again out back. Years ago, Ben had asked the landscaping company he hired to make the gardens around Pleasant View Manor an inviting, peaceful place, and they had done exactly that. The walkway was lined with countless ornamental bushes, flowers, and shrubs.

Vera-Lee preferred sitting out back, where she had a clear view of the river valley below. Another woman, who'd lost her hair from chemotherapy treatments, slowly shuffled around the building every afternoon, doing laps that seemed to take forever, and yet she enjoyed the exercise. Often, Fran Wilson would tuck her Bible under her arm and head out the front door, sunglasses perched on her nose. "I'm off for a walk through the gardens," she'd say, giving Ellis a brisk nod. And given Joseph's increased dementia, he was no longer allowed outside without an escort.

Nina Ballard had also been making her daily treks to the cedar bench out front. The day before, she'd told Ellis she was going to Niagara Falls, that her husband would be picking her up soon, and she hoped Ellis had a nice week while she was away. Then, like clockwork almost four hours later, Louie Johnson made his way out front, tucked Nina's hand into the crook of his arm, and escorted her back inside.

Ellis ran to hold the door open for them. As usual, Louie was carrying Nina's empty suitcase, covered in stickers from faraway places. A disposable camera dangled from Nina's frail wrist, her face flushed with pleasure as they discussed her trip.

"It really was something," she said, patting Louie's arm.

"You took photos?" Louie asked, nodding at the camera.

Nina stopped and glanced down with a blank look. "Yes," she finally said. "Yes, we did. Roy's always taking pictures, you know that."

"Tell you what," Louie said, guiding her down the hallway. "If you give me that camera, I'll get the pictures developed for you."

"Would you?" she said, giving his arm a squeeze. "Oh, thank you."

By this morning, she had forgotten all about Louie's promise and her trip to Niagara Falls, but it didn't matter because Ellis knew that Louie had already conjured up another trip for her. When he went outside to escort her in this afternoon, he would open her suitcase and pull out a new gem intended for her delight. It might be a handful of postcards from Norway, a Hawaiian lei made from silk flowers, a brochure from the Auckland Zoo in New Zealand. He was always coming up with something new.

Once, Ellis had watched him carefully drape a silk scarf around a sleeping Nina's neck and then, when she'd startled awake, disoriented and slightly confused, he had asked what she'd thought of the Taj Mahal. Was it truly as magnificent as he'd heard? And had Roy bought her that lovely scarf?

Her reaction was uncertain. "Scarf?" Nina repeated.

"Yes," Louie said, fingering the silk with admiration. "It really is beautiful."

Nina stared at it, and then she took it between her paper-thin hands and ever so carefully raised it to her cheek. "Oh, yes," she said. "It is, isn't it?"

The first time Ellis had stumbled across Louie doing this, she'd been curious. Now these daily exchanges moved her so much that she couldn't help herself—every afternoon she went out of her way to slip outside at two o'clock and stand quietly on a walkway hidden from view. Sadly, Nina's Alzheimer's seemed to be getting worse, and it was heartbreaking to watch this sweet woman float through her days in such a vacuous state. But Louie worked hard to give Nina these small gifts for a few brief minutes each day, and Ellis loved watching them from ten feet away, undetected.

By the time Ellis got to the lobby, Hadley was already chatting with Oliver. Leaning against the reception desk was a foam poster board Ellis had bought for Hadley, with two side panels that folded inward against the main section. Hadley had been working on the project for weeks, drawing and coloring pictures of eagles, Googling for data, even gluing on a bald eagle feather for impact.

"Hey, Mom," Hadley said. "Is Louie around?"

Ellis hooked a thumb over her shoulder. "He's just finishing lunch."

Hadley grabbed her poster board and disappeared down the hallway. Ellis decided to check on Nina. On his way out earlier, Ben had taken her a sandwich and a cup of tea. Worried about her sitting outside alone all this time, he'd ordered a thick cushion for the bench back in April, as well as a matching cedar side table for to put her tea on. Now, when Ellis stuck her head outside, Nina looked comfortable and relaxed, if not a little groggy in the warm sunshine.

"I see Ben brought you a cup of tea," she said.

Nina blinked up at her, her hair as fine as mist and her smile tentative. "Ben?" she said. Her eyes were milky, her fingers laced together in her lap in a dignified manner, but the eyebrow pencil she'd applied had been drawn half an inch above her actual eyebrows, giving her a comical look. Even so, for a split second Ellis could almost imagine her as a young woman standing next to her husband in a wedding dress, filled with dreams of one day traveling the world.

Ellis folded her arms across her chest and squinted up into the sun. "What a perfect day," she said, half to herself.

There was a beat of silence. "That's what the other two said."

Ellis frowned. "The other two?"

Nina lifted one of her gnarled hands and waved it vaguely toward the storage shed. "Yes," she said. "Those two."

Ellis went very still, looking from Nina to the storage shed visible behind a row of golden elder bushes. Was she talking about Ed Notton and his mystery lady? Glancing over her shoulder at the main doors, Ellis chewed on her bottom lip. Ben had left for the day, and other than her and

Oliver, there was no one else working until Murphy arrived at two. It really was none of her business, but she was dying to know who was sharing these clandestine meetings.

Just then a rusty pickup truck pulled in to the parking lot and an older man climbed out. He had a silvery gray brush cut and he wore jeans and a flannel jacket. Ellis recognized him right away. It was Hans Holt, Louie's Norwegian friend, the one who brought him a fresh bottle of scotch every few months. She smiled politely and waved at him. He gave her a shy grin and walked around to the passenger side of his truck, where he opened the door and pulled out what looked like a large Plexiglas box.

Ellis narrowed her eyes, trying to determine what it was. As he drew closer she could see a stuffed bald eagle mounted on a stand inside.

"Hello," he said, nodding to her and Nina as he set the eagle down at the far end of the bench so he could adjust his hold on it.

Ellis stared at the bird in amazement, noticing a brass plaque on the front of the encased box that read:

DECLARED THE UNITED STATES OF AMERICA'S NATIONAL EMBLEM IN 1782, THE BALD EAGLE'S RANGE STRETCHES FROM ALASKA TO FLORIDA
(1992 REPLICATED BALD EAGLE — TILLSON'S TAXIDERMY, MISSOULA, MONTANA)

"Think you could get the door for me?" he asked Ellis. "I promised old Louie I'd have this here by noon and I'm running a little late."

"You mean, he had you pick this up for him?"

Hans shrugged. "What's new?" he grumbled. "Louie's always getting me to hunt things down for him." Ellis held the door open as he carried the box inside. Never loosening his grip, he kicked off his boots and walked over to the reception desk. "A few weeks back he got me to hunt down a silk scarf made in India," he said, shaking his head. "Couldn't be made somewhere else either. Oh, no. It had to be India. Like I got time for that, right? Last fall he gave me a fistful of cash and told me to find him a piece of the Berlin Wall."

Ellis was speechless.

"I swear, the man's off his nut half the time," Hans said, smiling. "But we've been friends too long for me to give up on him now."

Hadley came around the corner and slowed to a stop, staring at the bald eagle with her mouth open. For an instant, no one said anything, and then Hans rubbed the palms of his calloused hands against his thighs. "Anyhow," he said, addressing Ellis, "can you let Louie know that I couldn't stay? Tell him I was able to rent it for two weeks, but if we don't get it back on time, there'll be a surcharge on top of the rental fee."

Ellis kept her eyes on Hadley. "Yes," she said softly. "I'll tell him."

The door closed behind him and Hadley turned to the window to hide her tears. "Mom, Louie's looking for you," she said. "He's in the dayroom and he asked me to come get you. Said there's a show on you might want to see."

Ellis ran a finger across the brass plaque. "Pretty amazing, isn't it?"

Hadley didn't speak. The fluorescent lights hummed against the ceiling. From the dayroom Rolly's voice could be heard raised in frustration. "Why would he do something like this?" she finally asked.

Ellis touched her gently on the arm as she walked past to go referee Louie and Rolly. "Because you're a great kid," she said, "and he has a soft spot for you. He also practices what he preaches. 'You get back what you put out,' remember?"

Hadley nodded, dragging her teeth across her bottom lip as she tried to regain her composure.

In the dayroom, Louie was sitting on the couch in front of the TV, clutching the remote control with both hands, a look of stubborn determination on his face. Rolly was rolling back and forth in front of him in his wheelchair, red-faced and flustered.

"It's not your television," he argued, "so why do you get to choose what we watch?"

"I don't mind," Vera-Lee said, shrugging. "It actually looks like a good movie."

Rolly swiveled to face her. "I wasn't asking for your opinion."

"Okay, okay," Ellis said, moving across the room. "What's going on here?"

"Thank God you're here to settle this," Rolly said, shaking a crooked finger at the TV. "Louie wants to watch a movie called

Harry and the Hendersons—he said you'd want to watch it, too—but I'd like to watch CNN."

A slow smile split Ellis's face. *Harry and the Hendersons* had come out years ago, about a family that accidentally runs over a Sasquatch with their car while on vacation. When they get out to see what it is, they find the seemingly dead body of a hairy Bigfoot-type monster. They take it home, planning to stuff it and put it on display in their living room, but the Sasquatch wakes up, all kinds of calamity ensue, and he is eventually adopted by the family as a pet. In her early teens Ellis had seen the movie at least a dozen times.

"Well?" Rolly said, crossing his arms. "What are you going to do?"

Ellis met Louie's eyes and smiled, sharing something private no one else could begin to understand. Then she turned and looked at Ben's locked office door through the dayroom window, letting her problem-solving skills kick into high gear.

"I'm going to make everyone happy," she said, tilting her head at Rolly to follow her.

Reaching into the front pocket of her smocklike top, she pulled out a set of keys on a silver ring and hurried into the hallway. Fitting one of them into the lock on Ben's door, she swung it open and waved Rolly inside.

Rolly gave her a skeptical look. "Here?" he said.

"You bet." She walked over to the long stretch of hip-high bookcases that had been built along the wall of the office under the windows and turned on Ben's twenty-inch television. Using the remote, she quickly flipped through the channels until she found CNN, and then she turned up the volume so Rolly could hear it.

"There you go," she said. "I'll leave the door open. If you need anything, call." She went back to the dayroom. "Louie?" she said, sticking her head inside the door.

His gaze flickered from the TV to her and then back again. "Eh?" he said.

"Make room for me on the couch, okay? I'll be there in two minutes."

Ellis rounded the corner into the lobby. Hadley was sitting at the reception desk, talking on the phone with her stocking feet propped against the edge of the desk. From the excitement in her voice Ellis guessed she had called Anissa to tell her about the bald eagle Louie had rented for her project.

Ellis was trying to get her attention, to ask her to join them in the dayroom for the movie, when Ed Notton stepped through the front door, smoothing down both sides of his hair. Curious, Ellis casually moved a few things around on the desk, watching him from the corner of her eye.

The door had barely closed when it opened again and in walked Fran Wilson, face flushed and hair askew. As usual, her Bible was tucked under her arm, but even from across the room Ellis could see that her red lipstick was smudged and the top two or three buttons on her blouse were undone. Ed leaned over and whispered something to her, wiggling his eyebrows suggestively, and Fran shot him a searing look and pushed him away with the flat of one hand, tilting her head in Ellis's direction.

Ellis pulled a rag out of her pocket and rubbed it against the bald eagle's Plexiglas case, removing a few smudges. *All righty then.* She fought back a smile. *This day has been one little amazement after another.*

Twenty

It was May twentieth, Louie's birthday, and to surprise him Ellis had roasted a turkey, his favorite, and prepared dressing and gravy. Ben had agreed to let her serve it to Louie and the rest of the aides in the staff lounge during the dinner hour. Since Ellis had begun working at Pleasant View, Louie had never stopped complaining about the meals.

"I don't care how old I am," he'd say, tucking his napkin into the neckline of his shirt. "Food should look like food when it's served. Who purees green beans? And who wants to eat reconstituted mashed potatoes?"

Ellis would listen and then dutifully respond as she'd been trained to. "I know it might not look appealing, but it is nutritional."

"Then why don't you eat it?" he'd challenge.

"Because I eat at home."

"And I'll bet you're having pot roast or turkey, aren't you?" He'd wave a hand over his plate with disgust. "Not pureed crap like this. Everyone's afraid we're gonna keel over, but while we're still alive and kicking we should get to eat whatever we want now and then. That's not asking too much, is it?"

That morning Ellis slipped on her coat and took two trips to load up her car. She opened the trunk and set the still-warm roasting pan inside, then went back to the house for her purse and the box she'd loaded up with all the trimmings. She and Hadley had bought Louie a CD for his birthday: John Denver's *Rocky Mountain Christmas*. Apparently he'd told Hadley that he loved John Denver but had never been able to find his Christmas CD.

Ellis pulled in to the parking lot at work feeling good about her upcoming shift.

Shouldering her purse, she opened the trunk, grabbed the roasting pan, and went inside, noticing Nina wasn't on the bench out front. There also wasn't anyone at the reception desk, which seemed odd. Lately it seemed someone was always there—Louie sifting through his mail, Gregory checking the massages Hadley had scheduled for him, Oliver calling the only courier in town to pick up medication from the pharmacy. Ellis hurried down the hallway into the kitchen, located next to the dining room, set the turkey on the counter, and decided to check in at Ben's office before making another trip out to her car.

Everyone was in the dayroom.

Slowing to a stop, Ellis looked through the glass windows. Ben and Murphy were sitting side by side, talking to a somber-looking group. Louie had his back turned to Ellis, so she couldn't see his face, but she could tell he was staring out the window into the distance. Vera-Lee's face was red and puffy, as though she had been crying. Ed, Fran, and Joseph sat across from her on one of the couches. Nina was dozing in the wheelchair she used now and then, next to Rolly, who was also in his. There were eight or nine others Ellis didn't know as well.

"Is everything okay?" she asked, stepping inside.

Ben looked up and paused for a split second. "Vern Heeley passed away."

Ellis's heart skipped a beat. "When?" she asked.

"Last night in his sleep."

She took a deep breath as she looked around the room. The painful truth of Vern's death was evident on all their faces. This was a group of individuals who'd been pulled up short.

"I phoned his son," Ben said. "He's flying in from Iowa tonight. Funeral arrangements will be made for Tuesday."

Oliver was sitting off to the side from Vera-Lee. His eyes were downcast and he was on the verge of tears. Ben had assigned him to Vern Heeley after Charlene quit. Oliver was only twenty-five, but he had a gentle empathy the residents responded well to, and Vern Heeley had thought the world of him.

Using both hands, Louie lifted himself out of his chair and straightened. On his way out of the dayroom, he stopped next to Ben and squeezed his shoulder, then continued out into the hallway, giving Ellis a polite nod as he passed.

Thinking of Vern, Ellis's throat tightened and she lowered her head. Grief seemed almost a physical thing in this room, its presence a dull reminder of a time not long ago when it had also paid an unexpected visit in her life. She glanced up and caught Ben's eye. She imagined him saying, *It comes with the territory*. Gently, but with a soothing calm to his voice.

"That poor man," Vera-Lee said, blowing her nose. "Lord, being old is terrible. Your body aches and your thoughts get muddy and you take more pills than the average pusher on the street. And then what happens? You die."

"He was eighty-seven," Fran pointed out. "He lived a good life."

Vera-Lee glared at her. "How would you know, Fran? You treated him like he had leprosy. You never even gave him the time of day."

Fran drew herself up straight. "Unlike you, Vera-Lee, I don't spend eight hours a day dressing a mannequin or jabbering and flirting with every man who happens to live here. I have a large family and a very busy life."

"Oh, yes, that's right," Vera-Lee said, folding her hands primly in her lap. "You are busy, aren't you, Fran? I think everyone here knows exactly how you spend your time, too, and it's certainly *not* helping your six grandchildren with their homework."

Fran suddenly looked homicidal.

"Okay, okay!" Ben said, lifting his hands in the air. "Ladies, please."

Ellis ran a finger around one of the buttons on the front of her coat. It no longer seemed appropriate that they should celebrate Louie's birthday on a day like this. Maybe she would give him his gift so he would know that she'd remembered and they would eat their turkey dinner another day.

The buzzer up front went off long and low. Murphy set her clipboard down, but Ellis waved at her to stay sitting; she would get it.

When she rounded the corner into the lobby, Ellis found her dad standing next to the reception desk, looking uncomfortable. He was holding a package wrapped in white tissue paper with a yellow ribbon. Louie's birthday gift. She must have forgotten it on the counter when she left for work.

"I thought this looked important," he said, holding it out to her. A note on top, written in Hadley's curlicue scrawl, read, "Happy birthday, Louie."

"It is," Ellis said, taking it from him. "Thanks for bringing it."

An awkward silence fell between them. Dennis stuck his hands in his pockets and looked around. "Seems like a nice place," he said, approving.

"It is," Ellis said, realizing with surprise how much she liked her job, how good she felt coming here every day.

Dennis's gaze wandered, taking in a painting tilted at an angle on one wall, the year-at-a-glance calendar tacked up behind the desk, the bulletin board where they posted weekly menu plans. Watching him, it occurred to Ellis how, as a child, she used to worry that she would be a disappointment to him when she grew up, yet now his opinion meant little to her: they were strangers who knew nothing of each other's inner workings, and in a swift and confusing rush this suddenly saddened her.

"Dennis Williams, right?" a voice said.

Ellis swiveled and there was Louie, making his way toward them, face drawn but with a polite smile. He walked up, held out his hand, and very formally shook Dennis's. "Louie Johnson," he said by way of introduction. "Nice to see you again."

Dennis stared, taking Louie in. "You too."

The phone rang and Ellis stepped away to answer it.

It was Jennifer Evans with the *Great Falls Tribune*. Could someone let Louie know that she'd called to wish him a happy birthday? Ellis tucked her and Hadley's gift for Louie behind the desk where he wouldn't see it and wrote down the message.

Then she studied Louie and her dad, feeling oddly displaced. For years now, her dad hadn't been in her life, as excluded from it as if he had died. Yet here he was, making polite conversation with Louie. To this day, Ellis could remember the smell of her dad's aftershave as she'd sat next to him in the grass the day he left Barrow. She could recall with equal clarity Louie's smile, one glorious flash of mischief and white teeth, before he'd pulled her into the river that morning so long ago. Two men: one who'd left her behind with apparent ease in his search for happiness, and another who'd refused to let her give up on herself.

They spoke briefly about the weather, Hadley and what a great kid she was, how Barrow hadn't changed much in the last twenty years. Then Dennis said good-bye and left. Ellis waited until he drove away before turning to Louie.

"You know my dad?"

He shrugged. "Not really. Before I was hired as a janitor at the high school I worked for your grandfather as the custodian at Williams Trucking. Your dad worked there, too, in a management job of some sort his dad had given him, but we rarely spoke. I left the year after your grandfather died and your dad inherited the business."

Ellis nodded. "Before it went bankrupt?"

Her mom had told her everything long ago. How the business had gone downhill so badly after Donnie died and how her dad had had to claim bankruptcy only weeks before he'd packed up and left Barrow.

"Yes," Louie said, shaking his head. "In the beginning, your dad got real caught up in all the money and power that came with running the business, but his heart was never in it the way your grandfather's was. I felt bad for him, though. He had big shoes to fill, and no matter how hard he tried, he couldn't do it. He went through some tough times. He lost his father, his son, and then the family business that had been his dad's legacy, a business that had defined who he was since leaving high school. After that, I think he lost his self-respect, and by the time he left Barrow he seemed like a broken man."

Ellis held herself very still, waiting to see if Louie would say anything else, wishing he could answer all of her questions about her dad. She picked at a torn fingernail, unable to meet his eye, feeling an old stab of anger. *I don't care how hard it was for him. He had a family. He had no right to leave the way he did.*

The front door opened and Hans Holt walked in.

"Hello," he said to Ellis. Then, addressing Louie, "Fancy meeting you here, old-timer." He handed him a lumpy package. "I got postcards from the Mirage Hotel and Casino in Las Vegas and a bathrobe from a hotel on Lake Lucerne in Switzerland." Reaching into his breast pocket, he pulled out a cigar. "Oh, and happy birthday. This one's straight from Cuba. It's probably as old as you are."

Louie clapped him on the back. "You sure know how to cheer a man up."

The phone rang and Ellis went over to answer it, holding the receiver with her shoulder as she wrote down another message for Louie. It was Lynn Fischer, a reporter from the *Billings Advocate*, calling to send her regards. Ellis wrote it down, watching Louie as he pulled cash out of his pocket to pay Hans, thumbing through a stack of bills, mouth moving as he counted.

Hans was on his way out the door, hand raised in farewell, when Ellis hung up. Before she could stop herself, she said, "So tell me, Louie, what's the connection with Nina anyhow, and how long have you been indulging her? Don't say, 'You get back what you put out,' either, because in this case I'm not buying it."

At first, the abruptness of her question seemed to surprise Louie, but after a brief pause, he winked at her. "I guess all that slinking around outside in the bushes listening to our conversations hasn't given you any answers, huh?"

Ellis's face burned with embarrassment. "You knew I was there?" Louie looked up at a small water stain on the ceiling, nodded.

"I guess that shouldn't surprise me," she said.

"Actually," he said, "Nina's husband and I grew up here in Barrow, and before he died twelve years ago he asked me to check in on her now and then and make sure she was okay. He was a good man, but he was dirt poor. He always felt Nina got shortchanged marrying him. He used to say she only ever wanted two things in life and he wasn't able to give her either. She wanted children, but they couldn't have any, and she wanted to travel. Instead, he bought an annual subscription to a travel magazine, said it was the highlight of Nina's month whenever an issue landed in their mailbox."

"He sounds like a nice man," Ellis said.

Louie smiled. "He was. You met him once, don't you remember?"

"I met Nina's husband?"

"His name was Roy Ballard," Louie said, watching for her reaction.

Ellis's face fell and she shook her head to clear away a foggy recollection. Searching her memory, she recalled Roy as a heavyset man with a good-sized paunch and a head of leonine white hair.

"He pulled us out of the river—"

"I remember," she said quietly, amazed at the many threads of her life that were weaving together since she'd come back to Barrow.

"Anyhow," Louie said, "when Nina's Alzheimer's took a turn for the worse a few years ago, it bothered me to no end to see her sitting outside on that bench every day, waiting for Roy to come pick her up, so I decided to make her believe for ten or fifteen minutes every afternoon that they had gone somewhere."

The phone rang again, interrupting them. "Hold that thought," Ellis said, stepping behind the desk to answer it. It was

Megan Read with the *Barrow Gazette.* Could she speak to Louie for a moment?

"It's for you," Ellis said, handing Louie the phone.

He took it and lowered himself into a chair behind the desk. Ellis listened as he thanked the woman for remembering his birthday and then made small talk for a few minutes. Had she seen the letter he'd written to the editor about the stupidity of wasting tax dollars to install a stoplight in the middle of Main Street? Had anyone asked the mayor why Barrow still wasn't offering town-wide recycling?

After he'd hung up, Ellis handed him his other messages. "You're a popular guy."

"Nah," he said, getting to his feet. "I'm just old. You spend fifty years writing letters to every reporter in the state and you get to know a lot of people, that's all." Louie pointed to the door, indicating that he was on his way outside. "If anyone's looking for me, I'll be taking a nap in my chair."

Before he took a step, Rolly came around the corner in his wheelchair. "Louie, I need to talk to you."

Louie's shoulders dropped. "What now?"

"I know today isn't the best time to bring it up," he said, lowering his voice a notch, "given Vern's passing and all, but I wanted you to know that I intend to ask Ben if I can move into Vern's room as soon as they've cleaned it out. I think everyone knows how much I don't like living next door to you."

Louie kept his face expressionless for a long moment, and then a big smile stretched across it. "I'll give you a week," he said, waving a hand at him as though dismissing a gnat. "You'll be back."

Rolly closed his eyes, took a deep breath. "Man, I hate you," he whispered, tilting his head back. Then, with an indignant huff, he swiveled his chair around and rolled down the hall, stopping briefly to reach up and adjust a crooked painting.

"I don't get it," Ellis said to Louie. "How can you be so nice to Nina and then turn around and treat Rolly so badly?"

Louie laughed as he buttoned his badly pilled pea green sweater. "Ack! I'm doing him a favor," he said. "Without me, Rolly wouldn't *have* any blood pressure. He's got no family, no friends, and he spends all his time reading karate books even though he hasn't done a move in forty years. If I didn't get his blood boiling every now and then, his arteries would clog up and he'd be toast. Ever watch him going around here straightening all the pictures? It almost drives him off the deep end, but it gives him something to *do*."

He turned to leave. "Oh, and Ellis?" he said, holding the door.

"Uh-huh?"

"Thanks for the present," he said, winking. "I'll open it later."

Ellis watched him leave, marveling at the almost gravitational force of Louie's personality. He was equal parts opinionated, eccentric, and cantankerous, but he truly was impossible to ignore.

TWENTY-ONE

On nights when Paulina made one of her trips into Great Falls, Ellis's dad usually prepared dinner. When Ellis got home from work, there would be soup on the stove, or stew in the Crock-Pot, or the hiss and spit of bacon as he prepared omelets. After dinner, he would do the dishes with Hadley, and Ellis would pluck towels from the dryer and fold them, pretending he wasn't there. What was she supposed to do, play cards with him? Discuss world economics? Chat about the weather?

On one of those nights when Hadley was at Anissa's studying for an exam, Ellis got stuck eating alone with her dad. She arrived home early, dumped a bag of bow-tie pasta into a pot, and adjusted the heat when the water foamed up. Minutes later, when her dad came in and said hello, she politely replied, fighting for some level of normalcy in an otherwise awkward situation. When the pasta was ready, she strained it and added meat sauce from a jar and grated asiago cheese. They ate in silence, she pretending to read a magazine and he doing the same with the newspaper.

"Would you like more?" she asked, motioning to the food.

"No," he said. "I'm good, thanks."

Ellis grabbed her plate and stood to clear the table. Dennis joined her, limping across the kitchen to put the salt and pepper shakers back in the cupboard, and snapping the lid onto the margarine container.

"She's seeing someone, you know," Ellis said, turning on the dishwasher.

Her dad had started to open the refrigerator door, but stopped and turned to her. "What makes you say that?"

Ellis poured a cup of coffee, determined

to dissuade him from any false hope of reconciling with Paulina. "She drives into Missoula at least once a week and she always stays the night. Hadley and I keep asking her about it: Who is this guy? When is she going to introduce us? But she just blushes and shrugs us off."

Dennis rubbed his sideburns, considering this. "Doesn't mean she's seeing someone."

"Sure it does. She's shy about introducing us to him, that's all, and now that you're here, she's showing a little decorum by keeping her private life even more private. He gives her flowers, too, if you hadn't noticed. She brings home a bouquet every time she spends the night, and I'm pretty sure he's the one who keeps buying her those nice clothes. Have you noticed her camel-hair coat? Or that she has four pairs of sunglasses when I can't remember her owning even one when I was a kid? How expensive her blouses are? She's not buying them at Wal-Mart. She's seeing someone," Ellis repeated forcefully. "I just thought you should know."

Dennis's whiskery face remained impassive. "I don't think you're right, but if she is, that'd be nice. Your mother deserves to be happy."

Ellis watched for a condescending smirk or a hint of superiority, but found neither. His eyes remained thoughtful and unreadable, although she was thrown off by his certainty.

The next afternoon, Ellis was late picking Hadley up at school. Racing around the kitchen to get out the door, she grabbed her jacket and bumped her coffee mug by accident, sending it flying across the floor. Ceramic shards sprayed everywhere and coffee splattered against her leg.

"Wonderful," she muttered.

Dennis limped downstairs. "Go," he said. "I'll clean it up."

"No," Ellis said. "I'll do it."

Hurrying to the utility closet, she reached in to grab the broom and a catalogue fell off the top shelf. Snatching it up off the floor, Ellis stood to put it back when she noticed a huge stack of catalogues and pulled them all down. What were these?

Across the room, Dennis stood watching her. Clearing his throat, he shrugged into his worn canvas jacket and snatched her keys off the counter. "I'm gonna go check your oil for you," he said, and slipped out the door and down the back steps.

Ellis set the stack of catalogues on the table, noticing they were all from the same company. *Ashford Essentials* was emblazoned across the top, with "Celebrate Yourself" in smaller letters beneath it. Perplexed, she began flipping through one, and came to an abrupt stop on page three.

Her eyes flew open, wide and disbelieving. There was her mom, posing like a seasoned professional in barely there ice blue lingerie against a simple linen backdrop. Around her neck hung a strand of pearls, and surrounding her on the floor were dozens of aluminum buckets filled with red roses. Stretched across the bottom of the page was *America's biggest online store for women over sixty*.

Ellis's heart began to pound. One after another, she paged through the catalogues, oblivious of the time. There were twenty catalogues in all, six issues per year, and her mom was on almost every other page, posing in slinky sleepwear, lingerie, underwear, even a variety of bathing suits.

Mom's modeling? she thought, incredulous.

In one two-page spread, Paulina was lounging next to a swimming pool in a form-hugging swimsuit, toenails painted, head tilted back and eyes closed, a look of contentment on her face. Flipping ahead, Ellis found another one of her mom and her friend Bonita, who often socialized with Paulina. Bonita was modeling a bathrobe, and Paulina looked stunning in a red slip-style nightgown that hugged her curves.

Ellis set the catalogue aside, suddenly understanding a truth that until then had been eluding her. Her mom had walked away from her old life and built an entirely new one. It seemed as though the phone was forever ringing and Paulina was constantly darting here or there—volunteering for Meals on Wheels, taking yoga classes, *modeling*—a busy lady with a busy life. Her behavior was at odds with the Paulina Ellis remembered from childhood, yet she seemed lit from within, happier than Ellis had ever seen her.

The porch door opened and Ellis heard

the *slap, slap, slap* of Hadley's feet crossing the room. "God, Mom, where were you?" she said. "Anissa's dad had to give me a ride home. . . ." Her voice trailed away. There was a pause, followed by, "Why is there a broken coffee mug on the floor? Mom? Are you okay?" Hadley gently touched her shoulder.

Ellis sighed. "I'm fine."

Hadley leaned over to look at the catalogue, her expression quickly registering wide-eyed amazement. She flipped through the pages. "Oh. My. God. You've got to be kidding me, right? Grandma's modeling *underwear*?"

Ellis straightened. "Looks that way," she said.

Hadley slid into a chair, her face taking on an expression of almost herolike worship. "Mom, she looks totally hot! These pictures make her look like a movie star. She should send some to Hollywood and get an agent." She paused, shaking her head as she continued to turn the pages. "Why didn't she tell us?"

"I don't know," Ellis said, resisting the urge to explain the power of a secret to her daughter. "But it obviously means a lot to her."

"Would it be okay if I ask her about it?" Hadley asked.

Ellis got to her feet and grabbed the broom. "No, please, don't," she said. "Things like this are private, Hadley. Grandma will tell us about it when she's ready to."

Outside, Dennis had raised the hood of her car and was pouring in a fresh can of oil, his movements slow and measured. As Ellis studied him through the window, it occurred to her how much her mom had had to overcome, and she felt a wave of undisguised pride—the same flash of pride she was certain she'd seen in her dad's eyes when he'd noticed Ellis holding that catalogue.

After accompanying Ellis to the two grief counseling sessions she originally committed to, Hadley had grudgingly agreed to attend a few more, so they had continued driving into Great Falls every Wednesday evening, but then the school running club started up and Wednesdays became double booked for Hadley. It had now been weeks since either of them had been to a session. However, during the last one they'd attended, Roma had touched on some points that didn't fully resonate with Ellis until now, as the anniversary of Mark's death crept closer.

"The first anniversary of your loved one's death can be especially hard," Roma had said that night. "It's a time to take stock of where you've been in the last year and where you're heading in the future. Intense feelings of grief often come rushing back and this can be overwhelming and confusing, almost as if you're experiencing your loss anew. Whether it is the first, third, or tenth anniversary, it can be a painful reminder of what once was. You may experience a range of unexpected reactions, including sadness, frustration, flashes of anger, fear, depression, or anxiety. Or you might choose to completely avoid any reminders of your loved one's death, finding this emotionally easier."

Ellis was amazed that so much time had passed since Mark's death. She'd seen summer come and go, had faced a tumultuous fall and winter, including a move across the country and a new job, and had watched spring arrive like a bright new penny. And yet, in some ways, it didn't seem as if any time had passed at all.

Sure, she had a job, her days were structured, and she spent as much time as possible focused on Hadley, but there were still moments when she felt cleft down the middle, her life utterly shapeless without Mark.

"Many people turn the first anniversary of their loved one's death into a special day of honoring his or her life," Roma had said.

From the corner of her eye, Ellis saw Hadley's mouth tighten almost imperceptibly.

Roma continued, fingers tented under her chin. "One family I know takes red helium balloons to the high school track where their daughter used to compete and lets them float up into the air with personal messages for her written on each one. Another meets at an Italian restaurant so they can eat their father's favorite pasta dish. Creating a positive ritual similar to these that's either fulfilled alone or shared with someone else can add powerful and supportive meaning to the death anniversary."

After Roma wrapped up, Hadley had gone out the door hopping on one foot, trying to pull her boots on without slowing down. On the drive home, Ellis had asked if she wanted to do something special to honor the one-year anniversary of Mark's death.

"No, thanks," Hadley said, holding her knapsack against her chest like a shield. "I don't need a ritual to remind me that Dad's gone."

"We could make it into a celebration of his life."

"Same thing," Hadley said.

Ellis stared at her for a long moment. "Okay," she finally said.

All day long, Ellis had been increasingly distracted at work. The anniversary of Mark's death was two days away. She kept thinking of him, and thoughts of him inevitably segued off into thoughts of Hadley. How much had she truly recovered? Yes, there were days when she seemed fine—Ellis could relate to those days herself—but over the last two weeks she had been exceptionally quiet and withdrawn.

After lunch, Gregory pulled Ellis to one side and handed her a slip of paper. On it he'd written a date and a time, nothing else.

"What's this?" Ellis asked.

He gave her an affectionate sideways hug, then stepped back and pressed his splayed palms against his chest. "It's an appointment slip for a complimentary ninety-minute massage with *moi*."

"I don't understand," Ellis said. "Why would you—?"

Gregory wagged a finger at her. "It's my way of thanking you for helping me get this job, and I won't take no for an answer."

"All right," Ellis said. She looked down at the paper, felt something pinch in her chest. "Oh, but Gregory, this is . . ." Her voice trailed away.

"I know," he said matter-of-factly. "I scheduled it for Saturday on purpose. I remembered you mentioning it once during a session. If you prefer, we can do it another day. I'll leave it up to you. But if you'd like some distraction to help you get through the day, I'll be here at ten."

Ellis watched him walk away.

Grasping the reality of his gift, she realized that she might not mind a distraction. After all, she'd already decided that if Hadley didn't want to do something special to mark the day, she didn't, either. Months ago, she'd asked Ben not to schedule her for work this coming Saturday, and now the idea of having no plans at all made her feel uneasy.

When Ellis got home from work, there were two voice mails from Anissa. "Hadley, it's me. Wanna go for a run tomorrow morning? Call me back." The second one was a mini-rant about homework. "Hadley, are you getting, like, any of this physics assignment? I mean, who *cares* about velocity and acceleration? It's not like I'm ever gonna be behind the controls of the space shuttle!"

Upstairs, Ellis found Hadley's bedroom door shut. She knocked on it and stuck her head inside. "Anissa left you two messages."

"I know," Hadley said, eyes locked on a textbook.

"Were you going to call her back?"

Pause. "Maybe later."

Most Saturday mornings, Hadley joined Anissa for a run, but not that Saturday. Paulina had left the day before for a weekend yoga retreat at a lodge near Kalispell, and Dennis was outside repairing the rotting front steps. Paulina had begged him to leave them alone, that she would hire someone to fix them, but Dennis had insisted. “I need to do something to pay my way while I'm here.”

Ellis woke to the shriek of rusty nails being pulled from wood followed by the sound of hammering. Rubbing her face awake, she walked over to the window and opened it. Her room looked down over the front yard, and when she stuck her head outside the air was filled with sawdust and the smell of freshly cut wood. Below her, Dennis was hunched over a Black & Decker Workmate he'd borrowed from a neighbor. He was cutting a board with a circular saw and Hadley was sitting in the grass off to one side, watching.

When Dennis finished, he unplugged the saw and asked Hadley if she would hold one end of the board while he pounded the other into place. She got up and helped him carry it over to the porch. Distracted for a moment, she reached under the open top step and pulled out the sun-parched skull of an animal.

“Hey, Grandpa, look at this.”

Dennis wiped his hands on a rag before taking it from her. He held it up so he could get a better look, turning it this way and that.

"It's a coyote skull," he said.

"Wonder what it's doing under here," Hadley said.

Dennis sat on the top step and rested his boots against the new wood below it. "Your grandma probably put it there," he said.

"Why would she do that?" Hadley asked, her face concentrated in a frown.

When Dennis answered, his voice sounded scratchy, as though he'd just stumbled across an old memory that had caught him off guard. "Because years ago, when we were still married and living in our big house outside of town, an old native guy who did our gardening told her that coyotes slept with one eye half open; that they did so to protect their family, and if she wanted to keep hers safe from harm, she should always bury a coyote skull somewhere in her front yard."

Hadley set her hands on her hips. "Did she?"

From where Ellis stood, she could see her dad nod. "Three or four," he confirmed. "Back then, every time she found one out in the wilderness or at someone's yard sale, she'd drag it home and bury the thing, so I'm not surprised that she did it here, too."

"Think it's true?" Hadley asked.

"What's that?" Dennis said, getting to his feet.

"That burying a coyote skull in your yard keeps your family safe."

"Certainly can't hurt, can it?" he said, reaching out and mussing up her hair.

Ellis's heart quickened and she stepped back and closed her eyes. It seemed such an unexpected and lovely moment, Hadley and her dad talking, that she thought she now understood why her mom had suggested he come here. Who could blame her for wanting them all under the same roof, if only for a short while? Their histories were woven together, each a fresh tendril off the same vine. Outside, their voices continued to rise and fall, soft murmurs followed by Hadley's quick laughter.

Moving back to the window, Ellis watched as Hadley turned the coyote skull over in her hands, examining it more closely. Then she reached down under the step and put it back where she'd found it. Moments later, Dennis lifted the last board into place and hammered a few nails into each end, sealing it off.

Maybe today won't be so bad after all, Ellis thought. *Maybe it'll be a lot like all the other days since Mark died.*

She knew now that when you first lose someone you love, you think it's going to destroy you, but it doesn't. In the beginning, your body aches, your mind can't focus, and your heart feels irrevocably broken. You believe the world should stop, that nothing else should matter. But it doesn't stop, and there are many other things that do matter. The world keeps moving, rudely rushing past as you struggle to get up off your knees, and before you know it you find yourself cautiously moving back into the mainstream—going to work, celebrating holidays, living your life.

TWENTY-TWO

Clad only in panties and the thin cotton gown Gregory had given her, Ellis climbed onto his massage table as if preparing herself for a doctor's examination. He had put in a CD before leaving her to get undressed, but the gentle swell of ocean waves mixed with flutes wasn't helping her relax. She was tense, anxious, slightly nervous—clearly the perfect candidate for a massage.

Gregory tapped on the door.

"Come in," Ellis called, pulling the gown tighter.

He slipped inside and closed the door,

holding up a sheet still warm from the dryer.

"This is my first time," she announced, feeling shy.

"Are you *serious*?" Gregory said. "Well, girl, trust me. By the time I'm done today, you will be signing up for weekly visits."

He shook out the sheet and held it up between them, asked her to take off the gown and lie facedown. Ellis did, stretching out on her stomach and positioning her face into the cushioned hole built into the table. He covered her and folded the sheet discreetly across her backside. Underneath the table, in Ellis's line of vision through the cushioned face hole, she could see a wooden bowl filled with stones and what looked like potpourri sprinkled on top. Seemed a little artsy to her, but a nice distraction nevertheless.

"Ellis, I like to keep my sessions as tranquil as possible," Gregory said softly, "so unless you talk, I won't. I will be giving you what's called a classic massage because I want to relax you and reduce stress, not energize you." The entire time he talked, he kept the flat of one hand firmly on her back. "Please tell me if you want me to ease up a bit or else go deeper. I'll start with long gliding strokes on your upper back, shoulders, and neck, and then, depending on how bunched up your muscles are, I may use my elbows or knuckles to work out the kinks. I'll move down your back to your legs and feet and then finish with the base of your neck and your temples."

"Sounds great," Ellis said.

Gregory was good. So good, in fact, that at some point Ellis fell asleep. When she finally did wake up, groggy and disoriented, he was gone. Music was playing in the background and there was a note taped to the inside of the door that read, "Enjoy the rest of your day ☺" Minutes later, she walked out of Pleasant View feeling like a worked-over tub of bread dough, her knees boneless and every inch of her elasticized.

By the time she arrived home, smiling and relaxed, the front steps were repaired and her dad had strung rope between the porch columns with a handwritten FRESH PAINT sign draped over it, warning everyone away. Ellis noticed that his car was gone when she pulled in to the driveway.

She parked, turned the car off, and rested her forehead against the wheel for a second, listening to the engine tick and sigh.

Inside, she dropped her purse on the kitchen table and called out to Hadley, but there was no answer. Ellis slid into a chair. Obviously she was on her own today. Maybe Hadley had gone out somewhere with her granddad. Ellis hoped so. Today, of all days, she didn't want her daughter facing the same dilemma she was—what to do with the next eight hours.

She was about to make coffee when she heard a loud thump upstairs. Someone was home after all. "Hello?" she called out from the foot of the stairs. "Hadley, is that you?"

There was no answer, yet seconds later she thought she heard something being dragged across the floor above her.

Ellis cautiously made her way upstairs, stopping first to check Hadley's room. It was empty. Where had the noise come from then? Noticing that the door to her own room was half open, Ellis crept over and placed her hand against it, giving it a quick push.

There was Hadley, on the floor in front

of Ellis's closet, rearranging her legs, an open cardboard box beside her.

"Hadley, is everything okay?" Ellis said, moving closer, then noticing that her daughter's face was puffy and her eyes were red from crying. "What's wrong?"

Hadley's hands fluttered up and then back down. "You said—" She ducked her head, hiding the naked grief on her face. "You told me you were going for groceries after your massage." Her voice was shaky, her hands restless. "I didn't think you'd be back for another half hour."

That had been Ellis's original plan, but after Gregory's massage all she had wanted to do was come home.

Risking that Hadley might pull away as she often did, Ellis reached down and touched her hand lightly to Hadley's cheek.

"What is it?" she said. "You're scaring me."

Hadley twisted her hands together in her lap. "You're gonna hate me when I tell you."

What was she talking about? She could never hate her. She sat down on the floor next to her, and she hugged her the way parents were supposed to hug when their kids' lives went off the rails: with them doing all the work. "I've got news for you, Hadley," she said. "There is nothing—absolutely nothing—you can do that will ever change how I feel about you."

Hadley pulled away and looked at her, desperate relief on her face.

"What is it?" Ellis asked.

"I took half of Dad's ashes," Hadley whispered.

Ellis blinked, taken aback. "What for?" she finally asked.

Swallowing, Hadley shifted sideways and set her hand on the urn that was sticking out of the cardboard box beside her. "I picked a spot," she said. "I went there and I spread them. I thought it was fair. That half of them should be mine."

Ellis heard her but she was so thrown off she felt like she hadn't.

She glanced at the urn that held Mark's ashes tilted sideways in the box, and then she looked at Hadley, sitting next to it, rumpled and upset from crying, wiping her nose with the back of her hand. Ellis quickly tried to imagine what this act might mean for them, what the ramifications might be.

Nothing, she decided. *It means nothing. We're fine.*

Ellis suddenly felt lighter, relieved even. So Hadley had spread half of Mark's ashes, so what? He would have wanted her to, and if the two of them had done it together, he would've been happy with that, too.

"I didn't want my half stuck inside a box somewhere," Hadley said, waving a hand at Ellis's open closet door, the jumble of boxes stacked inside.

Ellis nodded, not trusting herself to speak.

No, of course you didn't, she thought, wishing she had discussed it with her, wondering now why she hadn't.

Hadley looked up and then quickly away. "I'm sorry, Mom," she said. "I didn't know how to talk to you about it."

Ellis felt herself go still inside; her heart sank.

This comment rocked her more than any other, one small statement that brought with it the oddest sensation that she was slipping backward down a rocky hillside. Growing up, Ellis had never felt that she could talk to her mom—not when she was bullied at school, not after she got raped, not when she learned she was pregnant, certainly not before or after she jumped off that bridge—and that inability had had a profound impact on her. By the time Mark asked her to marry him, she knew she loved him, but more than anything, she had wanted to be taken care of, a difficult truth she'd only recently admitted to herself.

Ellis took Hadley by the shoulders and leaned closer until their foreheads were almost touching. "Look, as a teenager you're going to have your own secret life," she said. "Every kid does. And I don't expect to be your best friend—that's not what I'm saying. But I do need you to know that you can talk to me." She stopped and took a breath to quell the sob working its way up her throat. "About anything, Hadley. *Anything*. I'll never turn you away or judge you or tell you I've got too much on my plate. I need you to know that I'll always be here for you. Please know that, okay?"

Hadley nodded. "Okay," she said.

Ellis stared at the algae-colored urn and tried to gather her thoughts. She could barely recall choosing it, although she could remember the balding salesman at the funeral home, the cloying feeling that made her want to leave as quickly as possible, the way she had lifted a hand in the air and cut him off in midspeech, asking him to please just recommend an urn—any one would do.

After Mark's memorial service, she'd tried three times to pick up the ashes from the funeral home. The first time, her heart was pounding so hard she drove past without stopping. The second time, she parked across the street and stared at the building for half an hour, but couldn't bring herself to go in. Finally, she phoned ahead and asked if someone could meet her at the door.

Even now, those first few months following Mark's death were a haze. To anyone who knew her, it may have seemed as if she was handling everything well, but it'd been a fragile façade. Without the Xanax her doctor prescribed, she wouldn't have gotten out of bed each morning. She carried them everywhere, the way a bum might carry a flask of rum hidden in his trench coat. If she took too many, it was hard to talk or swallow, but that was okay. She didn't feel like talking anyhow, and at that point swallowing seemed overrated. In fact, preparing and eating meals had quickly become exhausting.

Then she'd come home one day and found Hadley's friend Rhea waiting for her outside their apartment in Dallas. When she'd opened Hadley's note and read, "Tell my mom I won't be coming home for a while, okay?" it was as though someone had flipped a switch. *Enough,* Ellis had thought. *Is this what I want for Hadley? For either of us?* After that, she'd stopped taking Xanax, determined not to repeat the same mistakes her mom had made.

Now, making a snap decision, Ellis leaned past Hadley and lifted the urn out of the box, surprised as always by its weight. She got to her feet. She'd been avoiding this for a year; now was the time.

"I want you to take me there," she said.

Hadley's face went blank for a moment. "Take you where?"

"To the spot you chose."

Hadley stared at the urn in sudden understanding. "Mom, you might not want to spread them there. It's not a fancy spot."

"I don't care," Ellis said, cupping a hand under Hadley's elbow and urging her up.

"Because you chose it, then that's exactly where I want to spread my half. Let's go."

Minutes later, Hadley was leading her down a path toward the river, the same path Ellis herself had followed many times as a child. Together they bobbed and weaved around tree branches and fallen logs, until finally Hadley stopped at a low spot along the riverbank, turned, and flung out an arm.

"Here," she said. "I let him go here."

Ellis stared out across the river. *I let him go here*. Yes, somehow that seemed right. That they should let him go and move on with their lives; that the truest part of him would remain in their hearts, not at the bottom of an old clay urn.

Mark would have liked it here.

Ellis took off her shoes and socks and rolled up her pants to her knees. Moving slowly, she waded out into the river, sucking in her breath as the cold water cut circles around her ankles and then her calves. She inched along until she was almost knee deep, one arm wrapped around the urn and the other stretched out to help keep her balance.

Holding the urn against her chest, she worked the lid off. She tilted it sideways, held it out in front of her, and turned slowly in a circle with her arms extended, watching the ashes gently fall. There were no gusts of wind, just a hazy arc of airborne ashes before they landed on the water. Ellis watched them float away in the current, quickly moving out of her reach. As the finality of what she'd just done took hold—Mark truly was gone forever now—she felt something akin to a vise grip take hold around her chest.

She clapped a hand over her mouth and briefly closed her eyes. Like a clear pinpoint of light igniting within her, she found herself thinking about the words on the back of her silver compass: *You're braver than you believe, and stronger than you seem, and smarter than you think.* She had shown it to Mark once years ago and he'd marveled at the inscription, telling her that he could imagine giving something exactly like it to Hadley; that he could understand how much comfort it would have brought Ellis.

Ellis heard splashing and then Hadley was standing in the water next to her, pants rolled up to her knees.

"Are you all right?" she asked.

Ellis nodded, then reached for Hadley's hand and gave it a squeeze. She opened her eyes and looked up at the sky, thinking how much she liked the sting of the cold water against her calves, the warmth of the sun beating down on her upturned face, the feel of her daughter squeezing back.

TWENTY-THREE

Paulina was setting the table and Ellis was stirring up a second batch of pancake batter when Hadley and her dad came downstairs for breakfast. School had been out for a week, Anissa had left days ago to spend the summer with her grandmother in California, and Hadley had been moping around the house ever since.

"Guess what," Hadley said, grinning. "Yesterday, Ben asked if I want to work full-time for the summer."

"Did he?" Ellis said. Ben had actually pulled her aside to make sure she didn't mind.

Paulina handed her the syrup. "You must like it then, huh?" she said, addressing Hadley. "Working at the nursing home?"

Hadley shrugged. "Depends on who I get to spend time with or what Ben wants me to do," she said, giving a self-conscious smile. "I hate working in the kitchen, but I like cutting the lawn 'cause I get to use the rider mower."

Dennis poured himself coffee, listening with interest.

"Nina's the sweetest lady, even though she, like, always asks me to read the same book over and over 'cause she can't remember that we've already read it. And Anissa's grandpa Joseph is a nice man—he likes to play cards. But I don't like Fran Wilson. She's always preaching to everyone in her big explaining voice about what's right and wrong, but the only time I ever see her treat anyone halfway decent is when she's talking to Mr. Notton. He's, like, this ancient guy, but when he walks around, he kinda struts like he thinks everyone's watching and he's always flirting with Fran and pinching her butt. It's *so* gross."

Ellis flipped a pancake, smiling. "When have you seen him pinch Fran?"

Hadley took a sip of juice. "He does it all the time," she said, blowing her bangs off her forehead. "The last time I saw them, they were coming out of the storage shed, where all the garden tools are kept? Fran said he helps her weed and prune those flowers she likes so much. I think anybody who believes in God as much as she does should be nicer, that's all." She took a bite of pancake. "My favorite is Louie Johnson, though."

Ellis turned off the grill and joined them at the table with a plate of fresh pancakes. She gave her dad a nod and passed them to him first.

"Thanks," Dennis replied.

Hadley kept talking. "Louie wasn't born in Germany but he has a cousin that moved over there a long time ago and they're always writing each other. Louie sends him newspaper clippings and magazine articles, and his cousin and his wife do the same."

Remembering something, Hadley got up and hurried over to where her knapsack was hanging on a hook next to the door. Licking syrup off her fingers, she dug around inside and pulled out a binder.

"His cousin mailed him this picture a few weeks ago," she said, sitting down and taking out a photograph she'd slipped inside the binder. "How cool is this?" She held it out for closer inspection. "Since 1674 swans in northern Germany have been moved to warmer waters when their home on the Alster River freezes. Every year, one man—they call him the Swan Father—gathers, like, seventy of them and then he moves them to this pond in the city of Hamburg. And then, when the weather warms up again in March, he moves them back to the river for the summer. Louie's cousin said tourists come from all over the world to watch the whole strange journey of the swans."

Curious, Ellis leaned over her mom's shoulder to take a closer look. It was a sepia snapshot of a tugboat chained to two large wooden fishing boats. Inside each were at least thirty snow-white swans, huddled together and straining their elegant necks to take in the scenery around them, looking incredibly well behaved given the circumstances.

At first, she had been apprehensive about allowing Hadley to work at Pleasant View, but more and more she could see that the experience was a positive one. Last week, she'd seen Hadley give Louie a big hug before showing him the mark she'd received for her bald eagle presentation. Apparently, it'd been a hit. Then, when Vera-Lee's mannequin toppled over, she'd called out down the hallway in desperation and Hadley had been the first person there to help her stand it back up again. Ellis had watched Joseph smooth back his shoe-polish hair and put his hands up in surrender, a grin on his face as he and Hadley played cards, and she'd listened to Oliver teasing Hadley more than once when it came time to do the laundry. "Listen and learn," he'd say, laughing. "You're watching an expert here."

All signs of a likable and empathetic young girl, Ellis thought. *Qualities Mark would have loved to have seen for himself.*

Twenty minutes later, when everyone had finished eating, Hadley helped clear the table and Dennis began washing the dishes. Paulina's friend Bonita picked her up for yet another yoga class and Ellis took a wet dishcloth and wiped down the table.

"Hey, Mom?" Hadley said, fiddling with her iPod.

"Uh-huh?" Ellis said.

"You know that Swan Father? The one in the picture Louie gave me?"

Ellis straightened a chair. "Mmmm?"

Hadley moved her hair out of the way to put in her ear buds. "I think that's something Dad would have done, taking those swans back and forth every year and never caring if he ever got any credit for it."

Ellis felt herself go still inside. The night before, while watching a reality TV show, Hadley had burst out laughing at a contestant who was trying to sing "American Woman" and doing it badly. "God, even Anissa can do better than that," she had howled. Later, Ellis came out of the bathroom and caught her dancing around the kitchen with her eyes closed, iPod volume on high as she'd attempted a few low, long hip swivels just like she'd seen one of the contestants do.

Both wonderful flashes of normal, Ellis thought. *Talking about her dad like this and dancing around the kitchen.*

"Yes," she said, smiling. "I think you're right."

A month passed and before they knew it the state of Montana was at the tail end of the hottest July on record. Forest fires were a concern. Grass turned brown and the town posted water usage bans, threatening to fine anyone who watered his lawn or washed his vehicle until further notice. On one of those whisper-hot days Ben stuck his head into the staff lounge looking for Ellis.

"Can I see you for a few minutes?" he asked.

Ellis paused, sandwich midway to her mouth. "Sure."

In his office, she slid into a chair, and Ben got straight to the point. "I need a favor. I know you aren't scheduled to work on Friday, but Louie Johnson's brother died yesterday." He held a pencil between his two forefingers. "I need someone to drive him to the funeral." He flipped open a file folder on his desk. "It's in a town called Milford, two hours north from here, and it's scheduled for Friday at two."

Ellis immediately thought of Hadley.

She'd promised to take her to Great Falls on Friday to do some shopping. "Ben, could you ask someone else?"

"No one else will take him."

"But it's his brother's *funeral*," Ellis protested.

"I know," he said, nodding pointedly.

Ellis glanced through the interior floor-to-ceiling window built parallel to Ben's office door. She could see Murphy and Oliver in the dayroom. Oliver was busy fluffing cushions on the couch and Murphy was tidying up the coffee table. Both had their eyes on her.

"What about Murphy?" she said.

Ben's forehead crinkled. "She's taking Friday off to fly to Minneapolis for the weekend to see her son."

Ellis snapped her fingers. "Maybe we could ask Hans Holt, Louie's Norwegian friend. I'm sure he wouldn't mind."

Ben was already shaking his head. "He had hip replacement surgery last week. He just got home from the hospital."

Ellis sighed, noticing that Oliver was now perched on the end of the couch, pretending to flip through a magazine as he shot furtive looks in her direction, and Murphy was consoling Fran Wilson, patting her back as she wept into a handkerchief—her daylong reaction to the news that Ed Notton would be leaving Pleasant View Manor at the end of the month to move to a nursing home in Florida. Louie was sitting across from them, his eyes locked on Ben's office door, obviously concerned about whether he could make it to his brother's funeral.

"I'd take him myself," Ben said, "but I've got a meeting with my accountant that was scheduled months ago and—"

"All right," Ellis said, shrugging. "I'll do it."

Ben's shoulders relaxed. "You'll be paid time and a half."

"Sounds good," she said, pushing to her feet.

"And, of course, I'll cover your gas."

Ellis nodded. "Okay."

He was smiling now, unable to hide his relief as he spread a map across his desk and waved her over with his free hand. "Milford is two hours northeast," he said, running a finger along a route highlighted in yellow. "It's north of Fort Peck, between Glasgow and Wolf Point. You take Highway Eighty-seven, make a right onto Highway Two, and you can't miss it."

He lifted the map and pulled out a slip of paper. "Weather permitting, the family has requested a graveside ceremony, so you should go straight to the cemetery when you arrive. Here are the directions." He handed them to her. "It shouldn't be hard to find. I was told that you should drive straight through town, take the second left at the lights, drive another mile and it's on your right."

Ellis glanced at Louie through the window. "What was his name?"

"Who?" Ben asked.

"Louie's brother," she said.

"I don't know," Ben said, frowning. "I've got so many residents and relatives to keep track of, I can't remember." He ran a finger down the first page in the folder, flipped it over, and did the same on the second. "Stan," he finally said, looking slightly embarrassed that he'd had to look it up. "His name was Stan Johnson."

Ellis and her dad ate dinner alone that Wednesday. Hadley was out with the running club and it was Paulina's week to do deliveries for Meals on Wheels. As always, Dennis was unerringly polite, the way a stranger often is in someone else's home—offering to set the table, helping dish up their plates, pouring them each something to drink. Earlier, when Ellis got home from work, there'd been a notepad with his handwriting on it by the phone. Curious, she had tilted her head and read, "Appleton Ranch. Full-time handyman (inc. room and board). Starts August tenth." He was leaving? All through dinner, she kept thinking he might bring it up, but he didn't. Later, after he'd helped her with the dishes, he went into the living room and dragged out Paulina's old Electrolux vacuum. The motor had been whining and he said he wanted to see if he could fix it.

Since his arrival, Ellis had been wary of his intentions, staying away from him as much as possible, but now she could see that her aloof approach wasn't doing either of them any good. Following an impulse she couldn't explain, she took her silver compass out of her purse and slipped it into the front pocket of her sweater. Minutes later, she stuck her head into the living room. Vacuum cleaner parts were spread here and there, and her dad's face was scrunched in concentration as he tried to tighten a belt that looked like a super-sized rubber band.

"Want to walk down to the river?"

Dennis turned to her in surprise. "The river?"

"I made coffee," she said, holding up two travel mugs.

"I guess I could use a break." He got to his feet and wiped his hands on a rag.

They took the long way, walking to the end of the street and then through an open section of trees before cutting down to the main path Ellis and Hadley had recently taken. To Ellis's surprise, her dad was in a talkative mood. He pointed out half a dozen trees that beavers had downed to repair their dam on the creek. He griped about a scarred piece of earth in the bush where someone had built an open fire. Then he segued off into talk of car repairs, suggesting she consider investing in a good set of winter tires this fall.

Ellis listened, remembering the time she had fallen down an embankment when they'd gone camping as a family. She was ten years old. They were out walking and she'd slipped and tumbled end over end all the way down to the bottom of a rocky hill. She'd sat up, crying, and when she brushed her hair out of her eyes and looked up, her dad was standing at the top of the hill with a rope.

"Come get me," she'd howled.

"Where's the fairness in that?" he said, tossing down the rope. "This is a steep hill and you're not little anymore. Grab hold and I'll pull you up."

He never coddled me, Ellis suddenly realized. *Not even then. He always pushed me to be independent, to take care of myself.*

When they finally reached the river, Dennis stared out at it with a distant expression in his eyes. For a long time Ellis stood very still. Then she reached into her pocket and rubbed her thumb against the inscription on the back of the silver compass. The child in her wanted to show him that she still had it, tell him how much it had meant to her over the years, but suddenly bringing up the past felt wrong.

Ellis sneaked a look at him, fighting a sad smile. She was old enough now, experienced enough, to know that he had never been the man she'd once believed him to be. He was not tall and he was not especially strong and he could not leap tall buildings in a single bound.

Her dad cleared his throat. “How’s Hadley doing?”

Ellis shrugged. “She’s fine. I worry about her, but I’m starting to realize she’s a lot tougher than I give her credit for.”

“She takes after you,” he said softly, “and you take after your mother, who’s an amazing woman, as kind and consistent and steady as the day is long. She deserved a lot better than what she got with me.”

Ellis blinked a few times, close to tears. Then she tilted her head back and gazed toward heaven, as though asking for help. “Dad?” she said.

Pause. “Uh-huh?”

“I’m glad you came back.”

For a long moment, they stood absolutely still next to each other, and then Dennis coughed into his hand and said, “If I remember right, there used to be a bald eagle’s nest somewhere around here.”

“Yes,” Ellis said. “I think you’re right.”

After they returned to the house, Ellis sat down to read the newspaper and stopped when she saw a photo of a homeless man sitting next to a garbage can, with a caption beneath it: *There is not much appealing about a broken man, but there is even less about a person unwilling to lend him a hand.*

Dennis was in the living room. Ever the hockey enthusiast, he had put in a DVD of the final NHL hockey playoff game, which had obviously been taped months ago. Ellis slowly folded the paper, thinking of something Louie had said that morning. He'd been in a surly mood, instigated by an article he'd read in the *Billings Advocate* about two young men who'd robbed an elderly woman at a bus stop.

"What people don't understand," Louie said, "is that time does not move in a straight line from point A to Z. It actually circles around like this"—he had demonstrated by waving a hand up and around his head—"and when it finally makes its way back around to where it all started, it'll bite you hard in the ass for every time you weren't good to someone. You get back what you put out," he'd said, flustered and upset.

Ellis set the paper aside and went into the living room, resolving to be nicer and less judgmental, determined to make the best of what she had to work with at this moment.

"What are you watching?" she asked.

"The final Stanley Cup play-off game," Dennis said, startled. "I know who won," he added, waving a hand at the TV, "but I wanted to see it again."

"Mind if I watch with you?"

He blinked at her, caught off guard. "No, not at all."

For the next hour, Ellis watched hockey with her dad. Now and then, she made a comment about a bad play, and he inched forward in his armchair, nodding in agreement. Soon, he began pointing things out to her—a weak goal here, a bad penalty call there. When there were only ten minutes left in the third period, Ellis stretched out on the couch and decided to close her eyes. A while later, in the blurred edges that sleep often brings, she was aware of her dad turning off the TV and the almost imperceptible touch of his lips against her forehead before he turned off the lights.

TWENTY-FOUR

Ellis pulled up to Pleasant View Manor Friday morning, and Louie was waiting for her on the bench out front, a canvas bag at his feet. He was wearing a hat, his favorite pea green sweater over a white button-down shirt, and a pair of sludge-colored pants. Smiling, he made his way to the end of the sidewalk and climbed in next to her.

"Morning," he said. "Looks like it's going to be another hot day."

"It sure does," Ellis replied, unfolding the map to give it a final once-over.

Louie leaned over and looked at the

route Ben had highlighted. "If it helps, I know a shortcut that will cut half an hour off the drive," he suggested.

Ellis hesitated, gnawing on the inside of her cheek.

"I've lived in Montana my whole life," Louie reminded her. "Trust me, I know every back road within five hundred miles. If we take this road"—he pointed to it on the map—"it'll take us straight through the east side of Choteau County."

"All right." Ellis handed him the map. "You navigate, I'll drive."

They weren't even out of the parking lot before Louie asked if he could listen to some music. "I brought along a few CDs."

Ellis agreed, although listening to Christmas music in July was the last thing she wanted to do. Ten minutes later, Louie was singing "A Christmas to Remember" with Dolly Parton and Kenny Rogers, and Ellis felt a dull headache forming behind her eyes.

"I've had threats, you know," he said, turning the volume down.

Ellis frowned. "What do you mean, *threats*?"

Louie shrugged. "Notes slipped under

my door warning me that my La-Z-Boy is going to get trashed if I don't stop playing my Christmas music." He shook his head sadly. "I'm pretty sure it's old Rolly working himself into a fit. Can you imagine? Threatening someone 'cause he likes to listen to Christmas music?"

Half an hour north of Barrow, Louie instructed her to turn right off the main highway and soon they were swooping along a narrow, winding gravel road. They crossed the Missouri River and Louie pointed out a tree farm. They wound through a series of twisting hills and valleys, and when they came around a wide corner near a power plant, Louie noticed an eagle's nest built around the soaring steel girders and begged her to stop so he could take a better look.

Making a visor out of his hand, he opened his door and climbed out. He'd brought along binoculars and he insisted that Ellis join him. Fifteen minutes later, after a lot of prodding from Ellis, they were finally back on the road.

Lulled by the hum of the tires, and the air shimmering with heat outside, Louie talked nonstop, telling Ellis stories about his life. How his wife, Ruby, had never seen snow until she moved to Barrow. How, until Arla was born, he'd never fully appreciated the magnificence of a rainbow. How he loved living in Montana. The words spilled forth out of him as though he'd been saving them up for a long time.

Then, on a deserted stretch of road, Ellis heard a definitive pop—not unlike the sound of a gunshot—and the car pulled sharply to the right.

"That didn't sound good," she said, easing down on the brakes.

"We've got a flat tire," Louie said with confidence.

"Are you serious?"

Her shoulders fell as she pulled onto the side of the road. She climbed out and circled around the front, then made her way to the back, where she came upon the offending tire on Louie's side.

Wonderful, she thought.

She opened the trunk and emptied it so she could locate the spare tire. She made a pile on the ground behind her: jumper cables, a wool blanket, a pair of rubber boots, two old lawn chairs. After finding the tire and the laminated instructions outlining how to change one, she lifted it out and swung it down next to her.

Louie opened his door. "You ever changed a flat tire before?"

"Nope," she replied, squatting in front of it. "But I guess there's a first time for everything, isn't there?"

Louie turned sideways on the front seat and lowered his feet to the ground. He straightened, set one hand on top of the roof for support, and made his way over to her. "Maybe I can help," he said.

Ellis skimmed the directions, turning the jack this way and that as she determined what had to be done. "It's okay," she assured him. "I've got it under control."

She pushed to her feet, grabbed one of the lawn chairs, and snapped it open. Then she set it off to one side in the grass and said, "Grab a seat, sir. We'll be back on the road in fifteen minutes."

Shrugging, Louie sat down and lit a cigar.

Half an hour later, a spasm shot across Ellis's lower back as she tried for the third time to wiggle the flat tire off.

"You can't just *loosen* the bolts," Louie pointed out. "You actually have to take them right off."

Grabbing the wrench, she worked her way around the tire, removed each bolt, and set it carefully to one side. Then she sat down on the ground, braced her feet against the wheel well and pulled, swearing under her breath. When the tire finally popped off, it did so with such force that she fell flat back against the hard earth, pinned under the tire.

At that moment, a rusty farm truck came up over a rise in the distance, backfiring on its way down the other side. Relieved, Ellis pushed to her feet. *Good,* she thought. *Maybe I can get some help*.

She stepped out onto the road, waving her hands in the air. The truck slowed as it got closer and then rolled to a stop. The driver was wearing a beat-up cowboy hat that looked as though someone had taken a bite out of the rim.

"Having some trouble, ma'am?" the man said. He was past middle age, with a grizzled gray beard and a nose that looked like it had been broken a few times.

Ellis indicated her car. "We've got a flat."

He climbed out and Louie walked around the front of Ellis's car and introduced himself. After a brief examination of the situation, the farmer tipped his hat back, turned to Louie and said, "She's got the jack set up wrong."

"I do?" Ellis said, frowning.

"I'm gonna need a lug wrench," the farmer said.

Grunting, he lowered himself to his knees and set to work. It took him almost an hour to lower the car, set the jack up properly, and change the tire. From Ellis's standpoint, it was painful to watch. He moved as slowly as a turtle, whether he knew what he was doing or not, and the entire time, he and Louie chatted like the best of friends—about baseball, a local politician who had been caught pilfering funds, a recent newscast trumpeting record-breaking weather for this year's crops. When the farmer finally finished and pushed to his feet, declaring the deed done, Ellis cocked her head, inspecting his handiwork.

"I don't know how to thank you," she said.

"Aw, it was no problem," he said.

Moments later, after Louie wrote down the man's phone number so they could stay in touch, Ellis put everything back in the trunk and they were on the road again.

Milford wasn't hard to find, but they were almost late when they arrived at the cemetery. At the entrance, Ellis gazed with interest at the graves they rolled past. Some were plain and bare, but as they followed the road to the far side where a large crowd had gathered, the stones became more ornate and lavish, most laden with fresh flowers, some with stuffed teddy bears or framed photographs leaning against the headstones. A child's baseball cap hung from one marble cross.

"Beautiful cemetery," she commented.

Louie glanced sideways at her. "They're all the same."

She pulled over to park, watching for chinks in Louie's armor now that they had finally arrived at his brother's funeral, but his face was unreadable. She started to open her door, but Louie lifted a hand to stop her.

"I'd like to go alone if you don't mind."

He pushed his door open and straightened, then shuffled across the grass making his way around to where he stood facing Ellis between two elderly couples.

Ellis moved across the seat and rested both of her elbows on Louie's open window.

"Family and friends," the minister began in a booming voice, "we are gathered here today to say farewell to Stan Johnson. . . ."

Maybe he'll break down and cry on the drive home, she thought.

"He was a man who lived a full life. . . ."

Or maybe this will put him in a bad mood, sensing that his time might not be that far off, either.

"Stan's life was rich with good health, family, friends, and the kind of financial success most people only dream of in their lifetimes."

Ellis perked up, curious.

"He was a man of many dimensions," the reverend said. "From the millions of dollars he donated as a philanthropist each year to the number of hours he personally spent helping to build Habitat for Humanity houses in this good country of ours."

Louie's brother was rich?

Louie's face remained impassive as he stared at the flower-laden coffin, his misshapen hat held respectfully against his chest. The minister continued, a charismatic force himself as he shared a few humorous anecdotes about Stan that sent ripples of appreciative laughter through the crowd. When he was finished speaking, he extended his hands toward the coffin and somberly invited everyone to say their last good-byes.

An older woman, dressed completely in black, including a veil that fell across her face, took the arm of the young man sitting next to her. He clasped his hand on top of hers, and they stood and took two halting steps forward to the coffin.

Obviously Stan's wife, Ellis thought, watching with interest.

When the woman lifted her veil, Ellis saw that she was Caucasian. Had Stan's marriage to a white woman caused a rift between him and Louie? Or had they been estranged for so many years because Louie was jealous of his brother's wealth? It was curious how important it had been for Louie to attend the funeral when he and his brother obviously hadn't been close. The minister signaled for the coffin to be lowered. Stan's wife broke down sobbing, as did her son and a few other people.

Not five minutes later, after shaking his nephew's hand and giving his sister-in-law a warm hug, Louie was back. He climbed into the car and snapped on his seat belt.

"It was nice that so many people came," Ellis said.

"Yes," Louie said. "Stan would have been pleased."

Mourners were squeezing each other's hands in silent recognition of their collective pain, embracing each other, calling out good-byes. Everyone slowly made their way to their cars and the vehicles parked in front of Ellis finally began to move.

"Who should I follow?" she asked.

"What do you mean?"

"There's almost always a get-together after a funeral," she said.

"It's okay," Louie replied. "I don't want to go."

Ellis gazed at him, baffled. "But, Louie, we've come all this way."

He grabbed his canvas bag and pulled out another CD. "I said I don't want to go."

She watched the last car in the procession pull out and fade into the distance. "Okay," she said, shrugging. It seemed odd, though, that they had come so far yet Louie didn't want to join his family for a visit.

Once they had left Milford behind and were back on the highway, Louie unfolded the map and suddenly got all cheery. "All right, then, how about if we head west and go straight through Havre and then cut down Highway Fifteen on the way back to Barrow?" he suggested.

Ellis stared at him. Who was this man?

"No point taking the same way back, right?" He pushed the map closer, showing her the new route he was talking about. "I've never been through Havre. It was founded as a major railroad service center for the Great Northern Railway, built by James J. Hill. It was originally know as Bullhook Bottoms, and is said to be named after the city Le Havre in France, although some people who live there dispute this."

Ellis evaluated the route he was proposing. How could he be more interested in driving to and from his brother's funeral than in the funeral itself?

Louie continued. "There's a statue of Hill near Havre's Amtrak station. If you like, we could stop for a break and have a look at it."

She was only half listening to him, still trying to piece together his disinterest in joining his family. Had he only attended the funeral out of duty? Over guilt from a long-ago argument with his brother he'd never apologized for?

"Tell you what," she said, handing him the map. "I don't care which way we go, as long as we don't take any back roads."

"Okay then," he said, rubbing his hands together. "Let's take the route I mentioned."

Soon, Louie had Boney M cranked up on Ellis's CD player and was singing "Feliz Navidad," snapping his fingers along to the beat, as if they were on a Thelma and Louie–like adventure. Ellis glanced in the side mirror to check for traffic before pulling out to pass a slow-moving Volkswagen van.

"Were you older than your brother?" she asked.

Louie stopped snapping. "Eh?"

"Who was older, you or your brother?"

Louie paused. "He was."

"Were you close growing up?"

"Not really." He picked a ball of lint off his sweater.

"Did you fight a lot?" she pressed.

A longer pause. "Think we could talk about something else?"

"Sorry," Ellis said, signaling to pull back

in front of the Volkswagen van. "I'm just interested, that's all."

The next few minutes went by like the slow tick of a clock. Maybe it was the lack of vulnerability she sensed in Louie, or the way he was always the first person in line to give everyone else a hard time, but Ellis couldn't help herself. Bored, she decided to tease him. The drive had been long, the day had been trying, and she suddenly felt punch-drunk goofy from the relentless heat.

"Don't tell me," she said, lifting a hand. "Let me guess. You and your brother robbed a bank as teenagers, but then Stan ran off with all the money and left you in an unpaid hotel room without a nickel to your name, and you never heard from him again. Not, that is, until Ben told you about his funeral last week."

Louie opened his mouth to interrupt.

"Wrong?" she said. "Okay, how about this one. Years ago, Stan was engaged to a beautiful woman, but you fell head over heels in love with her and she ditched him, forever causing a rift between the two of you. . . ."

Louie shook his head.

"Or better yet, he made a ton of money in the stock market and—"

Louie turned off the music. "I never had a brother, Ellis."

She gave him a long blink, followed by a blank expression.

"From what I heard today, though, if I ever did, this guy would have been a good pick, money and all."

"You never had a brother?" she said, incredulous.

"I was an only child," Louie confirmed. "Only thing I have in common with Stan Johnson is his name, and that was a complete fluke."

"You tricked me?" She hesitated, recalling how Oliver and Murphy had refused to take him to his brother's funeral, the look on Ben's face when she'd agreed to. And then the truth blossomed and she felt like an even bigger fool. "Oh, my God," she said. "You've done this before, haven't you?"

Louie's gaze flitted over to her and he shrugged when he saw the look on her face. "So what?" he said. "I'm not hurting anybody. Stan Johnson doesn't care and his family is so wrapped up in their grief that having one more person come to his funeral—a friend? an old coworker?—that's not such a bad thing, is it? Matter of fact, it usually gives people a little extra comfort, knowing someone they loved touched another person's life enough that they took the time to come to his funeral."

Ellis stared at him, speechless.

Louie threw a hand in the air, laughing. "Lord, I went to one last year where only four people showed up. Four people! Can you imagine? Makes you wonder what kind of life the guy lived. His wife and daughter were so happy to see me there, they insisted we join them for dinner. Went to a wonderful restaurant, too," he said, looking past her with a smile. "We had fresh lobster tail, and escargot—"

"They insisted *we* join them?" Ellis said. "Who was with you? Who took you to that funeral, Louie?"

He folded his hands in his lap. "Oliver," he said.

"And before that?" she asked. "How many have you been to in the last—oh, I don't know, three years? And who took you to them?"

He tilted his head to one side, thinking.

"Four," he finally said. "Oliver took me to one in Billings, and Charlene drove me to one in Miles City. But then they caught on and told Murphy, so Ben had to take me to the other two."

Ellis frowned, confused. "How can that be? Ben's not stupid! He's the one who—"

Louie raised an eyebrow, waiting for her to connect the dots.

When she did, Ellis was amazed at Ben's gall, at Louie's nerve, at her own stupidity. Oliver and Charlene had taken him to funerals in the past, and Murphy knew about the whole charade, not to mention Ben, who had blatantly manipulated this situation in the first place.

Spotting a gravel road up ahead, she signaled and pulled safely off the highway. She rolled her window down and rested her forehead against the steering wheel, trying not to laugh. She wasn't sure which revelation amazed her more: the fact that Louie didn't have a brother or that Ben had arranged for her to take him to a stranger's funeral.

A metallic green fly buzzed around the car and landed on her hand. She flicked it away, then looked at Louie for a moment, feeling light-headed, unsure if it was from the awful heat outside or the oddball secret he'd just dumped in her lap.

She opened the door and got out of the car. She started walking down the road, tilting her face to the hot afternoon sun.

"Where you going?" Louie called out after her.

She shook her head and kept walking, not bothering to turn around.

"Ellis?" he shouted, trying again.

"Open the trunk and set up a lawn chair," she yelled back. "There's ice water in a cooler in the backseat. You had your fun, now I'm going to have a nice, relaxing walk. I'll be back in a while."

The road she was on didn't seem to lead anywhere. It stretched empty as far as she could see, heat shimmer making the air ahead of her seem wavy and miragelike. She passed a thick grove of trees on her left, an abandoned farmhouse with broken windows, an old barn with a bowed roof that had caved in on itself long ago. Still, she kept walking.

In the distance she could hear water

rushing over rock and soon she found herself following a path off the road and down a hill to her right. When she came to a thick ridge of scrubby trees, she pushed through them, determined to find the source of the sound. Finally, she broke through a thicket and found a natural pond of fresh water alongside a river, curled inward like a bent spoon.

Ellis stripped off her clothes and dropped them on the ground. Setting her watch on top, she climbed down the embankment in her underwear, sticky with sweat, and walked barefoot straight into the water. She gasped as it cut sharp circles around her ankles and moved up her calves to her thighs, the sandy bottom locking around her feet like suction cups. Dropping to her knees, she scooped up handfuls of sand and let them drizzle from her fingers. She sat cross-legged, the water touching her chin, then sank down even farther as she pulled her hair free from its clip and let the water seal itself over her entire body.

By the time she returned to the car, Louie was asleep, his head tilted back and mouth open. The door on his side was ajar and Billie Holiday was blaring "I've

Got My Love to Keep Me Warm." As soon as she opened her door and slid in, Louie startled awake.

"Eh?" he said, sitting up.

Ellis started the car. Eyes focused on the road, she turned it around and pulled back onto the main road. Her wet hair was dripping down the back of her blouse, but Louie pretended not to notice.

For a while, they drove in silence, the steady hum of the tires almost hypnotic. Eventually, curiosity got the best of her and Ellis cleared her throat. "Okay then, tell me. What's this all about?"

Louie frowned. "Eh?"

She waved a hand. "Going to strangers' funerals. What's it about?"

Louie looked out the window. "Respect," he said softly. "It's about respect."

Ellis stared straight ahead, but she was a captive audience and he seemed determined to make a few points. "Just you wait. When you get old, much of what happens to you either happens without your knowledge or your consent, and you quickly reach the point where you'll do whatever you can to bring a little joy to each day, even if that means showing some stranger respect for the life they lived on this crazy earth of ours.

"You have no idea what it's like to be old, what it's like to be dependent on others, how it feels to lose the freedom you once took for granted. Imagine what it would be like to have a stranger help you bathe every day or how Vern must have felt wearing a diaper because he could no longer count on his body not to humiliate him. How demeaning it must be to get spoon-fed because your hands shake so badly you can't do it yourself. How would you feel inside being told what to eat and when to sleep and what kind of music you are and aren't allowed to listen to?"

Ellis tightened her hands on the wheel, uncertain of what to say.

"I'm old, Ellis," Louie said, his voice suddenly thick with emotion. "And because of that, I appreciate life more now than I ever have. I realize what matters and what never did. I know exactly where I'm going, and that makes me treasure where I've been, but it also makes me appreciate others who get there ahead of me."

Ellis swallowed hard, listening to him.

"I've lived a full life," he said, sighing. "But

the days are long now, filled with too many hours with nothing to do. My hands shake like a palsied old man's and lately my body refuses to cooperate with my mind." He dipped his head to his chest. "And I miss my wife. I miss her more than you can imagine. I can't remember the last time I spoke to my daughter. Twenty years ago? Twenty-five? I don't know if she's happy, if she ever got married, had kids, if she's divorced."

"Why don't you track her down?" Ellis asked.

Louie stared out the window. "I don't need to. I know where she lives. She mails me a Christmas card every year. The return address is always the same."

"Why don't you phone her then?"

Louie shrugged. "Sometimes the hardest thing is to let a child go."

"But she's not a child anymore," Ellis insisted.

"She is to me."

Ellis considered this. "What would you say to her if you could?"

"That I love her," Louie said.

"Anything else?" she prompted.

"Nothing else matters."

For a few minutes, they drove in silence,

each lost in thought as the tires hummed like a distant insect whine. Finally, Ellis bounced the heel of one hand against the steering wheel. "I think you should call her anyhow. Can't hurt, right?"

Louie paused as though weighing his options. Ellis wasn't looking at him, but she could sense a shift in the air, a sudden sadness that was almost palpable.

"You know, Ellis," he finally said, "the funny thing about a person's pride is that it always seems to show up when we can least afford it to, like a bad houseguest. I'm a logical man and I have considered calling her many times, but each time I reach for the phone it dawns on me that she was the one who left. My daughter walked away, even though I begged her to stay, and as she did, she said, "I'll never speak to you again." And she never has. Arla doesn't want me in her life."

"People change," Ellis offered.

"Maybe," he conceded. "But you don't know my daughter."

They stopped for something to eat in a town called Big Sandy, and by the time they had finished their meal, any conversation about Arla was a distant memory and Louie seemed mostly back to himself.

"Did you know," he said, pointing his dessert fork at Ellis, "that less than eight hundred people live in Big Sandy?"

Ellis shook her head.

"Or that this little town was once home to a guitar player from some world-famous rock band and a U.S. senator?"

"Really?" Ellis said, trying to sound interested as she signaled their waitress for the check. "Isn't that something?"

When they finally pulled in to the parking lot of the nursing home, it was dark except for the lights on the dashboard and the ever-present Pleasant View Manor sign stretched across the front entrance like a beacon.

Louie climbed out of the car and stretched, working out a few kinks. Ellis followed him to the door and handed him his canvas bag. He gave her a formal half bow. "Thank you," he said. "It was a pleasure spending the day with you."

Ellis shook her head, equally amused and astounded by him, then she reached out and gave him a quick hug. "Good night, Louie."

"Are you working tomorrow?" he asked, sounding hopeful.

"No, but I'll be in on Sunday."

"Hey, Ellis?" he called out when she was halfway to her car. "You've never asked what my secret is."

"Your secret for what?"

"For staying young and living happy."

"Okay, Louie," she said and laughed. "What's your secret?"

He shot her a wink. "It's the dancing."

TWENTY-FIVE

Saturday afternoon, Ellis opened her closet to look for a jacket, and stopped and stared at all of Mark's things, stacked in boxes waist-high across the back. Most had "Clothes" scribbled across the top and two said "Mark's desk." Before leaving Dallas, she'd sold his tool bench, the teak patio furniture he had loved, his climbing gear. Gone too was his mountain bike, although she'd stored his kayak in Lance's garage for Hadley when she got older. She had kept their wedding rings, a box of photo albums, and a digital picture frame he'd given to her years ago, his and Hadley's voices captured forever in a tinny echo that made her heart sink each time she heard it.

And now these boxes are all that's left.

Suddenly intent on making a few changes, Ellis went downstairs. She opened a bottle of wine, grabbed a knife, a handful of garbage bags and a roll of packing tape, and then she went back up to her bedroom. *It's time,* she thought. *No more false starts where I drag a box out and then nudge it back into the closet ten minutes later because I feel like I can't breathe.*

She shook open two garbage bags and set them on the floor: one for giveaway, the other for trash. Next, she poured herself a glass of wine, reached inside her closet, and tugged four boxes off the top of the stack. Kneeling on the floor, she sliced open the first one.

Inside was Mark's collection of hockey jerseys. She remembered packing them, deciding to keep them for Hadley, especially the Wayne Gretzky autographed Edmonton Oilers jersey he'd treasured. Folding the flaps shut on the box, she taped it up again and relabeled it before pushing it to one side. The second one was crammed with golf shirts and T-shirts. The third was filled with jeans and dress slacks. The fourth bulged with sweaters. She put all of it aside for giveaway and dragged four more boxes out of the closet.

Half an hour later, almost done, Ellis felt stronger than she had in months. Mark would be proud of her. She imagined him lying on the bed, chin propped on his hands, elbows sinking into the mattress. "I never did like that suit jacket," he'd say, trying to make her smile. "And let me tell you, the idea of wearing those dress shoes after going barefoot for a year holds zero appeal." He'd had a good sense of humor, and at that moment, Ellis felt its presence as palpably as though he were sitting next to her.

The last two boxes had "Mark's desk" scribbled on top. Cutting them open, she slowly began going through what she found inside. She had avoided packing his desk until the last possible moment, and when she finally did, she'd done so quickly, stopping now and then only to wipe away her tears. Inside were picture frames he'd kept on the credenza behind his desk. There was a photo of Hadley with a front tooth missing. Another in which she was holding up a medal at a swim meet. A snapshot someone had taken on their wedding day. All reminders of a time when their lives had been whole.

Ellis pulled out a stack of postcards Mark had brought home from business trips to Venezuela, Kuwait, and the Canadian Oil Sands in northern Alberta. There were books, half a dozen Beatles records, swim meet buttons with Hadley's face on them, a brochure promoting a zip-line tour through the rain forest in Costa Rica, a printout of qualifying times for the Boston Marathon: all private, personal items that had been important to Mark.

Lost in thought, she lifted out a large yellow envelope. Inside was a handful of smaller envelopes, each one labeled with the word "January" and a corresponding year; each one sealed with tape. She felt her insides pitch.

Oh, my God. Mark's January letters.

It was a tradition Ellis had introduced years ago, something she and her mom had done on New Year's Day for as long as she could remember. They would sit across from each other in front of the fireplace and write a letter meant only for their eyes that covered two issues: how they felt about the year they had just been through, and what their hopes and dreams and goals were for the upcoming year. When they were done, they would open the January letters they had written twelve months earlier and see how many of their personal goals they had achieved and how happy they were with their lives.

At first, Mark had thought it odd. "You want me to write a letter to myself?"

"That's right," Ellis said, handing him a pen and paper.

"And no one's ever going to read it but me?"

"Exactly," she said.

By the time they'd written two January letters, Mark got into it in a big way, often writing three pages or more before declaring the mission accomplished.

Their January letters were private. Ellis had never once shared hers with Mark, and she had never read any of his. Turning them over now, she chewed on her bottom lip. She kept hers tucked away in an old tin box on the top shelf of her closet, but until now she'd had no idea that he'd also kept all of his.

Starting with an envelope dated ten years ago, she opened each one and read what he'd written, savoring the tiny vulnerabilities he'd never shared with her—*This year, I'd like to learn another language; I want to try running a marathon*—and fighting tears over others—*Help Ellis find a job she enjoys more than nursing; work less, play more; register Hadley for self-defense classes*. In more than one, he'd written about his dream of owning his own business; in another, his worries about growing old; and in the letter he'd written six months before he died, he expressed disappointment over how the company was doing and concern over how to tell Ellis they might lose everything.

There was one envelope left.

Ellis pulled it out and froze when she saw the return address: People Scan Incorporated—Legally Admissible DNA Results. Her hands trembled when she turned it over and saw that it was still sealed.

Mark had never opened it.

She tilted her head back and closed her eyes, recalling the day she'd given it to him.

She'd paid for two copies of the results and asked to have them sealed in separate envelopes: one for her, one for Mark. She had hoped the odds were in their favor, that Mark would look at it as a gift of sorts. Hadley was almost four by then and they had just moved into their house in Dallas.

When Ellis gave Mark his envelope, he shot her a puzzled look, squinting to read the return address. He stopped, caught his breath, wiped his brow. "Why did you do this?" he said.

"Because I need to know."

He ran his hands through his hair. "Well, I don't."

Ellis felt a quaver in her throat. "I'm sorry. I thought—"

"Don't you understand?" Mark said, his jawbone jumping. "It doesn't matter, Ellis. It never has. She's my daughter. I don't need a piece of paper to tell me so."

"Of course she is," Ellis said. "It's just . . ." Her voice trailed away. She struggled to find the right words. Hadn't it been on his mind as much as it was on hers? Didn't he want to know the truth? She had imagined them opening their envelopes together: Mark grinning with relief if the results confirmed he was Hadley's biological father— something Ellis felt more confident about all the time, given her daughter's blond hair—or else Mark giving her a reassuring hug if he wasn't, both of them resolute about how much they loved Hadley, but relieved now that her parentage had been confirmed and they were able to move forward without this unanswered question hanging over them.

Mark stared at the envelope, turning it this way and that, as though considering the magnitude of what it held.

"I want to leave it alone, Ellis."

"But, Mark, I think we need to—"

"No." He lifted a hand to stop her. Then he stood to go, pausing in the doorway. "I'm done. Do whatever you need to do, but I don't want to hear about it."

They had never talked about it again.

Mark didn't want to know the truth, and yet whether the results were good or bad, Ellis knew that she couldn't move forward without knowing. She believed it was the only way she could finally put the rape behind her.

Days later, when Mark was at work and she was alone, she'd finally worked up the nerve to open her envelope. She hadn't slept well the night before, and as she slid into a kitchen chair, she caught herself wishing she felt the way Mark did. Since Hadley's birth, she'd watched to see if he was holding back, but never—not once—did she see him express anything less than an over-the-top adoration for Hadley. It was clear in the way he held her against his chest when she was tired, how he rocked her to sleep, how he had lovingly strapped a faux diamond bracelet onto her twiggy wrist the day she turned three. Mostly, though, it was clear in the way his face lit up whenever Hadley entered the room.

Ellis's hands trembled when she ripped the envelope open. What happened to her on that deserted service road years ago had been horrific, but the fact that she'd had to question Hadley's parentage every day since then had been even worse.

It's as if he wins every morning all over again when I wake up.

She needed to know.

Her palms were beginning to sweat as she removed the report. Setting it on the table, she wiped her hands on her jeans, telling herself the sudden taste in her mouth wasn't fear, that whatever the results, she'd finally be free.

Gingerly, she unfolded the paper and took a deep breath. Her head was pounding and the room suddenly felt much too hot. Flattening the paper out with her hands, she edged forward on her chair and read, heart racing so fast she felt dizzy from its force.

Moments later, she sucked in her breath.

And, just like that, she began to cry.

Ellis ran a finger over the typewritten words and the formal signature scrawled across the bottom of the page that made it true. Then she lifted her gaze and stared at a picture of her daughter hanging on the wall across from her, looking at her, really looking at her, as though for the first time. *Thank God,* she thought. *You are your father's daughter.* She walked to the window and pressed her forehead against the glass, feeling as though something old and tired and heavy had finally been lifted off her chest.

TWENTY-SIX

Ellis arrived at work Sunday morning to find Nina sitting outside, head dozing against her chest and wearing a shirt that read "I've been to the Great Wall of China." Ellis sneaked past her and there was Ben waiting inside the door, hands stuffed into his pockets. Gone was the ready smile that usually lit up his face; it was replaced with a drawn, weary look that made him seem older than he was. She studied him when he held open the door. Twice he started to reach out his hand to touch her arm.

"What is it?" she said. "What's wrong?"

"Come in," he said, tilting his head toward Nina.

"Is it Vera-Lee?" Ellis asked once the door closed behind them, thinking about the harsh, wheezing cough that had been worrying her for weeks.

"No," he said, dropping his gaze.

She lifted a hand to her chest. "Did Joseph have another stroke?"

"No, Ellis. It's Louie." She held her breath as she waited for him to finish." "He died last night," Ben said softly.

"Louie?" she said, feeling her heart shrink inside her chest. *But he was fine when I dropped him off Friday*.

"Oliver found him outside in his La-Z-Boy after dinner," Ben continued. "At first, he thought he was asleep, but it looks like he had a heart attack. . . ."

Louie's gone?

At first, Ellis couldn't shake the feeling that maybe this was one of Louie's bad jokes, but as she searched Ben's face, there was only deep sadness. "He died in his La-Z-Boy," she whispered. She imagined him with the chair kicked all the way back, his arms and legs thrown wide, eyes open and mouth frozen into a surprised *O* because even though he knew his time was coming, he would have been surprised when it finally did arrive.

Ellis looked up. Murphy was standing next to a group in the lobby, blowing her nose. Oliver was there, too, eyes red-rimmed, and Rolly looked unusually frail in his wheelchair. Fran Wilson hung back a bit, standing next to Joseph and Vera-Lee as she cradled her Bible against her chest.

Ben touched her shoulder. "Louie left this for you."

He handed her a blue envelope, similar to one she now noticed sticking out from Fran's Bible, and ones Joseph and Murphy and Vera-Lee each held. Ellis opened it and pulled out an invitation with silver embossed lettering and a snapshot of Louie in the top right-hand corner. It was a picture someone had taken of him sitting in his La-Z-Boy years ago in front of Bianca's Café, cigar propped between two fingers and a newspaper spread across his lap.

You are invited to my funeral. Please come. Wear your best clothes, bring your friends, circle my grave and send me off with flair. And as you

say good-bye, keep these things in mind: I wasn't a wealthy man, but my life was rich. I wasn't brilliant, but I never got tired of my own company. Most important, I lived my life believing happiness is something a person has to decide on ahead of time. It doesn't arrive at your door and knock. You need to unwrap each day like a gift and find your own tiny piece of it, sometimes in the middle of pain and sadness. So eyeball each other and share stories about me, good and bad. If you smoke, light a cigar. If you drink, pop back an ounce of scotch. If it rains, slip off your shoes and go barefoot. Cry if you need to, but at the end leave happy, and weeks and months and years from now, tilt a few pictures sideways for me, would you?

Ellis felt a quaver in her throat, but she managed a dry, hard swallow. She lifted her head and noticed that each and every picture in sight was tilted off center an inch or two. The group was silent as it broke up, and as everyone went their separate ways, not one person reached out to straighten a picture. Ben put a hand on Ellis's shoulder and gently squeezed, giving her a show of support before heading to his office, discreetly ignoring the tears that were now sliding down her cheeks.

Ellis grabbed a Kleenex off the reception desk. Louie had had the ability to light up any room he entered, whether he was complaining about the food or working the room like a politician seeking support for some cause. Either way, he had filled every inch of this place with his personality. He had lifted people up and he wore them down, but he always added something to their lives.

Feeling dazed, she slipped the invitation back into its envelope and made her way down the hall to Louie's room. Nothing would be the same without him.

Reaching his room, she opened the door and paused. "Oh, I'm sorry. . . ."

Sitting on Louie's bed with her back to Ellis was a middle-aged black woman cradling a cardboard box. She was tall and her arms looked flabby in the sleeveless white blouse she wore. From behind, her tight polyester slacks strained against her backside, and yet when she turned around, sniffing and wiping her nose with a tissue, her chiseled face looked as dark and exotic as it always had.

Ellis blinked in surprise. *Arla Johnson.*

Arla squinted at her for a moment, face screwed in thought. "You don't remember me, do you?" Ellis said.

"No," Arla admitted, sounding disappointed, as though she'd just failed at something important. "I'm sorry. I don't."

Ellis hesitated, her mind scrubbed clean and raw from the news that Louie was gone. Her mouth opened and she touched a hand to her chest. Growing up, Arla had never really acknowledged her. Ellis knew she had been insignificant in her life, and yet she found herself grappling for the right words to tell her how important her father had been in hers. How, at the lowest moment she had ever known, he had saved her.

Arla raised her eyebrows. "Ellis?" she said. "Ellis Williams?"

Ellis leaned against the doorframe without answering. The sound of the lawn mower outside got loud and then faded away again as someone drove it up and down the length of the grass. "It's Ellis Semple now, but yes, you're right."

"You work here?" Arla said, taking in her uniform.

Ellis followed her gaze, glancing down at the olive green outfit. "I do."

Arla thought about this for a moment. "Did you take care of my dad?"

"Yes, I did."

A wistful look flitted across Arla's face, coupled with a flash of something akin to envy. Ellis studied her. She seemed softer now, more accepting of life's uncertainties and less cocky than she had once been. Arla nodded at an empty chair. "Want to sit with me?"

Ellis did. She set her purse on the floor and slid into the chair. Arla set the cardboard box beside her on the bed, fingering one ragged corner. "I still can't believe his life has been reduced to the contents of one small box," she said. "He was always larger than life to me, a bear of a man who seemed untouchable. Bigger than anybody I have ever known, and just as stubborn."

"He was stubborn," Ellis agreed.

Reaching into the box, Arla pulled out

Louie's favorite pea green sweater. "Did you know I gave him this stupid old thing?"

Ellis shook her head no, she didn't.

"It was a late Father's Day gift. I bought it for half price when I was seventeen and then I gave it to him the night I graduated from high school. I think it was on sale because it was such an awful color, but I'll never forget the look on his face when he opened it that day. He acted like I'd just handed him the moon on a silver platter." She shook her head. "Good Lord, why would he wear the same old sweater for so many years?"

"Because he loved it," Ellis said in a half whisper. *It reminded him of you.*

A shadow of self-doubt passed Arla's face and then she suddenly leaned forward, her face in her hands, and started to cry. Ellis tried to find words to comfort her, sensing that Arla had more regrets than she could imagine, knowing now, the way a person does when you've had your own share of hurts, that it doesn't get any worse than this—losing someone who was once your anchor.

"We had a fight that night," Arla whispered into her fingers. "One of our worst."

Ellis had often heard them arguing, Louie begging Arla to keep her voice down, and Arla yelling at him, "I will not waste my life in this stupid town!"

She had seen Arla storm out the front door in a near-hysterical rage, walking down the street in stocking feet with no shoes. She had watched her crawl out her bedroom window, drop barefoot onto the grass, and then run to a waiting car idling on the street. Once, she'd seen her tear through Louie's prized sunflower plants with a butcher knife, cutting them down one by one, complaining that he embarrassed her, that he had no idea what it was like to have such an oddball father.

Arla glanced up at Ellis and then her gaze drifted away again.

"He came to my high school graduation ceremony that night and he took pictures when I walked across the stage to pick up my diploma. He even went out of his way to be polite to my date, some guy I'd met the week before at a party in Billings. Then I went home to change. I told him I was going to Missoula for a few days, that we were leaving after the grad party. He told me I couldn't go. Said I was too young to be gallivanting all over the state with someone I hardly knew. Said I needed to put some serious thought into my future or I'd end up on the street with nothing to show for myself. That until I was eighteen, and I wouldn't be for another two months, he was responsible for me. . . ."

Riveted, Ellis went very still. Invited by Arla, she had crossed into a private and personal place, a place where a father adored his daughter, and more often than not she had brushed him off like a bad itch. Ellis had seen it herself.

"He gave me a gift before the ceremony," Arla said, chin quivering. "A beautiful gift. It was on the table when we were fighting, and after he told me I couldn't go, that he'd pick me up at the grad party no later than one that morning, I ran upstairs to my room." Arla was staring at the floor. "I screamed downstairs at him. I told him he could go straight to hell and then I packed my suitcase. Said I didn't need him telling me how to live my life, that I'd do as I pleased, he didn't have to worry about me anymore. And when I came back down to the kitchen, I grabbed his present and I threw it in the garbage." She glanced at Ellis, her face twisted with shame. "I don't think he even noticed. He was too busy trying to calm me down. But it was right there on top, so I know he would have seen it later. And to this day, I regret it," she admitted, wiping away tears.

"We all do stupid things when we're young," Ellis said.

"Maybe," Arla conceded. "But can you imagine being so pigheaded that you decide to write your father off and never speak to him again?"

Yes, Ellis thought. *I can easily imagine being that pigheaded.*

She'd never asked Louie why Arla had stopped talking to him and he'd never volunteered an answer, but she suddenly understood that he wouldn't have had a clear answer to that question any more than she could've told him why her dad had left all those years ago.

"After my mom died, my dad used to read to me every night when I was little," Arla said suddenly. "At bedtime, he'd grab a book and stretch out next to me on my bed. *Winnie-the-Pooh* was my favorite. I swear, I had every book ever written by A. A. Milne . . ."

Ellis shifted in her chair, trying to remember if her dad had ever read her bedtime stories, waiting for the memories to come back, but there were none.

". . . and then, after he'd finished reading," Arla continued, "he'd tuck me in and whisper in my ear something Christopher Robin says to Winnie-the-Pooh. *Promise me you'll always remember: You're braver than you believe, and stronger than you seem, and smarter than you think.*"

Ellis's chest tightened; all at once she felt light-headed.

Arla tilted her head back, trying not to cry. She waited for a long moment and then lowered her chin again. Softly, less to Ellis than herself, she said, "You know that gift he gave me for my graduation? It was a silver compass. He had that saying engraved on the back, and I know it probably sounds dumb," she said, wiping her eyes with the back of one hand, "but when I came here today, I was hoping I'd find it among his things, that maybe he'd picked it out of the garbage and put it away for me."

Ellis had to work hard to keep her face blank. At the very center of her, where everything came together, she felt something slowly splintering apart.

She realized what must have happened all those years ago. At twelve, she had often sat outside on the back steps, crying because she missed her dad, unaware that Louie was listening next door. And then the day after her thirteenth birthday, a birthday her mom had tried to make happy by hanging balloons from the trees, an unexpected gift had arrived wrapped in brown paper with her name on it. A silver compass she thought her dad had left for her; the same silver compass Louie had picked out of the garbage the night his daughter ran away from home.

"I only asked my dad for advice once that I can remember," Arla said, smiling at the memory. "I was maybe fourteen at the time and I wasn't sure what I should do with my life, so I sat him down and asked him what direction he thought I should go. I wanted a solid answer, you know? Something I could hold on to and build from. But he just smiled and said, 'Forward would be good.'"

Ellis leaned her cheek against the cool glass of the window, remembering the lie Louie had so graciously told for her—*She didn't jump to* jump, *Roy. She jumped to save me*—how he hadn't even hesitated to do so. And she suddenly knew what she needed to do now. The back of her throat tightened and she closed her eyes for a moment, thinking it through. She pictured Louie sitting in his La-Z-Boy, a cigar forked between two of his fingers, shooting her an encouraging wink.

"Your dad didn't throw your silver compass away," she said. The lie slipped out of her mouth easily, as though it had been slowly forming there for years, just waiting to be told.

Arla seemed genuinely confused. "He didn't?"

Ellis could see the wind outside stirring the leaves beyond the glass. She wanted to make this good, the lie so convincing and the gesture so sincere that Louie would have been proud of her. She lifted her purse off the floor, took out the hinged box she had treasured for years, and held it out to Arla.

"He gave it to me for safekeeping," Ellis said. "And he made me promise to give it to you when he died."

Arla looked startled, her eyes red-rimmed and swollen. Suddenly there was confusion mixed with curiosity in her face, followed by relief so huge and grateful it made her look like a kid again as she opened the box and stared.

"Oh, my God," she said. Her hands were trembling as she lifted the compass out and turned it over with a reverence only Ellis could fully appreciate. She traced her fingers over the inscription on the back and then she started to cry, pressing the sobs back into her mouth with her hand.

"He knew you'd want it," Ellis said. "He told me nothing mattered more than making sure it found its way back to you."

It was a beautiful lie, the sort Louie would have told, but there was also gravity in that moment and a feeling of loss for Ellis.

For a long moment, Arla stared at the compass in amazement. When she finally looked up, she wiped her hands across her cheeks and said, "My dad always liked you."

Ellis's heart caught. "I liked him, too."

Arla put the compass back in its box. "I don't know how I can ever thank you."

As Ellis stood to leave, she touched Arla's shoulder. "You just did," she said.

That afternoon and into early evening, Ellis moved through her shift with a heightened sense of awareness. She'd agreed to cover for Oliver for a few hours so he could attend a family dinner. It was a long day, and there was a definite strangeness in not having Louie around, an empty pocket of loss that had temporarily taken claim to every room and conversation that Ellis happened upon. When she stopped briefly for dinner, she considered calling her family to give them the news, but decided to wait.

Later, when Ellis got home, her parents' vehicles were in the driveway, so she parked out front. She sat in silence for a few moments, gathering her thoughts before going inside, struck once again by how fragile all their lives were in the end.

Finally she got out of the car. She glanced up at the living room window. Hadley came into the square of light and Ellis felt something catch in her throat. Her daughter's hair, long enough again that it now touched her shoulders, was held back with a headband, making her resemblance to Mark unmistakable: there was his smile, his nose, the way his forehead used to crease when he was trying to figure something out. Hadley passed out of Ellis's line of vision and returned, yanking a sweatshirt over her head. She was tugging it down when Ellis's dad came in with a bowl of popcorn. He said something that made Hadley laugh, and then Paulina joined them, juggling three glasses.

Ellis stood transfixed, marveling at the pull of her family, at her sudden need to join them. She took a preparatory breath, listening to the sounds of birds building a nest under the eave of the roof next door, the gentle flutter of their wings mixing with the rise and fall of voices through her mom's open living room window. Tilting her head back, she felt a rush of pleasure. She closed her eyes, and for one moment—one perfect moment—she was certain she could hear the distant sound of the river, as swirling and alive and unstoppable as the world around her.

About the Author

Holly Kennedy is the author of *The Penny Tree.* She currently resides in the foothills of the northern Rocky Mountains with her husband and two sons. Visit her Web site at www.hollykennedy.com

CONVERSATION GUIDE

The Silver Compass

HOLLY KENNEDY

This Conversation Guide is intended to enrich the individual reading experience, as well as encourage us to explore these topics together—because books, and life, are meant for sharing.

A CONVERSATION WITH HOLLY KENNEDY

Q. The Silver Compass, *while ultimately hopeful and uplifting, begins with Ellis Williams as a teenager attempting to take her own life. Why did you choose to start the story there?*

A. The prologue came to me swiftly, almost fully formed, six months before I began writing the novel. I wrote it while I was finishing my second book, *The Penny Tree,* and then I put it aside. There were numerous changes made to *The Silver Compass* while it was being written and rewritten, but it always began with that prologue. That was the scene that hooked me and made me want to write the rest of the story. I knew Ellis and Louie would meet again years later. I also knew Ellis would one day return Louie's favor of saving her life in a special way all her own. It was the contrast between them—a pregnant seventeen-year-old girl and an eccentric sixty-year-old janitor—that was most compelling to me; I was fascinated by the idea that the lives of such different people could become irreversibly entwined. Also, none of the other characters in the book ever know what happens that day between Ellis and Louie, which, for me, makes the opening all the more powerful.

Q. Do you find it hard coming up with story ideas?

A. The ideas are the easy part. It's the *writing* that's hard. I'm always tearing articles out of magazines or newspapers that spark ideas, and I'm forever writing things down I've seen or overheard. At the end of every day, I stuff it all into a twelve-inch-high aluminum garbage can labeled "story ideas" that I keep on my desk, and every few weeks I dump it out and go through it, taking what I want for the book I'm currently working on and putting back whatever I've decided to reserve for another novel.

My imagination always seems to be in high gear. When I'm driving to the grocery store, I get bored and my mind starts to wander. I'll stop at a red light and start making up stories about the people in the next car. Things like: That balding driver is a henpecked alcoholic; his wife, sitting next to him, is having an affair with her boss; and their teenage son slumped in the backseat secretly robbed a bank the day before. Then—*boom*—the light goes green and I drive away. That sort of thing.

Q. Where did you get the idea for this book?

A. I was teaching a creative writing workshop to a group of teenagers. We were discussing opening lines and scenes that would grab your attention enough that you'd want to read on. They were bored and I needed to perk them up. I wrote a few opening lines on the blackboard. One was *Ellis Williams was seventeen when she jumped off the town bridge.* I have no idea where it came from, but they loved it, and for days afterward I couldn't stop thinking about it. What would bring a girl to that point? I wondered. Why would she jump off a bridge? From that point forward, I was hooked.

Q. Do you have any favorite characters?

A. Louie, for sure. I admire nonconformists who do their own thing and refuse to act the way society says they should act. Often, such people seem happier and more whole than those who let money or power or public opinion define their lives. Anissa is another favorite. She was fashioned after a childhood friend I once had who made a big impression on me. My friend's sense of adventure and exuberance drew people to her. She was an off-the-wall goofball who was crazy about Lindsay Wagner and *The Bionic Woman*. She was also the first person I ever met who honestly didn't care what anyone else thought of her, something I greatly admired. I also have a soft spot for Joseph, the elderly man who keeps forgetting to wear his trousers, and Vern Heeley, the old guy who soils himself; my heart went out to both of them.

Q. Which character do you feel the strongest connection to?

A. That would be Ellis. I'm a Gemini, so I can be gregarious and outgoing—get me talking about writing and I'll go on for hours—but I also have a shy, private, and somewhat reclusive side that can relate to Ellis's fascination with Sasquatches and her desire to observe without getting involved.

Q. After Ellis finds the silver compass it becomes a talisman of sorts, a source of comfort and strength. Is there a similar object in your own life?

A. I don't have a silver compass, if that's what you mean, but I do have keepsakes I treasure. They are stored in an old tin box at the back of my closet. All of them are priceless to me and I draw strength from each one at different times, for different reasons.

Q. Terri Schlichenmeyer with the Albany Democrat Herald *(Oregon) said this about your last novel,* The Penny Tree: *"Kennedy has a knack for mentioning tiny details and making those little items important later on in the story. I liked that, being surprised over and over." This description might apply to all your stories. Is it a deliberate technique?*

A. Yes, it is. I aspire to write stories that are entertaining and thought-provoking, but I also want them to be uniquely mine. It is my hope that by weaving in seemingly irrelevant details that become significant in later chapters, I will make the story richer and more rewarding for readers. I like the idea that the technique might become a recognizable style.

Q. Much of this story is structured around a dark and shocking event that happens to Ellis, something that is kept secret from the reader until midway through the novel and isn't fully resolved until near the end. Did you find it difficult writing that section?

A. I found it challenging, yes. As I wrote and fine-tuned that scene, I had to disassociate myself from the emotional side of it, focusing instead on the issue of realism. It was important to me that the scene be visual without being too raw or visceral, and realistic enough that readers would see how quickly a situation like that could turn bad and how it might forever change a person's life.

Q. It's interesting that you chose to write a novel in which much of the action involves a number of elderly characters. What made you decide to do so?

A. In general, sadly, we tend to dismiss the elderly, people who can teach us most about life. We are all going where they are now. We will all get old and wrinkled. We may lose physical control of our bodies while our minds remain sharp, or lose our mental faculties while our bodies stay strong. How will we want to be treated once we get like that? In this story, I wanted the elderly characters at Pleasant View Manor to be living in a relatively appealing environment, and I wanted to show them actively engaged in life and with each other, since the need to connect with other people never leaves us.

Q. Do you think it's realistic that Paulina goes from being tentative and submissive during and after her marriage to modeling lingerie in her later years?

A. Absolutely. I believe our capacity for growth is endless and that it's deeply affected by the people with whom we choose to journey through life. For example, the wife of a controlling husband will either be docile and subservient or she'll buck the system, say "no, thanks," and the marriage won't work. Once you remove that domineering man and leave the woman to make her own choices, she is free to discover fully who she truly is.

Q. At twelve, Ellis copes with her father's abrupt desertion and her mother's depression by withdrawing from people and trying to solve her problems on her own. Do you think she would have become a different person if her father hadn't left?

A. Yes, I think so. I believe there is a great deal of commonality in our lives between the ages of, say, twelve and eighteen. Those are such formative years, often characterized by confusion and angst as we try to figure out who we are and what we want to do with our lives. Ellis's teenage pregnancy is obviously life-altering, but the damage done by her father's rejection is equally harmful and irreversible.

Q. Did you yourself experience the pain of a broken home? Did you draw on personal experience in describing Dennis's desertion?

A. No. My parents were married for thirty years and they raised all five of us kids. We were not a wealthy family, but we were fortunate to have each other. Whereas Ellis spends a lot of time alone in her preteen and teenage years, I was rarely alone. There was a time when four of us shared the same bedroom—my sister, two of my brothers, and myself: two of us on the top bunk, two on the bottom. I was a tomboy, forever climbing trees or jumping in the creek or riding my bike down a staircase, no joke. I preferred fishing and camping to baking and sewing, but through it all—good and bad—I was fortunate to have both of my parents.

Q. In the book, you write: It took her a long time—long after she'd had Hadley and married Mark—to fully understand that the biggest impact her dad made on her life occurred not during the twelve years she knew him, but in the ten-minute conversation when she realized she didn't. *This is a very telling statement.*

A. Oh, I agree. As children, our love for our parents is unconditional and often tinged with hero worship. That image is shattered at some point in our growing up, when we see our parents as real people who make mistakes and have strengths and weaknesses. In *The Silver Compass*, in her early childhood Ellis idolizes her father and believes him to be someone he isn't. Then there is Louie, quietly in the background, a relative stranger, whose influence on her life proves to be rich and rewarding in ways she never could have anticipated.

QUESTIONS FOR DISCUSSION

1. Do you think Ellis's decision to move back to Barrow with her daughter shows strength or weakness?

2. To what extent do you feel Ellis's deep sense of abandonment after her dad leaves shapes her as a woman, wife, and mother?

3. Paulina seems relatively unfazed by her husband's sudden appearance after twenty years. In Paulina's situation, what would you do? Do you believe she feels obligated to her ex-husband or is she simply being kind?

4. Father-daughter relationships are prevalent in this story—Ellis and her

dad; Hadley and Mark; Louie and his daughter—yet the main narrative focus is on Ellis learning how to be a mother to Hadley. How is Ellis a better mother at the end of the novel than she is at the beginning?

5. The novel is also about grieving for the death of a husband and father. In what ways do Ellis's and Hadley's responses to Mark's death ring true for you? Are there any ways in which they do not?

6. If you were Ellis, would you be able to move past your father's abandonment and allow him back into your life twenty years later?

7. Has this story changed your perception of elderly people and their role in your life? You might include Dennis and Paulina in your discussion, not just the characters in the nursing home.

8. Secrets are prevalent throughout this book. Were you surprised by any of them?

9. Do you have a "silver compass" in your own life, a talisman from which you draw strength and comfort?

10. Were you surprised by what happens with the silver compass in the final scene of the book? If you were in the same situation as Ellis, would you have done the same thing?